THE DEPUTY'S LOST AND FOUND

BY

STELLA BAGWELL

AND

HER SECOND CHANCE COP

BY

JEANIE LONDON

Dear Reader,

Like the pages of a book, our minds are layered with memories and as the years pass we're able to look back, read those pages and revisit the moments that make up our lives. Memories tell us the type of person we've been, point out our accomplishments and failures, and invariably guide the plans we map out for our future.

However, in *The Deputy's Lost and Found,* the pages of my heroine's memory are frighteningly blank. She has nothing to guide her, except the feelings in her heart. Can she trust them? And even more importantly, can she trust the sexy deputy, who's vowed to keep her safe?

To find the answers, come with me and saddle up for another trip to Lincoln County, New Mexico, where the desert meets the mountains, old friends welcome new ones, and the youngest Donovan brother helps my heroine find her true home!

Thank you all, dear readers, and may God bless each trail you ride.

Stella

DID YOU PURCHASE THIS BOOK WITHOUT A COVER?

If you did, you should be aware it is **stolen property** as it was reported *unsold and destroyed* by a retailer. Neither the author nor the publisher has received any payment for this book.

All the characters in this book have no existence outside the imagination of the author, and have no relation whatsoever to anyone bearing the same name or names. They are not even distantly inspired by any individual known or unknown to the author, and all the incidents are pure invention.

First published in Great Britain 2011
by Mills & Boon, an imprint of Harlequin (UK) Limited,
Eton House, 18-24 Paradise Road, Richmond, Surrey TW9 1SR

ISBN: 978 0 263 88904 8

23-0811

Harlequin (UK) policy is to use papers that are natural, renewable and recyclable products and made from wood grown in sustainable forests. The logging and manufacturing processes conform to the legal environmental regulations of the country of origin.

Printed and bound in Spain
by Blackprint CPI, Barcelona

Stella Bagwell has written more than seventy novels. She credits her loyal readers and hopes her stories have brightened their lives in some small way.

A cowgirl through and through, she loves to watch old Westerns, and has recently learned how to rope a steer. Her days begin and end helping her husband care for a beloved herd of horses on their little ranch located on the south Texas coast. When she's not ropin' and ridin', you'll find her at her desk, creating her next tale of love.

The couple have a son, who is a high school math teacher and athletic coach.

Chapter One

"The woman is turning into a pest, Hank," Deputy Brady Donovan said as he steered the official SUV around a mountain curve. "Last week I told her flat out that I didn't want to go out with her again, but she's still jamming my cell phone with text messages."

The junior deputy sitting in the passenger seat offered his best explanation. "Maybe Suzie has a hearing problem?"

"Only when it comes to the word *no*," Brady muttered.

Groaning, Brady's young partner rolled his eyes toward the ceiling. "Man, if I could just be you for one day I'd overdose on women."

Brady chuckled wryly. "Trust me, Hank, a daily diet of females can be hazardous to your health."

"So is starving. And I don't want a diet of women. I want a feast. Like you."

Brady tossed his partner a droll look. "I don't know where

you get your ideas, Hank. If you ever expect to be a good deputy you've got to do a better job at sizing up people."

"Yeah. Just like you could size up Suzie's figure?"

Chuckling again, Brady rolled his head to ease the stiffness that had been building in his shoulders for the past hour. "You sound just like my family. They have this notion that I'm a cowboy James Bond. Thrilling chases after criminals and making love to a bevy of beauties. They don't understand that we spend hours on the road, talking about nothing, and wishing an antelope would cross the road just to break the monotony."

Moving to the edge of his seat, Hank twisted the rearview mirror so he could study his freckles. "Cowboy James Bond. I wish. Maybe it would change my luck if I ordered my iced tea shaken and not stirred?"

"Damn it all, Hank, straighten that mirror before it snaps off. Or do you want to explain to Sheriff Hamilton why our vehicle needs repairs?"

It was nearing ten-thirty on a pitch-black Sunday night in August. For the past two hours Brady and Hank had been patrolling the southeastern corner of Lincoln County. Not a simple feat, considering the New Mexican county covered more than four thousand, eight hundred square miles and some of the roads were rough dirt, winding through steep mountains. But Brady and his partner both knew that if criminals were out to smuggle drugs, do illegal deals or rustle some rancher's livestock, it would most likely occur on these secluded back roads. And there was nothing that Brady liked more than catching a criminal in the act. Liked it much more, in fact, than cozying up to Suzie Pippin on a cold night, or even a hot one, he thought wryly.

But so far this evening, everything appeared to be quiet. Another quarter mile to go and they'd be at Highway 380 near Picacho. Brady would be glad to get back on asphalt. Deep winter snows, followed by unusually heavy spring rains, had washed out huge sections of this particular road. He'd spent the past thirty minutes wrenching the steering wheel one way and the other in order to dodge deep holes and road ledges that were crumbling away to the steep canyons below.

"Aw, Brady, you're no fun tonight. You could've let me dream for another minute or two." Hank readjusted the mirror to its proper position and settled back in the bucket seat.

"You can dream while you're in bed," Brady retorted.

Hank sighed as he stared out at the empty dirt road in front of them. "Okay, I'll put the dreaming on hold. When we get to 70 let's head into Ruidoso. The Blue Mesa stays open all night and I want some coffee and maybe a piece of cherry cream pie," Hank said as the SUV bounced over another rough spot. "No. Make that apple. With cinnamon on it. And some ice cream on top of that."

"Forget it. We're driving on to the county line. Sheriff Hamilton didn't send us over here to eat pie. Or dream about women. Which is all you seemed to be doing tonight."

"Hell, what else is there to do?" Hank countered. "This night is as dead as a doornail."

Brady slowed the vehicle as they crossed a washboard surface in a road that had narrowed down to little more than a dirt track hugging the side of the mountain.

"Okay," he relented. "After we reach the county line, we'll head back to Ruidoso and—" All of a sudden, Brady stomped on the brakes and the vehicle skidded to a stop in the middle of the road. "Hellfire! What's that, Hank?"

Sensing the urgency in Brady's question, the other man bolted upright in his seat and leaned toward the windshield. "Where? I don't see—"

Before he could finish, Brady rammed the gearshift in Park and jumped to the ground. Grabbing a flashlight, Hank quickly followed and lengthened his stride to catch up with his partner.

"Over there," Brady instructed. "To our left. In the ditch. It looked like a body to me."

The orb of the flashlight swung to a steep cliff covered with boulders, scrubby pinyon pine, juniper and tall clumps of sagebrush, then dropped to a white object lying in the ditch.

"Man, oh, man, somebody met up with some trouble!" Hank exclaimed in a hushed tone.

"Yeah."

Before moving to the downed figure, Brady took a few seconds to assess the situation. There were no other vehicles to be seen or any evidence of a driving mishap. No persons or animals. Nor a sound to be heard. Like Hank had said earlier, the night was dead. Brady only hoped to God that wasn't the case for the person lying several feet away.

"Call this in, Hank."

To the onlooker, the two deputies appeared equal and for the most part they shared duties just as they shared a friendship. But during critical calls, Brady's position of chief deputy demanded that he take control. Thankfully Hank was more than happy to accept the protocol.

"Right," Hank replied. "An ambulance, too?"

"Let me have a look first. We might need the coroner."

The other man tossed Brady the flashlight, then made a quick U-turn back to their unit. Brady moved purposely forward, his gaze surveying the body lying facedown on the rocky ground. The person was slender, dark-haired, dressed in blue jeans and white shirt and unfortunately showing no sign of life.

Homicides were extremely rare in the county. In fact,

during his seven years at the sheriff's department, Brady had only worked two murder scenes. The last thing he wanted was a third.

His senses on keen alert, he squatted near the body and, using one hand, swiftly slid his finger to the artery at the side of the victim's neck, the flashlight throwing a narrow beam of light. The faint pulse fluttering against the pad of Brady's finger sent relief rushing through him.

Behind him, the sound of crunching gravel alerted him to Hank's approach.

"Is he alive?" the other man asked quickly.

"Yes. But unconscious."

Very carefully Brady rolled the person to a face-up position and was instantly whammed with shock as he found himself staring at a young woman! One side of her black hair was wet with blood, while dried smears marked her forehead.

"Hank, get a blanket from the unit and call for an ambulance," Brady ordered swiftly. "It's a woman. And she has a nasty gash on the forehead."

While the other deputy hurried away, Brady carefully searched her limbs for obvious broken bones or visible injuries. Other than the head wound, there didn't appear to be any, but he could only guess what might be going on internally. Except for a crumpled tissue, there wasn't anything in her pockets.

Hank arrived with the blanket and as Brady folded it to make a cushion for her head, the woman suddenly made a faint groaning noise.

Encouraged by the sound, Brady stuffed the makeshift pillow beneath her head, then questioned, "Miss? Can you hear me? Wake up and tell us what happened! Is there anyone else injured?"

She groaned again and Brady glanced at Hank. "What's the ETA on the ambulance?"

"Twenty-five minutes. When it's time, I'll drive to the highway to signal them," Hank told him. "Unless you'd rather me stay with her and you do it."

Brady wasn't about to leave the woman. Everything about the situation was screaming that some sort of foul play had taken place and he wanted to be around to make sure nothing else happened. "I'm staying," he said bluntly.

"What the hell could she have been doing way out here?" Hank wondered aloud.

"I can't make sense of it," Brady responded. "She doesn't look like the typical person involved in drug use or trafficking. And this area isn't a national forest with camp sites or hiking trails for nature lovers. I don't want to start speculating, but I'm getting a bad vibe."

"Could be she had a simple accident," Hank suggested.

"Yeah. But why did a simple accident happen in the middle of nowhere?"

"Maybe she's been out hunting. Her vehicle might be parked on one of the offshoot roads and we didn't spot it."

"Maybe. But there's no rifle or bow and hunting season is closed. Besides, she isn't dressed for that sort of thing. Look at those cowboy boots. Small fortune for those hand-stitched babies. And she's wearing turquoise—the expensive kind—on her wrist and neck. A robber wouldn't have left that behind."

"Hmm. That's why you're the chief deputy," Hank said wryly. "You don't have to study about noticing things. You just see them."

Brady glanced up at Hank. "Walk the edge of the road and see if you can spot a wallet or handbag lying around," he ordered, then, turning his attention back to the victim, he lifted her hand and patted the back of it. "Come on, miss, wake up!"

This time his voice must have penetrated. Her eyelids fluttered, then slowly lifted. Brady anxiously watched her gaze attempt to focus on him.

"Hello," he said to her. "Welcome back."

She stared blankly at him. "What—where…am I?"

Even though her voice was dazed and weak, Brady was relieved to hear her speak. Bending near, so that she could get a look at his face and official uniform, he explained, "I'm Chief Deputy Brady Donovan."

"A deputy?" she repeated dazedly. "Have I…been in some sort of accident?"

"It appears that way." He squeezed her hand. "An ambulance is on the way. Other than your head, does it feel like anything else is injured?"

Her free hand slowly lifted to her temple. "My…head is…pounding."

"Anything else hurt?"

She closed her eyes and for a moment Brady feared she was going to lose consciousness again.

"No— I…don't think so," she mumbled.

Encouraged that she might not be as badly injured as he'd first feared, he asked, "Can you tell me anything? What happened?"

Confusion puckered her forehead. "No. I— Where am I?"

Brady pulled a handkerchief from his pants and began to wipe at the blood trickling near her eye. If someone had deliberately struck this lovely young woman, they'd obviously left her for dead. The idea sent a shudder down his spine. "You're on a mountain road in Lincoln County, New Mexico. You don't remember?"

Her eyes widened and Brady could see they were a deep gray, the color of a snow cloud on a stark winter day. They were framed by black winged brows and long thick lashes that fluttered like a silk curtain caught in the wind.

"New…Mexico? I—" She broke off as her trembling fingers traveled from her forehead down to her dirt smeared cheek. "That doesn't…make sense to me."

"Why?"

"I…don't know! It—" Suddenly in a panic, she attempted to rise. Not wanting her to struggle and perhaps worsen her condition, Brady helped her to a sitting position. By now, her whole body was beginning to shake, a signal to him that she might be slipping into shock.

Supporting her with an arm around her shoulders, he wrapped the blanket around her, then tucked it close to her body to help hold in the warmth. "Don't worry about it now, miss," he gently instructed. "You've had a nasty knock to your head. Just try to relax and we'll start from the beginning. Can you tell me your name?"

She looked at him and Brady felt something twist in his gut as he watched her lips tremble with fear and uncertainty. He'd never seen a woman look so lost and vulnerable and the protective side of him ached to reassure her, yet the lawman in him yanked those emotions back and ordered him to remember that his first priority was doing his job.

"I…no! Oh, God help me, I don't know my name!"

Over the years, Brady had learned that people who found themselves in trouble with the law oftentimes conveniently forgot their identities. That could be the case with this gray-eyed gal, but he didn't think she was acting. The shock on her face looked far too genuine.

Before he could decide how to reply to her anguished

plea, Hank walked up carrying nothing but a flashlight. Brady rose from his squat to talk to his partner.

"Nothing, Brady. Maybe we'll find something after daylight."

With a pointed glance at the blanket-wrapped woman, Brady gently elbowed Hank in the ribs and the two men walked a short distance away before stopping to converse in low voices.

"She's claiming she doesn't know who she is or where she is," Brady told him. "I'm thinking she has a heck of a concussion. It might be tomorrow before we find out what took place."

Frowning, Hank glanced over his shoulder at the injured woman. "Yeah. But she could be lying. Especially if there was a drug deal gone wrong. By tomorrow, she might lawyer up and decide not to tell us anything."

Brady's lips stretched into a grim line. He wasn't buying that scenario. He'd sensed something innocent about the woman. No doubt Hank would laugh at that notion, so Brady kept the opinion to himself. "Let's hope that doesn't happen."

"Is she Apache? Maybe she's from the res."

"No. She's white. Somewhere in her mid-twenties, I'd say."

Hank shook his head with disbelief. "Boy, oh, boy. And I thought this was going to be a boring night."

Brady slapped him on the shoulder. "You'd better get down to the highway. The ambulance ought to be here soon."

Forty-five minutes later, the ambulance had picked up the injured woman and carried her to Sierra General Hospital in Ruidoso. Brady and Hank arrived directly behind the emergency vehicle and followed the paramedics as they pushed the injured woman through the swishing doors.

Once they were inside the building, Hank said, "Guess we'd better give Admitting what information we have. But that's not a heck of a lot."

Brady's expression was rueful. "We have nothing but white female. Black hair, gray eyes, mid-twenties. They'll have to admit her as a Jane Doe."

As Brady and his partner paused in the middle of the corridor, two nurses hurried out and ordered the paramedics to take the patient farther down the hallway. As he watched the gurney and medical attendants make a sharp left and disappeared from view, Brady had the oddest urge to follow. He wanted to see for himself that the woman was going to be okay, that the nurses and doctors did everything they could to alleviate her pain and fears.

The urge was totally out of character for Brady and made him feel foolish. He'd always made it a policy to never let his emotions get tangled up with his job. It was easier that way. Easier to go home at night and forget the victims who'd been battered or robbed or abused. As a deputy, his job wasn't to fix personal problems, but to put criminals away so that no one else might be harmed.

Sure, when a young child was involved, there wasn't an officer on the force who wasn't emotionally affected. But the woman he'd found on the road tonight was hardly a child and what happened to her next shouldn't be on Brady's mind.

"Hey, Brady, you here on official business tonight? Or just to see your sister?"

At the sound of the female voice, Brady turned to see Andrea, a nurse who often worked the night shift in emergency.

"Bridget is working tonight?" he asked.

Brady's sister was a medical doctor with a very busy practice. She wasn't a hospital resident, but if any of her patients needed hospitalization she treated them here at Sierra General. If he could find her, he might be able to talk her in to taking over Jane Doe's case.

The tall, blonde nurse nodded. "I saw her a few minutes ago. She had some sort of emergency with a patient on the third floor."

Brady turned to his partner. "Can you deal with admitting her on your own?"

Hank shrugged. "Sure. Why?"

At that moment a male nurse at the front desk called to Andrea and as she quickly excused herself, Brady told the deputy, "I'm going to look for my sister."

Hank's brown brows pulled together to form a puzzled frown. "Bridget?" he asked blankly. "Why in heck do you need to see her right now? Your family having problems you haven't told me about?"

Brady had two brothers, three sisters, parents and a grandmother. And, except for one sister, they all lived in the same house on the Diamond D Ranch. Among that many relatives there were always problems arising, but thankfully usually minor ones.

"No, Hank. No problems!" Trotting toward the elevator, Brady said over his shoulder, "And don't run off to the coffee shop until I get back!"

On the third floor, Brady stepped off the elevator and headed to the nearest nurse's station. But before he reached the post, he spotted Bridget striding toward him.

When the petite redhead reached his side, she looked at him with faint alarm. "Brady! What are you doing here? Nothing is wrong with the family, is it?"

"Relax. As far as I know everyone is okay. I'm here on business."

Looping her arm through his, his sister pulled him to one side of the wide corridor so as not to clog the pathway. "Oh, I hope it's not a domestic battery," she said quickly. "I hate to hear about those victims, much less see them in the hospital."

Removing a gray Stetson from his head, Brady raked a hand through thick, tawny-colored waves. "Actually, I'm not sure what this woman is a victim of. Hank and I found her on a back mountain road a few miles from Picacho. The paramedics just brought her in a few minutes ago. She's had sort of trauma to the head. And I was…hoping you'd take a look at her."

His sister frowned. "Isn't one of the emergency doctors dealing with her?"

Brady felt like an idiot. The hospital was full of competent doctors and no doubt Gray Eyes would get the best of care. That should be enough for any patient. So why was he trying to garner her more attention?

"Yes. She's…being treating now. But I thought—well, I'd just feel better if you'd stop in and look at her."

"Who is it?" Bridget quickly questioned. "A friend? Someone we know?"

Shaking his head, he said, "Never seen her before. She doesn't know who she is."

Bridget started to ask another question, but at that moment, a small group of people walking past them called greetings to his sister, momentarily distracting her from their conversation.

"Sorry, Brady," she said, once the medical personnel had moved on down the corridor and away from them. "You were saying—"

"She's blank, Brita. Not her name, where she was or why. Nothing. And no ID to tell us."

A thoughtful frown crossed his sister's face. "A head injury, you say?"

Brady nodded. "A bad gash near her temple."

Suddenly she patted his forearm in a placating way. "I think Dr. Richmond is on emergency call this evening. He's certainly capable of taking care of this type of injury."

"I'm sure he is. But she'll have to be handed over to the care of a permanent physician. And she doesn't know anyone and—"

Sensing his urgency, she released a sigh of surrender. "Okay, Brady, okay. I'll take a look. But mind you, when her family steps forward and requests another doctor, I'll be gone. Understand?"

Smiling with relief, he clasped a loving arm around her shoulders and squeezed. "Did you know that you're my favorite sister?"

She shot him a tired look. "Yeah. Your favorite is the one you happen to be with at the moment. And do I need to remind you of the messes you've gotten me into? That time—"

"We don't have time to go into my transgressions now, sis," Brady interrupted as he urged his sister toward the nearest elevator. "I promise I'll make everything up to you. Someday."

The cubicle behind the plain beige curtain was cold and smelled faintly of disinfectant. Standing a few feet away, at the foot of the narrow, railed bed, a middle-aged doctor with dark blond hair and black rimmed glasses was scratching notes on a clipboard, while barking orders at the attending nurse.

Since arriving in the emergency unit, she'd been stripped of her boots and clothing, sponged clean and dressed in a blue cotton gown that tied at the back. The doctor had poked and prodded, asked her questions that she couldn't answer and generally done little to assuage her fears.

Now that he'd ended his examination and was conversing with the nurse, her mind vacillated between sheer panic and a pit of total emptiness.

Scans. Sutures. Neurological tests. The medical words she managed to catch here and there made little to no sense to her.

Oh, God, who was she? Where was she? The questions pounded through her head, adding to the horrible throb in her right temple.

Thinking was like bouncing herself off a black wall where there was no door or crack of light to lead her either forward or backward. Other than waking up to see a deputy sheriff hovering over her, there was nothing in her mind, except icy, paralyzing fear.

She tried to push the terror back and keep from sobbing as the doctor exited the cubicle and the young nurse with a kind face bent over her. The name tag pinned to the left side of her chest said her name was Lilly.

"All right, miss," she said warmly. "Let's get some pain medication started and then we'll see about taking you down to radiology. When that's done someone will come around to put some stitches in your scalp."

During the ambulance ride, the paramedics had started an intravenous drip. Now the nurse simply pushed a syringe full of medication into the tube already affixed to her hand.

"Why am I going to radiology?"

"To take pictures of your skull and brain," the nurse replied. "Dr. Richmond needs to see if you have internal injuries."

"Oh." She didn't want pictures or stitches, she wanted

to scream. She wanted her memory back. "Will that take long? The tests?"

"No," the nurse assured her. "They won't hurt, either."

She closed her eyes. "Um—the deputy who found me. Is he here?"

Lilly answered, "I saw Hank Ridell out in the corridor a few minutes ago. Is that who you mean?"

She opened her eyes to see the nurse was writing something on the chart the doctor had left behind.

"No. His name was Donovan, I think. He was tall and had on a gray hat and he had a little scar right here." She touched a finger to a spot on her cheekbone near her eye.

Lilly suddenly smiled a knowing smile. "Oh. That's Brady. He's the chief deputy of Lincoln County. And considered quite a catch by most of the young women around here."

The pain medication was beginning to course rapidly through her bloodstream, easing the pounding in her head. "Including you?" she asked the nurse.

Lilly blushed and laughed. "No. I have a boyfriend. Besides, I'm not in Brady Donovan's league." She placed the chart in a holder at the foot of the bed, then studied her more closely. "Did you need to talk with the deputy for some reason?"

There were a thousand things she wanted to ask the man, things that might help jar her memory. But that wasn't entirely the reason she wanted to see the deputy again. He'd been nice and gentle. He'd held her with strong hands and soothed her with his low voice. At some point during their wait for the ambulance, he'd become her light in a heavy fog. She'd not wanted to leave him and now she fervently wished he was back by her side.

"I would like to speak with him. If you think that's possible."

Smiling, Lilly winked at her. "While you're in radiology I'll do my best to find him."

The nurse quickly swished out the door and as she watched her go, she desperately prayed the woman would find the deputy.

Her world had gone crazy and he was the only person, the only thing her memory had to go back to. She was totally and utterly lost. And without Deputy Donovan, she didn't know if she'd ever be able to find her way back home.

Chapter Two

More than an hour later, Brady and Hank were sitting in the hospital coffee shop, finishing off huge slices of pie when Bridget walked up to their table.

Shaking her head, she looked at the crumbs on their plates. “Looks like both of you are really worried about good nutrition,” she said wryly.

“Pecan pie must be good for you or the hospital wouldn’t serve it, right?” Hank asked.

“Wrong. But it looks delicious,” she said with a weary sigh.

Immediately, Hank jumped from his seat and pulled out a chair for her.

“Did you see our Jane Doe?” Brady questioned before she had time to get comfortable.

The doctor thanked Hank, then pushed a hand through

her tumbled hair. "I did," she said to Brady. "And I've become her doctor. For the time being."

"I'm glad. So what about her condition?" Brady questioned.

His sister frowned at him. "I can't give you details, Brady. You know that's invading a patient's privacy."

Brady muttered a curse word under his breath. For the past two hours he'd not been able to think about anything except the gray-eyed woman he'd held in his arms. Now his sister wanted to act all professional with him.

"Damn it, Brita, just tell me—is she going to get better? Is she going to be able to remember? Tell us who she is?"

Bridget studied him keenly, and then glanced pointedly at Hank. "What has he done, had a love-at-first-sight experience?"

Hank grinned. "You mean another one?"

Normally Brady liked to joke. In fact, Fiona Donovan had often called him her most lighthearted child, full of happiness and humor. But at the moment he wasn't feeling anything of the sort. In fact, he was getting a tad angry at both his sister and his partner.

Scowling, Brady muttered to the both of them, "I'm not in the mood for this!"

Seeing he was serious, Bridget relented. "Okay, brother, I'll be straightforward. Your Jane Doe will get better. The good news is that physically she's fine. She wasn't raped, and aside from some bruising on her arms and legs she isn't seriously injured. As for her memory, how long that might take is a question I can't answer."

"Are you kiddin' me?"

Reaching across the table, she patted the back of his hand. "No. Medicine is not always an exact science. And head injuries are sometimes tricky. She might remember everything in the next few minutes, years from now, something in-between, or never."

The picture of awful uncertainty his sister was painting hit Brady like a fist to his mouth. No matter the circumstances that caused the injury, the woman didn't deserve this.

"Isn't there something you can do to make her remember? Give her some sort of drug?"

"Trust me, Brady. If she doesn't improve quickly, I'll be calling in a specialist. But since she's a ward of the county, cost has to be considered—there's just so much the hospital will allow. And quit staring at me like you expect me to perform some sort of miracle. I'm just a doctor."

Hank suddenly interjected, "Look, Brady, it might be that we find her ID when we return to the scene in the morning. Who knows, we might even find an abandoned vehicle in the area."

Brady wished they didn't have to wait until daylight to return to the scene. He wanted answers now. But the department's manpower was already stretched across the enormous county. To bring in searchlights would be costly, time-consuming and perhaps even worthless in the long run.

"Yeah," Brady agreed. "Let's hope."

Bridget suddenly squeezed his fingers and he glanced back at his sister.

"I almost forgot—she's asking for you."

Brady's mouth fell open. "Me?"

Bridget's smile was wry. "Yes, you. She wants to see you. I expect the meds we've given her will be putting her to sleep soon, so you'd better get going."

Gray Eyes wanted to see him? The news didn't just stun Brady, it pleased him in the goofiest sort of way and he hurriedly scraped back his chair.

"I'll be back in a few minutes, Hank." Rising to his feet,

he pulled out his wallet and tossed several bills at Hank. "Here. Buy Bridget a piece of pie. She looks hungry."

He headed toward the plate glass door leading out of the coffee shop when suddenly his sister's voice called out to him.

"Brady, where are you going?"

Frowning with frustration, he glanced over his shoulder. "Where do you think I'm going?" he asked impatiently.

With a shake of her head, she looked drolly over to Hank, then back to her brother. "I don't know. There are nearly five hundred rooms in this hospital. Don't you think you need the number to find her?"

If Brady didn't feel like an idiot before, he certainly did now and he was glad he was standing a few feet away from the table. Otherwise Hank could easily see the red on his face.

"All right," he conceded. "I wasn't thinking. What's the number?"

"Two-twelve. And Brady, be easy," she warned.

A lazy smile crossed Brady's face. "Don't worry, sis. If there's one thing I'm good at, it's handling women. Especially damsels in distress."

When a knock sounded on the door, she didn't bother to open her eyes. For the past thirty minutes the nurses had been coming and going from the hospital room like ants on a picnic blanket. She expected the footsteps she heard approaching her bed belonged to yet another nurse who was there to take her blood pressure for the umpteenth time.

"Excuse me, miss. It's Deputy Donovan. Do you feel like talking?"

The sound of his voice set her heart to pounding and her eyes popped open to see him standing near the head of the bed. His gray hat was in his hand and beneath the dim lighting she could see rusty-gold hair waving thickly about his head, tanned features molded in a sober expression.

He was a young man, she decided. Somewhere in his late twenties or early thirties. *Handsome* was not the word to come to her mind as she studied him more closely. But *rugged* and *sexy* certainly did. Sharp cheekbones, a thrusting chin, hazel green eyes and a full lower lip merged together to form one strong face.

Suddenly feeling as weak as a puny kitten, she cleared her throat and tried to speak in a normal voice. Instead, it came out raspy. "Thank you for coming, Deputy Donovan."

A faint smile tilted the corner of his lips and her gaze was drawn to his mouth and the dimple marking his left cheek.

"My pleasure," he said. "How are you feeling?"

That voice. It was her first memory of anything and she clung to it like a child with a blanket. "Lousy. But better."

"I'm glad to hear it. Hopefully, you'll be right as rain real soon."

She swallowed as hopeless emotions thickened her throat. "Doctor Donovan was very positive about that. She…told me that she's your sister."

His smile deepened. "That's right. We're from a big family. We all live together in a big ranch house."

Family. Parents. Siblings. Did she have any? And if she did, where were they? Nearby? Far away? Maybe she had no one. Oh, God, let her remember, she prayed.

Her gaze fell from his face and settled on the folds of her blue hospital gown. "No one here at the hospital seems to recognize me. I…don't know if I have any…family."

His hand was suddenly touching her shoulder and the warmth from it spread through her, easing the chill that she couldn't seem to shake in spite of the extra blankets the nurses had spread over her.

"If you do, we'll find them. Trust me on that."

He sounded so confident, so firm in his conviction, that she had to believe him. Her gaze fluttered back to his face. "I can't remember anything about the place where you found me. Was it near a house or anything?"

"No. The road is a back road that leads into the mountains. Ranchers use it to move their sheep and cattle from one range to another and hunters travel it during open season. That's about all. The nearest house to where we found you is probably six or seven miles away."

She shook her head with dismay. "What could I have been doing there? Was there a car? Anything?"

"Not that we've found yet. We'll be examining your clothes and scouring the area in the morning. If you left anything behind, we'll find it."

She drew in a deep breath and let it out. She was exhausted and her body was screaming for sleep, yet she fought the fogginess settling over her. She wanted to be with this man a little longer, absorb the security he lent her.

"If I—don't remember, is there much you can do to find out who I am?"

His fingers tightened reassuringly on her shoulder. "Don't worry about that tonight. Everything is going to be all right. I promise."

He was trying to make her feel better and oddly enough, he was. "I don't even have a name for you to call me," she said, then tried to laugh at the ridiculousness of her situation. "I guess I'm a Jane Doe, aren't I? But please don't call me that. I never liked the name Jane that much."

His brows arched. "How do you know something like that without remembering?"

"I—well, I don't know why I dislike the name. I just

know that I do," she said with faint surprise. "But I guess you're right. Subconsciously I must be remembering something."

Brady had never wanted to take anyone in his arms more than he did this woman at this very moment. She looked lost and wounded and utterly beautiful. And everything inside him wanted to make her better.

"See," he said gently, "your memory will all come back and then you can tell me your real name. But for now let's give you another one. What would you like to be called?"

One hand lifted, then fell helplessly back to the bed covers. "It doesn't matter."

"It must have," he said with an easy chuckle. "You didn't want to be called Jane."

A tiny smile curved her lips and he felt instantly better.

"Well. That's different," she said. "I don't want to be a Jane. I want to be someone real."

"All right. Then I'm going to call you..." He thought for a moment, then smiled with satisfaction. "Lass."

Even though her gray eyes were full of sleep, he could see surprise flicker in their drowsy debts.

"Lass," she repeated as though testing the name on her tongue. "Why?"

Brady couldn't stop his fingers from moving to her forehead and gently pushing a strand of shiny black hair away from the bruised flesh near her eye. Did this woman have a husband somewhere, he wondered? A husband that often touched her this very same way?

During the time the two of them had spent waiting for the ambulance to arrive, Brady had studied her hands. From a professional standpoint, he'd wanted to see if there had been defensive wounds on her hands or traces of flesh or hair beneath her fingernails from fighting off an attacker.

From a personal position, he'd wanted to see if she was wearing a wedding band or engagement ring.

Except for a bit of grime on her palms, her hands had been clean. But that might not mean she was single. Her ring could have been stolen or she could have simply not been wearing it when she'd left home. Or not had one on for very long—not long enough to get a tan line or callus.

"Well, Lassie got lost lots of times," he reasoned, "and she always found her way back home to her family. Then everyone was happy again. That's the way it's going to be with you, Lass."

She reached for his hand and as her fingers curled loosely around his, her eyelids drifted downward

"Lass," she repeated sleepily. "That's very pretty. Thank you, Deputy."

Brady was about to tell her that no thanks were needed, but at that moment the muscles in her face went lax and the fingers wrapped around his lost their grip and dropped to the white sheet covering her body.

She'd fallen asleep and it was time for him to go, he realized. Yet he lingered beside the bed, unable to tear his gaze away from the woman.

She was smaller than he'd first estimated, but her arms appeared toned and muscled. No doubt the rest of her was as fit, he thought. This told him she wasn't someone who sat around all day. She either worked at something that required manual labor or she made frequent visits to the gym. Her hair was shiny and well cared for, the straight ends trimmed to blunt precision. Pale pink polish covered her short, well-manicured nails and her satiny smooth skin looked as though it had been pampered since birth.

She definitely wasn't blue collar, he thought. Along with her grooming habits, there were also the earrings attached to her lobes. If he was a betting man, he'd wager the glittering stones circling the chunks of turquoise were real diamonds. A fact that only added to her strange circumstance.

If someone had whacked her in the head to rob her, why hadn't the thief taken the pricey jewelry? No, something else had gone down with this little, lost lassie and he was going to do his damnedest to find out.

His thoughts were interrupted by a faint knock on the door and Brady turned from the bed just as his sister stepped into the room.

"I think she's gone to sleep," Brady said, hoping he didn't look as sheepish as he felt. "And I…was just about to leave."

Bridget peered around his shoulder at her sleeping patient, then back at him. "I'm on my way home. I wanted to see if she recalled anything that might be helpful."

Brady shook his head. "No."

"Well, it will come." She rose on tiptoes and planted a kiss on his cheek. "Good night, Brady. And don't look worried. You've always been good at your job. You'll figure out where this Jane Doe belongs."

"She's not Jane Doe. I've named her Lass and that's what she's going to go by. Until—well, until she remembers or we figure out her real identity."

Bridget appeared amused. "Lass, eh? That ought to fit right in with our Irish brood. What are you doing, making plans to adopt her?"

"Damn it, Brita, that remark was uncalled for."

Frustrated, he stepped around his sister and headed out of the room. Bridget followed closely on his heels and once they were out in the corridor, she grabbed him by the arm.

"Okay. I'm sorry," she apologized. "I was only trying to lighten things up with a little humor. What's the matter with you tonight, anyway? You're as prickly as Grandma's rose bushes."

Brady sighed. He honestly didn't know what was eating at him. He was thankful, very thankful, that he and Hank had just happened to be traveling the road where Lass had lain unconscious. If not, well, he didn't want to think about the outcome. And yet, the whole ordeal had shaken him, affected him like nothing he'd dealt with before.

"You're right." Pinching the bridge of his nose, he momentarily closed his eyes. "I guess…it's not every day that we find someone left on the side of the road for dead. I keep thinking, if that was you I'd want someone to do everything they could to help you."

Bridget rubbed his forearm with understanding. "I always thought you were too soft-hearted for this job," she said gently.

A dry smile curved his lips as he opened his eyes and looked down at her. "Hell, other than Grandma, you're probably the only one in the family who thinks I have a heart."

Her soft laugh was full of affection. "That's because they don't know you like we do."

Were his sister and grandmother the only ones who realized he was more than a lawman, covering his heart with a bullet proof vest? How did Lass see him?

Forget that last question, Brady. How Gray Eyes sees you is irrelevant. She's just a part of your job. Nothing more. Nothing less.

The next morning, Brady and Hank and two other deputies returned to the mountain road near Picacho to search the area for clues. Thankfully, the day was bright and no rain had fallen during the night to wash away evidence. But unfortunately, they found nothing, except a crumpled betting ticket from Ruidoso Downs Racetrack. The twenty-dollar bet, found lying against a clump of sage, about a hundred yards down the road from Lass, had been for a trifecta on the fifth race of yesterday's card. After a quick call to the track, Brady had learned that the ticket was worthless, so there was no other record of it.

But the money, or lack of it, was inconsequential at the moment, Brady figured. The main question was why the ticket was here on this back road where there was nothing but wilderness? Had a group of party-goers from the track driven out here just to find an isolated place to whoop it up? Teenagers might do something that foolish. But teenagers couldn't wager. And Lass wasn't a teen.

None of it made sense to Brady or his partner as they exchanged speculations.

"Maybe Lass was at the track yesterday and the ticket fell out of her pocket when she whammed her head," Hank said as the two men stood in the middle of the quiet dirt road.

"Or when someone whammed it for her," Brady said grimly. "We'll post a few pictures of her at the track. We might get lucky and one of the clerks working the betting cages will recognize her."

Last night, after Brady and Hank had left the hospital, they'd driven the thirty-mile trip to their headquarters in Carrizozo to finish the remainder of their shift. Before he'd gone home, Brady had looked through as many missing cases that could possibly be tied to the area and he'd come up with nothing that matched Lass's description. No calls had come in to the sheriff's office reporting anyone missing. Nor had there been any calls for domestic disputes, robberies or assaults. Other than the incident with Lass, the only thing that had gone on was a few public intoxication and DUI arrests. Like Hank had said, last night had been as quiet as a sleeping cat.

This morning, after a lengthy meeting, Sheriff Hamilton had turned the entire case over to Brady and now as he scanned the rough terrain beyond the smoky lens of his sunglasses, he was feeling a heavy weight on his shoulders. For years now, Ethan Hamilton had been his mentor, even his hero. He never wanted to let the man down. Yet incredibly, it was Lass and her pleading face that was weighing on him the most.

Hank's voice suddenly interrupted Brady's deep thoughts. "It's too bad we couldn't have found her in the daylight. We might have been able to pick up on more footprints. Looks like most of them were blown away with last night's wind."

"No one ever said our job was supposed to be easy," Brady replied as he continued to study the area around them.

The trees and vegetation weren't exactly thick, but there was enough juniper and pine for a person to hide or get lost in. Not that either scenario applied to Lass, he thought. But his gut feeling kept telling him that she'd come out of the mountains and then ended up at the road's edge, rather than the other way around.

"I think I'll have a talk with Johnny Chino and see if he'll come have a look at things," Brady said after a moment. "It might help us to know what direction Lass came from before she ended up in the ditch."

Hank tossed him a skeptical glance. "Good luck. Johnny hasn't done any tracking since—well, not for years."

Brady sighed. The Apache tracker was one of the best. But for a long time now the man had turned his back on a job that had once taken him all over the southwest. Brady didn't exactly know what sort of personal demons the tracker was carrying around, but he figured working again would be the best way for Johnny to get rid of them.

"He might do it for me. We've been friends since we were kids."

"Like I said, good luck," Hank muttered.

She was running through inky darkness. Stumbling over rocks and fallen branches. Her breaths were gasps of fire, burning her lungs and stabbing her chest with searing pain. Somewhere, far in front of her, she would find light and safety. If only she could keep running. If only…

"Lass? It's Dr. Donovan. Wake up and talk with me."

The firm voice penetrated the dark terror around her and Lass jerked awake with a jolt to see Deputy Donovan's sister standing next to her bed.

"Oh! It's you, Doctor." Shoving a handful of disheveled hair off her face, Lass eased to a sitting position in the bed and blinked her eyes. Her whole body felt damp and her heart was pounding with lingering fear. "I guess I dozed off. I must have been dreaming or maybe I was trying to remember—I don't know."

The redheaded doctor studied her closely. "Do you remember your dream?"

Nodding, Lass shivered. "I was running in the dark. Away from something. And I was terrified. That's all I know."

The doctor pulled out a pin light and flashed it in both of Lass's eyes. "Mmm. That's a common nightmare. It could be a result of the trauma you've gone through or you could be remembering something that happened. Hard to say. In any case, I'm happy to report that your scans have been read and there are no fractures to your skull or any other major brain damage. You have a garden variety concussion and it should go away in the next few days. And it's a positive sign to see that your short-term memory is working. You obviously remember that I'm your doctor and you remembered your dream."

The doctor put the pin light away and placed a stethoscope to Lass's chest. Once she'd listened to her satisfaction, then hung the instrument back around her neck, Lass asked, "What about the rest of my memory? I keep working my mind, trying to think past last night. I can't."

The doctor gently patted her shoulder. "I'm hopeful that once the swelling in your brain starts to recede and everything begins to heal itself, your memory will return. But in the meantime, I'm going to have a specialist come in this afternoon and speak with you."

"A specialist?" Lass asked warily. "What kind of specialist?"

Dr. Donovan's smile was meant to be reassuring. "A psychiatrist."

Lass stared at her in horror. "Do you…think I'm crazy? Oh, God, I never thought about that! I might have been institutionalized and wandered away. Maybe I hurt someone and they put me away! I—"

With each word that passed her lips, Lass grew more and more agitated.

"Lass," the doctor said gently. "You need to stop this. I can assure you that no one here has detected any sort of mental illness. The psychiatrist will simply talk to you and perhaps help coax some of your memories to return. That's all."

Lass's shoulders slumped with relief. She didn't know why her thoughts kept running toward such negative speculations. Had she been in some sort of trouble? Criminal trouble?

What a stupid question, Lass. Trouble might as well be written across your forehead. Anyone who's found on the side of the road with a head bashed is bound to be connected to some sort of trouble. What do you think you were doing out there in the mountains in the middle of the night? Admiring the wildflowers?

Swallowing, she forced the troubling questions aside and tried to focus on the doctor. "So—how much longer will I have to be in the hospital?" she asked.

"If no complications pop up, I'll be releasing you tomorrow." Dr. Donovan smiled with encouragement. "As for this morning, the nurses are going to come in and help you shower and dress. And if you're steady enough on your feet, you can move around somewhat. But I don't want you overdoing it, okay?"

Lass agreed and the doctor continued to give her a few more orders before she finally said goodbye and left the room.

Once she was gone, Lass let out a heavy sigh as her gaze surveyed her surroundings. For the moment, the small, stark room was her home. But tomorrow she'd be leaving. To where? Where was her home? Oh, God, if she only knew.

Chapter Three

Later that afternoon while Hank questioned workers at the racetrack, Brady drove to the hospital to check on Lass. From the report Bridget had given him earlier this morning, the young woman's memory was still a blank. But he was hoping each hour that passed would bring her closer to recalling her identity and, moreover, what had happened to her the night before.

On the second floor, he stepped off the elevator and turned right in the direction of Lass's room, but before he could get past the nurse's desk, a young woman with long brown hair wrapped in a knot atop her head waved and called to him.

"Hey, Brady! Are you going to the concert next weekend at the rodeo arena?"

He paused as the nurse came rushing up to him. Miranda was a sweet girl he'd once dated a few times, but it had quickly become obvious to both of them that she'd wanted more than just a good time together. Thankfully, she'd understood that he wasn't looking for a permanent partner and they'd parted on friendly terms.

He shook his head. "Not unless I have to provide security. And right now the city police are planning on handling it."

With Lass's case thrown on his plate, he wasn't going to have much free time in the coming days. Unless, she miraculously recovered, or someone showed up to identify her.

"Guess you're busy with the Jane Doe thing," she commented. "I think I ought to tell you that most of the hospital stopped by to see her. We'd been hoping someone would recognize her, but nobody does."

"Thanks for letting me know, Miranda. I appreciate the attempt."

Miranda grimaced with regret. "Poor thing. And she's so pretty, too. What will happen to her? I mean, if she doesn't remember? I guess she'll have to go to one of those shelters." Miranda shuddered with distaste. "Maybe you'll figure it out, Brady, before that happens."

He nodded and she quickly excused herself as the phone on the nurse's desk began to shrill loudly. Brady hurried on to Lass's room and as he went, Miranda's suggestion plagued him. To think of Lass thrown in a rescue mission or a shelter for battered women sickened him. And whether she remembered or not, he couldn't let it happen.

After a short knock on her door, he stepped inside the room and was pleasantly surprised to find her dressed and sitting in a cushioned chair positioned near the room's only window.

"Well, you look much better than the last time I saw you," he greeted. "How are you feeling?"

She was wearing the clothes he'd found her in and though they were smudged with dirt in spots, they made her look far more normal than the hideous hospital gown. Her long hair had been pulled back from her face and fastened at her nape with a rubber band. The style exposed her swollen eye yet at the same time revealed the long, lovely line of her neck.

"Stronger," she answered. "And my head doesn't hurt nearly as much."

He moved across the room, then stopped a couple of feet from her chair. The late afternoon sun slanted a golden ray across her lap and cast a sheen to her crow-black hair. Except for her cheeks, her skin was as pale as milk and he found himself tempering the urge to reach over and touch it, test its softness with the pads of his fingers.

Clearing his throat, he said, "That's good. Bridget says you're on the mend."

Her features tightened. "Did she also tell you that she sent a psychiatrist to talk with me?"

Brady looked at her in surprise. "No. But I'm glad. I told her to help you in every way that she could. Obviously she's not going to leave any stone unturned." He took a seat on the edge of the narrow bed. "So what did the psychiatrist have to say?"

She rubbed her hands nervously down the thighs of her jeans. "Well, that I'm not crazy or anything like that."

Brady grinned. "I could have told you that much."

She darted a sober glance at him. "He also said that I might not be remembering because I'm afraid to remember."

Folding his arms against his chest, Brady studied her with interest. "Like a psychosomatic thing," he said.

Her brows arched with surprise. "Why, yes. How did you know that? Have you studied medicine, too?"

Brady chuckled. "No. I left that to my sisters. I'm a lawman. I study human characters. And believe me, seeing people under stress and in trouble makes for a good psychology class."

Dropping her head, she let out a heavy breath. "Well, I've not remembered anything. Unless you count the dream I had. And that didn't tell me much. Except that I was running in the dark and whatever was behind me was scaring the living daylights out of me." She looked up at him, her expression twisted with something close to agony. "Your sister says she's going to release me from the hospital tomorrow. What does that mean, Deputy Donovan? What will happen to me then?"

He swiftly shook his head. "I'd be pleased if you'd call me Brady. And don't worry—we'll find some place nice for you to stay until we can get a fix on where you really belong."

Suddenly it dawned on him that she had nothing but the clothes on her back. No handbag with all the little necessities women carried with them. No cell phone filled with numbers of friends and family that she might call for help. No credit cards or checkbook or any sort of means to provide for herself. She was totally dependent and, at the moment, looking straight at him for answers.

She didn't make any sort of reply to his comment and Brady figured there wasn't much she could say. She was at the mercy of the county and what it could provide for her. Unless he stepped in, he thought, as his mind suddenly jumped forward. Since his older sister, Maura, had married Quint Cantrell, her room had become empty. Brady's home, the Diamond D Ranch, was a huge place with plenty of space for a guest. What would his family think if he showed up with Lass? He and his sister Dallas had always been guilty of picking up strays that needed a home. Well,

Lass was no different, he rationalized. She needed a home in the worst kind of way.

"Thank you, Brady. I guess… Well, you know the old saying—beggars can't be choosers. I'm obviously in that position now."

Changing the subject for the moment, he suddenly asked, "Did someone from the sheriff's department come by to take your picture?"

She nodded. "Yes. A lady. She said you were going to be putting it on posters around town and posting it on the Internet."

"That's right. We also plan to put it in the area papers. See if that will turn up any leads. But in the meantime, you'll need some help. A place to stay, clothes and things like that. I'm thinking—" His gaze zeroed in on hers. "How would you feel about staying at my home? Until we get your problem worked out?"

Her gray eyes narrowed with something like mistrust. "I don't understand. I'm not your responsibility. I mean, I know that you and your partner are the ones who found me, but that doesn't mean—"

She broke off as he quickly shook his head. "Look, Lass, I'll be frank. I don't think you'd much like living in a shelter. You wouldn't have much privacy and some of the women there—they're dealing with some pretty bad problems."

Her lips quivered. "And I'm not?"

He tried to give her the same sort of smile Brady's mother gave him when he was fretting over an issue that was beyond his control. "As of right now, Lass, the only problem we're certain that you have is amnesia. And the way I see it, you could've had a whole lot worse things happen to you."

"Maybe I did. And we just don't know. Maybe I'd bring

trouble to your family and—" Her words abruptly trailing off, she shook her head and rose slowly from her chair. "I don't want to be a burden or a…problem. Thank you for your kind offer, Brady, but I can't accept."

Feeling ridiculously squashed, he watched her move to the window and stare out at the small manicured lawn at the back of the building. To one side of the grassy area, a patio had been constructed and offered a group of comfortable lawn chairs to visitors who needed a break from the confines of a sterile hospital room.

At the moment a young woman with two small children in hand was strolling among the potted desert plants that adorned the patio. Lass appeared to be focused on the sight of the playful youngsters and Brady wondered if she might have children of her own, children that were missing their mother. For some reason he didn't like the image of her being a mother, or a wife. And yet, he realized that if she did have a family waiting for her somewhere, she needed to get back to them as quickly as possible. More importantly, it was his job to see that she was reunited with her loved ones.

"I assure you, Lass, you're not going to cause trouble. And even if you did, we Donovans know how to deal with trouble. Besides, you being on the ranch would be a big help to me."

A frown puckered her forehead as she pulled her attention away from the children and over to him. "Really? How is that?"

"Well, until we discover your identity, you're going to have to keep in close contact with the sheriff's department. Since I'm in charge of your case that means me. And having you on the Diamond D will make it convenient for the two of us to work together."

"The Diamond D," she repeated thoughtfully. "I think I recall you saying last night that you lived on a ranch. Your family raises cattle?"

"Horses," he explained. "Racehorses."

"Oh." The frown on her face deepened. "What do you do with racehorses around here? The nurses tell me that this is a relatively small town. Most of the major tracks are on the east and west coasts."

Rising from the bed, he joined her at the window. As he rested his hip on the wide seal, he studied her keenly. "If you remember such things as that, then apparently a part of your memory is working. As for our horses, we—or I should say my brother Liam—hauls them cross-country to race. But Ruidoso has a track and it's becoming significant in its own right. It's the home of the Million Dollar Futurity that takes place every Labor Day."

"I see," she murmured, then thoughtfully shook her head. "I wonder why I knew about the major tracks? Perhaps I'm connected to the business in some way. But I'm…only guessing. It's just a feeling I have. Not a memory."

Brady's mind was leaping in all direction as he attempted to connect what dots he had. "I don't know if this means anything, Lass, but one of the deputies found a wagering ticket from Ruidoso Downs not far from where you were found. The track, betting, horses—do any of those things ring a bell?"

She stared out the window for long moments, then with a groan of defeat, pressed a hand to her forehead. "I'm sorry, Brady. When I try to think of anything personal, it's all a blank. And the harder I try to think, the more my head aches."

"Then don't try to think," he urged with concern. "Bridget would have my hide if she found out I'm making your condition worse."

Quickly, as though to reassure him, she reached out and touched his arm. "It's not your fault. Please don't think so. You're only trying to help me."

The touch of her hand on his bare forearm was as light as a butterfly and though her fingers were cool, Brady's reaction was just the opposite. Heat flowed along his arm as though he'd been touched by a torch, and for a moment he was lost for words, lost in the gray depths of her sad eyes.

"Don't worry about me, Lass. I've got a thick hide." At least, he'd believed he was tough-skinned, until she'd touched him. Dear Lord, he had to get out of here before he did something totally unprofessional. Like gather her into his arms and cuddle her against his chest. "And right now I have to get back to work."

Unable to tear his eyes away from her, he began to move backward toward the door.

"What about tomorrow?" she asked in bewilderment.

He flashed a smile. "Bridget will let me know when to be here to pick you up."

"But I—"

Placing a finger against his lips, he said, "I promise, my folks will be thrilled to have you."

And so would he, Brady silently admitted. But how long would it be before the thrill turned into a problem? Before good intentions turned bad?

Brady wasn't going to let himself think about those questions. Right now Lass needed him. And that was all that mattered.

The next morning Brady had been at his desk for over an hour when Sheriff Hamilton arrived at work. As the tall, dark-haired man sauntered through Brady's small work area, he stopped in his tracks and stared at his chief deputy.

"It's not even daylight yet. What are you doing here?"

Brady glanced up from his computer screen. Ethan Hamilton was a big man in stature and presence and held a lifelong connection to the area he served. Eleven years ago, when Roy Pardee had retired, Ethan had stepped into a pair of mighty big boots. Roy had been loved and revered, a living legend as far as citizens of the county were concerned and being the man's nephew had only made it harder for Ethan to prove himself. Down through the years he'd done that and more. He'd married the county judge, Penelope Parker, and they were now raising twin sons, Jake and Jase.

"I could say the same about you." Even though Ethan was clearly the boss, the two men were longtime friends and they conversed as such. Now Brady swiveled the rolling chair away from the desk and stood facing the sheriff. "Is something going on with you?"

"Penny's still feeling puny and she was up early," Ethan explained. "Once she gets up, I can't sleep."

"Again? Maybe you should take her to a doctor. See what's wrong with the woman," Brady suggested.

A slow smile spread across the sheriff's face. "I don't need to. She went to the doctor yesterday and he assured her everything would get back to normal—in seven months. Or as normal as it can be with another baby in the house."

Brady was stunned. Ethan and Penny's twins were nearly twelve years old. After all this time, he'd never figured the couple wanting more children. "Penny is...pregnant?"

"Yeah," he said with a beaming smile. "Isn't it great? We'd been wanting more children for a long time, but she's had health issues. Her having the twins was a miracle, so we figured it would be a second miracle if she could get pregnant again. We'd almost given up, but now it's happened and the doc says everything is going along fine."

The sheriff was a true family man and nothing made him happier than his wife and children. Brady could only wonder if he'd ever want to be that settled, that focused on one certain woman. So far he'd not found one that could hold his interest for more than a month, much less forever. Where women were concerned, Brady's mother accused him of being a selfish alpha male who expected too much from a lady. But Brady would hardly classify himself in those terms. He'd rather think of himself as smart and practical. And he was smart enough to know that he wasn't ready or willing to turn his life over to a woman. For that to happen, he'd have to be head over heels in love. And so far, that malady had never struck Brady.

Shaking the sheriff's hand heartily, Brady expressed his congratulations. "Wow! This must have been a pleasant surprise for the whole family! You must be walking on a cloud right about now!"

The sheriff chuckled. "The whole Murdock clan has kept the phone lines hot with the news. And me, well, I'm not even complaining about having to cook breakfast for me and the boys for the past week. Penny can't stand the smell of food early in the mornings. She won't even let me make coffee. And speaking of coffee—" he glanced over his shoulder to a corner where the coffeemaker was located "—has anyone made a pot yet?"

"Yeah. Me. I'll get us both a cup," Brady told him. "I need to talk with you."

"Fine. Bring it on to my office," he said. "I want to see if Dottie has left any notes on my desk."

Moments later, carrying two cups steaming with coffee,

Brady entered the sheriff's office and took a seat in front of the other man's desk.

"So," Ethan said as he sipped from the cup and rifled through the scraps of paper scattered in front of him, "you have something personal on your mind? Or business?"

Feeling sheepish and not really knowing why, Brady cleared his throat. "A little of both, I suppose. It's about the Jane Doe case. She's getting released from the hospital today. And I…plan on taking her out to the ranch."

Ethan's head shot up. "The Diamond D—?"

"That's right. Do you have any problems with that?"

The sheriff rubbed a finger along his jaw. "Well, I don't think there's any law against it. But I…wouldn't advise it, Brady. The county has places for people like her. They'll look out for her until we get this thing straightened out."

Frowning with disapproval, Brady leaned forward. "Sure. In that women's shelter down in Ruidoso. That wouldn't be good."

"Why not?"

Brady slowly sipped his coffee while he tried to gather all the legitimate excuses he could think of. "Well, it's right next to the mission for people with addiction problems."

"She won't have to mingle with those people."

Drawing in a deep breath, Brady tried again. "The women's shelter is small and they rarely have enough room to spare. Lass wouldn't have any privacy and she'd have to wear whatever she could find out of the charity box."

Ethan picked up another note and scanned the brief contents. "I could think of worse things."

Brady's jaw tightened. "She doesn't come from that sort of background, Ethan. She doesn't belong there."

The sheriff shot him a wry look, before he carefully sipped his coffee. "None of the other women belong there, either, Brady. Bad circumstances put them there. Just like the Jane—" He suddenly paused, his eyes narrowing on Brady's face. "Did I hear you call her 'Lass'? Has she remembered her name?"

Brady couldn't stop a wave of red heat from crawling up his neck and onto his face. "No. Unless her condition changed overnight." He made a dismissive gesture with his hand. "I gave her the name. We had to have something to call her."

"Yeah," Ethan said dryly, "guess the name Jane wouldn't work for that."

Knowing the other man could see right through him, Brady tossed up his hands in surrender. "Okay. Okay. So I'm a sucker for a stray. What can I say?"

Ethan settled back in his chair and Brady could feel the full weight of the other man's attention.

"Like I said, there's no law against you taking Lass or Jane or whatever the hell she's calling herself, home with you," the sheriff said, "but you could be asking for a whole heap of trouble. This thing with her smells fishy to me. And the stink could rub off on you or your family. Are you prepared for that?"

Unease prickled down Brady's backbone. He'd been a law officer long enough to know that Ethan was right. Lass could mean trouble. Yet his job was to serve and protect. And right now he couldn't think of anyone who needed his services more than Lass.

"All the more reason to have her in a safe, secluded place. Where I can keep watch on her."

Ethan studied him for long, thoughtful moments, then shook his head. "All right, Brady. I'm not going to buck you on this. Just remember not to let your personal feelings get in the way of the case."

Brady grinned with relief. "I'm not going to stop until

I solve it. In fact, that's why I'm here so early this morning. I was trying to go through the system, see if she might match any new missing person's case."

"What about her fingerprints? Have you already run them?"

Nodding, Brady said, "Did that yesterday. No match there. But then she would've had to have been in the military, the government or arrested to find them in our database."

"What about medical progress?" Ethan asked. "Hank tells me that your sister has taken her case. What is Bridget's medical opinion?"

"That time will heal her. But she can only guess as to how much time."

"Hmm. Let's hope her recovery is speedy. In the meantime, the woman has to be connected to someone. Boyfriend. Husband. Family. Someone who cares enough to start a search for her."

Someone who cares. Ethan's words jerked Brady back to the everyday reality of his job. Of course there were people out there who cared about Lass, he thought. A woman who looked like her most likely had a special man in her life. And it was Brady's job to see that she got safely back to that man's arms.

Chapter Four

Shortly after lunch that same day, Lass's paper work for her release from the hospital was completed and Brady picked her up in a black pickup truck with a sheriff's department seal emblazoned on the doors.

The day was warm and bright and as he drove slowly along a mountain highway, Lass felt her spirits lift. It felt wonderful to be out of the confines of the hospital and even more wonderful to know that she wasn't going to be deposited in a charity ward, where she'd be pushed aside and her plight ignored for those persons with more serious problems.

Turning her gaze away from the passenger window, she glanced over to the man behind the wheel. Brady Donovan was not just a regular deputy, she decided. He was a tall, sexy angel who had rescued her from possible death. If she'd lain on the side of the road throughout the night, she could have succumbed to exposure to the elements or wild animals, particularly black bears. Now he'd come to her rescue again and she wasn't quite sure why.

"You're sure that your family won't mind me staying at their home for a few days?" she asked.

"It's my home, too," he reminded her. "And stop worrying. I spoke to my parents this morning. They're glad to help."

Lass sighed. Most of last night and this morning, as she'd struggled to remember anything about her life up until a day ago, she'd felt totally disconnected, as though she'd been defeated by something or someone, even before she'd received the whack on her head.

"They must be very generous people to allow a stranger into their home." Bending her head, she squeezed her eyes shut as tears threatened to fall. "It would be impossible to express my gratitude to them—to you."

"Forget it, Lass. My family has plenty to give. And they like helping others. They're that sort of people."

Raising her head, she glanced his way. Now in the bright light of day, she was getting an even clearer image of the man and she had to admit that the sight of him was a bit breathtaking. Did that mean that she'd not been accustomed to having a sexy man like him for company? If her memory were working normally, would he still look just as special? Something told her that he would and that she'd never encountered a man like him before.

His tawny-colored hair was shaggier than she'd first noticed and subtly streaked with shades of amber, copper and gold, a perfect foil for his dark green eyes. But the rich colors were only a part of what made his looks so striking, she realized. It was his bigger-than-life presence, the personality that simmered behind his twinkling gaze and enigmatic smile.

"Well, I won't forget this kindness you and your family are showing me. I'll repay you somehow. I promise."

A corner of his mouth lifted in a wry grin. "We don't expect that, Lass. Giving doesn't mean much if you give only to get something in return. That's what my mom always taught me."

Her heart heavy, she gazed out at the desert mountains. They were dotted with twisted juniper, scrubby pinyon pine and clumps of sage. To her right, at the bottom of the mountains, the highway shared part of the valley floor with a river. The Hondo, Brady had called it earlier, was lined with tall poplars, willows and evergreens, while in between the meandering ribbon of water and the roadway, green meadows were covered with grasses and wildflowers. Pretty as the scenery was, nothing about it seemed familiar to her fuddled brain.

"I wonder if I have a mother," she murmured. "I wonder what mine might have taught me."

He was silent for a moment and then the two-way radio on the dashboard began to crackle yet again as a busy dispatcher issued information to an officer on call. By the time the female voice had finished, Lass figured Brady's thoughts had moved on to things other than her miserable plight.

He surprised her by picking up the conversation exactly where Lass had left off. "You're a young woman, Lass. I'm betting you have a mother somewhere. She's probably hunting for you right this moment, and so is…your father."

Lass's heart winced with a doubt she couldn't understand. Why did she have this notion that her parents might not be hunting for her? Wasn't that what normal parents did when their child went missing? Only if they were normal, she mentally pointed out, and God only knew if hers were alive, much less normal.

"I can only hope," she replied, then forcing her mind to move on, she asked, "Does this area have a name? I've noticed we've passed a few homesteads."

"It's called the Hondo Valley. People around here raise cattle and horses and lots of fruit in the summer. Does that ring a bell?"

She bit back a sigh. "Not really."

"Well, if you're not from around here, it probably wouldn't. And I'm positive you don't live anywhere close."

"How could you know that?"

His chuckle was warm and husky and filled Lass with unexpected pleasure.

" 'Cause I know all the pretty women in Lincoln County. And believe me when I say I would know your name."

Forty minutes from the time they drove away from Sierra General, Brady steered the truck off the highway and onto a graveled dirt road lined with a white board fence and towering Lombardy poplars. Along the way, the land opened up to wide meadows with tall dense grass.

When Lass spotted the first mares and foals grazing along the roadside, she squealed with delight.

"Oh! How perfectly lovely!" Leaning forward, she gazed raptly at the horses and, as she took in their grace and beauty, emotion suddenly overwhelmed her to the point that she had to swallow before she could say another word. "Could we…stop for just a minute, Brady? For a closer look?"

"Sure. We're not in a hurry."

He pulled the truck to the side of the road and after carefully helping her to the ground, wrapped his hand firmly around hers, then led her to a spot where the fence was shaded by one of the poplars.

"This is part of the Diamond D's brood stock," he explained as they looked out over the meadow dotted with mares and babies at their sides. "And I'll admit without a speck of modesty that we have some of the finest horses in the southwest."

"Mmm. I wouldn't argue with that," she said as she deliberately fixed her gaze on the horses and tried to ignore the fact that he was still hanging on to her hand. But that was impossible to do when the tangle of their fingers was sending all sorts of hot currents pulsing through her, sensations that she was certain she'd never felt before. Something this strong couldn't be forgotten, she decided.

"You must like horses," he observed. "Maybe you have one of your own somewhere."

She could feel his glance sliding over her and like a magnet it drew her eyes back to his rugged face. Drawing in a deep breath, she replied, "It doesn't make sense but I know…without even thinking about it, that I love these beautiful animals. Strange, isn't it?" she murmured with despair. "I don't know if I have a job, or home or…anything. Yet I feel this affinity to horses."

"We're going to find answers for you, Lass. I promise. And Brady Donovan never makes a promise he can't keep."

Glancing up at him, she gave him a shaky smile and tried not to notice the gentle gleam in his green eyes. As far as she was concerned, Brady Donovan didn't need to carry a firearm. His smile was lethal enough to stop a woman dead in her tracks.

Her heart kicked into a faint flutter, making her words little more than a husky whisper when she said, "I'm going to hold you to that, Deputy."

Carefully extricating her hand from his, she moved a

step forward and leaned against the white fence. The afternoon was warm and a southwesterly breeze ruffled her black hair against her shoulders. The wind carried the scent of pine and juniper and though pleasant, the smells seemed unusual to her. But not nearly so much as the strong reaction she was having to Brady Donovan.

"It's very beautiful here," she went on nervously. "Have you always lived here in this valley?"

"Always," he answered. "All of us six children were born here. My paternal grandparents came from Ireland and settled for a while in Kentucky. That's where my father was born before they moved out here and built the ranch in 1968."

"Are your grandparents still living?"

"My grandmother Kate lives with us. She's eighty-four now and still going strong. My grandfather Arthur died of a stroke nine years ago. He was quite a bit older than Kate. And mean as hell when his temper was riled. But he was a wonderful man."

It was easy to pick up the fondness in Brady Donovan's voice and Lass didn't have to ask whether he was close to his family. Obviously they were a close-knit bunch. And that notion could only make her wonder about herself. Did she have sisters, brothers or both? Was she carrying a family in her heart? One her mind had forgotten?

She was straining to remember the slightest image from her past when a bay mare and brown colt ambled near. Gripping the top rail of the fence, Lass was once again struck with an overload of emotions.

"Oh, what a perfect little filly! She's all brown. Not a speck of white on her!"

Brady smiled fondly at the curious filly drawing near to them. "My sister Dallas calls her Brownie. Of course, that's not her real name. Dad makes sure all of the horses' names go back to their dams and sires. But we usually give them nicknames."

Brownie stuck her nose toward Lass's hand and as she touched the filly's velvety nose, tears blurred her eyes, then fell like watery diamonds onto her cheeks.

Seeing them, Brady softly exclaimed, "Why, Lass! You're crying!"

Instantly, her face blushing with embarrassment, Lass dashed away the emotional tears. "I'm okay," she said with a sniff. "Just feeling a bit…sentimental."

Bending her head, she wiped at the moisture that continued in spite of her effort to gather herself together. Oh, God, what was wrong with her? she wondered. Why would a brown filly with big, sweet eyes reduce her to tears? She was losing it!

Without warning, his arm came around her shoulder and its steadying strength allowed her to lift her head and look at him. The concern on his face touched her, made her long to lay her cheek upon his broad chest and weep until she was too weak to be frightened by the past or worried about the future.

"Have you remembered something, Lass? Is it something about the horses?"

With a brief shake of her head, she forced herself to turn her gaze back on the filly. At the most, the baby horse was probably six months old and would no doubt be weaned in the near future. Her body was long, her tall legs gangly. She was bred for speed and in a couple of years those legs would stretch into a gallop so fast they would appear as little more than a blur.

How did she instinctively know all these things? How did she know about a horse's conformation? Without even thinking she could point out the animal's cannon bone, or hock or withers or any other body part.

"I…don't know, Brady. Something about the horses… When I look at them—especially this brown filly—I feel happy and sad all at the same time. It doesn't make sense. But somehow I'm certain that I know how to ride and ride well."

"Well, that's good news," he said with gentle humor. "That means you're going to fit right in with my family. And while you're here on the ranch you can ride to your heart's content."

She nodded and he squeezed her shoulders.

"We'd better get on to the house," he suggested. "I don't want you to overdo on your first day out of the hospital."

Embarrassed that she'd gotten so inexplicably weepy, she straightened her spine and gave him a grateful, albeit wobbly, smile.

"Thank you, Brady, for stopping and letting me have a few minutes with the horses," she said softly. "And for… everything you're doing for me."

Without warning, his hand lifted to her face and her heart jumped into a rapid thud as his forefinger slowly, gently traced the line of her cheekbone.

"I don't want you to keep thanking me, Lass. I have my own selfish reasons for giving you a temporary home."

Instead of the wild race it had been on, her heart geared itself to a near stop.

"Oh." She unconsciously moistened her lips. "Um…what reasons are you talking about? Making your job easier?"

A lopsided smile twisted his lips. "My job actually has little to do with inviting you to the Diamond D. I like your company. It's that plain and simple. And I guess you could call me a naughty boy for taking advantage of your homeless situation."

She'd not expected anything like this to come from the deputy's mouth and for a moment she was too stunned to make any sort of reply. "Well," she finally whispered, then cleared her throat and tried again, "I have to admire your honesty."

Chuckling lowly, he squeezed her shoulder. "Sorry, Lass. I'm not very good at being subtle, I guess. But don't worry, I promise not to take any more advantages. Unless you…invite me to," he added with a sinful little grin.

Feeling flattered and naive all at once, she drew in a deep breath. "Brady, I—"

Keep everything light, Lass. This lawman is just enjoying a little flirtation with you. That's all.

After her long pause, he prompted, "You what?"

Plastering a playful smile on her face, she said, "I was just going to say that you probably won't enjoy my company for long. Without a memory, I'm pretty boring."

His eyes softened. Or did she just imagine the elusive change in the green depths?

"Let me be the judge of that," he said, then before she could possibly decide how to respond, he turned her toward the waiting truck. "Right now, we'd better get back on the road."

They traveled two more miles before Brady finally stopped the truck in front of a massive two-story house built of native rock and trimmed with rough cedar. Arched windows adorned the front and overlooked a deep green lawn shaded by tall pines.

A brick walkway led to a small portico covering the front entrance. At the double wooden doors fitted with brass, Brady didn't bother knocking. He opened one and gestured for her to precede him over the threshold and into a long foyer filled with potted plants and lined with a selection of wooden, straight-backed chairs.

Instantly Lass caught the scent of lemon wax and the distant sound of piano music.

"That's Grandma Kate pounding the ivories," Brady informed her as they stepped into a long, formal living room.

As they walked forward, Lass caught glimpses of antique furniture covered in rich colored brocade, elaborate window coverings and expensive paintings. The room looked stiff and lonely.

"Is your family musical?" she asked, while trying not to feel conspicuous in her mussed shirt and blue jeans.

Lass would've liked to have purchased something clean to change into before she left the town of Ruidoso, but without money or credit cards, she was hardly in a position to buy anything. And she would have bitten off her tongue before she would've asked Brady for financial aid. He was already bending over backward to help her.

In a flirtatious way, he'd called it taking advantage, but now that she'd had a couple of miles and a few minutes to think about it, she realized he'd only been trying to make her feel as though she wasn't going to be a burden on him, or anyone. There hadn't been anything personal about the look in his eyes or the way he'd touched her. He probably treated all women in that same familiar way and the best thing she could do was put the moment out of her mind.

"Only Grandma and my sister Dallas are the musical ones in the family. I can't tell one note from the other," he answered. With his hand at her back, he guided her through an arched opening and into a long hallway. "The family room is right down here. That's where everybody relaxes and gets together when they're not working. There and the kitchen. Forget the front parlor. That's only used for meeting with people we don't like."

Lass couldn't help but laugh. "Then I'm glad your family didn't meet me there."

After walking several feet down the carpeted corridor, Brady ushered her through an open doorway to their right. The family room, as he'd called it, was a long space, comfortably furnished with two couches and several armchairs, a large television set and stereo equipment, one whole wall of books and wide paned windows that overlooked a ridge of desert mountains. At the far end, a tall woman with graying chestnut hair sat playing an upright piano. The instrument looked as though it had to be near a hundred years old, but the woman pressing the keys appeared surprisingly vital for her age.

At the moment she was playing a boisterous waltz that went a long way in lifting Lass's drooping spirits.

"Grandma! Stop that confounded noise and come meet Lass!" Brady yelled loud enough to be heard above the piano.

Abruptly, the woman lifted her fingers from the keys and turned with a frown. "What? Oh, Brady, it's you."

She rose spryly from the piano stool and walked over to greet them, while Lass studied Brady's grandmother with a bit of shock. She'd been expecting a frail woman with white hair and pale, fragile skin dressed in a flowered shirt-waister. Kate Donovan was a tanned, robust woman, with a short, sporty hairdo and heavy silver jewelry adorning her ears and neck. She was wearing Levi's, cowboy boots and a generous smile on her face. Lass instantly loved her.

"Yes, it's me." He reached out and fondly pinched the woman's cheek and she immediately swatted at his hand.

"Stop it! You big flirt!"

Brady grinned. "That's because you're looking so pretty today."

The older woman feigned a bored sigh, then thrust her hand out to Lass.

"I'm Kate Donovan," she said warmly. "And you must be the little lost lady that my grandson found on the roadside."

Shaking the woman's firm grip, Lass smiled back at her. "Yes, ma'am. And please call me Lass." She glanced shyly toward Brady, then back to the matriarch of the Donovan family. "That's what Brady named me. And I'd like to say how very grateful I am to your grandson—to you and your whole family for allowing me to stay here in your home for a few days."

Kate patted the back of Lass's hand. "You're perfectly welcome, honey. We like having company. When an outsider is around, it keeps the family fights down to a minimum," she added with a wink.

"Grandma, don't make her any more nervous than she already is!" Brady scolded his grandmother. "You'll have her thinking we're a bunch of heathens."

"Nonsense!" Kate shot back at him. "She's probably used to family bickering."

Brady tossed his grandmother a look of exaggerated patience. "Grandma, Lass can't remember anything. She doesn't know whether she has a family, much less if they argue among themselves."

Kate scowled at him. "All right, all right. I wasn't thinking," she admitted. "But it looks as though you don't have an iota of sense in that brain of yours, either."

Confusion caused him to arch one of his brows. "Why do you say that?"

Frowning at him, Kate moved to Lass's side and curled a protective arm around her shoulder. "What do you mean letting the girl leave the hospital in dirty clothes? Shame on you, Brady!"

Brady opened his mouth to speak, but the older woman didn't allow him the chance.

"Don't bother with excuses," Kate said, then turned Lass and began leading her out of the room.

Brady followed on their heels. "What are you doing?"

"Taking Lass upstairs," the older woman answered. "Fiona is already up there, making sure everything is ready for our guest. We'll find Lass some clothes and get her all settled. You don't have to concern yourself now."

"But I—"

Kate Donovan paused in her forward movement long enough to shoot Brady a pointed frown.

"Don't you need to get back to work?" she interjected.

He looked helplessly at Lass, who was still standing beneath his grandmother's protective wing, then shrugged. In all honesty, he wasn't yet ready to leave the ranch and Lass behind. He'd been planning on taking a few more minutes to show her around the house, introduce her to his mother and generally make her feel welcome.

"Ethan lets me be my own boss."

"Poor man," Kate said. "You've got him confused."

Brady hurried over to join the two women as they headed out of the room and quickly looped his arm through Lass's.

"Confused, hell," Brady retorted, then directed his next question at his grandmother. "Have you heard that Penny's pregnant again?"

The older woman paused long enough to gape at him. "Penny? Pregnant again? Why, no! But how wonderful!"

"I'd think shocking is a better word for it," Brady replied. "She's got to be pushing forty."

Kate Donovan laughed and winked at Lass. "Maybe there's still hope for me yet."

"Grandma! Why don't you quit embarrassing me? Old

people should be seen and not heard and you're quickly falling into that category," Brady chided the woman.

Lass gasped while Kate's robust laughter rang through the hallway. "Why don't you move out, big boy?" she suggested to Brady. "And then this house might not feel so much like a mental ward."

Chuckling, Brady bent his head toward Lass's ear. "Grandma and I love each other," he explained. "Very much."

By now the three of them had reached a wide, carpeted staircase, but before they started the climb, Kate stopped and leveled a stern look at Lass.

"Honey, I'm going to warn you right now. Whatever you do, don't believe a word this young fool tells you. He's full of Irish blarney. Or full of himself. Either one is bad for a pretty girl like you."

Before Brady could defend himself, the cell phone in his pocket rang. After one swift glance at the number, he answered, listened briefly, then briskly replied, "Take Tate with you. I expect they'll be some resistance. Yeah. Thirty minutes."

Snapping the phone shut, he dropped the phone in his pocket. "Gotta go," he explained to the two women. "Trouble in the Valley of Fire."

Picking up the urgency in his voice, Lass watched him turn and trot off in the direction from which they'd just came. And as she watched him go, she was suddenly reminded that for all his playfulness, Brady was a lawman and his job no doubt often put him in danger. The idea left her very uneasy.

Kate Donovan patted her shoulder. "Don't worry, Lass. My grandson is a fine deputy. He knows what he's doing."

Yes, but did Lass know what she was doing? She'd come here to the Diamond D to stay until she could figure out where she really belonged. So why did one touch, one smile, from Brady Donovan make her feel like she'd just found home?

Chapter Five

Much later that evening, as night fell over the Diamond D, Lass sat quietly in an armchair in her bedroom. As she watched stars emerge in a purple sky, and wondered how she'd gone from lying unconscious in a mountainside ditch to a luxurious ranch, a light knock sounded on the door.

Maybe Brady had finally returned home, she thought hopefully. All afternoon she'd been thinking about him, imagining him in all sorts of dangerous, life-threatening situations.

Glancing over her shoulder, she called, "Come in."

Instead of Brady pushing through the door, a tall, young woman with light auburn hair and a cheery smile stepped into the room. A crinkled floral skirt swirled against her brown cowboy boots while a coral-colored blouse flattered her vibrant hair. To Lass she looked like a beautiful ray of sunshine.

"Hi," she said. "I'm Dallas. Brady's and Bridget's sister."

Smiling, Lass quickly rose from the chair and walked over to the other woman. Extending her hand, she said, "I'm very happy to meet you, Dallas. I'm...well, I'm Lass." Her short laugh was a mixture of helplessness and humor. "At least, that's what Brady has christened me."

Dallas laughed along with her and Lass instantly realized she was going to like this woman.

"Well, that's much better than the name he gave one of our barn cats. I won't repeat that one to you." She glanced appreciatively over the pale blue dress Lass was wearing. "Hey, that looks great on you. Grandma said that she and Mom found you some of Bridget's things to wear. Since the two of you are both petite and about the same size. But listen, if you'd like to go on a shopping trip, just let me know. We'll take an afternoon and raid all the shops in Ruidoso. My treat. After all, a girl needs intimate things of her own."

"Oh, I couldn't. I mean, Brady didn't find a pocketbook, money, credit cards or anything on me. I'm a—" She held up her palms in a helpless gesture. "I suppose I'm what you call a charity case."

The tall redhead shrugged one slender shoulder. "So what? You won't always be dependant. Besides, I just might put you to work," she added with a wink, then touched Lass's shoulder and urged her toward the door. "If you're ready, let's go down. Dinner is close to being served and the family is having drinks."

Lass followed her out of the bedroom and as they descended the steps, she couldn't stop herself from asking, "Has Brady made it home yet?"

Dallas shook her head. "No. None of us have had any contact with him. One of the hands down at the barns heard over the police scanner that shots had been fired, but that was more than an hour ago."

A heavy weight sunk to the pit of Lass's stomach. "That…sounds ominous."

"Well, Brady has worked as a law officer for a long time and it's pretty rare for shots to be fired. But we try to take it all in stride. He knows what he's doing. And he doesn't want us sitting around worrying about him. But it's definitely hard not to worry. Especially when he was shot last year during a drug sting."

Lass felt chilled. "Shot? Was he wounded badly?"

"A flesh wound in his arm. We were all thankful it wasn't worse."

Hoping the other woman couldn't see the fear in her eyes, Lass murmured, "I'm sure."

The two women descended the last few stairs, then made their way to the family room where Fiona pressed a glass of port into Lass's hand. While she sipped the sweet wine, the woman introduced Lass to Brady's father, Doyle, and his two brothers, Conall and Liam. Surprisingly, the three men were nothing like Brady. Conall was dark and quiet, Liam polite, but with an air of indifference, while Doyle appeared to be a blunt, no-nonsense sort of man.

When the family finally gathered around a long dining table, Lass couldn't help but notice the empty chair to Fiona's left elbow was conspicuously empty. And as the conversation flowed back and forth between the family members, she got the feeling that they were all concerned for his safety, but doing their best to make light of the situation.

"It's probably a drug bust," Fiona said as salads were served by one of the housemaids. "What else would anyone being doing out in the Valley of Fire? There's nothing there but miles and miles of lava beds."

Liam said, "The way Reese heard it over the scanner, the call had something to do with a domestic dispute."

"Way out there?" Dallas countered. "That doesn't make sense. There aren't any homes out there."

Liam frowned impatiently at her. "I'm just repeating what I heard, sis."

"It doesn't matter what the call was about," Doyle said brusquely. "Brady's simply doing his job. He'll be fine. Now let's talk about something else."

At the opposite end of the table from Doyle, Kate cleared her voice loudly. "You're right, son. We have a guest and I'm fairly certain she'd like to talk about something else besides shootings and criminals."

Lass looked up from her salad to find several pairs of eyes on her. Feeling more than conspicuous, warm color flushed her cheeks.

"Oh, please, don't let me interrupt," she said in a small voice. "I'm very happy to just listen."

The older brother—Conall—looked straight at her. Lass got the impression he'd been carved from a chunk of ice.

"So you don't know where you come from?" he asked. "No clues at all?"

"Well, hell no," Kate boomed back at her eldest grandson. "If she did, do you think she'd be wasting her time sitting here, listening to you?"

"I don't know, Grandmother," he said with exaggerated patience. "Maybe she doesn't like where she came from."

Her lips pressed into a grim line, Kate shook her head at him. "Sometimes you can really disappoint me."

He shrugged. "Sorry. I guess I was just made that way," he quipped.

Feeling worse than uncomfortable and wishing Brady was at her side for more than one reason, she tried not to squirm on her seat. She hated to think that some of this family thought she might be faking her amnesia, or that perhaps she might be part of a con, directed at the Donovan family. Didn't they realize that it was all Brady's idea to bring her here? As far as she was concerned, things would have been much simpler if she'd gone to the women's shelter in Ruidoso rather than try to integrate herself into this large, complex family.

"Actually," she said in a low, but steady voice, "I don't know where I used to live. But I believe Brady when he says he'll find my family."

To her surprise, it was Doyle who looked at her with empathy and understanding. "I believe him, too. And until he does, we want you to make our home your home, Lass."

Gratitude poured through her and she smiled briefly at him. "Thank you, Mr. Donovan. I'm very grateful."

Dallas quickly interjected. "Well, I'm happy to learn that Lass remembers something about herself. She knows all about horses and knows how to ride."

Liam's brows lifted with faint curiosity while Conall muttered, "How convenient."

"That's right," Dallas went on, clearly ignoring her brother's sarcasm. "I'm going to take her over to the stables tomorrow and show her around. I think I might have found a great assistant. That is, after she gets over her concussion."

Over a small glass of wine before dinner, Lass had learned that Dallas operated a therapeutic riding stable for handicapped children. Angel Wing Stables, as Dallas had called it, was entirely nonprofit and considered a labor of love. If Lass could help out around the stables in some way, she'd be glad to. She needed something to keep her mind occupied as it tried to heal. And she loved children.

How do you know that about yourself, Lass? Do you have a child of your own? Were you a nurse? A teacher? A mother?

The voice in her head was like tormenting drips of a leaky faucet. The questions were endless and unstoppable.

"By the time she gets over her concussion," Liam reasoned, "she'll probably have her memory back."

"Let's pray that happens," Kate said, then leveled sharp eyes on her grandsons. "You two tough guys over there would be as scared as hell if you woke up some morning and didn't have any roots, or home, or family or a dime in your pocket. Think about it."

They must have thought about it, Lass decided. Because after that, the subject of her amnesia wasn't brought into the conversation again. Talk around the table turned to racing and the fact that Del Mar would be opening for the late summer season soon. In a couple of days, Liam planned to ship several horses out to the historic track in Southern California and would be staying with them until the meet was over in September.

From what she could gather, the Donovans owned several grade I and II thoroughbreds, which was impressive indeed. Horses of that caliber were worth at least a million dollars each and oftentimes more. Which explained the comfortable, but elaborate, house and grounds, the large diamonds on Kate's and Fiona's hands, their casual, but well-tailored clothes. And yet, none of this awed Lass nor made her feel out of place. What did it all mean? That she was also from a rich background? Lass certainly didn't feel rich. But perhaps her inner self wasn't measuring her wealth by money. Thank God.

Not long after the meal, Lass excused herself and climbed the stairs to her bedroom. Brady still hadn't come home and after a few minutes, she climbed into bed thinking about the deputy and listening for the sound of his footsteps on the bedroom landing.

You're clearly unstable, Lass. You don't know your name, where your home is, or if you have one relative on the face of this earth. But instead of worrying about that, all you can think about is a sexy deputy with a head full of tawny waves and hazel green eyes glinting with mischief.

Eventually the nagging voice in her head quieted and Lass fell asleep from the exhaustion of the past two days. She must have slept soundly because the next morning she didn't hear a thing until Brady's voice sounded just above her ear.

"Wake up, sleeping beauty. Coffee has arrived."

The fog of sleep was slow to move from Lass's brain, but when it did, the realization that Brady was standing over her bed and that she was wearing a skimpy gown had her eyes flying open and her hands quickly snatching the cover up to her chin.

"Brady! What…are you doing in here?"

Grinning as though he was pleased with himself, he gestured toward the nightstand and a tray holding a small insulated coffeepot, a fragile china cup and saucer, cream pitcher, sugar bowl and a small branch covered with red blossoms.

"What is that?" she asked.

"Coffee. I took it for granted that you liked it. But if you'd rather have tea, I'll have Reggie prepare another tray."

With a death grip on the sheet, she propped herself against the headboard. A dose of caffeine to wake her up was hardly needed, she thought, when just looking at him was already making her heart pound. "No. I love coffee. I was talking about the flower."

"Oh. That." He picked up the branch of blossoms and handed it to her. "I don't know what it is. I broke it off one of the bushes in Grandma's flower garden. Because it was pretty. And I thought you might like it."

Lass lifted the flowers to her nose, while an awkward feeling suddenly assaulted her. She didn't know why having Brady see her in bed was bothering her. It wasn't like it was the first time. But that had been a narrow hospital bed and she'd been garbed in a thick, unflattering cotton gown. Now she was in an opulent bed wearing a piece of red silk that revealed every curve of her body. And he was giving her flowers as though she was special.

Keeping her eyes carefully on the red, trumpet-shaped blooms, she said, "I do like it. Very much. But Kate's going to get you for meddling with her flowers."

He chuckled. "She'll forgive me. Especially if I tell her I did it for you. She likes you. I can tell. And Grandma doesn't just take to any and everyone."

Turning away from her, he poured the cup full of coffee. "Cream? Sugar?"

It felt ridiculous having this macho man of a lawman standing beside her bed, serving her as though she was a princess. Yet it also made her feel cared about and very special. Was that his motive? she wondered. Or was he this way with all the females who visited the Diamond D?

"Just a little cream, please. But I can do it," she insisted. "You don't need to do…all of this for me."

"Why not? I'm here and I'm capable."

Thrusting her disheveled hair from her face, she placed the flower on her lap and took the cup he offered. While she sipped, he pulled the chair away from the vanity, positioned it next to the bed and took a seat. This morning he was dressed in faded jeans and a black, short-sleeved polo shirt and though his hair was combed neatly back from his face, she could see a hint of rusty whiskers shadowing his chin and jaw. That and the faint lines beneath his eyes were the only signs that he'd had a late night.

"Tell me, Brady, do you do this for all house guests that come to the Diamond D?" she asked as she peered demurely at him over the rim of her cup.

He grinned. "Only the ones I want to leave a lasting impression on," he teased, then his expression sobered. "You have a concussion. You need to be taking it easy."

Unconsciously, her fingertips fluttered to the stitched wound hidden by her hair. "Bridget says I can move around. As long as I don't rush or exert myself. And I'm feeling much stronger today."

"That's good. Real good."

He stretched his long legs out in front of him and crossed his ankles as though he was planning to stay there for a while. Apparently it didn't make him the least bit uncomfortable to visit a woman's bedroom. But then a man who looked like him had probably had plenty of practice at it, she thought.

"We…were all worried about you last night," she murmured. "I'm glad to see you made it safely back home."

He simply looked at her, his eyes warm and appreciative. "It was nothing to get worked up about. Just a little scuffle. A man with a gun got upset and went a little off the beam. That's all. He's safe behind bars now. And we're all just fine."

The first few hours after she'd gone to bed, she'd imagined him in all sorts of dangerous situations and she'd been desperately afraid for his safety. Now, she felt foolish for letting her imagination and her feelings get so out of hand. "Does that sort of thing happen often?" she asked.

"No. But neither does finding a pretty girl with amnesia," he answered, a faint grin lifting one corner of his mouth. "The stars must have gone off-kilter this past week. The department's been extra busy."

"Well, I wish the stars would realign themselves," she did her best to joke. "Maybe then I'd get my memory back."

"Still nothing?"

Staring down at her cooling coffee, she said dismally, "No. Apparently nothing up there in my head is regenerating."

"If Brita says it will, then it will. You just need time," he said with encouragement. Pulling his legs toward him, he leaned forward and rested his forearms across his thighs. "Later this morning Hank and I are going to the track and plaster your picture throughout the clubhouse and betting area. It could be that some of the employees will remember seeing you there last Sunday."

Brady was being so kind and positive the least she could do was be hopeful and optimistic, too. But that was rather difficult to do when every path her mind took, it ran into a black wall.

"But how will that help, Brady? More than likely I didn't give my name to anyone."

"Probably not. But just having someone witness seeing you in a certain place is a big start. If we can confirm that you were at the track that will give us a starting place. From there we can try to trace your steps forward and backward."

She gave him the bravest smile she could muster. "Okay. I trust you."

He chuckled. "Really? Then you're the first woman who ever has."

Was he saying she was gullible where he was concerned? It didn't matter. As far as her missing person case was concerned, she had to trust him. As a man, it shouldn't matter. Even if he wasn't involved with one special wom-

she was in no position to get her feelings tangled up with him. With her past a blank, her future could be nothing but uncertain.

Not really knowing what to reply to his sardonic remark, she sipped her coffee and waited for him to take the conversation elsewhere.

"So what are you going to do today? Sit in a stuffed armchair and read a book?"

Wondering if he was serious, she glanced at him. "I have amnesia, not paralysis."

A dimple came and went in his cheek. "Well, if reading sounds too boring you can get Grandma to tell you stories about when she and Grandpa first came here. She has some real humdingers."

"I'm sure. She's quite a colorful woman. But I already have something planned. Later this morning Dallas is taking me over to her stables to have a look around."

He groaned. "Listen, Lass, if you let her, Dallas will drive you crazy talking about all her kids and horses and work. If you get tired, don't be afraid to tell her to hush and bring you home."

Home. Funny how he said it that way, she thought. As though this place was her home, too. The idea touched her and yet at the same time it made her feel a bit weepy. Somewhere there had to be walls and floors and rooms that had made up her home. Had anyone lived in it with her? Had she been loved? The way the Donovans loved each other?

"I'm sure Dallas and I will get on just fine," she told him. "I like her very much."

"Well, as much as I like sitting here with you and seeing you in that pretty red thing you're wearing, I've got to get to work." He rose to his feet, but instead of heading toward the door, he picked up the thermos and refilled the china cup she was balancing on her knee.

His remark about her gown had her eyes flying downward and she realized with a start that the sheet had slipped to expose her bodice. Thankfully, the paper-thin silk was still covering her breasts.

With a tiny gasp, she started to reach for the sheet, but realized the movement was causing the coffee to slosh dangerously near the rim of the cup.

"Don't worry about it," he said with a little laugh, then taking pity on her, started toward the door. "You look beautiful. Just the way I imagined you would." With his hand on the knob, he gave her one last glance. "Unless an emergency comes up, I'll see you later this evening. And who knows, by then someone searching for you might contact the sheriff's department."

"I guess that could happen," she said, while wondering why she couldn't muster up more enthusiasm over the idea.

"Sure it could," he said cheerfully. "And then all your problems will be solved."

He gave her a little salute then stepped out the door. Once it clicked behind him, Lass's shoulders sagged against the pillows. Would finding her past really solve all her problems, she wondered.

Somehow she didn't think so. Something kept swirling around in her brain, some dark elusive thought that kept whispering the words *danger* and *fear*.

Later that morning, dressed in her own boots, and the jeans and blouse that the maid had laundered for her, she climbed into a pickup truck with Dallas and the two of them headed south on a graveled road toward a ridge of desert mountains.

"Looks like we're going into the wilderness," Lass commented. "I thought your stable was probably located close to the highway. For convenience."

Smiling, Dallas shook her head. "When I first got the idea to build the stables, I knew I wanted it to be far away from the things that most town kids see every day. Like concrete, asphalt and the whiz of vehicles. I wanted it to be an escape for them." She jerked the steering wheel to avoid a pothole. "I admit that the trip back here isn't like a drive to the country club. But I believe all in all, it's worth it for the children." She glanced at Lass. "I guess this is a silly question, but do you think you have children or a child of your own?"

Sighing, Lass stared out the window at the passing desert landscape. Instinctively, she felt she'd come from a place where huge trees shaded deep green lawns. Yet when she thought of something personal, like a husband or children, her mind revolted and turned as blank as a clean blackboard.

"That's a question I've been asking myself, Dallas. And when I try to remember if I ever held a baby of my own..." She paused and shook her head miserably. "I don't feel as though I've ever had a child. Dear God, I hope there's not a baby out there somewhere crying for me and I have no way of knowing—of getting back to him or her."

Brady's sister nodded grimly. "Yes. I can see where that thought would be torturous."

"Bridget did say that it's unlikely I've given birth. Still, that doesn't mean there isn't a child out there waiting for me."

Three miles from the Diamond D ranch yard, beyond the mountain ridge, two huge barns and several smaller buildings were erected in a meadow not far from a small creek. Dallas wasted no time in taking Lass through the barns where the horses were stalled, the tack and feed kept and the outside riding arena. Because the day was growing very warm, Dallas had decided to move the riders to a smaller, indoor arena where the temperature was regulated.

Whenever they stepped inside, Lass was surprised to see several stable assistants had children already mounted and moving slowly over the carefully raked ground. Some had outward problems that were obvious to any onlooker, like leg braces or a missing limb. Others suffered the less obvious, such as mental and emotional handicaps. But to Lass's delight, they were all smiling and having a good time.

"This is wonderful!" Lass exclaimed as she twisted her head in an effort to take everything in. "The children appear to love it!"

Dallas's eyes twinkled with pride. "They do. And the interaction with the horses helps them in ways you wouldn't believe. I hope while you're here you'll get a chance to see all the positives that go on here," she said.

"I think I'm seeing it right now," Lass told her.

Taking her by the arm as though she'd known her for years, Dallas urged her forward. "C'mon and I'll introduce you to everyone."

Much later, while Dallas went to deal with a few of the more problematic riders, Lass was content to find a seat on a hay bale behind the fenced arena. She was concentrating on the children and watching the interaction between them and Dallas, when a slight movement caught her eye.

Turning her head slightly, Lass saw a tall, dark-haired man tethering a white horse to a hitching post. There was nothing unusual or out of sorts with the man or the animal and she was on the verge of turning her attention back toward the arena when images suddenly began to flash in front of her eyes.

A steel-gray horse wearing a bright red blanket, a saddle being tossed upon its back. A tall, faceless man in tan chinos, his hand gripping her wrist.

You're coming with me. Coming with me. Coming with me.

The male voice chanted the words over and over in her head, wrapping the phrase around the flashing images until everything became a violent blur.

Releasing a faint sob, she dropped her head in her hands and supped in long, cleansing breaths. If she was actually remembering, she didn't want any part of it.

"Lass? Are you okay?"

Dropping her hands away from her face, she looked up to see Brady's sister standing over her. The woman was looking at her with concern and for a moment Lass wondered if she'd unconsciously cried out in fear.

"I…um, my head is starting to pound again. That's all." She didn't want to tell Dallas about her visions just yet. Not until she'd spoken to Brady. He was the one who'd rescued her. He was the one who was working to find her identity. And he was the one she trusted to make some sort of sense of her predicament.

"Oh. I'd better get you back to the house!" With a hand on Lass's arm, she helped her to her feet. "I'm so sorry, Lass. I've probably put too much on you this morning. Brady is going to be furious with me."

"Bridget is my doctor. Not Brady," Lass pointed out.

A knowing smile crossed Dallas's pretty face. "Yes. But my brother considers you his lost and found."

Dallas's words should have lent her some sort of omfort. After all, what normal woman wouldn't want to ucked under the protective wing of a sexy lawman dy?

s wasn't a typical woman. And after experiencing those strange visions a few moments ago, she feared her hopes for a normal future were in jeopardy.

For the remainder of the day, Lass stuck close to the house and generally tried to relax. But that was difficult to do when her head was spinning with the unbidden images she'd experienced at Dallas's riding stables. Everything about them had scared and confused her and she was desperate to see Brady again. Not only to tell him what had happened, but also to see his smile, to hear his strong voice assuring her that everything would be all right.

She was sitting on a covered porch at the back of the house, two of the family's pet cats curled at her feet, when she heard footsteps behind her. Expecting it to be Fiona or Kate inviting her in for drinks, she was more than surprised to see Brady.

"Mom told me where you were," he explained as he approached her chair. "Why are you sitting out here all by yourself?"

Even though he was still in his work clothes, he looked wonderful to her and before she could contain herself, she jumped to her feet and threw herself against his chest.

"Oh, Brady, I'm so glad you're home!" she practically sobbed.

His face a mixture of pleasure and confusion, he wrapped his arms around her and held her close. "Whoa now, Lass, there's not any need for you to be so worked up. I haven't had anybody shooting at me today. That was last night."

Sniffing, she tilted her head back and looked up at him with misty eyes. "I'm sorry for being so…melodramatic, Brady. You must think I've lost my mind. And I—" With an anguished groan, she twisted out of his arms and turned her back to him. "I'm afraid I have. I apologize for throwing myself at you like that."

His low chuckles were suddenly brushing against the back of her neck and suddenly the quivering in the pit of her stomach had nothing to do with fear.

"You think you need to apologize for hugging me? I just wished you'd hung on longer."

His suggestive remark had her swallowing, fighting the urge to turn to him once more. "I don't think…that would be wise," she said, her voice breathy and broken.

"Why?"

She couldn't summon an answer and then it didn't matter as his hand pushed the curtain of her long hair to one side and his lips settled softly on the back of her neck.

"Because I might do this," he whispered against her skin. "Or this?"

With his hands on her shoulders, he turned her toward him and all Lass could do was stand motionless and wait for his kiss.

Chapter Six

Since the night Brady had found her in the ditch and propped her limp body in the circle of his arms, he'd wondered how it would feel to hold this woman in a romantic embrace, imagined how her lips would taste. Yet none of those mental images had come close to the actual thing he was experiencing now.

He knew he should be resisting her. He should remember how vulnerable she was, that she looked to him for protection. But she'd made the first move, and he wasn't the type to refuse a beautiful woman. Especially not this one.

Tucked close against him, her body felt small and soft and incredibly warm, while her lips tasted like sweet fruit. Ripe. Juicy. Delicious. Her hands were planted against his chest and though her fingers were small, they were sending shock waves of heat straight through the fabric of his shirt and onto his skin.

Brady could have stood there kissing her forever if she'd not finally broke the contact of their lips and squirmed her way out of his arms. And even then, as she stood there looking at him with wide, wondrous eyes, he wanted to gather her back against him, to experience the pleasure of her all over again.

"I'm sorry. I…must have sent you the wrong signal," she finally said in a raw whisper.

He couldn't stop a grin from lifting one corner of his mouth. "Which time? When you hugged me? Or when you kissed me?"

Groaning with embarrassment, she covered her mouth with her hand. As though he'd just marked her in some way and she didn't want him or anyone to see the change in her.

"Both times!" she exclaimed, then dropped her hand and stared at him in a beseeching way. "Please forget that. Every bit of it!"

Brady could see she was deadly serious, but still he couldn't prevent the low chuckles that rippled up in his throat. She was just too precious, too beautiful. "Are you kidding? I'm not about to forget something that wonderful."

Her nostrils flared and he watched the rapid rise and fall of her bosom as images of her in bed this morning assaulted his already lust-filled brain. The thin red silk had revealed the exact shape of her nipples, the perfect round curves of her breasts. He'd wanted to touch her then. Just as badly as he wanted to touch her now.

"Brady, I need to explain. I—"

"Lass, there's no need for you to break apart over a little kiss. You're carrying on as though you've never been kissed before," he teased in an effort to ease the moment. Clearly she was distressed and he didn't understand exactly why. He knew enough about women to know when one was enjoying being kissed and Lass had clearly been enjoying it.

She grimaced. "I wouldn't know! I don't remember what I've done in the past! Or who I've done it with," she practically snapped, then shook her head with dismay. "Forgive me, Brady. I…seem to be breaking apart, don't I? And I'm trying so hard to hold myself together. But this morning—"

She trailed off and Brady stepped forward and reached for her hand. To his relief, she wrapped her fingers around his and held on tightly.

"What about this morning?" he urged. "Did something happen while I was gone?"

Sighing, she closed her eyes. "I'm not sure. Maybe I've worked myself up over nothing," she told him. "But whatever I saw in my mind won't go away. That must mean it happened. Wouldn't you think?"

Not fully understanding what she was trying to say, he led her to a wicker love seat shaded by a curtain of morning glory vines.

"Okay, Lass, start over. Are you trying to tell me that you've remembered something?"

She nodded soberly. "I think so. But I'm not sure. I was with Dallas at her stables this morning. Just sitting there watching the children. And then I saw one of the stable helpers tending to a horse and something happened in my head. All of a sudden images were flashing in front of my eyes."

"What sort of images?"

"A steel-gray horse was being saddled by someone. I don't know who. The blanket was bright red and the saddle was the English sort. Then the horse was suddenly gone and a man was standing in front of me. He was gripping my wrist. Really hard. And he kept saying over and over, 'You're coming with me.'"

Everything inside Brady went still. "Did you recognize this man?"

"No. It was like a dream where you never see the face. It was someone tall with dark hair."

"What about the voice? Did you recognize it?"

Shaking her head, she said, "It seemed familiar, but I can't identify it. To be honest, the voice scares me, Brady. I—" She gripped his hand even tighter. "All day it's been haunting me. Now, after desperately wishing I could remember something, I'm wishing I could forget this."

Placing his free hand on top of hers, he said, "I wouldn't put much stock into the whole thing, Lass. Whatever you saw could be something that happened years ago. Or maybe you had a dream last night and it suddenly came to you."

She didn't look at all convinced and to be honest Brady found it hard to dismiss her images as dreams. From the small amount of time he'd been around this woman, she didn't appear to be an airhead or a drama queen. True, she was a bit upset at the moment, but anyone in her predicament had a right to feel unsettled.

"I don't think so, Brady. I think those were glimmers of things that happened—before I was injured."

"Could be, Lass. But we won't know for certain until you have more of them, or I manage to get a toehold on some relevant information. And I hate to tell you, but that hasn't happened yet. No one at the track seemed to recognize you. A waitress in the club house restaurant thought she recalled seeing you, but she wasn't sure. When they see hundreds of faces a day, it's hard to single out one from the crowd."

"Oh, well," she said, trying to put a bit of cheer in her voice, "someone might eventually see my picture and identify me. I mean, I couldn't have come from Mars. Martians don't wear cowboy boots and Levi's, do they?"

Glad that she could see a bit of humor in the whole thing, he smiled, then leaned forward and pressed a light kiss against her forehead.

Behind them, a door opened, and Kate made a production of clearing her throat. "The family is having drinks. Are you two going to join us?" she asked.

Knowing this intimate time with Lass was over, at least, for now, Brady rose from the love seat and reached for Lass's hand.

"Grandma, did anyone ever tell you that your timing is rotten?"

Kate grinned. "Looks to me like my timing was perfect. I saved Lass from your clutches."

Easing his arm around Lass's waist, he urged her toward Kate and a door that would take them back into the house. "What's wrong with my clutches?" he asked his grandmother. "Lass just might like them."

With a good-natured snort, Kate turned and entered the door before them. "She's too smart a girl for that, sonny."

Lass was quickly learning that dinner at the Donovans' was a special affair. Tonight, Opal, the family's longtime cook, had prepared prime rib, and as each course was served, the conversation seemed to change to a different subject. By the time dishes of strawberry torte arrived for dessert, Conall was giving a production report of a gold mine that belonged to their sister, Maura. Since the elder brother was manager of the Golden Spur's operations and part of the profit was distributed to the whole family, it was a subject that held everyone's attention.

Except Brady, it seemed. He seemed more interested in Lass than anything and each time he turned his twinkling eyes on her, her mind insisted on replaying the kiss he'd given her on the back porch.

What had prompted him to do such a thing? But then what had been behind her behavior? The moment he'd walked onto the porch, she'd thrown herself at him like some sort of starved lover. Was that the way she normally acted around attractive men? Before she'd lost her memory had she been promiscuous?

No, Lass refused to believe that. Deep down, she felt certain it wasn't her nature to casually jump into a sexual relationship with a man. She hadn't felt anything for Hank, or the doctors or even Conall. So she couldn't exactly understand what had come over her with Brady. Except that all day long she'd been desperate to see him, talk with him. She'd certainly not had kissing the man on her mind. She'd been all wound up about those memory flashes and then when he'd finally shown up, relief and joy had shot her straight to his arms, nothing more. Now he was looking at her as though she was part of the dessert. And all she could think about was the magic she'd felt when his lips had touched hers, the way his hands had caressed and pulled her close.

For the remainder of the meal, she tried to push the whole incident out of her mind and by the time everyone finished dessert, she'd convinced herself that she was being silly to dwell on one little kiss. Brady hadn't taken it seriously and neither should she.

As everyone filed out of the dining room, Brady excused himself to make an important phone call. Since it was still too early to retire to her room, Lass followed Kate and Brady's parents to the family room.

While Kate played a medley of Irish folk songs on the piano and Fiona and Doyle started up a card game, Lass picked up a newspaper and began to scan the headlines.

She was reading about a government proposal to bring aid to drought-stricken ranchers, when Brady eased a hip onto the arm of her chair.

"Catching up on the news?" he asked.

She glanced at him, while wishing her heart wouldn't jump into high gear every time the man drew within ten feet of her. "Trying," she admitted, then gave him an encouraging smile. "You know, when I started reading the headlines, I realized that I remembered who our president is and most of our national officials. Strange, that I can remember something like that, but not my own parents."

His brows peaked with interest, and he gestured toward the paper. "Were there any stories in there that sparked your memory? A town? A name?"

"Not really. But that's not surprising. I'm obviously not a local." A thoughtful frown puckered her forehead. "When I look at some of the addresses listed on these advertisements, I keep thinking I should see a TX rather than NM."

"So you're thinking you might be from Texas?"

Nodding stiffly, she said, "I'm hardly certain of that. It's just a gut feeling." As she looked at him her eyes suddenly widened. "Brady, maybe I had a rental car! You could trace it! Or perhaps I flew in from Texas to the Ruidoso airport? Will they have records?"

"I've questioned the staff at the airport. None of them recalled seeing you. As for passenger records, the personnel at the airport has promised to go through them, but since we don't have your name, it's impossible to know when you arrived, or even if you arrived by plane. So that effort might not lead to any sort of productive information. Hank has already checked all the car rental places in town. Nothing there. So that means you probably took a taxi. We've left your photo with all the cab services. But I'm not expecting much to evolve there. There are simply too many tourists and strange faces in town and a cabbie would've only seen you for few short minutes at the most. Plus there's still the possibility that someone else drove you to the track."

"Someone else drove me to the track," she repeated blankly. "Like who? If I was with a friend or relative where are they now? Why did they leave me on that mountain road?"

"I understand that possibility doesn't make sense to you, Lass. But as a lawman, I have to go at things from every angle. Some person you met in town could have simply offered you a ride to the track out of kindness, then left town after the races."

"I see," she murmured, while wondering why this news left her feeling so confused. She wanted Brady to discover her real identity, didn't she? Of course, she did. Her whole life was missing. And yet, a part of her didn't want to return to who she'd been before. A part of her wanted to start her life right here. Right now. With him. Oh, God, what was happening to her?

"Come on, you've worried about all that stuff enough for one day. Do you feel like a walk?"

Grateful that he understood she needed a break from the turmoil going round in her head, she smiled at him. "I'd love to take a walk."

He helped her from the chair, then ushered her out of the room before his parents or grandmother even noticed they were leaving. At the end of a long hallway, near a door composed of paned windows, he snatched a white shawl from a rack on the wall.

"You might get a little cool," he explained as he draped the crocheted lace around her shoulders. "Mom won't mind if you borrow her shawl."

Swallowing nervously, she focused on the front of his pale yellow shirt instead of his face. "Thank you, Brady."

"My pleasure."

When they stepped outside, Lass could see they were at the side of the house. It was shaded deeply by tall ponderosa pines, but footlights illuminated a graveled path leading to the front and back of the huge rock structure.

"Let's go to the backyard," he suggested as he splayed a hand against her back. "Have you been down to the pool yet?"

"No. I've only gotten as far as the porch," she admitted.

He ushered her forward and they began to slowly walk abreast. He'd been right about the air turning cool. The temperature felt as though it had dropped several degrees, but the touch of his hand felt so hot against her, it chased any chilliness away.

Breathing deeply, she tried not to think of his nearness or the way it had felt to kiss him.

"Do you like living here with the rest of your family?" she asked as they strolled along a walkway of loose river gravel.

"I can't imagine living anywhere else." He darted a glance at her. "That probably sounds like I lack ambition, doesn't it? You're probably wondering why a man like me doesn't want a place of his own."

"I'm not wondering anything like that," she admitted. "I see a man who loves his family."

"Hmm. That's true. But I don't hang around here because I'm too green to cut the apron strings."

Lass smiled in the darkness. Green was the exact opposite of the image he portrayed, she thought. He was strong, brave and independent. The exact opposite of… whom? For a split second, a man's image almost popped into her head, but it was so fleeting and her mind so weary, she didn't bother to try to catch it.

"I would never think that," she assured him.

His hand moved downward until his fingers were curled snugly around the side of her waist. "You're being very polite."

"I'm not just being polite. I'm being honest."

He chuckled then. "Well, I guess to the outward person my brothers and I look like mama's boys. But that's not the case at all. Conall and Liam run the ranch operations. Without all their work, Dad wouldn't be able to retire and enjoy these years with Mom. And me, well, I don't do ranch work on a day-to-day basis, but I help as much as I can."

"That's something I've been curious about," Lass told him. "Why did you become a lawman? Particularly, when your brothers are ranchers like your father."

They walked for several yards before he finally answered and by then they'd entered a garden filled with ornamental bushes and low, blooming flowers. The graveled path had turned to stepping stones and the sweet smell of honeysuckle filled the night air.

Brady paused to face her. "I'm lucky, Lass. From the time we were young children, our father has always encouraged us to follow our own dreams. If that meant something other than raising thoroughbreds, then that was okay with him."

"You don't like working with horses?"

There was a perplexed frown on her face, as though she couldn't imagine anyone opposing such a job. It made Brady realize just how much she loved horses and that she'd no doubt been involved in the equine business in some form or fashion. But that was a wide-ranging possibility that included farms, ranches, tracks, trainers, stables and veterinarians, coupled with all the offshoot jobs from those businesses. Unless she remembered something helpful, finding her identity was going to be like searching for one tiny mosquito in the middle of a giant swamp.

Keeping that worrisome thought to himself, he said, "Oh, sure. I love horses. But I never had that special touch with them. Not the way my father and brothers have always had. They understand what a horse is thinking and planning way before the horse even knows it. And I…well, I learned the hard way. By being bit or kicked or bucked off. You get the picture. But that didn't matter. I just happened to have other ideas about my career. And it wasn't breeding or racing horses."

She nodded that she understood his independence wasn't born out of retaliation. "How did you decide you wanted to be a lawman? You have other relatives in the business?"

He chuckled. "I wish. Then everyone wouldn't look at me like I'm the lone wolf of the bunch." Curling his arm around her shoulder, he once again urged her forward. "Actually, I first planned to be a lawyer. A horse farm of this size always needs legal work and I liked the idea of laying out rules and regulations."

"A lawyer," she repeated with faint amazement. "I can't imagine you in a courtroom."

"No? Well, Grandma could imagine me in that role. She said I could argue better than anyone she knew," he teased. "But after I started college it didn't take me very long to realize I didn't want to be confined behind four walls for the rest of my life."

"So you quit college and went to work for the sheriff's department?"

"Not exactly," he answered. "I went to work part-time for the sheriff's department, did my rookie training and continued earning a degree in criminal justice during my off hours. All of it together was tough going for a while.

But now I'm glad I put out the effort." With a wry smile, he glanced down at her. "I took the long way about answering a simple question, didn't I? So I've talked enough about myself. Let's talk about you."

By now they had reached a long, oval-shaped pool surrounded by footlights. The crystal clear water sparkled invitingly and as she stared at the depths, she envisioned herself in a similar pool, the water slipping cool against her arms, the night air above her hot and humid. She tried to hang on to the image, to memorize every detail, but like before, it was gone almost as quickly as it came and with a frustrated sigh, she said, "We can't talk about me, Brady. I don't know anything about me."

Seeing the whole thing disturbed her, Brady urged her over to a flowered lounge positioned a few feet from the edge of the pool. After she took a seat on the end of the long chair, he sank next to her and reached for her hand.

"I'm sorry, Lass. I wasn't thinking. Damn it, I've never been around anyone who can't remember who they are and I keep forgetting to watch my words. Everything I say seems to put a glaring light on your predicament."

Shaking her head, she stared pensively into the darkness. "That's all right. I don't want you to watch your words around me, Brady. I want you to be yourself. I don't want you to try to isolate or cushion me from reality. I'm tougher than you think. Really I am."

Brady couldn't stop his hands from wrapping around her slender shoulders or turning her toward him. There was something sweetly endearing about her that pulled at everything inside of him. Something about the trusting look in her gray eyes that made him want to be her protector, her hero, her everything.

"Tough is not the way I'd describe you, Lass," he said

lowly. The holes in the crocheted shawl exposed patches of skin to his hands. The soft feel of it excited him, almost as much as gazing at the moist curves of her lips. "Strong. But not tough."

Her lashes fluttered demurely against her cheeks. "Brady, we came out here for a walk," she pointed out. "In case you hadn't noticed, we're sitting."

He rubbed the top of his forefinger beneath her chin and swallowed as the urge to kiss her threatened to overtake his senses.

He murmured, "As a deputy of this county, I can assure you that sitting isn't a crime."

The tip of her tongue slipped out to nervously moisten her top lip. "Brady, that kiss…earlier—"

"Yes?"

"I don't think we should repeat it."

She looked confused and worried and for the first time in his life, Brady felt a bit of unease himself. Which didn't make any sense. Kissing a beautiful woman had never concerned him before. He didn't know why it should give him second thoughts now. But kissing Lass had been different, he realized. So different that he wanted to do it over. He wanted to make sure it had actually felt that amazing.

"Why?"

Her mouth fell open. "You have to ask? Brady, I can't even tell you my name! I don't even know how old I am!"

He cupped his palm against the side of her face as his thoughts rolled back to the night he'd found her lying lifelessly in the ditch. When she'd finally regained consciousness and he'd sheltered her in his arms, he'd experienced some very unprofessional feelings and since he'd gotten to know her, those unprofessional feelings had only deepened. Hell, that was enough to scare any tried and true bachelor. But it didn't scare him enough to make him rise to his feet and walk away from her.

"Of course you can tell me your name," he insisted. "It's Lass."

"Only temporarily."

Ignoring that, he said, "And you certainly look old enough to kiss."

She sighed. "Kate says you're somewhat of a ladies' man."

He grimaced. "Grandma has a motormouth."

"Then she was speaking the truth?"

Since she wasn't trying to pull away, Brady made the most of the close proximity by delving his fingers into her silky hair, sliding them downward through the long strands.

"Look, Lass, I'm not going to pretend I've been some sort of saint. Especially when—"

"When I can't even tell you what I've been," she finished miserably. Then biting her bottom lip, she looked away. "I'm sorry, Brady. I had no right to question you about your past. Not when mine is a complete blank."

"Lass, Lass," he softly scolded, "no one has to give me your résumé for me to know that you are and were a lady. And in spite of what Grandma says about me, I'm a gentleman."

Her eyes softened and then to Brady's amazement, her face drew near to his. "Yes, I think you are," she whispered.

The moment their lips touched, Brady realized he'd made a mistake. Her kiss didn't just taste amazing; the sensations went far deeper than that. Like tremors of an earthquake, waves of pleasure vibrated through him, urged him to crush her close, to search out the mysterious sweetness of her lips.

Seconds could have passed or minutes, he didn't know, but suddenly he felt her arms go around his neck and the sign of surrender brought a groan of triumph deep in his throat. Her lips parted wider and he took advantage, slipping his tongue past their sweet curves and into the honeyed cavity of her mouth.

The intimate connection caused his head to reel and before he could get a grip on his senses, their surroundings began to float away. His hands began to urgently roam her body, his lips fought to totally capture hers and in the process he forgot everything but making love to the woman in his arms.

Until her hands slipped to his shoulders and pushed, her lips abruptly jerked away from his.

The sudden break jolted him and as he attempted to gather himself together, he wanted to ask her what was wrong, why had she interrupted something so incredible.

But one look at her face answered those questions for him. The two of them had been on the verge of losing control, of making love right here beside the pool. And she wasn't all that happy about it.

Pushing a tangle of hair from her eyes, she said in a husky voice, "I think we've 'walked' enough for one night. Don't you?"

Did she really expect him to answer that? He looked away from her and drew in several long, mind-cleansing breaths. What was happening here? He wasn't supposed to want Lass this much. He wasn't supposed to want any woman this much.

Rising from the chair, he reached for her hand. "You're right, Lass. We'd better go in. Before our walk turns into a run."

Chapter Seven

He'd been wrong to kiss Lass.

The next morning, as Brady drove south to the Mescalero Apache Indian Reservation, that dismal thought continued to swirl through his head. He'd misjudged the whole thing and instead of it being a pleasant little connection of the lips, the kiss had turned out to be a heated embrace that had turned him on his ear and left her strangely quiet for the remainder of the evening.

Now, all he could do was relive the experience over and over in his mind and wonder what it all meant. That the two of them had great chemistry together? There was no doubt about that. But he'd dated attractive women before and some of those occasions had turned into overnight delights. Yet he could easily admit that nothing about those unions had messed with his thinking or left him in such a mental fog. Lass was doing something to him. Something that he didn't understand or want to acknowledge.

Sighing, he glanced over to the empty seat of the pickup truck outfitted with a two-way radio, weapons and other police equipment. This morning he'd left Hank back in Ruidoso, scouring the more popular restaurants and motels where Lass might be remembered by the staff.

Normally, a case like hers wouldn't receive this much investigative work from the sheriff's department. Instead, Lass's case would have fallen under the health and welfare services. But thankfully Sheriff Hamilton had agreed with Brady that the circumstances surrounding Lass's amnesia smelled of criminal mischief and needed to be resolved.

Brady had no idea how long Ethan would keep the case open or how much time and manpower he would expend toward it. With county cost a factor, Brady knew the search couldn't last forever. He couldn't imagine having to tell Lass the effort to find her home and family had to come to an end. In fact, if it came down to it, Brady would use his own resources to find Lass's identity.

But he prayed to God before any of that happened, something would turn up. Or even better, Lass would start to remember. Until then, Brady had his work cut out for him. Not only to find Lass's past, but to also keep his growing attraction for the woman in a proper perspective. And his hands to himself.

Yeah, right, he thought, as he turned down the bumpy dirt road to the Chino homestead. That was like telling himself to quit eating whenever he was hungry.

Johnny Chino was two years older than Brady and had lived with his grandparents, Charlie and Naomi, since he was a tiny infant. His mother had been an unwed teenager, a wild and irresponsible girl who'd been spoiled since her parents were older when she was born. She'd brought much shame on the Chino family. Shortly after Johnny had been born, she'd dumped the baby into her parents' lap and left for parts unknown. A few years later, they'd gotten word that she'd been killed in an alcohol-related car crash.

Now Johnny's grandparents were both in their nineties, but were still in good enough health to do for themselves. Even so, Johnny didn't stray far from the home place and Brady often wondered if they were the reason the man had quit taking on tracking jobs. Rumor had it that he'd quit because of some tragedy that had occurred out in California. But Brady wasn't one to listen to rumors. Nor was he one to question a friend just to satisfy a curiosity.

When Brady parked the truck in front of the house, two dogs, a red hound and a black collie, barked and ran toward the vehicle. Trusting that the dogs would remember him from his last visit a couple of months ago, he stepped to the ground.

By the time the dogs had surrounded him, a door slammed and he looked up to see Johnny stepping onto the long, wooden porch spanning the front of the small stucco house.

He was a tall, strongly built man, his long black hair pulled into a ponytail. His right cheekbone carried a faint scar, but it was his dark eyes that bore the true marks of his past. He stood where he was and waited for Brady to join him in the shade.

Lifting his hand in greeting, Brady approached the porch. Their tails wagging, the dogs trailed close on his heels.

"They remember you," Johnny said, nodding toward the dogs.

"Why wouldn't they?" Brady joked. "I'm pretty unforgettable."

A quirk of a smile moved a corner of Johnny's mouth as he motioned to a tattered lawn chair. "Come sit."

Brady climbed the steps and took a seat. Johnny slouched against the wall of the house and pulled a piece of willow from his pocket and opened his pocket knife.

"How are your grandparents, Johnny?" he asked politely.

"Old. Very old."

Well, his friend always did have a way of summing up a situation with very few words, Brady thought wryly.

"You probably know why I'm here," Brady said. In spite of this part of the reservation being remote, he knew that news of any sort traveled quickly from one family to the next. No doubt Johnny had already heard a woman had been found in the mountains.

"Maybe."

Brady did his best to contain a sigh of impatience. This was one man he couldn't hurry and if he tried, he'd probably blow the whole reason for the visit.

"The girl doesn't know who she is," Brady explained. "And I can't figure out what happened. At least, I haven't yet."

"I'm no lawman."

"No. But you'd make a good one," Brady said honestly.

Johnny's knife blade sliced through the piece of willow and a curl of wood fell to the porch floor.

"I don't track anymore."

Brady couldn't let things die there. Lass and her happiness meant too much to him. "I was hoping you'd break out of retirement for me. Just this one time."

"The dogs don't track anymore, either."

Brady looked around to see both dogs had flopped down in a hole they had scratched near the end of the porch. Their energy level appeared to match Johnny's.

"Since when have you needed dogs to help you?" Brady asked.

"I don't track anymore," he repeated.

Rubbing his hands over his knees, Brady tried to hide his frustration. "Johnny, I thought we were friends. Good friends."

Johnny's rough features tightened, but he said nothing.

One minute, then two, then three finally ticked by in pregnant silence. If it had been anyone else besides Johnny, Brady would have set in with a long speech about how they'd stood up for each other in high school, how they'd always had each other's backs on the football field, and how after Brady's grandfather had died, they'd camped together on Bonito Lake for a whole week. Because at that time, Johnny had understood how much Brady had needed to be with a friend.

But Brady didn't remind the other man of their close ties. He knew that Johnny hadn't forgotten anything.

"This girl," Johnny said finally, "she means a lot to you?"

Brady let out a long breath. Means a lot? Leave it to his old buddy's simple question to make Brady really think about what Lass was becoming to him, how important her happiness had come to mean to him. "Yeah. She…well, I like her better than any girl I can ever remember."

His friend didn't make an immediate reply to that and while Brady waited, he watched a pair of guinea hens strut across the dusty yard. He tried to imagine Johnny living in Albuquerque or Santa Fe, but that was like picturing a mountain lion in a cage.

"Show me where you found her," Johnny finally said. "And I'll try to get the dogs interested."

More grateful than he ever expected to feel, Brady swallowed a sigh of relief, then rose to his feet and walked over to Johnny.

At that moment, he could have said a lot of things to his old friend. Like how much he valued their friendship. How much he appreciated his help and how much he thanked him for always being around whenever he needed him. But Johnny already knew all of that. And the quiet Apache would be insulted to hear such platitudes from Brady. To Johnny a true bond needed no words to keep it strong.

Instead, Brady touched a hand to his shoulder. "Fine. But before we go, I'd like to say hello to your grandparents."

Johnny opened the front door of the little stucco and motioned for Brady to precede him into the house. As Brady stepped into the cool, dimly lit living room, all he could think about was that he was now one giant step closer to finding Lass's identity.

But what was that going to bring to her? To him? Was all of this effort to find her past, eventually going to tear her from his arms?

Brady couldn't let himself think about those questions. Because the minute he did he would quit being the Chief Deputy of Lincoln County and simply become a man.

At the same time, some twenty miles away, in a small boutique in downtown Ruidoso, Lass ambled slowly through the aisles of lingerie while close behind her, Dallas made helpful suggestions.

"I love this pink lace," Dallas said, pausing to examine a set of bra and panties draped from a padded satin hanger. "This would look great on you, Lass."

A faint blush colored Lass's face. "Those are very expensive. Especially when…well, no one is going to see what I'm wearing underneath," she reasoned.

"Lass! Since when did a woman start worrying about that? We wear this stuff because it makes us feel sexy and pretty. And who's worrying about the cost, anyway? I'm not."

Following up on her invitation from yesterday, Dallas

had insisted on bringing Lass to town today to shop for personal items. So far she'd purchased a sack full of inexpensive makeup, hair-styling tools, two pair of shoes, a handbag and wallet. Though what she expected to put inside the wallet, she didn't know. Without money, ID, credit cards, or a checkbook, she had little use for one. But Dallas had insisted, saying eventually that Brady was going to solve the whole thing and then Lass would need a place to put her driver's license and other important information.

"I can see that you're not concerned about the expense. But I am," Lass told her.

Dallas rolled her green eyes. "Oh, Lass, I rarely leave the stables to do anything. Much less shopping. And to have someone else to buy for makes this spree all that much better. Now please don't spoil my fun. Come on and loosen up. Pick out your size in this pink and then we'll find something in black. With your hair color you'll sizzle!"

Sizzle? Lass didn't need black lingerie to make her sizzle. Brady could easily get that job done.

Oh, Lord, why couldn't she quit thinking about the man? Why couldn't she get last night out of her mind? she wondered, as a flush of embarrassed heat warmed her cheeks. She'd never behaved so recklessly with a man. Never felt such a raw, unbridled urge to make love.

So how do you know that, Lass? Your mind is a blank blackboard. It can't tell you whether you've had a boyfriend or lover or even a husband! How can it tell you that Brady made you feel things you've never felt before?

Because something deep down, something more than her mind was speaking to her, she mentally flung back at the little voice.

To Dallas she said with a measure of uncertainty, "I'm not really sure I want to sizzle, Dallas."

Dallas laughed. "Honey, every woman from nine to ninety wants to feel a little spark now and then. And even though no one can tell us your exact age, I think we can safely assume you fit somewhere in that category."

With a good-natured groan, Lass followed Dallas's orders and searched through the pink lingerie until she found the correct size. But as the two women moved on down the aisle, past the cotton undergarments, Lass touched her friend's arm.

"Dallas, wait a minute. Look at this stuff. Have you stopped to consider that I might be a cotton sort of girl?"

Dallas shot her a look of wry disbelief and Lass made a helpless gesture with her hands.

"See what I mean! I don't remember anything about myself. It's…scary. I could have been a mousy little librarian afraid to date even a nerd or—God forbid—maybe I was one of those women who flaunted themselves and had boyfriends scattered all over town!"

Dallas began to laugh, then, spotting the distress on Lass's face, she gently curved a reassuring arm around her shoulders.

"I'm sorry, Lass, I know that none of this seems funny to you. But the idea of you being either one of those types of women is ridiculous. You have amnesia, not a personality disorder. Believe me, if Brady had thought you were wild and crazy, he wouldn't have brought you home to the ranch. And trust me, he's a good judge of character."

After last night, there was no telling how he was judging her character, Lass thought. Stifling a groan, she said, "Well, I'm just very grateful that he decided to help me. That all of you are helping me."

Dallas gave her shoulders another squeeze. "Look, Lass, I'm actually a selfish person. I love having your company. Brita's so busy with her career as a doctor and Maura's time is consumed with her own family. She has an eighteen-month-old son, Riley, and two weeks ago she gave birth to another son, Michael, so I don't have a sister to pal with anymore and you're the next best thing. The fact that you're a horsewoman like me just makes it even better." She shook her head with wry disbelief. "Isn't it destiny," she went on, "that you ended up on our horse farm?"

Destiny? Sometimes Lass felt as if she were in the twilight zone or some freakish dream that was too good to be true. She worried that at any moment she would wake and be jerked back to some dark place she didn't want to be.

"Very," Lass agreed. "And if your brother hadn't found me that night—I might not even be alive today."

Dropping her arm from her shoulders, Dallas urged her on down the aisle and away from the cotton underwear. "I can tell my brother likes you," she declared. "A lot."

Lass glanced around the store, as though she suspected anyone hearing such a comment would burst out laughing. From what Kate had told her, Brady's acquaintances with women ranged all over the county and beyond. He'd never lacked female attention. In fact, Kate said that more often than not, Brady had more trouble getting rid of a girlfriend than acquiring one. And after that kiss he'd given Lass last night, she could certainly understand why. The man's charm was so strong it deserved a warning label.

Picking up a black camisole, she studied the lace edging that would frame her bosom in a very provocative way. "I understand that Brady likes *a lot* of women," Lass murmured as she fingered the whisper light silk.

Dallas grimaced with disapproval. "Yes. But not like this. Not like you."

Lass jerked her gaze to the other woman's face. "Why do you say that?"

"Because he's never brought any woman home to the ranch before. And he darn sure wouldn't let one near Grandma. Not unless he considered her to be *really* special."

Could Dallas be right? Lass wondered. Did he consider her special? As soon as the question crossed her mind, she berated herself for even thinking it. She couldn't allow herself to get all dreamy-eyed about Brady. Any hour, any day, someone could show up to claim her. And then what would happen? Where would she be? What sort of life would that someone lead her back to? No, getting involved with Brady would be the same as asking for a heart ache.

Later that evening, more than thirty miles away at the sheriff's department in Carrizozo, Brady was sitting at his desk, searching through page after page of data on the computer screen, when a cup of steaming hot coffee appeared a few inches from his right hand.

Glancing up, he saw Hank's beaming face.

"What's this for?" Brady asked the junior deputy.

"I just made a new pot and you looked like you needed it."

"Thanks. I do need it. It's been a hell of a day and it's not over yet."

"You're telling me. Ever since I came back from lunch, the darn phone has been ringing off the hook." Hank motioned toward the monitor. "Find anything on there that fits Lass?"

"This is the first chance I've had to look today. And so far I'm not finding any missing persons alerts that even come close to Lass's description." He reached for the foam cup and took a cautious sip while Hank pulled up a folding metal chair and flopped into it.

This afternoon, while Brady had driven Johnny to the mountains, the department had been flooded with an array of calls. For the past several hours, Hank had been out doing his part to deal with the problems. Brady glanced at his watch. It was getting late, but before he left for the ranch, he needed to talk over Johnny's findings with Ethan. But for the past hour Ethan had been tied up with meetings and phone calls. Today had been a busy day for all of them and Brady was feeling more than tired. He was frustrated and troubled and more than a little anxious to see Lass again.

"I'm glad you showed up before I head home," he told Hank. "I need your reports from this morning. Have you had a chance to type them up?"

Hank looked at him with a bemused expression. "Reports? I didn't go out on any calls this morning."

Brady slowly lifted his gray hat from his hand and stabbed his fingers through his flattened hair. "Hank, I sent you out to question the businesses on Sudderth and Mechem Drives. You were supposed to ask if anyone working in those businesses recalled seeing Lass in the days before we found her. Remember?"

"Well, sure I remember what I was doing this morning. I just wasn't considering that the same as going on a call. You sent me on that job. It wasn't the same as somebody calling in and wanting help. Don't you see?"

Brady sighed. "Yeah. I see. So where are your notes? I understand that you've been tied up most of the day, so if you've not had a chance to type them up, we'll worry about that later. Just give me what you have and I'll try to decipher your handwriting."

Hank's expression turned sheepish. "I ain't got no notes. Nobody knew nothin'. So there wasn't any use in taking down notes."

Screwing his hat back onto his head, Brady narrowed his eyes on the hapless deputy. Hank was usually a dedicated deputy. And ever since he'd been hired on at the department, he'd been a good friend to Brady. But at this moment he wanted to wring the man's neck.

"No use, huh? I don't know what makes me angrier at you, Hank. Not following orders or using double negatives!"

His face red, Hank cringed back in his seat. "Brady, that's not fair! I talked to a bunch of people. Waitresses and clerks and cleaning people. You name it and I talked to 'em. They all looked at Lass's photo and none of them remembered her."

Frustration boiled over and Brady's hand slapped down so hard on his desk that the coffee came dangerously close to slopping over the rim and spilling onto the ink blotter.

"Since when did Sheriff Hamilton decide to change department policy around here?" Brady boomed at him. "Maybe we should call him out here and ask him? He might need to know that you've taken it upon yourself to decide what information is worthy of being noted or ignored."

"No! Oh, hell, Brady, please don't tell him about this!" Hank pleaded, then suddenly his expression turned hopeful and he dug into the front pocket of his jeans until he pulled out a small scrap of paper. Tossing it onto Brady's desk he added, "I almost forgot. That's for you."

With a cursory glance at the paper, Brady asked, "What is it?"

"A telephone number. From that little redhead at the desk at the Aspen Hotel. She asked me to give it to you."

His back teeth grinding together, Brady wadded the paper into a tight ball and threw it at the junior deputy. "I'm not interested in some little redhead!" He regained control, stabbing a finger toward the outer office. "Go type up your work, and if nobody knew anything, then put it down that way! And I expect you to list each business you walked into and each person you said one word to. Got it?"

Hank jumped up from the chair so fast that it tipped over and clattered loudly to the hard tiled floor. Before Brady could say more, he scrambled to right the chair, then scurried from the room as though a bolt of lightning was nipping at his rear.

On the opposite side of the room, the door to the sheriff's office opened and Ethan's face appeared around the edge of the wooden panel. "What in heck is going on out here?"

Brady wearily wiped a hand over his face. "Sorry for the interruption, Ethan. Hank knocked a chair over."

Sensing that Brady was dealing with more than a tumbled chair, Ethan stepped into the room.

"I heard yelling. That's not like you, Brady."

Brady grimaced. It was rare that he raised his voice to anyone. But this whole thing about Lass, about what Johnny had discovered about the night she was injured, was tearing at him. "No. Hank set me off and I…lost my cool with him."

Ethan took a seat in the chair that Hank had vacated only seconds ago. "Well, Hank can be a handful to deal with. But he means well. What has he done now?"

Sighing ruefully, Brady rubbed the tight muscles at the back of his neck. In spite of his frustration, there was no way he wanted to get his partner in trouble. "Nothing that bad. He…just needed a reminder to follow orders. That's all."

Accepting his explanation without further question, Ethan glanced thoughtfully at the computer screen, then back to Brady. "Any leads about Lass?"

"Only what Johnny found."

Ethan arched a quizzical brow at him. "You got Johnny Chino to venture off the res for Lass's case?"

There had been a time when the department had relied on Johnny's tracking skills to help them solve cases or find lost children. But that had ended long ago when Johnny had abruptly called it quits. No doubt the sheriff was surprised to hear the man had emerged from the reservation to offer his help.

"We were in the mountains all afternoon."

"And?"

Brady fought the urge to bend his head and close his eyes. This was business, not personal, and he needed to treat it as such. Yet the whole idea that Lass had possibly been running for her life haunted him in ways he'd never expected it to.

"Plenty. He found the spot on the side of the highway where the vehicle she'd been riding in had stopped. A scuffle ensued there and then Lass ran into a nearby ravine. Her attacker—companion, or whatever the person was—followed. But he must have lost Lass in the dark because his tracks climbed back out of the steep crevice and returned to the car. Lass's tracks continued on up the mountain. Johnny found where she'd tripped over a fallen branch and hit her head on a slab of rock. After that, she wandered due west until she reached the road and collapsed in the ditch."

Ethan's thumb and forefinger stroked his chin as he silently digested this new information. "Did Johnny think the car drove up the mountain to look for Lass? After four days the elements have probably erased most of the readable evidence. But that Apache can see things no one else can see."

"Actually, I asked him that same question," Brady told him. "And Johnny believes the car pulled back onto the highway, headed east and never returned. After Lass fell and wandered to the road, no one else's tracks appeared."

"Hmm. So in other words, whoever was driving the car left Lass alone in the mountains. And so far, he hasn't shown his face to us. That tells us plenty."

"Yeah," Brady said grimly, "he was up to no good. And he has no intention of showing up to claim her."

Ethan nodded. "Even if the wound to her head occurred because of the fall, that doesn't clear the jerk from wrongdoing. Clearly he was trying to harm her. But who and why? Has she remembered anything else?"

"Only confusing fragments. I talked to Bridget about it and she seems to think that remembering things, no matter how small, is a hopeful sign. She believes Lass's memory will return sooner than later."

Ethan rose to his feet. "This is not just a case of amnesia, Brady. It's a criminal case, but we pretty much assumed that from the very start. So I don't expect you to sit around and simply wait for Lass to remember who tried to hurt her. Keep doing what you're doing. Searching—for anything and everything."

Brady nodded soberly. "I will."

His expression full of concern, Ethan laid a hand on Brady's shoulder. "So what are you going to tell Lass about this? About Johnny's findings?"

Brady glanced up at him. "I have to tell her everything, don't I? What other choice do I have?"

Ethan released a heavy breath. "None, I suppose. It's her life, she deserves to know what happened." Giving Brady's shoulder another pat, the sheriff gazed pensively off in space. "I'm thinking back to a time before Penny and I were married, when she was still the county judge. A crazy escaped convict was sending in threats to the sheriff's department that he intended to kill her. I had to be the one to tell her that some other human being hated her that much.

Then I had to try to capture him and keep her safe. It wasn't an easy task."

"Was that before you two started a relationship?" Brady asked curiously.

One corner of Ethan's mouth lifted wryly. "That's when I fell in love with her."

Something inside Brady tumbled, then hit with a hard jolt. What was Ethan trying to tell him? That if he didn't watch his step he'd be falling in love with Lass?

His mind was spinning, searching for some sort of sensible reply to the sheriff's remark when Ethan spoke again, thankfully on a different subject.

"So what are you going to do about Hank?" Ethan asked. "We don't want him moping around here like a whipped pup for the rest of the week."

"I'll make it up to him," Brady assured him.

Ethan chuckled. "How do you plan to do that? He's not yet ready for a promotion."

A tired grin crossed Brady's face. "I'll set him up with a blind date. He thinks having a woman in his life will fix everything."

Grunting with amusement, Ethan headed back to his office. "Don't we all?"

Thoughtful now, Brady watched the sheriff close the door behind him. Having Lass in his life for these few days had been nice. No, he corrected, it had been more than nice. The time with her had been special. Really special. But that didn't mean his life before Lass had needed fixing. Did it? That didn't mean he'd become a broken man if she suddenly went back to her old life.

Turning back to the computer screen, Brady muttered a curse under his breath. He was damned stupid for letting Ethan's simple question get to him. After all, he'd always been a strong guy. He'd always been in control of his emotions, his happiness. One pretty little gray-eyed lass wasn't going to change that. Was she?

Chapter Eight

In spite of the heavy workload, Brady managed to make the drive home to the Diamond D and shower before dinnertime. Once he dressed and combed his hair into a semblance of order, he left his room, then stopped at Lass's door on the chance that she'd not yet joined the rest of the family downstairs.

Rapping his knuckles on the wooden panel, he called to her in a low voice, "Lass? Are you in there?"

After a couple of moments he heard her light footsteps and then the door swung wide. Brady's pulse stumbled, then leaped into a fast race as he drank in the sight of her petite figure sheathed in a pale blue dress that fit at her waist and flared at her knees. The neckline was daringly low. At least, in his mind, it dared him to take a second and third look at the tempting hint of cleavage exposed above the fabric.

"Brady," she greeted with faint surprise. "Am I…late for supper or something?"

He smiled gently while he tried not to stare. There was a faint bit of makeup on her face and her black hair was coiled into intricate loops atop her head and fastened with rhinestone pins. She looked so lovely it made him ache in a way he'd never ached before.

"Don't worry. I doubt the family has gathered yet. I…wanted to talk to you before we went downstairs," he told her.

Her gray eyes earnestly searched his face. "Oh. Is anything wrong?"

He said, "Not exactly. May I come in?"

"Of course."

With slightly flustered movements, she pushed the door wider and Brady entered the bedroom. The faint scent of her flowery perfume lingered in the air and from the corner of his eye he could see a few silky undergarments scattered across the end of the queen-size bed. For one reckless moment, Brady easily imagined himself pulling scraps of satin and lace from her slender body, of laying her on the bed and…

Before he could let his mind finish the erotic vision, he grabbed her by the elbow and maneuvered her over to a sliding glass door that opened onto a balcony.

"Let's go out here," he suggested. Where he could get some fresh air and hopefully forget how much he wanted to make love to this woman.

The balcony floor was made of planked timber and spanned the whole width of the house. Furniture made of redwood and covered with cushions of bright floral fabric was grouped along the wide expanse, so that each bedroom was provided with a variety of comfortable seating. Potted bougainvillea, agave and aloe plants were scattered here and there, but it was the huge loblolly pines towering over the front edge of the deck that made the spot feel truly outdoors.

As Brady helped her into one of the chairs, she spoke in an attempt to lighten the moment. "Should I be whispering? We'd have to go down to the barn to get much farther from your family."

Brady eased onto the edge of the chair facing hers and leaned toward her. He'd never brought his work home with him before. And he'd always made a point of never getting personally involved with victims of a crime. A lawman had to work with his head, not his heart. But with Lass he'd broken his own rules.

Now he understood why Ethan had initially discouraged him from bringing Lass into his home. Danger could possibly be following her right here to the Diamond D. Yet he'd known that from the very start. And from the very start, he'd not been able to resist her.

"They'll hear it later. Right now— I wanted to discuss this with you first."

Her gray eyes suddenly filled with uncertain shadows. "You've discovered something. About me. About what happened."

He nodded, then awkwardly broke his gaze from hers to stare over her shoulder at the gathering clouds. Ethan was right again, he thought bleakly. It wasn't easy to tell a person that someone had intentions to harm them. Especially a soft, gentle woman like the one sitting in front of him.

"Yes. This afternoon, my friend—Johnny Chino, an Apache that I grew up with—scouted the area where we found you in the mountains."

She looked completely puzzled. "I don't understand,

Brady. It's been four, nearly five days since the accident. What could this man possibly find after that length of time?"

A corner of his mouth lifted in a wan grin. "You'd be surprised. He can pick up a trail that most normal people would fail to see. And, we've had a bit of luck with very little wind and no rain occurring these past days."

She drew in a bracing breath and Brady couldn't stop himself from reaching for her hand and wrapping his fingers around hers.

"So what did he find? My handbag? Pieces of clothing? More wagering tickets from the track?"

"No. He didn't find items, Lass. He found a story."

Her pink lips parted as she stared at him and Brady fought the urge to pull her out of the chair onto his lap, to kiss her until the lipstick was gone, along with the burning need inside him.

"A story?" she repeated blankly.

Brady nodded. "It has a few holes, but enough of the plot is there to tell us part of what happened that night you lost your memory."

Her free hand crept up to her throat, as though she feared his next words, as though the unconscious part of her mind already knew it was an ugly story. Brady desperately wanted to ease her fears, to assure her that he would always keep her safe. God, what was it about this woman that made him feel so protective? he wondered. Until Lass came along, he'd never wanted to be any woman's knight in shining armor.

"Tell me," she whispered.

As concisely as possible, Brady related the evidence that Johnny had found, including the exact way she'd fallen and struck her head, to the direction she'd been walking when she'd collapsed in the ditch.

When Brady's words finally died away, Lass closed her eyes and tried to digest it all, tried to attach it to the strange images that had continued to flash through her mind at odd moments, but it was all so horrifying, so confusing, she could pull none of it together.

"Oh, God, Brady, someone really did try to harm me!" Her eyes flew open and looked straight into his. "I mean, logically, I knew that I hadn't just wandered off in the mountains on my own. Without any car it was obvious that someone had driven me there. But this—why? Why would I have been struggling with someone?"

Before Brady could answer, she jumped to her feet and walked blindly over to the wooden balustrade surrounding the edge of the balcony. Tears burned her eyes as she stared past the pine boughs, to the distant mountain ridge. At the moment, dark clouds were churning over the tall peaks, while intermittent flashes of lightning warned of oncoming rain. She could only think how the turbulent weather matched the turmoil inside her.

"Lass, I'm sorry," Brady said softly as he walked behind her and wrapped his hands over her shoulders. "I wish… that none of this had happened to you."

A hysterical sob bubbled up in her throat. She not only had amnesia, she thought sickly, but she'd gone crazy along with it. Because a part of her wasn't sorry that someone had nearly killed her. Otherwise, she would have never met Brady. Otherwise, she would have never known his touch, his kiss, the pure joy of being near him.

Twisting around to face him, she said in a stricken voice, "But it has happened, Brady! And where is this person now? What if he's hanging around, waiting to hurt me again?"

With a heavy groan, Brady circled his arms around her and Lass gladly settled her cheek upon his broad chest.

Bending his head, he whispered against the top of her hair, "No one is going to hurt you here on the Diamond D, Lass. You may not realize it, because they're dressed like the rest of the cowboys around here, but we have plenty of security roaming the ranch. Many of our horses are worth six and seven figures each. You don't take chances with them. So if anyone shows up without a reason for being here, the security guys will know it."

"But Dallas and I went shopping in town today!" she exclaimed. "He could have been stalking us. He—"

His arms tightened to pull her even closer. "Is more than likely long gone from this area. And if he isn't, then I'll catch the bastard. In the meantime, I don't want you leaving the ranch alone for any reason. And if you do leave with anyone, I want to know about it first. Okay?"

Lass couldn't stop a sliver of fear from snaking down her spine. "I understand."

His forefinger slid beneath her chin and lifted her face up to his. "You trust me to take care of you, don't you?" he asked softly.

With her safety, yes. Her heart? That was another matter. Yet where this man was concerned, it seemed to ignore the fact that he was a self-admitted bachelor and her future was a big question mark. At this moment, she couldn't stop it from pounding with joy at being in his arms, feeling the warmth of his hard body pressed against hers.

"Yes," she murmured. "I trust you."

The pads of his fingers gently brushed her cheek, then trailed downward along the side of her neck. Without looking up at the sky, Lass sensed that the distant clouds had now moved over them. But to her, the oncoming storm wasn't nearly as dangerous to her well-being as this man she was clinging to.

"I hear a 'but' in your voice, Lass."

She sighed as his hand moved to the skin of her bare back. "That's because I'm afraid I'm beginning to trust you too much, Brady."

"That's impossible," he whispered. "Just like it's impossible for me not to kiss you."

This time Lass didn't hide her desire for him or wait for him to bend his head to hers. Rising up to her tiptoes, she angled her mouth to his, then moaned with satisfaction as he took what she offered.

The tender movement of his lips against hers was the complete opposite of the fiercely heated kiss they'd shared by the pool, yet it was equally potent, touching her senses, her heart so deeply, that her hands clutched him for support, while her body wilted and wallowed in the pleasure he was creating inside her.

Brady's body was burning, his mind threatening to lose all common sense, when suddenly a whoosh of cold wind swept across the balcony and, close on its heels, fat rain drops spattered around them like warning signals from heaven.

Lifting his head, Brady grabbed her hand. "We'd better get inside before we get drenched."

By the time they entered the bedroom and Brady had safely secured the glass door behind them, lightning was cracking ever so close. Thunder rumbled loudly, followed by more wicked flashes of raw electricity.

Clutching her arms to her waist, Lass looked at him and tried to push away her disappointment, to tell herself that it was probably for the best that Mother Nature had decided to interrupt their embrace.

A few steps away, Brady spoke her same thoughts, only for a different reason. "It's probably a good thing the rain ran us inside," he said as he shook a few drops from his hair.

"It's time for dinner and if we don't show up soon, Grandma will come looking for us. She's just like Dad, grumbling and groaning if one of us is late to the dining table."

Lass suspected he was right. The older woman had already come searching for them last night when she and Brady had been kissing on the porch. If Kate had seen then what was going on between her grandson and Lass, she'd never mentioned it. But Lass figured the woman missed nothing that went on in the Donovan house.

After the kiss Brady had just given her, she needed to repair her lipstick, but she wasn't going to waste the time. Instead, she said, "In that case, we'd better hurry. I don't want her upset with me."

Chuckling, he put his hand to the back of her waist and ushered her out of the bedroom.

As they quickly crossed the landing, Lass said in a thoughtful voice, "I wonder if I had a grandmother like Kate."

"Let's hope not," he teased.

Lass cast him a hopeless look. "What am I doing wondering about grandparents, anyway? I'm a woman who doesn't even know if she has parents!"

"Of course you do. Someone gave birth to you, raised you."

"Then why aren't they looking for me?"

As she and Brady reached the stairs, he paused to look at her. "Your parents could be looking for you, Lass. Just not in the right place yet."

Regret clouded her eyes. "When you tell Fiona and Doyle about…what happened to me on the mountain, they're not going to be pleased. They might even want me to leave before trouble follows me here to the ranch. And I probably should."

His hands were suddenly gripping her upper arms. "Not

in a million years, Lass! My parents already understood there was a possibility you'd met with foul play. They'll be concerned, but they'll hardly be afraid or want you to leave. They've dealt with trouble before. And they have six children of their own. They'd want someone to shelter and care for one of us if we were in your predicament."

Sighing, she pressed fingers to the tiny ache in her forehead. Since she and Brady had ran in from the rain, her head felt odd and it was a struggle for her to keep her thoughts focused on anything. What was the matter with her?

"Well, I can only hope that my parents come close to being as kind and generous as yours."

With a confident grin, he tucked his arm through hers and guided her down the long staircase. "They'd have to be, Lass, to have a daughter as lovely as you."

His compliment put a wan smile on her face and as they continued on down the stairs, she tried to put the troubling thoughts out of her head, but the more she tried to push them aside, the more her mind began to jump erratically from the story that Johnny Chino had revealed, to the faceless man gripping her arm, gritting out a menacing order to follow him.

"Oh!" Without warning, everything began to swirl wildly around Lass. She swayed drunkenly and grasped blindly for the staircase railing.

"Lass!" With his arm planted firmly around her waist, Brady steadied her on her feet and helped her off the last stair. "What is it?"

Squeezing her eyes shut, she pressed a palm to her forehead. Her breaths were coming short and fast and a fine layer of sweat now covered her face.

"I—I don't know. I..." The rest of her words trailed away as behind her closed eyes, the vision of a woman's face suddenly appeared. She had graceful features and coal-black hair, but it was her soft smile that pierced Lass right in the middle of her chest. That gentle, understanding smile was the same one that had soothed Lass down through the years, had encouraged her to face her fears and always put forth her best effort.

Mother? Yes. Her dear, sweet mother.

Bending her head, Lass fought to hold on to the image, to connect it to a name, a place. And then without warning, Lass could see herself standing next to a grave. The mound of dirt was covered with fresh flowers and a crowd of mourners was gathered in the quiet cemetery. She sensed that her father was at her side, but she couldn't look at him. Couldn't bear to hear him say that her mother was truly gone.

"Oh, God. Oh, no!" With a sob catching in her throat, Lass lifted her head to stare at Brady. Sorrow, dark and heavy, fell over her, while angry fists pounded at her heart. "I—I've remembered my mother," she finally managed to say in a broken voice. "And—she's dead, Brady. I don't have a mother anymore."

Clearly stunned, Brady studied her wounded face. "Lass," he began softly, "are you certain about this? Maybe you're seeing some other relative, or a friend?"

"No. It's my mother. My heart is telling me it's my mother. I can't give you her name or where we lived, but I do know that the image was her and that she…is gone."

As she spoke the last word tears welled in her eyes and spilled onto her cheeks. Brady gathered her into his arms and cradled her head against his chest.

"It'll be okay, sweetheart. I promise."

He was stroking her back, waiting for her sobs to subside, when footsteps sounded on the hardwood floor and he looked around to see his grandmother approaching them. No doubt she and his father had grown tired of waiting and Kate had come to let the hammer down.

But after one sweeping glance of the situation, Kate's annoyed expression turned to concern. "What's happened?"

Brady was shocked to find he had to swallow before he could answer his grandmother's question. "Lass has remembered her mother."

Kate arched a brow at him. "That's good, isn't it?"

Over Lass's head, Brady exchanged a troubled look with his grandmother. "It would be—but she's remembered that her mother has passed away."

"Oh, the poor little darling." Immediately, Kate marched forward and gently eased Lass out of Brady's arms. "Come on, honey," she said to Lass, "let me take you to the family room where you can lie down."

As Brady watched his grandmother slowly lead Lass away, he felt oddly empty and more than shaken. To see Lass in such grief had been the same as someone stabbing him with a knife. And the moment Kate had pulled Lass from his arms, he'd wanted to snatch her back.

He was the one who should be consoling Lass. He was the one who wanted to soothe her tears, make her happy. But how could he ever expect to do that? He couldn't even give her something as simple as her real name.

Chapter Nine

For the next week and a half Lass tried to come to terms with her mother's death and the reality that something unhappy had been going on in her former life. Along with reflections of her mother and the menacing man gripping her wrist, snippets of another person had been entering her mind at unexpected moments. Even though names and places still eluded her, Lass was quite certain the image was that of her father—although she'd not yet gotten a clear picture of his face, she recognized his big frame and deep voice.

Each time her father's image flashed through her mind, she was consumed with sadness and confusion. Clearly, all had not been right between father and daughter. But Lass had no idea what had brought about such dissension in the family. She only knew that whatever had occurred now left her feeling cold and empty.

Bridget had continued to check on Lass every day and

the family practitioner kept insisting that Lass needed to start talks with a mental therapist. But so far Lass was reluctant to begin. She'd already remembered enough to tell her that she'd left bad things behind her. Why should she let a therapist, or anyone for that matter, send her back to that place? Lass didn't want to go back. She wanted to move forward. And perhaps that was the crux of the matter, she thought dismally. Like the psychiatrist in the hospital had initially suggested, her mind refused to remember, because she simply didn't want it to.

Still, Lass was smart enough to understand that she couldn't live in limbo forever. The time would soon come when she would be forced to seek help from a medical specialist. But in the meantime, she wanted to live as though she was as normal as the next person.

These past days, Lass had worked at Dallas's riding clinic from early in the mornings to late in the evenings. She'd been doing everything from grooming and tacking the horses to assisting the children with their rides.

The task of dealing with both children and horses couldn't have been more perfect for Lass. The job had given her more than pleasure; it had filled her with new confidence. Now she felt as though she was serving a useful purpose rather than sponging off the Donovans. And the fact that Brady had been showing up at the stables these past few evenings made the job doubly pleasurable.

Dallas had told her that occasionally in the past, whenever his work schedule allowed, Brady showed up at the stables to donate his time and labor to whatever was needed around the place. But she insisted that her brother had never appeared at the stables for several days running. Usually his social calendar took up most of his free time.

Dallas attributed his sudden interest in the stables to

Lass's presence, but Lass wasn't convinced that was the only reason Brady had been spending time at the riding clinic. He seemed to genuinely care for the children and went out of his way to make them happy. On one particular evening, he'd ridden for nearly an hour behind the saddle of one very small girl just to help her gain confidence in handling her mount. And last night after everyone had dismounted and gone into the barn for refreshments, he'd gathered the children together and told them a funny story that had kept them all laughing.

Seeing Brady at the stables had shown Lass a side of him that she'd never expected to see. In spite of his single-guy image, he dealt with the children as any good father would. And even though he'd told Lass that he didn't have a special touch with horses, he handled and rode them better than she and Dallas put together.

Lass was learning there were many more sides to the man and each one he revealed drew her to him even more. Yet she continued to remind herself that her time with Brady was borrowed. Where he was concerned, she couldn't give her emotions free reins. Not if she ever expected to leave this ranch with her heart fully intact.

They had not kissed again, though Lass hadn't been able to forget that last kiss. An occasional holding of hands and a few touches and gentle kisses had been all the contact they'd had. And Lass had tried to convince herself that it was what she'd wanted.

Even so, this particular evening, she'd found herself glancing around, wondering if or when he was going to show up. After a very busy day, things were beginning to wind down and now only a handful of children were mounted and circling their horses around the outdoor arena.

Earlier this afternoon, Dallas had gone to Ruidoso for

business reasons and left Lass in charge of operations. So far Lass hadn't run into any problems. Except for one little boy with dark brown hair, a metal brace on his leg and a very sad look on his face. His name was Tyler and since his arrival a couple of hours ago, he'd never left his seat on the bale of hay stacked near the arena fence. Earlier Lass had tried to coax him into the saddle, but he'd refused to budge.

Now, with plans to try again, she walked up to the boy. "Tyler, aren't you getting tired of sitting there? Would you like to walk with me over to the saddling corral?"

"Nope. I like it here," he said stubbornly.

"Oh. Well, I think it's time I rested my feet. Do you mind sharing your seat?"

He shrugged one slender shoulder. "Suit yourself."

After easing down beside the child, Lass crossed her boots out in front of her. "Is this your first visit to the stables?"

Looking bored now, the boy shook his head. "Nope. I was here once before—a long time ago."

"Hmm. I guess that was before I started helping around here," she said thoughtfully. "Did you ride a horse then?"

"Nope. I didn't want to ride then and I don't want to ride now," he said flatly. "The only reason I'm here is because my mom made me come."

"Awww," Lass groaned with disappointment. "That's too bad. When I first saw you sitting here, I thought to myself, now I'll bet that young man loves horses almost as much as I do. I guess I was really wrong about you."

His lips clamped into a tight purse, but it was simply taking more strength than he could muster to hold them that way for long. Suddenly words began to burst from him like air from a balloon.

"That ain't so! I love horses!"

Lass smiled to herself. "Really? That's great to hear. So why aren't you riding today?"

He pulled a face at her that said she must be blind or stupid, or both. "Can't you see? I gotta wear this brace. I can't bend my leg."

Lass had already talked to Dallas about Tyler's condition and she'd learned that eventually the brace would be removed and the boy's leg would be straight and perfect enough to walk, run and jump like any normal child. But in the meantime, Tyler clearly thought that day was a lifetime away.

"So? That doesn't mean you can't sit in the saddle. You're sitting on this hay bale, aren't you? And Ms. Dallas has already saddled Cloudwalker for you. He's a pretty black-and-white paint and he loves attention. Wouldn't you like to ride him?"

He looked angry and hopeless at the same time and then his bottom lip thrust forward and began to tremble. "Yeah. But I don't want to fall off."

Easing her arm around the child's slender shoulders, she said, "Look, Tyler, it's okay to be scared. I know just how you feel."

"I doubt it," he mumbled. "I'll bet you didn't wear any ol' brace like this."

"No. But I once had to wear a cast on my arm for a long time. And at first I was very sad about it. Because I was afraid to ride my horse. His name was Rusty and I loved him more than anything, but I was sure if I got on him I'd fall and break my arm all over again."

Interest sparked in the child's brown eyes. "So what did you do?"

"My father finally reminded me that Rusty was special. The horse was my best friend and he understood that he needed to take extra care of me and not go too fast or make sharp turns. My father told me that if I couldn't trust my best friend, then I would be scared of all sorts of things for the rest of my life. So I decided I wasn't going to let a cast on my arm make me scared or ruin my fun."

Tyler digested this, then thoughtfully tilted his head to one side. "Yeah, but Cloudwalker ain't my friend," he pointed out. "He don't even know me."

"Not yet. But he'd like to make friends with you. And he's like Rusty, he's a very special horse. You can trust him to take care of you. I promise."

"Say, what is this? Are you giving my girl a hard time?"

Both Tyler and Lass turned their heads to see Brady had walked up behind them. He was still dressed in his uniform, but she was grateful to see he'd considered the children and put away his handgun and holster.

Lass rose to her feet to greet him and he quickly slipped his arm around her waist and gathered her to his side. As she smiled at him, she couldn't stop her heart from jumping with joy or stop it from thinking how right it felt to be wrapped in the sheltered circle of his arm.

Rather than appearing intimidated, Tyler surprised her by taking the offensive. "Who says she's your girl?"

"I do. That's who," Brady shot back at him.

Backing down, Tyler mumbled, "Oh. Well, I wasn't tryin' to steal her from you or anything."

"That's good to know. For a minute there I thought you were giving her the eye." Brady gave Lass a discreet little wink. "So why aren't you riding…uh, what did you say your name was? Jim-Bob? Frankie?"

The child rolled his eyes. "No! It's Tyler!"

"Okay, Ty. So why aren't you riding? Think you're better than all the other kids? Or are you afraid you'll fall off and everyone will laugh at you?"

Lass very nearly gasped, but stopped just short of it. Clearly, Brady understood what it was like to be a little boy of Tyler's age. He ought to know how to handle the child better than she. But wasn't he being a little tough?

She didn't have to wonder for long. Tyler instantly hopped off the bale of hay and squared around to face Brady.

"I ain't afraid to ride any ol' horse here!" he exclaimed. "And I won't fall off, either! I'm just as good a cowboy as you are!"

Chuckling now, Brady reached out and affectionately ruffled the child's hair. "Probably better. Now come on and show me what you're made of. Guts or sawdust?"

Tyler thrust his little stomach forward and pointed to the pouch he'd made. "I've got plenty of guts! See! I'll show ya!"

"I can't wait," Brady dared.

Tyler tugged on Lass's sleeve. "Come on, Miss Lass. Let's go get Cloudwalker!"

With a groan and a grin, Lass shook her head. "Male mentality. I don't understand it."

Ten minutes later, Tyler was in the saddle and insisting he could take the reins and handle the horse on his own.

Brady lifted the bridle reins over the paint's head and placed them in Tyler's hands. After a few last-minute instructions, he said, "Okay, off you go. And if you need me or Miss Lass we'll be right here."

"I won't," he said, then confidently set the horse in forward motion.

Standing at one end of the arena, Lass and Brady watched him slowly clop toward the rest of the children.

"Well, I guess he showed you he had guts," she said.

Brady chuckled. "Yes. But you'd already talked him into facing his fears. I just put the rest in motion."

She glanced at him. "I didn't know you heard my story."

"I'd been standing there longer than you think. You've got a pretty good imagination. At least, it worked on Tyler."

Her brows arched. "Imagination? I'll have you know that was a true story."

It was Brady's turn to look surprised. "Really? You actually broke your arm and had a horse named Rusty?"

"Yes. And my father did tell me those things about facing my fears." With a helpless sigh, she pinched the bridge of her nose. "It's crazy, isn't it? I can remember those sorts of things yet I can't remember names or where I lived—except that I believe it was somewhere in Texas."

"Your memory is returning, though. You're recalling more and more. Who knows, in a few days everything may come back to you."

"You could be right," Lass murmured. Each day that passed brought more and more snippets of her past to mind. Bridget called them small signs that her memory was healing. So why didn't that idea bring her more joy? Because she didn't want to face her past? Or because she didn't want to leave this man? A man she'd already fallen in love with?

"Lass, this horse, Rusty, can you remember where you got him? What he looked like?"

Her forehead puckered as she contemplated his questions. "Not exactly. He was sorrel with a long flaxen mane and tail. And I think he had a blaze down his face."

"What about a brand?"

She glanced at him. "A brand?"

"Yes. It's a long shot, but if he had a brand we might trace his ownership."

"I see." She closed her eyes and tried to picture her beloved childhood friend more clearly. "I think—I'm not sure, but I seem to remember there was something on his left hip. Something like an initial. Like a—a *P*. Yes, it was a *P!*"

Encouraged, he nodded. "Good. That's a start. But I doubt one single letter would be used for a brand. It would need a distinguishing mark with it. Like a Bar or Rafter. Rocking. Wings for Flying P. Does any of that ring a bell?"

For several moments, she rolled those possibilities around, then shook her head. Brady was trying so hard to move her case forward. She didn't want to disappoint him. And yet when he asked her to try to remember, her mind recoiled. Dear God, she felt torn in all directions.

"None of that sounds right," she told him. "But I'll try to remember. I promise."

"Don't worry about it, Lass. We still have more options to put into motion."

He glanced thoughtfully out at the children who were presently riding in an obedient circle over the tilled ground. Following his gaze, Lass was happy to see that Tyler was already mixing with the other children, and from the smile on his young face, appeared to have forgotten all about the brace on his leg.

"Since we've been busy with Tyler, I haven't had a chance to tell you yet," he said. "This afternoon, before I left headquarters, I obtained a bit more information about your case."

Lass suddenly froze. "Information? From where? Whom?"

"A jockey. He'd been riding at Ruidoso Downs earlier that Sunday afternoon on the day you were injured. Seems this jockey recalls seeing you at the track that day."

Her heart leaped with something akin to fear. So it was now confirmed. She had been at the local racetrack before she'd been injured.

"Why is the jockey just now coming forward with this information?" she asked, her mind swirling with confusion. "Does he know me personally?"

Brady frowned at her last question. "Why, no. Should he? I mean, do you think in your past that you might have rubbed shoulders that closely with people in the racing circle?"

Tormented by the empty spaces in her mind, she looked at him. "I can't explain it, Brady. It's impossible for me to recall my parents' name, or mine for that matter, but these past few days I've come to realize that I can name every racetrack in the southwest and most of their leading riders, including Ruidoso Downs. I even recall visiting most of the tracks. That has to mean that I was closely associated with the business somehow. But if that's true, then someone should have recognized me before now—-before this jockey. Oh, Brady, this is crazy, I know. I'm crazy!"

"Lass!" he gently scolded, "don't ever say that about yourself. You've had an injury and you can't remember everything. That doesn't mean you've lost your mind. There could be all sorts of explanations why no one has recognized you," Brady reasoned. "Could be you've been away from the business for a few years. Or your appearance has changed. That's not uncommon with young women changing their hair color or style. I've had Liam asking around his racing circles to see if anyone has been reported missing, but no one he contacted knows you. But then if you were associated with quarter horses or standard breds he wouldn't be familiar with you or your connections."

She let out a heavy sigh and tried her best to smile at him. "That's true. And I'm sorry, Brady for being so negative. Please—go on about this jockey."

"Well, he says that after the meet that Sunday, he flew out to California to ride at Hollywood Park. He didn't return until yesterday and that's when he saw your picture posted in the clubhouse."

"And out of a crowd of thousands, he remembers seeing me? That sounds highly unlikely."

He continued on in a patient voice, "Lass, you were supposedly standing outside of the saddling paddock just where the horses start onto the track for the post parade. He says he remembers this because his mount tossed him to the dirt right in front of you and he was naturally a little embarrassed about losing his seat in front of an attractive young woman."

Jockeys often lost their seat in the saddle, she thought. It wasn't like that would have been a major occurrence. Still, with it happening right in front of her, she should be able to remember the incident. And yet, she couldn't even recall being at the track that day. "Did he have any other information that might help identify me?"

The corners of Brady's mouth curved downward. "Not exactly. But he does recall that a man was with you. The jockey described this man as being tall, dark-haired and somewhere in his mid- to late-twenties. This new information doesn't necessarily move our case forward," he added, "but it underscores everything that Johnny Chino uncovered. I believe this man at the track is the same man you struggled with on the mountain highway."

Inside her, fear and confusion roiled like a black cloud. She felt suffocated and shaken. "Oh, God, Brady, who was that man?" With both hands, she reached for his arm and clung to him tightly. "Why was I at the track with someone who wanted to…hurt me?"

"Lass, have you ever stopped to think you didn't want to be there with him?"

Her brows pulled together. Could that have happened? Or had she been with this man because she'd wrongly trusted him?

Oh, come on, Lass. It was just a kiss. You know you liked it. Show me again, baby, show me how much you want me.

Suddenly an image was exploding behind her eyes and in it the man's lips were grinding down on hers, bruising, hurting, repulsing her in every way. She pushed hard against his chest and turned to run.

"Lass? Honey, what's wrong?"

Brady's hand stroked her upper arm as Lass struggled to jerk her thoughts back to the present.

"I— Nothing is wrong," she said in a strained voice.

"Nothing! You're trembling, Lass." He wrapped his hand firmly around her elbow. "I want you to go to Dallas's office and lie down on the couch. I'll see after Tyler and the rest of the kids."

Shaking her head, she suddenly set her jaw with determination. Before her accident a man had been trying to manipulate her. She was certain of that now. But who and why? Why had he been kissing her and why had she hated his very touch? Clearly, he was a part of those bad things she'd been running from. And was still running from. Sooner or later, she was going to have to turn and face the shadowy man. Face everything she'd left behind.

"I'm okay, Brady. And I really don't want to talk about this anymore." She pulled her elbow from his grasp. "I'm going to check on the children."

As she walked away, Brady didn't try to stop her. But he desperately wanted to. There was something troubling her. Something more than having to accept that another human being had tried to harm her. He almost got the feeling that a part of her didn't want him to solve the mystery of her identity.

But then, a part of him didn't want to solve it, either.

Chapter Ten

On certain days of the week, Dallas kept the stables open and running so that working parents could bring their children after work hours. But the next evening wasn't a day with extended hours, which allowed Lass to return to the ranch house well in advance of dinnertime. After showering and changing into a peach-colored sundress and a pair of sandals, she started down the stairs with plans to head to the family room.

Normally Kate was the first one there to drink a glass of wine and play her beloved piano. During these past weeks Lass had been on the Diamond D, she'd grown close to the older Donovan woman. Kate was gruff and forward in many ways, but there was a calm strength to the woman that comforted Lass.

"Now this is what I call perfect timing. And you're even dressed for the part."

Hearing Brady's voice, Lass glanced up to see him standing at the foot of the stairs. Apparently he'd been home long enough to change out of his uniform. A pair of worn jeans hugged his thighs and hips while a navy blue T-shirt was tucked into the lean waistband. He looked handsome and sexy, yet it was the warm smile on his face that drew her to him, touched her just as deeply as his kiss.

"Hello, Brady," she greeted, her heart booming in her chest. "I wasn't expecting to see you. Last night at the stables, you said your schedule was changing and that you'd be working late."

She stepped off the bottom stair and he immediately pressed a kiss to her cheek and slung his arm through hers.

"My schedule changed at the last minute. I'm going to a party. Sheriff's orders. And I want you to come along with me."

Unconsciously her palm flattened against her chest. "Me? But I don't know the sheriff, Brady. And I—" biting her lip, she glanced awkwardly away from him "—I really don't want to discuss my case with a...group of strange people."

He gave her arm a reassuring squeeze. "Trust me, honey, there won't be any talk about work. Not from me or the sheriff. If anyone else brings up your situation and you don't want to talk about it, then tell them to mind their own business."

"Oh, Brady," she lightly scolded. "That would be rude and uncomfortable."

"Listen, beautiful, what would be rude and uncomfortable is for you to make me to go to the party tonight without a date. Especially when I was counting on you."

A wry smile of surrender touched her lips. How could she say no to him, when every cell in her body wanted to be with the man? Since that night she'd remembered her mother's death, their relationship had taken a different turn. He seemed to be more gentle, more concerned about her feelings. And whenever he kissed her, it was more than fiery lust. Now when their lips met, she tasted tender passion, felt emotions gently knocking on her heart and begging to come in. If he was seeing other women while he was away from the ranch, she didn't know. Nor did she feel she had the right to question him. But deep down, whenever he looked at her, touched her, she wanted to believe she was special to him. More special than any other woman had been to him.

"All right. I suppose I can go. But what about dinner with your family? And—" she glanced doubtfully down at her dress "—am I dressed appropriately for this outing?"

"Forget dinner with the folks. We'll be eating at the Hamiltons. Their twin boys are turning twelve this week and they're having a little family celebration."

"Oh. And you're considered family? Or was the rest of the sheriff's staff invited, too?" she asked.

The impish grin on his face told Lass that he and the sheriff were closer than he wanted his coworkers to know.

"Some of them will be there. The rest had to stay behind and work." He gestured up to the second floor where the bedrooms were located. "If you want to take a purse or anything, now would be the time to get it. We need to be leaving."

She rolled her eyes. "You believe in giving a girl plenty of notice, don't you?"

He winked. "Gives her less time to back out on me," he teased.

Sure, Lass thought, as she hurried up the stairs to fetch her purse. She doubted Brady had ever been stood up by any woman. And here she was falling over herself to have an outing with the man. What did that say about her? That she was gullible? Vulnerable? Foolish? Or all three? The answer hardly mattered, she told herself. Her resistance had crumbled the moment she'd looked up to see him at the foot of the stairs, smiling as though she was the only woman in his life.

The Hamilton ranch, the Bar H Bar, was located several miles east of Carrizozo, the little county seat where the sheriff's department was located. Just as the sun was setting, Brady drove slowly through an open mesa covered with creosote, grama grass and blue sage. Here and there, prickly pear and cholla cacti grew at the road's edge. Some of the pear cactus was in bloom and the bright yellow roses reminded her of some distant place in her mind, a place where the sun was hot and horse's hooves thundered over a plowed track, giant live oaks spread like deep green umbrellas, shading the lawns and pastures with their sheltering arms.

Home. Was that her home? The snatches of memory caused a part of her heart to ache with longing. Yet when she turned her gaze upon Brady, she realized the thought of leaving him made her ache even more.

"You've gone quiet, Lass. What are you thinking?" Brady asked as he steered the truck over the graveled road. "Are you nervous about meeting my friends?"

By now the mesa was behind them and they were traveling into a group of low-rising hills. Juniper and pinyon dotted the desert slopes while spiny yucca plants dared to grow between slabs of rock.

"A little," she admitted. "But I was mostly thinking how beautiful this land is. How different it is where I came from."

He darted a sharp glance at her. "You're sure about that?" he asked, then grimaced. "Sorry. I forgot that you didn't want to talk about your amnesia this evening."

"It's not a pleasant topic," she said flatly. "But I'm beginning to see that it's a subject I can't avoid entirely. Everything I look at, think about, talk about, connects to my memory. I'm beginning to think I've lost the most important part of my brain."

"You're going to get it back, Lass. I'm as sure of that as I'm sure my middle name is Roark."

Turning slightly in the seat, she studied him instead of the darkening landscape. "Well, to answer your earlier question, yes, I'm sure I didn't live in a desert area. But I'm fairly certain I've been to New Mexico before. It all feels familiar to me now. But then maybe that's because your family has made me feel so at home."

"I'm glad," he said, then slanted a look her way. "And as for my friends, Lass, don't worry about them. They're all just plain folks like us Donovans."

There was nothing plain about the Donovans, she thought. Especially Brady. On the surface he appeared to be a lighthearted, easygoing guy, but that was only one slice of the man. She'd seen it that night he'd found her in the ditch, when he'd stood over her hospital bed and held her hand. And last night, when he'd helped her with Tyler, she'd known he was doing it from his heart and not just for effect.

"I doubt you've ever been described as plain," she said to him. "Why, I even bet in high school you dated the football homecoming queen or the captain of the cheerleading squad, didn't you?"

"Me? Not hardly. Those sorts of girls were too conceited for my taste. They'd rather look at themselves than at me."

Smiling now, Lass glanced curiously over to him. "I'm shocked. So what sort of girls did you go for? I won't believe you if you say the studious type."

He pulled a playful face at her. "Actually, I did have a

studious girlfriend once. She was an honor student. Unfortunately she liked boys as much as she liked getting straight A's. She was a fickle little thing."

"Hmm." She gave him a furtive peek from the corner of her eye. "So what sort of girls do you like now?"

"Oh, that's easy enough to answer. I like the kind of girl who can't remember her own name."

It took a few seconds for the meaning of his words to sink in and then she began to laugh.

Chuckling with her, Brady reached for her hand and as their fingers entwined, she wondered how she could feel so warm and happy at a time like this. Someone had tried to injure or kill her. She didn't know who she was or where she belonged. Yet as long as she was with Brady she could laugh and hope and dream.

She was falling in love with him. To admit it to herself was somewhat of a relief. But to admit it to him would be something altogether different. To reveal her feelings to him now would either draw the two of them closer, or pull them apart. And she was desperately scared of either outcome.

Thankfully, the party at the Hamiltons' proved to be big enough that she didn't have to spend a lot of time making one-on-one conversation with Brady's friends and acquaintances. Instead, he squired her from one group to the next with hardly a chance to make more than small talk.

The twins, Jacob and Jason, were a polite, good-looking pair and at the age where they weren't quite sure if they were still rowdy boys or know-it-all teenagers.

Clearly, their parents understood them, and after the children and adults had partaken of a big barbecue spread, the twins and their young guests were excused to the barn, where they were going to have their own little party.

Penny, their mother, told Lass that the twins' idea of fun was a bucking barrel, a churn of homemade ice cream and a group of girls to watch while the boys made fools of themselves.

Later that evening as Lass sat with their hostess on the edge of a large patio, sipping punch from a paper cup, she commented, "It must be a labor of love to raise twin boys."

Smiling, the dark-haired woman nodded. "They're a handful, but more than worth it."

Three hours had passed since the party first started and now all the adult guests had departed, except for Lass and Brady. While she and Penny enjoyed the quietness, Brady and the sheriff had disappeared into the house. In spite of him assuring Lass that work wouldn't be discussed, she figured that's exactly what the two men were doing. And she wondered if the sheriff might have uncovered something about her case, but hadn't wanted to say anything in front of her.

God, she hoped not. Tonight she simply wanted to pretend that her name really was Lass and that she belonged here. With Brady.

"Brady tells me you're expecting another baby soon," Lass said to the other woman. He'd also revealed to Lass that Penny had once been the county judge for Lincoln County, a position she'd held up until the twins had been born. Since then, the woman worked at her own private law practice.

Penny's eyes glowed as she smiled at Lass. "That's right. I gave birth to the twins shortly before Christmas during a snowstorm." She patted her slightly rounded tummy. "This one is supposed to arrive a little after New Year's and I'm hoping that this time a blizzard won't come with it."

How wonderful that would be, Lass thought, to be having a child with a man you were madly in love with, to plan together for its arrival. Instinctively her hand settled against her own flat midsection.

Now that she'd had plenty of time to think about it, she believed Bridget that she'd never gone through the miraculous experience of childbirth. Yet she knew that having a child was something she'd always longed for. But had there been a man to make that wish come true? No. She refused to believe she'd been madly in love with a man before she'd met Brady. As far as she was concerned, Brady was the first and the last man to step into her heart.

"Do you know if you're going to have twins again?" Lass asked.

Penny laughed. "Oh, dear. That's something Ethan and I have been thinking about. Ethan wants a pair of girls. But the doctor says he can't yet discern whether there are two."

Smiling, Lass told her, "I'll keep my fingers crossed that you'll get those girls."

Playfully wrinkling her nose, Penny leaned forward and said in a low, conspiring tone, "To be honest, I wouldn't know what to do with little girls. I love having rough and tumble sons. But I guess I could learn how to tie ribbons and fix ponytails."

The two women shared a chuckle and then Penny said in a more serious voice, "Brady tells me you've been helping Dallas at the stables."

"That's right. And I'm loving every minute of being with the children," Lass admitted.

"Then I'm sure that someday you'll be like me," Penny replied. "With a house full of kids and more on the way. "

Could Lass allow herself to dream about such things? she wondered. And more important, would Brady want to be a part of those dreams?

You're being very foolish, Lass. Brady is thirty years old and from what his family says, he's shown no interest in getting married or having children. He's not even been engaged. He's not thinking of you in those terms. Besides, you might already have a husband somewhere. A husband who wanted to hurt you.

Doing her best to push away the dark, mocking voice in her mind, she smiled wanly. "I hope you're right, Penny. But until that day comes I'm happy helping Dallas. Kids and horses. It's a combination I can't resist."

She couldn't resist Brady, either, Lass thought with a heavy dose of unease. From the moment she'd opened her eyes and seen his face hovering over hers, she'd felt a sudden connection. And with each day, each hour that passed, that connection continued to deepen.

How soon would it be, she wondered sickly, before that man in her past, the man with the repulsive kiss, showed up on the Diamond D and put an end to all her hopes and dreams?

Later that night, on the way home, Brady was mostly quiet and Lass was content to lean her head back and let her thoughts stray to nothing in particular. But by the time he turned the truck onto Diamond D property, she was beginning to get the sense that something was wrong.

"Brady," she asked, as he let the two of them into the house, "have I…done something wrong? Did I embarrass you in some way tonight?"

He curled his arm around the back of her waist as they began to climb the long wooden staircase. "Are you kidding? You were perfect. Everyone loved you. Why would you think such a thing?"

"You haven't said much since we left the Hamiltons'," she reasoned.

"I'm sorry, Lass. I've been a little distracted."

A little, he thought ruefully. Why the hell couldn't he be honest with her? He was downright troubled. And not just because her identity was still a mystery. Tonight, while she'd stood next to him, her slender arm resting casually on his, he'd felt something he'd never felt before. He'd experienced a sweet connection, a contented ease with her company. Those sorts of feelings about a woman had never struck him before and the whole thing had left him more than a little dazed.

"You and Ethan disappeared into the house for a long while. You were talking work, weren't you?"

He released a guilty groan. "I confess. We did talk a little work. Mostly about you."

"Oh, Brady," she wailed under her breath in order not to disturb the sleeping household. "I've been nothing but a headache to you. If I had any sense at all, I'd leave here and let you and your family get some peace."

By now they had reached her bedroom door and he caught her by the upper arms and turned her to face him. "Is that what you really want, Lass? To go off somewhere—to be a charity ward of the county?"

"I'm not helpless. I can work and support myself," she shot back at him, then groaned with regret. "I'm sorry, Brady. I'm sounding very ungrateful and I don't want you to think that. I—" Her hands gently rested against his chest. "No. I don't want to leave here. But I'm—"

"Look, Lass, I haven't mentioned this to you, but after I got the call from the jockey, I made a decision to flood several Texas newspapers with your photo and story. That was early yesterday. Now a few calls and tips are starting to come in and we're trying to sift through them as quickly as we can to see if any are legitimate. So far you've been identified as everything from an elementary teacher in the

Texas panhandle to a PFC in the Texas National Guard and a sales clerk at a Neiman Marcus in Dallas. It will take us a while to confirm if any of the callers actually know you or your family. But I have a gut feeling I'm going to have some answers for you soon."

She looked up at him and through the dim lighting of the landing, he could see turmoil swirling in her gray eyes. To his wonder, she looked exactly the way he was feeling inside.

"And how do you feel about that?" she whispered.

He groaned, then, bending down, he pressed his cheek against hers. "I feel torn, Lass. I don't want anything or anyone to come between us," he murmured against her ear.

She pulled her head back to look at him and as his gaze settled on her lips his gut twisted with a need so great it was almost painful.

"Do you really mean that?" she asked.

"I can't believe you have to ask me that, Lass. Since you've came into my life everything has changed. I've changed. You and me together. That's the most important thing to me now."

Without saying more, he angled his head to kiss her. She tasted soft and sweet and giving, and when her arms slipped up and around his neck and her lips unfolded beneath his, he felt more than pleasure, he felt totally and strangely happy.

Quickly, he deepened the connection of their mouths and just as instantly passion fired, then exploded like flint against rock, flame to dead grass. From somewhere in the core of him, heat spread, then raced outward, downward until desire was gripping his whole body like a red-hot vise. The need to make love to her was searing a hole in his brain, turning every scrap of common sense into useless ashes.

Somehow, he managed to tear his lips from hers and as

he sucked in deep, ragged breaths, he caught her by the hands and tugged her toward the end of the landing, where his bedroom was located.

She followed his lead, but whispered as they went, "Brady, what are you doing? My bedroom is…behind us."

Opening a carved wooden door, he flipped a switch and a small lamp at the head of the bed instantly shed a shaft of soft yellow light across a dark blue spread.

"But this is where we're going," he explained. "To my room."

She didn't say anything until they were standing inside the dark room and he'd locked the door securely behind them.

"Brady! This is risky! What if someone comes to your room?"

With his hands against the back of her waist, he groaned and pulled her close. "In the middle of the night? No chance. No one ever disturbs me. Besides, the door is locked. The two of us are finally alone and together."

"Together," she repeated wondrously, then shyly pressed her cheek against his. "Oh, Brady, I do want us to be together."

Her softly spoken words filled him with an urgency he could hardly contain. Swiftly, he picked her up in his arms and carried her over to the bed. After he'd laid her in the middle of the wide mattress, then stretched out beside her, he framed her face with his hands and simply gazed at her, letting his eyes fill with the lovely sight of her.

"Why are you looking at me like…I'm strange?" she whispered.

The corners of his mouth tilted, his eyes gentled. "*Strange* is the wrong word, Lass. Try special. I've never seen a woman lying in my bed before. I didn't realize it would look this good. Feel this right."

Between the loose hold of his fingers, her head twisted

back and forth. "Don't talk to me as though I'm naive, Brady. I know you've had other women in your bed."

One hand slipped to the back of her neck and pulled her face forward so that their eyes and lips were level and only scant inches apart. Her heart was pounding and she must have forgotten how to breathe because her lungs were burning almost as much as the rest of her body.

"Lass, my little Lass, you misunderstand. Yes, I've had a woman in *a* bed before. But not *my* bed. *This* bed. Since I was a small boy, this is where I've always slept. It's my private place where I rest and dream and, these past few weeks, pictured you in my arms. Now here you are and I can't look at you enough. Can't touch you enough."

He closed the last bit of space between their lips and as the connection deepened, she groaned softly and rolled toward him. With his mouth fastened hungrily to hers, he gathered the front of her body close to his, then his hands went on a reckless exploration across her back, down her hips, then up to the small curve of her breasts. The dress she was wearing zipped in the back and his fingers trembled as he searched for the handle, then slowly tugged the fastener downward.

Beneath the tough pads of his fingers, her skin felt like satin and when he slipped the piece of fabric off her shoulder and bent his head to the curve of her neck, it tasted like smooth cream sweetened with sugar.

As a lawman he'd always thought of himself as a protector, but with Lass in his arms the feeling intensified a thousand times over. He wanted to shelter her, worship her, bind her to him so closely that nothing or no one could touch her or tear her from him.

Savoring the fine texture of her skin, his lips moved across her throat, then upward to the tender spot beneath her chin. He could feel her soft sighs brushing his cheeks, the beat of her heart pounding against his, her hands gliding over his shoulders and across his back.

The need to feel those hands against him, to have her slender fingers playing over his bare skin, was so fierce he drew back from her and quickly began to deal with the buttons on his shirt. Lass followed his cue and while he shrugged out of his shirt, she pushed her dress over her hips and allowed it to fall to the floor.

The sight of her wearing nothing but pink lace caused blood to pound in his ears, his loins. His body was screaming to make love to her, yet at the same time his mind was gearing down, commanding his hands and lips to linger, to investigate and memorize every curve, every inch and every pore of her heated skin.

Up until this moment, Lass hadn't really understood what being lost meant. With her lips consumed by his, her body turning to soft putty in his hands, she was as lost as a raindrop falling into a wide, dark ocean. He was her only anchor and she clung to him, her mouth a willing prisoner to his as he kissed her over and over, while his tongue tangled, plunged and teased.

By the time he pulled away from her and began to deal with the rest of his clothing, Lass's body had become a heated coil, winding itself tighter and tighter until every cell in her body felt as though it would explode.

Shamelessly, her breaths coming hard and fast, she removed the last flimsy remnants of her clothing and waited for him to rejoin her on the bed. When he finally turned back to her, she could see that he'd already taken care of protection and for one split second, the reality of what they were about to do whooshed like a chilly breeze through her mind. But that one brief second ended as soon as his hands reached for her, then pressed her back upon the mattress.

Stretching next to her side, he spoke against her cheek. "From the first time I kissed you, I've wanted you like this."

Her hands left his shoulders to gently frame his face and he paused to gaze into her eyes.

"And I've wanted you," she murmured.

A soft, inviting light flickered in her eyes and he felt something in the middle of his chest jerk, then like a broken fountain, emotions flowed unchecked, drowning him, terrifying him with their intensity.

"Lass," he uttered hoarsely. "My Lass."

It was all he could say as his throat closed together and his arms instinctively tightened around her.

Tilting her head back, she offered her lips up to his and this time when he kissed her, his body won the war over his mind. He could no longer slow this trip they were taking. He needed her. All of her. Nothing else could quench the violent force driving his movements.

Beneath him, her legs parted with invitation, and with one smooth thrust he sank into her soft wetness. As her warmth surrounded him, pleasure such as he'd never experienced wrapped around him, snapped his head back and momentarily paralyzed his movements.

And then he felt her hips thrusting toward his, her back bowing, crushing her breasts against his chest. With a guttural growl of desperation, he began to move inside her and with each exquisite thrust he felt himself falling, tumbling to a place he'd never been before.

Beneath him, Lass tried to keep up with his frantic pace, tried to knead, touch, taste every bump and hollow on his hard, muscled body. Like a strong wine, she wanted to drink him, savor every taste, every magical sensation that was intoxicating her senses.

Soon she was gasping for air and the need inside was clawing at her like a fierce cat, hissing, twitching, readying itself for the final pounce. When that final leap came, she swallowed her cries and gripped him close. And like water over a fall, she was suddenly flowing wild and free, drifting languidly, until finally she ebbed onto a soft, sandy shore.

The second Brady felt her velvety softness tightening around him, heard the low, keening moan deep in her throat, he lost all touch with his surroundings. Unbearable pleasure burst inside him, flung him upward and outward until he was sure his heart had split open and everything it held was spilling into her.

The urge to shout was so great that he buried his face into the curve of her neck and kept it there until the shudders in him subsided.

Once the walls of the room quit spinning, Brady realized he was sprawled over Lass and she was supporting the brunt of his weight. Quickly, he rolled to one side of her and lying flat against the mattress, stared in stunned wonder at the shadowed ceiling.

So that was making love, he thought. He'd not known or ever imagined that such give and take could go on between a man and a woman. She'd taken him over a precipice, and even if he'd known the fall would kill him, he still would have gone willingly, happily.

Somewhere from the dark corners of his mind, fear pricked like a cold, evil blade and he turned his head to look at her.

At that moment, she rolled to face him and strands of her long black hair spilled over a flushed cheek and swung a modest curtain over one breast. Her lips were dark pink and puffy, her skin covered with a sheen of sweat. He'd never seen anything so lovely, so perfect. And though he'd not yet caught his breath, he felt desire stir in him all over again.

Shifting toward her, he reached out and gently tucked the errant strands of hair behind her ear.

"What are you thinking?" he asked gently.

The corners of her mouth tilted wanly and then to his dismay, her gray eyes glazed, then pooled with tears.

"I think," she whispered huskily, "that I love you, Brady Donovan."

Chapter Eleven

I love you. Those three little words were the last thing Brady expected to hear from Lass. For a second time tonight she'd stunned him and as he gazed at her, his thoughts were spinning, searching for a way to reply that wouldn't make him sound insensitive or patronizing or, God help him, an enchanted fool.

In spite of his reputation for having racked up more dates than Abe Cantrell had cattle, Brady had never had a woman tell him she loved him. Well, maybe once in high school, but that had been from a silly little drama student, who'd not really known the meaning of the word, but truly believed she was destined for a star on the Hollywood walk of fame. So as far as he was concerned that one time hadn't counted.

But tonight, with Lass, he'd felt the emotion in her voice, saw a glow in her eyes that made him feel amazed, yet at the same time terribly unworthy. She deserved the best. She deserved to be loved in return. But was he capable of that?

His hand trembling, he trailed his fingertips down her damp cheek. "Lass, I don't know what to say. I—"

Her forefinger touched his upper lip, stopping anything else he might have said. "You don't have to say anything," she gently insisted. "I don't expect you to tell me that you love me back."

She scooted closer to him and the musky, womanly scent of her swirled around him, caught his senses and sent them dancing away to hide in a shadowy corner. Then just as he was trying to drag them back, her hand drifted onto his shoulder and glided down his arm. Her touch scattered goose bumps across his skin.

"I just…thought you should know how I feel," she went on, then with a sigh, she pressed her cheek against his chest. "That's all."

His throat thickened, his eyes closed. Was that his heart tearing down the middle? Did love feel like a fist punching him in the gut, making his whole chest ache? If so, then he was scared. Scared that the pain might never stop.

"Lass, maybe…what you're really feeling for me is gratitude. Because I found you—that night on the road."

An objective groan sounded in her throat. "Look, Brady, I'm grateful to anyone who helps me. And I may not remember my own name, but I don't believe that I ever went around thanking the men in my life like—" she reared her head back to look at him "—like this."

"God, I hope not."

She slanted him a wry look. "I should have never said anything to you about my…feelings. Now you're uncomfortable and I don't know how to put you at ease, to convince you that I'm not expecting vows or pledges or flowery words from you. I'm not blind. I can see that you don't want to be serious about any woman."

He was shocked at how much of him was insulted by her not so flattering assessment. "Really?" he asked sardonically. "You can see that about me, through all the muddy conceit and selfishness?"

Disappointment filled her eyes and Brady was suddenly ashamed of himself. He didn't know what was pushing him to say such things. It must be that odd pain in his chest that was putting words in his mouth.

Sighing, she rolled away from him and climbed from the bed. Confused, Brady watched her walk over to the nearest window and stare out at the dark, moonless sky. And though the lovely sight of her nakedness was riveting, it was the wistful expression on her face that caught his attention and pushed him to leave the bed and go stand behind her.

Sliding his arms around her waist, he bent his head and pressed a kiss to her bare shoulder. Her skin was warm and salty and he had to catch himself before his teeth began to nibble, his hands lift to cup her breasts.

"I'm sorry, Lass. I guess I'm not saying anything right."

"Maybe it would be better if you didn't say anything at all," she suggested, her voice painfully distant.

Lifting his head, he rested his chin on the top of her head. "I can't do that, Lass. I want you to understand that… well, you threw me for a loop."

Twisting in his arms, she looked up at him, her gaze searching. "Why?"

Grimacing, he shook his head. "I don't know. Lass, this is all new for me. I don't know what being in love feels like and I've never dated any woman long enough to give her the chance to fall in love with me."

"Why?" she asked again.

Her simple question pulled a groan from his throat.

"This is probably going to sound corny to you, but to me love means forever. It's like marriage—once you do it, it ought to be for life."

Her gray eyes suddenly softened. "Is that why you've not yet loved or married? Because you don't want to be connected to someone for life?"

With a rough sigh, he pulled her to him and cradled her head against his shoulder. As his fingers meshed in the silky strands of her hair, he asked, "Did you know that both of my brothers have been married?"

"Yes. Kate told me that Conall is divorced and Liam is widowed."

"That's right. Conall was married for a few years and then things went wrong between him and his wife. Liam's wife was killed in a car accident. She was pregnant with their first child at the time."

Lass gasped. "Oh, how tragic!"

"Yeah. Both my brothers have endured too much heartache."

Her gaze sharpened on his face. "So you're afraid to try love or marriage? Afraid that tragedy will strike you, too?"

"Not exactly," he answered, then his mouth twisted wryly. "Funny you should think that about me. My family tends to think I'm a shallow fellow when it comes to women. That I'm some sort of heartbreaker." Snorting softly, he shook his head. "I guess to them it does look that way. I have to admit that I've dated plenty of women over the years, but I don't have anything against love or marriage. It's just something…well, I want to be cautious about it. I need a woman strong enough to cope with my job, with the worries and fears, and realize that I truly want to keep being a deputy. A lot of the girls I dated couldn't really cope with the hours and the schedule and the job. And I want to get a little older and wiser before I take the plunge and then maybe I'll have a marriage like my parents have."

Her palms rested upon chest. "And that's what you want, a marriage like your parents'?"

His fingers stroked the silky hair lying upon her shoulder. "I want a woman I can love. The way my dad loves my mother. The way my grandpa loved my grandma. What they had, what my parents have now, is that forever kind of thing. Nothing can rattle it or break it. That's what I want. And I'm not going to make a vow to God to love, honor and obey, unless I can truly mean it."

One corner of her mouth slowly curved upward. "Why, Brady, I never suspected you of being such an old-fashioned sort of guy."

Her arms were sliding around his waist, her warm little body leaning into his and that in itself was enough to put a smile on his face. "Is that what you call it? Mom calls it being too particular," he said, then brushing his knuckles against her cheek, he added thickly, "But I'm beginning to think you're absolutely perfect—for me."

"Oh, Brady, I—"

"Shh. Let's not waste any more of this night talking," he gently interrupted. "Morning will be here soon enough."

Apparently, she agreed with him. Without another word, she rose on tiptoes and fastened her mouth over his. And as desire for her began to burn all over again, Brady was content to let his mind go blank and ignore the restless questions in his heart.

The next morning, Brady had to be at work early, but thankfully not as early as most mornings when he headed to Carrizozo long before daylight. When the alarm finally jolted him awake, he expected to see Lass's head on the pillow next to his. Instead, he found himself alone with nothing but memories of the love they'd made in his bed.

The fact that she'd chosen to leave him sometime while he was asleep, stung him a bit. He'd thought their night together had changed everything. He'd thought she'd grown as close to him as he had to her. Maybe he'd presumed too much.

Rolling to his side, he wiped a hand over his face and told himself he was becoming downright maudlin. He couldn't expect Lass to simply stay in his room all night, then go down to breakfast together as though they were a married couple. She had more respect for herself and his family than that. And he had more respect for her than that.

So what do you want, Brady? For her to be your wife? Do you want the right to have her in your bed, your life for always? Is she that woman you've been searching for?

Always. Always was a long time, Brady mused, as he pushed himself out of bed and walked toward his private bathroom. Would having only one woman in his life get boring? Would he regret not being able to play the field?

Something made him suddenly stop in the middle of the room and gaze back at the bed he'd shared with Lass. Nothing about Lass could ever be boring. Even if she was gray and wrinkled he would want her. Love her.

Yes, he could admit it to himself now. But saying those words to Lass were quite another thing. Her past might have already promised her future to someone else. And if that turned out to be the case, what would he do? What could he do?

After a quick shower, he hurried down to the kitchen in hopes of catching Lass before she left with Dallas to work at the riding stables. But when he reached the kitchen, Conall was the only person he found.

Of the three Donovan brothers, Conall was the enigmatic one. With hair as dark as their mother's and eyes as green as an Irish shamrock, he was a handsome devil. Or at least he would be, Brady thought, if he'd find it in himself to smile as though he was enjoying life. But with a natural head for business, that side of the ranch had been handed over to him and with the job came heavy responsibilities. Brady couldn't remember the last time Conall had taken time off for himself or left the ranch for anything more than business.

Dressed in a starched white shirt and dark tie, Conall was sitting at a small breakfast bar located at the end of the cabinets, nursing a cup of coffee and rifling through the *Lincoln County News* when Brady walked into the room.

At the sound of his footsteps, Conall peered over the top of the newspaper, "You're getting around late this morning, aren't you?"

"Not exactly," Brady explained. "Yesterday my schedule changed a bit and I have to work later."

He poured himself a cup of coffee, then peered at the breakfast food that Opal had left in the warming drawer. The eggs and bacon still looked fresh so he helped himself to a plate full, then carried the meal over to a table situated near a sliding plate glass door. Beyond it, he could see his grandmother trimming her roses. The sight comforted him.

"Where is everyone?" he asked.

"In everyone, you mean Lass?"

The faint sarcasm in Conall's voice jerked Brady's head up and he stared sharply at his brother. "Okay, have you seen Lass this morning?"

"She and Dallas have already left for the stables. You

should have gotten up earlier if you'd planned on kissing her goodbye."

Brady's jaw tightened. He and Conall had always been as different as daylight and dark, but they normally got along well. He didn't know why his brother was being so testy this morning, but he was hardly in the mood for it.

"What is that supposed to mean?"

Laying the paper to one side, his brother looked squarely at him. "Oh, come on, Brady, the whole family can see you've fallen for the girl. What have you done, turned into some sort of idiot?"

Falling in love with Lass made him an idiot? For an instance, Brady reverted to his childhood and wanted to jump up from the table and wrench Conall's arm around his back and twist until his brother took back every word he'd just said. But the days where they'd physically fought had ended years ago. Now that they were grown men, they had to fight with words.

"I ought to knock your damned head off for that," Brady muttered.

Unperturbed, Conall grimaced. "Why get mad just because I struck a nerve? I'm only trying to point out that you're making a mistake."

Even if he'd been starving, at that moment Brady couldn't have wedged a bite of food between his gritted teeth. "Oh, you're an authority on women now? That's a laugh." He jerked up his coffee cup and brought it halfway to his mouth. "Sometimes you're a real bastard, Conall."

Leaving the bar stool, his brother walked over to the small table, jerked out a chair and sank into it.

"Maybe I am a bastard," Conall said in deceptively soft voice, "but I'm just trying to keep you from being hurt."

"Like you?" Brady retorted.

"That's a low blow."

It was a low blow and the realization helped Brady put a lid on his rising temper. He shouldn't have let Conall's remarks get to him. But these past few days he'd been torn between his search for Lass's identity and his growing feelings for her. He was walking a tightrope and his nerves were raw from the strain. Wiping a hand over his face, he said, "I shouldn't have said that. But Lass is…important to me."

"That's the whole point," Conall replied. "You don't know who she is or where she came from. She could be carrying all sorts of trouble or baggage that you don't yet know about. Is that the sort of woman you want to bring into our family?"

At one time, Conall himself had brought a fairly disturbed woman into the family. But Brady wasn't going to point that out. He'd already suffered enough without him bringing up the subject of Conall's ex-wife.

"Lass is a good person. I don't have to run a police check on her to know that."

Rising to his feet, Conall shrugged. "I don't know what the hell I'm worrying about this for. You've never stayed interested in one woman for more than a week or two. Lass will be no different."

Like hell, Brady thought.

Forcing his attention to his plate, he shoveled up a fork full of eggs. "This is one time, big brother, you need to mind your own business."

Without another word, Conall turned and left the room.

For the next four days, Brady was relegated to working the night shift. Which meant he left the ranch while Lass was working at the stables and didn't return home until the middle of the night. She'd talked to him on the phone, but those conversations had been brief and while she'd been in the company of the stables staff. So she'd had little chance to say anything personal, like how much she was missing him, how much she was aching to have his arms back around her. But he'd let her know he'd not forgotten her or their night together. One evening she'd found a fresh flower on her pillow and last evening he'd left a gift wrapped box on her nightstand. Inside had been an ivory lace shawl with a short note telling her the gift was meant to keep her warm until he could wrap his arms around here once again.

She was totally and utterly besotted with the man and these last few days without him had only underscored how empty her life would be without him. The realization was weighing on her, adding to the confusion that continued to swirl through her mind.

Images of her past were coming to her more frequently now and the sights and sounds had grown intense and frightening. Out of the blue, flashes of that day at the Ruidoso track had been striking her, filling her with a sense of unease and then downright horror.

David. It was a man named David who'd been kissing her against her will, shoving her into a car, then chasing her into the mountain ravine. Yet she still couldn't put a last name to his face or what he'd meant to her past life. Then last night as she'd lain in bed, the image of her father had once again floated to the front of her mind. She'd not been able to focus directly on his face, but she'd known the big, towering figure was his. In the vision she'd been shouting at him, swearing that she never wanted to see him again. But why?

Oh, God, had her father tried to hurt her, too? Why had she been so angry with him? Because her mother was dead? Had he done something to her mother? Had Lass been running, trying to escape from David and her father?

If only she could put the pieces of the puzzle together, she thought, then all of her memory might fall into place. But what would that do to her and Brady? She loved him. But she recognized that for him, their relationship was only beginning and he might never love her in return. If her memory returned and she had to leave the Diamond D, the chance for her to earn Brady's love would be over.

"Lass? Are you out here?"

Turning at the sound of Dallas's voice, Lass saw the other woman stepping into the barn where they stored the feed and tack for the children's mounts.

"I'm here," Lass called out to her. "Just putting away a few bridles."

Dallas walked over to her. "The last rider just left," she said. "Are you ready to head for home?"

Lass looped a headstall over a wooden peg, then stepped off a short, wooden platform to join the other woman.

"You mean Tyler has already gone, too? I was going to tell him goodbye."

"His mother picked him up a few minutes ago," Dallas told her, "but I wouldn't worry about it. Tyler knows that you care about him. In fact, I'm amazed at the progress you've made. Once you and Brady got him on Cloudwalker, he's become a different child."

Lass's smile turned a bit dreamy. "Brady is very good with children. Did you know that?"

Dallas laughed. "Not really. I can't remember seeing him with a kid. But apparently my brother has a few hidden talents that his family doesn't know about."

Blushing, Lass glanced away from the other woman's perceptive gaze. "Yes, he does."

Wrapping her arm around Lass's shoulder, Dallas gave

her an encouraging squeeze. "You've been missing him these past few days, haven't you?"

Lass stared at the toes of her boots. "Oh, dear, is it that obvious?"

"You're not the one that's obvious, Lass. Brady is the one who's behaving like a man in love. At least, that's what Grandma thinks and so do I."

Something between a sob and a groan sounded in Lass's throat as she turned and walked to the open doorway of the barn.

Staring out at the distant mountains, she spoke in a heavy voice, "Oh, Dallas, I'm beginning to think I've lost more than my memory. I've lost my mind. I had no business falling in love with your brother. No right at all."

"Why?"

Jerking her head around, she stared in dismay at Dallas. "Do you honestly have to ask?"

Dallas turned her palms upward in an innocent gesture. "Well, yes. You're a young, lovely woman and he's single, employed and manages to keep his fingernails clean. What's wrong with the two of you getting together?"

Groaning with frustration, Lass shoved a hand through her black hair. "Dallas, I've…been remembering things. Bits and pieces of my life before I came here. A man was involved. I don't know who or what he was to me. And then there's my father—I can almost see him, but I can't speak his name. We're arguing terribly and I'm saying awful things to him. Something bad was going on in my life, with my family. I don't know what or why. But it's clear that I can't start any sort of relationship with that sort of baggage hanging over my head."

Tsking her tongue with disapproval, Dallas shook her head. "Lass, bad things happen to all of us from time to time. They can be resolved. And I happen to think that Brady is going to put this puzzle together." She reached for Lass's arm and urged her away from the barn door. "C'mon, honey, and quit worrying. Let's get home. Who knows, Brady might actually show up at the dinner table."

Later that night, Brady and Hank took a break from patrolling the western side of the county to enjoy pie and coffee at the Blue Mesa Café in Ruidoso. It was well past midnight and except for a hippie-looking couple eating burgers, the restaurant was empty.

"Brady, why don't you put those papers down and eat your pie. The whipped cream is melting."

Earlier this evening at headquarters, Brady had printed out a stack of information pertaining to Lass's case and this break was the first chance he'd had to look it over. Now he glanced impatiently across the table to Hank.

"I'm eating," he told the young deputy. To prove his point, he whacked off a piece of the apple pie and jammed it into his mouth.

Grimacing, Hank complained, "For all the company you've been this evening, I might as well have come out on this patrol by myself. Ever since we left headquarters you've been somewhere else."

"I'm working, Hank. Remember, that's what we're supposed to be doing."

"Yeah. One job at a time. You can't patrol and do detective work simultaneously."

Frowning with faint amusement, Brady looked at the junior deputy. "Simultaneously? Where did that come from?"

Hank shot him a bored look. "From the dictionary. Where else? It means at the same time. Like doing reading and eating together."

Brady slapped the tabletop. "Hellfire, I know what simultaneously means! What are you doing using it? It sounds ridiculous."

Hank pursed his lips together. "Ya know, Brady, a guy just can't please you. Remember how you're always gettin' on to me about my grammar? Well, I've been doing something about it. I've been studying the dictionary, building my vocabulary."

Pinching the bridge of his nose, Brady wearily shook his head. "I'm sorry I ever said anything about your grammar."

"Shoot, I ain't. You're only trying to give me a little class. And I figure if I can talk right, I'll be a lot bigger hit with the ladies. Like you."

"Not like me!" Brady blustered under his breath, then with a rueful sigh, reached for his coffee. "You're as bad as my family, Hank. They think I'm incapable of having a serious thought about a woman."

"I didn't say anything like that," Hank defended himself, then with a curious expression leaned toward Brady. "Are you?"

"Shut up. Just shut up and eat," Brady ordered, then snatched up the papers and tried to refocus on the list of names in front of him. He was fishing for one tiny minnow in a huge ocean, he thought wryly. But he had to start somewhere.

"What are you looking at anyway?" Hank asked as he went back to tackling the cherry pie on his plate. "Something to do with that knifing incident last night at the Bull's Head? I thought you'd already handed in that report."

"This is about Lass. It's a list of registered brands in the state of Texas."

Hank rolled his eyes. "Oh, well, that sounds logical. The woman can't remember her name, but she can remember her family's brand. You're reachin', aren't you, partner?"

Brady shot him an annoying glare. "And you're going to be hanging, partner, by your thumbs, if you keep it up."

Hank turned serious. "Sorry, Brady. I'm just thinking about you. You've been worrying me. Ever since we found that gal, you've been different."

Brady realized that this was one time Hank was right. He had been different. Now that Lass had come into his life, nothing felt the same. He wasn't that man who'd taken one day at a time and lived only to work and play. Now he was thinking forward, dreaming, planning, imagining a future with Lass.

But that couldn't happen, he realized, until he knew for certain that she was free to become his. Until she was free from her forgotten past.

"She's become important to me, Hank. And I want to be able to solve this thing, to give her back her real name."

"Or give her yours?" Hank countered.

Brady stared at him. Leave it to Hank to put everything in simple terms, he thought wryly.

"Maybe."

The deputy whistled under his breath. "Boy, you have got yourself in a fix."

"What is that supposed to mean?"

Hank swallowed the last bite of his pie. "Think about it, Brady. You believe a woman who looks like Lass didn't have a man hangin' close? Why, there's probably a husband or fiancé out there right now just combing the countryside for her."

That possibility was the one thing that Brady couldn't shake from his mind. The idea haunted him day and night.

"If that's the case, then why hasn't he shown up to fetch her back home?" Brady asked. "That's what I want to know."

Hank swung his gaze around the empty restaurant, as though he'd find the answers somewhere among the empty tables and booths. "Maybe he don't want to find her. Maybe he wants to keep her danglin' for a while. Just to teach her a lesson."

That idea made Brady's hands curl into fists upon the tabletop. "Only a sick bastard could do that."

"That's why you'd better find him first," Hank wisely replied.

His partner was right, Brady thought, as unease trickled down his spine. The only way he could keep Lass truly safe was to find her true identity. And the only hope he had to keep her in his arms was to hope she loved him more than the man she'd left behind.

Chapter Twelve

The next morning, shortly before lunch, Brady was sitting at his desk, continuing to pour over an endless list of registered Texas brands when he suddenly stumbled across the one he'd been looking for. At least, he believed it could be the one. The letter *P* merged with an *F*.

The brand had been registered some forty years ago by a Francis Porter for Porter Farms. Whether Francis was a man or woman, or whether Porter Farms was still in existence, he didn't yet know. But at least he had something to start with.

In spite of the three short hours of sleep he'd gotten before heading back to work, excitement rushed through him. These past few days, he'd missed Lass terribly and later this evening, he'd be off duty for the next three days. He couldn't wait to see her, hold her, make love to her again. And maybe, God willing, he'd also be able to also give her news about her case.

Ignoring the talk and commotion of the deputies working in the next room, Brady quickly began to search the Internet for anything related to a Porter Farms. Not expecting much, he was amazed when a whole Web site suddenly emerged on the monitor screen.

Porter Farms bred and raised quarter horse racing stock. That explained why Liam or anyone in his thoroughbred circle could identify her. The different breeds raced separately, their auctions were held at different times and places, and most all trainers specialized in one breed. Not both. She wouldn't have traveled in thoroughbred circles. But was this Porter Farms connected to Lass?

Although there was no family photo available, the Web site was full of photos of the ranch and many horses, yearlings, and weanlings presently for sale. It was a professionally done site, offering high class animals. The Porter family had to be rich, he decided. Rich enough to splurge on diamond and turquoise earrings and handmade boots, the sort that Lass had been wearing the night he'd found her lying unconscious on the side of the road.

An address, telephone number and detailed map of the ranch's location were all right there for him to see and Brady's hand shook as he scribbled the information down on a scrap of paper, then reached for the phone.

Surely it couldn't be this easy, he thought.

The phone rang three times before a woman picked it up. She answered in a business-like manner and Brady realized he'd reached the commercial part of the ranch, rather than the private homestead.

"This is Brady Donovan, Chief Deputy of Lincoln County New Mexico," he said, identifying himself. "Could I possibly speak to a family member?"

There was a long pause and then the secretary replied, "Mr. Porter isn't in right now. And Miss Camille is…away."

Miss Camille. Away. Could that be Lass? Brady's heart was suddenly pounding.

"Is that the daughter of the house?" he questioned.

"Yes. Yes, she is. Is this an emergency, Deputy? Is something wrong?"

He'd classify it as worse than an emergency if these people knew that Lass was missing and hadn't lifted a finger to do anything to find her. But why would anyone do such a thing? His teeth clenched.

"Not exactly. Is there another family member I could speak with? A son? Wife perhaps?"

"No. Mrs. Porter passed on a couple of months ago. And there are no sons in the family."

My mother is dead. Even though more than three weeks had passed since Lass had revealed that painful memory to him, he'd not forgotten the stricken sound of her voice, the tears in her eyes. This had to be her home and family or a very uncanny coincidence.

"I see," he said thoughtfully. "Well, could you please have Mr. Porter call me as soon as possible. It's very important."

He gave the woman his own personal cell number, then hung up. As he entered Ethan's office, his mind was spinning, wondering if he would hear from the man or if he'd have to take the investigation to another level. One that could involve the Texas Rangers.

For the next fifteen minutes, he discussed everything he'd discovered with Ethan about Lass's case and had moved on to a stabbing incident that had occurred near Ruidoso two nights ago, when his phone rang.

After a quick glance at the illuminated number, he motioned to Ethan that it was the call he'd been waiting for.

Swallowing away the tightness in his throat, he answered, "Deputy Donovan."

There was a long pause and for a moment Brady feared the connection had been severed, but then a man's voice sounded in his ear.

"This is Ward Porter. My secretary said you wanted to speak with me."

Brady hadn't realized he'd gotten to his feet until he looked down and saw Ethan sitting behind his desk, calmly waiting for him to finish the call.

This time Brady was forced to clear his throat. "That's right. I'm working on a missing persons case. A young woman in her mid-twenties. Black hair. Gray eyes."

"That's Camille—my daughter! But she's not missing."

"Your secretary says she's currently away from home."

"That's right. She went on vacation."

"Where?"

"I don't know. She wouldn't tell me where she was going."

"When was the last time you talked to her?" Brady persisted.

"I'm not sure. Three—no, something like four weeks ago."

The man sounded agitated now and Brady could tell he was holding something back.

"And that doesn't concern you?"

"Well, hell yes, it concerns me! But what's a father to do when his daughter refuses to talk to him? Look, I don't know what this is about, but Camille is wherever she is because she wants to be there. She damned well doesn't want to be on Porter Farms with me! She made that clear enough when she spun out of here in that damned sports car of hers. And the last time I checked it was still at the airport, so apparently she's not flown back into San Antonio."

And why was that, Brady wanted to shout at him.

Instead, he fought to keep his voice and his questions impersonal. He wasn't a judge or juror, he was simply a lawman. And he couldn't allow his love for Lass to interfere with his job.

"You're certain about everything you're telling me?"

There was another long pause and then the man said in a voice that had suddenly turned quiet and confused, "Wait a minute, are you telling me that you have my daughter for some reason? What's happened to her? Is she—"

"The young woman in question doesn't know who she is or where she came from. For the past three weeks or more she's had amnesia. The sheriff's department here is trying to contact anyone who might know her."

"Oh, God. Oh no," the man whispered in a genuinely stricken voice. "How did she get amnesia? Are you sure it's my daughter? That it's Camille?"

"We're not exactly sure what happened. She received a head injury." Brady went on to describe Lass in detail and finished with her apparent affinity for horses. "We do know she was at the racetrack some time before she was injured. Is that something your daughter would normally do?"

"Every chance she got. I—" He suddenly paused and Brady was amazed to hear the man choke up with emotion. If he cared about his daughter that much, why hadn't he made an effort to find her? "I'll be there by tomorrow afternoon," he finished. "Where will I find you?"

Brady gave him directions to the Diamond D, along with a reminder to bring the proper papers to prove his identity and his connection to Lass, then hung up the phone.

Behind the desk, Ethan shook his head. "Sounds like the man has some explaining to do."

"A whole lot of it," Brady muttered. He paced restlessly around the room, then stopped to stare at the sheriff. "You know, for a minute when I found the Web site for Porter Farms I kept thinking how easy this whole thing was. But I was wrong. It hasn't been easy. Nothing about it has been easy. If Lass hadn't remembered that brand on her horse we'd still be at square one. Because this Ward Porter, this man that claims to be her father, wasn't making any effort to find his daughter. He didn't even consider her missing."

Disgusted, Ethan shook his head. "Broken families. Uncaring relatives. In this business I've seen it all. You'd think I'd be hardened to it by now. But it still bothers the heck out of me."

"Yeah," Brady agreed, his voice thick. "Me, too."

"I feel badly for Lass," Ethan went on. "From what you tell me, and from what I saw at the party, she sounds like a nice young woman."

She was more than nice, Brady thought. She was compassionate, caring, genuine. She deserved a family who loved her. A family like his. But it looked as though Ward Porter was going to arrive tomorrow and change all of that.

"Well, to be fair, we've not heard his side of the story," Brady muttered. "All I can say is that it better be a good one."

Ethan cast him a narrowed glanced. "So when you get to the ranch, what are you going to tell Lass?"

Lifting his Stetson from his head, Brady swiped a shaky hand over his hair. "I don't have much choice. I have to tell her that her father is coming for her," he said flatly. "And I have no idea how she's going to react."

Rising from his chair, Ethan rounded the desk and with a hand on Brady's shoulder, urged him toward the door.

"You've done more than enough for today. Get home and give Lass the news. You can let me know what happens after Mr. Porter arrives tomorrow. And whatever you do,

Brady, don't let him take her without showing you the proper legal documents."

As far as Brady was concerned the man needed to show more than a few paper documents to prove himself worthy of taking Lass anywhere. But he was only a lawman, sworn to protect a person's legal rights, not their future happiness.

"You don't have to worry about that, Ethan. I'm going to make sure Ward Porter is the real thing."

An hour later, he arrived at the ranch and, other than the hired help, discovered the house empty. Even his grandmother was nowhere to be found, which was probably for the best, he thought, as he took the stairs to his bedroom two at a time. He wanted to go straight to Lass with this news. She deserved to hear it before anyone else.

Hurriedly, he changed out of his uniform, then drove over the mountain to Angel Wing Stables. The afternoon was warm and sunny and when he parked his truck in front of the main barn, he noticed that most all the activity appeared to be off to the right in the outdoor arena.

Climbing out of the truck, he headed in that direction only to be intercepted by Dallas, leading a chestnut pony behind her.

"Well, my little brother has finally resurfaced," she said with a grin, then teased, "We were beginning to think we were going to have to drag out the family album to remember what you look like."

"It's been hectic," he explained. "A couple of deputies have been off sick and another with a family emergency. The department's been flooded with calls and working shorthanded made things even worse."

"I'm sorry," Dallas said and as she studied his strained

features, her expression turned to one of concern. "You look so worn, Brady. Is anything wrong?"

He gave her a short nod. "I have news about Lass's case. I need to talk to her about it."

Sensing his urgency but having the tact not to question him, she said, "You should find her in the saddling corral."

"Thanks," he said, then turned to start in that direction.

Before he could take a step, Dallas caught his arm and he arched an inquisitive brow at her.

"What?" he asked.

Smiling, she suggested, "Maybe it would be better if you talked with Lass in private."

"It would. Are you offering me the use of your office?" he asked.

"No. That place isn't private. The staff comes and goes all the time. I was thinking you ought to drive her up to the old foreman's house. I'd been planning on taking a few of the kids up there for a little cookout sometime soon, so I stocked the place with food last week. The two of you could relax without anyone bothering you."

He couldn't have been more grateful to his sister and he quickly leaned forward and pressed a kiss to her cheek. "Thanks, sis. You're my favorite."

"And don't forget it," Dallas called out as he turned and trotted away from her.

The saddling corral was a small lot connected to a row of stalls where many of the Angel Wing horses were kept on a daily basis. When he stepped through a wide, wooden gate, he spotted Lass walking beneath the portico at the far end of the shed row. A saddle pad was bunched beneath her arm while Tyler was trailing after her, his gait stiff from the brace on his leg, but doggedly steady. She'd changed the boy, Brady realized. Just as she'd changed him.

"Hello, you two," Brady called out to them.

Both Lass and Tyler turned at the sound of his voice and as he watched a bright smile light her face, Brady felt something stab him directly in the heart. Was he about to lose this woman forever?

Oh, God, he couldn't think it. Not now.

"Hi, Brady," Tyler greeted. "Have you come to ride with us today?"

"Maybe some other time, partner," Brady told the boy. "Right now, I need to see if I can borrow our girl for a little while. Think you can manage without her?"

Tyler threw his little shoulders back proudly. "Sure, I can manage. Dallas is gonna let me brush Cloudwalker and help saddle him. So I'm gonna be busy anyway." He held up a bridle for Brady to see. "I got to pick out his bridle today. See, it has silver and—" he looked to Lass for help "—what is that other stuff, Lass?"

She smiled. "Copper."

"Yeah. Copper. It has all that fancy stuff on it. It's neat, huh?"

Reaching out, Brady gently scuffed his knuckles against the boy's cheek. "Hoppy couldn't have done better."

Tyler's expression wrinkled with confusion. "Hoppy? Who's that?"

Brady and Lass both laughed, then Brady promised, "Hopalong Cassidy, a famous cowboy. I'll tell you all about him sometime."

At that moment, Dallas hurried up to join them.

"Come on, Ty, let's get that horse of yours saddled before the sun goes down," she said, then gave a subtle signal to Brady and Lass to hit the trail.

As the two of them headed out of the corral, Lass shot him a glowing smile. "Do you know how happy I am to see you?"

At that moment, it was all Brady could do to keep from pulling her into his arms and kissing her. But with children milling about, he couldn't take the chance, because he knew that once his lips touched hers, he wouldn't be able to control his hunger.

"When you left my bed the other night, I had no idea we were going to be apart this long," he explained. "Things have been…worse than hectic. But I'll explain all that later. Right now we're leaving here. I've already talked to Dallas."

She stared at him in surprise. "Leaving? Why?"

He grimaced. "Because—we need to talk."

Picking up the serious note in his voice, she nodded in silent agreement. "I'll go get my things and meet you at your truck."

The old foreman's house was a small stucco structure built on the side of the mountain about a mile from where the riding stables were located. The road up to the old empty home place wasn't graveled, but since the last rain was long ago it had dried up to make the narrow path hard packed and easy to navigate.

As they climbed the twisting road, through a thick stand of juniper, Lass looked at him in confusion. "Why are we going on this road? I thought you said we needed to talk."

"We're going somewhere quiet," he answered. "You'll understand when we get there."

"Why don't we talk now?" she asked, and then slanted him a confused glance. "Are you angry with me about something, Brady?"

Realizing she didn't understand anything that was going on, he reached across the console between their seats, to clasp her hand. "No. I'm not angry at all. Why would I be?"

Her gaze dropped to her lap. "I'm not sure," she said

quietly. "You seem upset. Maybe…you're regretting the other night…when we made love." Her head came up and she squared around in the seat to look at him. "Maybe you're wishing that it never happened, that I…hadn't fallen in love with you."

She looked miserable and Brady felt even worse. Groaning, he shook his head. "No! I'm upset because—" His jaw tightened as they topped a steep rise then flattened out directly in front of the old stucco. "Here we are. Let's go in."

Even though the cool evening air had already started to move in, the house was stuffy from being closed up. While Brady opened the windows, Lass walked around, gazing at the rustic surroundings, but not really seeing anything. She was too anxious and keyed up to concentrate on her surroundings. Whatever it was that Brady had to say, she wanted him to get it over with.

The tenseness she was feeling must have shown on her face because the moment he returned to her side, he gently took hold of her arm and led her over to a small, wood-framed couch. "Let's sit down," he suggested, "so we can be comfortable."

Lass sank next to him on the green cushions and while she waited for him to continue, her thoughts rolled over the past few days since his work schedule had gone awry. Without his company, she'd felt empty and as each day had come and gone, she'd imagined how it would be once he was back home and they finally had a chance to be together. Her whole body had been hungering, pining for him, and she'd envisioned him swooping her up into his arms and kissing her until they were both breathless. Had their time apart caused his desire for her to wane?

"I have news for you," he said finally. "And I wanted us to be alone when I gave it to you."

The grim look on his face put a chill in her heart. "What sort of news?" she asked hoarsely. "Is it…about me? My case?"

He wiped a hand over his face, then swallowed as though his throat was so lodged with words none of them could get out. "I don't know any other way to tell you this, Lass, except that I—"

His troubled gaze caught hers and she inwardly shivered at the dark, foreboding shadows she saw in his green eyes. "I believe I've found your father."

Incredulous, her head reared back as she stared at him. "My…father!" she spluttered. "I thought— Oh, God, I thought you were only going to say that you'd found someone else who'd recognized me being in Ruidoso. This is… Are you sure?"

"Not a hundred percent. But close to it."

Unconsciously her fingertips lifted to her mouth as her breaths started coming fast and short. "Oh, Brady, how—"

"The brand on your old horse, Rusty. It was an *F* that went with the *P*. An *F* for Farms. Porter Farms. Does that ring a bell?"

She closed her eyes as all sort of images began to fly at her like whirling debris in the spin of a tornado. Rooms and furnishings. Barns and stalls. Large trees and thick St. Augustine grass covering the lawn like green carpet. She could almost smell the grill on the patio, the mockingbirds chirping in the live oaks, her mother's sweet voice calling to her, calling out her name.

"Oh, God," she whispered in awe. "My name is Camille! Camille Porter."

A heavy breath rushed out of him and she opened her eyes to see his expression had turned to one of a sad sort of acceptance. His reaction didn't make sense to her. In fact, it scared her and she flung her arms around his neck and held on tightly.

"Brady, what does this all mean? What's going to happen now?"

His arms circled around her and pulled her so close she could scarcely breathe. "Your father is coming tomorrow. I'm figuring he has plans to take you back home with him. Do you remember his name?"

Her face buried in the side of his neck, she continued to cling to him. "No. But I can visualize him now. He—I was very angry with him when I left the ranch. I remember that much. I think I've been angry with him for a long time. Each time I picture him—the two of us together—I feel this huge sense of betrayal and disappointment, but I can't remember why I should feel that way." Lifting her head from his shoulder, she looked at him with sudden conviction. "I don't want to go back with him, Brady. I—"

"Oh, Lass, sweet Lass, don't go getting all worked up right now. We don't know what's going to happen yet."

Another thought struck her, and she untangled herself from his arms and rose to her feet.

"Brady, did he… Did you find out about the man? The one who took me from the racetrack? Did my father mention him or a…husband?"

"No. If this man truly is your father, he didn't mention you having any sort of family. And when I first talked to his secretary she only mentioned Mr. Porter and a daughter. I didn't bring up the subject of the man at the racetrack. To him or the secretary. I didn't want to tip our hand."

She stared at him. "What do you mean?"

Rising from the couch, he closed his hands over her shoulders. "Lass, as a lawman I have to keep my mind open to any and every thing. If Ward Porter had any sort of connection to the man at the racetrack, I want to question him about it before he has a chance to plan his answers."

Stunned, her head jerked back and forth with disbelief. "Do you think… Oh, surely my father didn't send him to harm me?"

The horror of that thought filled her eyes with tears and then she gripped the sides of her head with both hands and moaned. "I can't think, Brady," she said, her voice full of anguish. "Everything is rushing at me. Emotions. Memories. Fears. Oh, God, it has to end! No matter what happens to me, it has to end!"

Her knees suddenly grew so mushy that she was forced to grab the front of his shirt to prevent her body from sliding to the floor.

Muttering a curse, Brady quickly swept her up in his arms and carried her to the back of the house to one of its two bedrooms.

As soon as he deposited her on the bed, she rolled to her side and pressed a hand to her forehead. "I'm sorry, Brady. I just got a little shaky there for a moment."

"Lie still and don't talk," he ordered. "I'll be right back."

By the time he returned with a cool glass of water, she was feeling stronger. After she took several long sips from the glass, he placed it on a nearby dresser, then took a seat on the edge of the mattress.

"Better now?" he asked.

She nodded weakly. "At least my head doesn't feel like it's going to rip apart."

"I should call Bridget to come look you over. Or take you into the hospital," he suggested, his expression tight with concern.

Sighing, she turned on her back and looked up at him. "I

don't need medical attention, Brady. I need time to absorb all of this. It's…too much for me to deal with all at once."

He stroked the hair off her forehead. "I knew this wasn't going to be easy for you. It's not…easy for me, either."

With a look of anguish she rose to a sitting position and cupped his face with her hands. "Brady, I'm so scared. What's going to happen to me?"

Gathering her close to him, he spoke close to her ear. "Nothing is going to happen to you, Lass."

"It will," she sobbed into his shirt. "If I have to leave you."

Suddenly his hands were on her face, tilting her head back and away from him. She blinked away the moisture in her eyes to see that he was gazing at her with hunger and need and something she'd not ever seen on his face before.

"Lass, ever since the night we made love—no even before that—I knew that you were special, I could feel something happening between us. I didn't want to think I was falling in love with you. I thought that was something that would happen a few years down the road, when I was good and ready to let it happen." His mouth twisted to a rueful grin. "I didn't understand it was something a person couldn't control."

Her heart seemed to stop as it waited, wondered, hoped that she was hearing the very thing it needed to survive. "Brady, are you—are you telling me that you love me?"

His fingers delved into her hair, stroked ever so softly against her temple. "I'm telling you that I love you, Lass."

Tears brimmed over the rim of her eyes and slipped down her cheeks. "Are you saying this because you…think it's something I want to hear?"

An anguished groan growled deep in his throat. "Oh, Lass, how could you think that? I…wasn't going to tell you. Not now. Not with everything else that's going on. You already have more than enough to deal with."

"But…don't you understand, Brady? All this other stuff about me—about my past—it doesn't matter. Hearing you say that you love me is all that I need."

With a rueful shake of his head, he pulled her back to him and buried his face in the side of her hair. "But it does matter, Lass. You can't just wipe away the life you'd been leading, as though it didn't exist. You need to go back—to remember—to face the problems you were having and deal with them. Unless you do that I don't think—" He paused as a heavy breath rushed out of him. "I don't think we could ever be truly happy together."

"But Brady—"

"That man, Lass, the one at the track. If you remember him kissing you, then the two of you must have had some sort of relationship. That's why you need to go back to Porter Farms, to give yourself time to remember what he meant to you. Because I…don't want us being together to be a mistake, Lass."

Pulling back from him, she stared at him in stunned wonder. "Brady, I told you that he was kissing me against my will! He was the one who was trying to hurt me! How do you think I could ever have feelings for him?"

Grimacing, he closed his eyes. "Because I don't know what he meant to you in the first place! Lovers have arguments, Lass. They do and say terrible things to each other. In my line of work I see it all the time. Then after a few days, everything is forgiven and forgotten and the two of them are back together."

"Not with me," she said flatly.

His eyes opened, then narrowed skeptically on her face. "All right. Maybe that man wasn't important to you. So how can you be sure there wasn't someone else?

Someone you'd fallen in love with and you just haven't remembered him yet?"

More tears formed in her eyes, then splashed onto her face. "Because I know I wouldn't feel what I do whenever I touch you, Brady. When I search my heart, all I can find is the love I feel for you."

He stared at her for long moments, and then with a stifled groan, he pressed his cheek against hers. "Oh, Lass, I hope you're right. Because I—I'm not sure I can live without you."

She wanted to assure him that he wouldn't have to, but she held the words back. She understood that nothing she could say now would convince him that her life was meant to be with him. The best she could do to convey her love was to show him, to let her lips, her hands and fingers do all the talking.

"Brady."

Whispering his name was all it took for his lips to latch over hers in a kiss so devouring it snatched her breath and pulled a whimper from deep in her throat. Her mouth couldn't begin to keep up with his rough, hungry search, so she simply surrendered to the thrill of being a captive to his kiss.

Mindlessly, her arms slipped around his neck, while one hand glided up the back of his neck and into his thick hair. The hard heat of his body ignited a fire that flashed through her veins, raced down her spine and blanketed her skin with a shiver of goose bumps.

With a guttural growl, he lowered them until they were both lying crosswise on the soft mattress. With their mouths still fused, their arms and legs entwined, he drank deeply from her lips, then nibbled and kissed his way across her cheeks, up her nose and onto her forehead.

By the time he raised his head and gazed down at her, she was weak with desire and nothing else mattered but him and this moment.

"Lass, this isn't going to fix anything," he murmured with anguish. "Tomorrow—"

"Is just that," she swiftly interrupted. "Tomorrow. I don't want to spend this precious time with you talking about what might happen in the next few days. Just love me. Love me now."

She didn't have to implore him a second time. After a moment's hesitation, his mouth crushed down on hers and for a while all thought of tomorrow was forgotten.

Chapter Thirteen

The next day, shortly after lunch, Brady was sitting in the family room with his grandmother when Reggie came to the door and announced that Ward Porter had arrived and she'd seated him in the parlor.

Thanking the maid, he rose from the long couch, then cast a grim glance at Kate. "Well, Grandma, looks like this is it," he said flatly. "Ever since I plucked Lass up out of that ditch, I've been working toward this day. Funny, now that it's here, I feel like hell."

Sensing her grandson's anguish, Kate laid a hand on his arm. "Do you want me to go with you?"

"No. I'd appreciate it if you'd give me a few minutes to go over a few details with this man, then go up and collect Lass from her bedroom," he told her, then with a grateful pat to her hand, he turned and left the room.

As he walked down the long hallway to the parlor, he

was confident that he could trust his grandmother to give Lass the emotional support she needed before facing her father. Since Lass had come to live on the Diamond D, she and Kate had grown close. The fact that his grandmother clearly loved her only proved to Brady that his feelings for Lass weren't foolish or misguided as Conall had tried to make him believe. But once Lass came down those stairs and met her father, how was she going to feel? Was she going to remember everything? Remember that there was a man somewhere back in Texas that she already loved?

Dear God, facing a gun barrel wasn't nearly as terrifying as the thought of losing her.

Once Brady reached the opening of the long parlor, he paused only for a moment before he stepped into the austere room that was relegated for guests such as Ward Porter.

The man was sitting in a green armchair, his elbows resting on his knees, a black cowboy hat dangling from his two hands. He appeared to be a tall, robust sort of man, but at the moment, his graying head was slightly bowed, as though he was in troubled thought. The idea suddenly had Brady wondering how his own father would be feeling if he learned one of his children had gone missing and couldn't even remember his name. Doyle would be devastated. Could be, this man was, too.

Clearing his throat, Brady swiftly crossed the room. Before he reached Ward Porter, the man lifted his head and studied Brady with a curious squint.

"Good afternoon, Mr. Porter. I'm Brady Donovan," he introduced himself. "The deputy you spoke with yesterday."

He extended his hand to Lass's father and with a look of faint surprise the man rose to his feet to shake it.

"I'm not sure I understand any of this," the man said, a frown furrowing his brow. "I've heard of the Diamond

D horses, of course, though I don't think we've ever met. Is this where Camille has been staying since she lost… her memory?"

Brady gestured for the man to return to his seat, then crossed a short space to sit on the edge of a straight-back chair with a cowhide seat.

"That's right, Mr. Porter. This is my family's home. We thought it would be better for her to stay here than in a shelter in Ruidoso."

"Oh. Well, I'm grateful to you for extending her the hospitality," he said, then added, "And by the way, just Ward will do. No need to be formal, is there?"

As far as Brady could see, Lass didn't physically take after her father. His face was broad, his features on the coarse side. The bit of hair that hadn't yet grayed appeared to be a dirty blond color and his eyes were dark brown, the complete opposite of Lass's soft gray. At the moment the man's narrow gaze was wary and full of confusion.

"No. Not at all," Brady agreed.

Ward suddenly reached for something lying on the floor next to his chair and it was then that Brady noticed the leather briefcase.

"I brought all the papers I think you'll need to verify my identity and my relation to Camille. And a few photos, too. Just in case you have any doubts."

Brady had all sorts of doubts, but he couldn't throw them at the man all at once. Besides, a person usually learned more by listening than questioning, he thought.

"I'll look at them in a few minutes," Brady told him. "Right now I'd like to hear about Lass. You told me yesterday you didn't know where she was or had been."

Ward's brown eyes squinted to mere slits. "Lass? You call her by that name?"

"We didn't know her name," Brady reminded him. "And she didn't want to be called Jane."

His eyes suddenly widened and then a faint pallor came over his cheeks. "Oh. I see."

"Do you?" Brady asked. "Because I'm not sure you understand the hell, the anguish, your daughter has endured these past weeks. No one came forward to identify her. No family or friends. I think she was beginning to think that she had no loved ones or family."

A ruddy red suddenly replaced Ward's ghostly white complexion. "Look, maybe I don't come across as father of the year here, but I was in the dark about this whole thing," Ward blurted defensively. "My daughter left the ranch of her own free will. She wouldn't tell me where she was headed. Nothing. And short of following her, there wasn't much I could do to stop her. She's twenty-six years old. That's a grown woman—with her own mind."

The man was clearly agitated, but underneath it all, Brady could see pain on his face, the sort that comes right alongside a dose of regret.

"So you don't know why she came here to New Mexico? To Ruidoso?"

"Not exactly. But I should have guessed. She always loved it out west and she's not going to go anywhere where there's not racehorses close by. That's for damned sure. Guess that's the one thing she got from me." He shoved a hand through his wavy hair, then looked straight at Brady. This time regret and concern were clearly written on the older man's face. "She hasn't remembered me or what happened?"

"Not completely. Only bits and pieces. She claims she was angry with you about something, but she can't remember what or why."

Ward's head suddenly dropped and when he spoke, his

quiet words were directed at the floor. "That much is true," he said with a sigh, then with a rueful twist to his lips, he looked up. "You see, a couple of weeks before Camille left the ranch, her mother passed away. She and Judith had always been really close and her death was almost more than she could bear. Camille is the only child we had and I guess in our own ways we clung to our little girl too much."

Brady leaned forward in his chair as his mind turned over the image of Lass grieving. Just the idea made his heart ache. "Was your wife's death sudden?"

"No. It was an expected thing. She had cancer and her health had quickly deteriorated these past few months. You see, she refused to take any sort of treatments to save her life. And…well, Camille blames me for that. She blames me for her mother's death."

Ward's voice cracked on his last words and Brady wondered how it could get any worse for this man and for Lass.

"Why is that?"

Ward suddenly rose from his chair and with his hands jammed deep in the pockets of his western trousers began to pace around the large room. "Because, damn it, she found out about Jane. My mistress."

"Oh, I see."

He stopped in midstride to look at Brady. "I doubt it," he said tightly. "I doubt your father is…as weak as I am. I'll bet he's always done the right thing, been a man you can look up to."

"Pretty much so. That's not to say he's perfect. He's made some mistakes, but when he does, he'll be the first to admit it."

Tilting his head back, Ward gazed at the high ceiling above their heads. "I could go into a lot of reasons why I've had Jane in my life for the past several years. But that won't fix anything with Camille. She's lost her respect for me. I doubt she'll ever forgive me."

Brady studied him thoughtfully. "I wouldn't say that. She has a huge, compassionate heart. She just needs time. She's been through some trauma and the doctors aren't certain when or if she might recover all her memory."

"Yeah. Well, once I get her back on the farm, I'm going to do everything I can to make it up to her. To help her remember."

Drawing in a deep, bracing breath, Brady rose to his feet. "Ward, I've not asked this yet, but before she left the ranch was Lass involved with anyone?"

Brady's question caused the older man's brows to arch with faint surprise. "Involved? You mean with a man?"

The urge to swallow at the hard lump in his throat was so great Brady finally had to cough before he could speak. "That's what I mean. Like a husband? Fiancé? Boyfriend?"

"No. Camille has only had a handful of boyfriends over the past years and none of them have been that serious. Her mother always said our daughter put her love into horses, not men. That's why she's not yet gotten married. I say she's just darned picky. I've tried my best to get her interested in David, one of my assistant trainers, but she wouldn't have any part of him." His gaze narrowed on Brady's face. "Why do you ask?"

Now was hardly the time for Brady to go into his feelings for Lass. There were still many blank spaces that needed to be filled in. If not by this man, then someone he might lead to.

"Your daughter was injured because she was running from a man. A man who was seen with her at the track. She remembers struggling with him, but she can't yet identify him. I thought you might have an idea of who this person could have been."

Ward looked disgusted and horrified at the same time and Brady instinctively knew that he'd played no part in Lass's injury.

"I don't have a clue. None of her friends back home would do such a vile thing. And she's…well, she's always been a good girl. She wouldn't have let herself be picked up by a strange man at the track. It would have been done against her will."

Yes, she was a good girl, a good person, Brady silently agreed. She deserved to be happy and now that he'd talked with Ward, he could see that she needed to return to Porter Farms, needed to get her feet under her and her past in order before she could truly be ready to start a life, a family with him. If that meant he had to hand her over to this man, for however long it took, then he would. Because he loved her. Because in spite of everything, what he wanted the most was her happiness.

Dear God, was this the first time in his life that he'd put a woman's feelings before his own desires? The idea stung him, made him wonder what he'd been doing, thinking?

Hell, you know what you've been doing, Brady. You've always thought love was just a game you could either play or leave on the table. Now Lass has come along and showed you that love is nothing about playing or lust or getting what you desire. It's about caring, protecting, giving.

Shaken by the idea that these past few weeks with Lass had changed him so much, he turned away from her father and swallowed hard. "That's my thought, too."

The sound of footsteps suddenly caught both men's attention and Brady turned to see Lass and his grandmother stepping into the room. Kate had her arm around Lass's shoulders, yet even with the older woman's support, Brady could see she was walking gingerly, as though meeting her father had left her weak and wary.

He could hear the slight intake of Ward's breath before he took one step toward his daughter, then stopped abruptly and stared at her.

Across the room Lass could feel Kate's strong arm at her waist, supporting her, comforting her, yet in spite of the woman's hold on her, she felt as though her legs were going to crumble.

The man standing in front of her was her father. All this time, how could she not have remembered his name, his face? Now that she was seeing him in the flesh, it seemed incredible that her mind could have erased so much.

"Camille. Honey."

From the corner of her eyes, Lass could see Brady moving to join them and her heart ached as she thought about the sweet love they'd made last night in the foreman's old house. Was he actually going to force her to leave the Diamond D? Leave him? She couldn't think about it now. If she did, she would totally break apart.

Once she was finally standing face-to-face with her father, Brady and Kate discreetly moved aside. Lass felt lost without them and the notion only proved how much at home she felt on the Diamond D, how much she considered Brady's family as her family. Even Doyle, who wasn't around all that much of the time, seemed more like a father to her now than Ward Porter.

"Hello, Daddy," she quietly greeted.

For a moment he said nothing and then his face crumpled and his voice was full of cracks when he finally spoke. "You…remember me?"

Lass nodded. "Much more clearly now."

Behind her right shoulder, Kate cleared her throat. "If you'll all excuse me, I'll get Opal to prepare a tray of refreshments."

"I'll carry it back for you," Brady said, then turned to follow his grandmother out of the room.

Panicked by the thought of being without him, Lass blurted, "No, Brady! Please, come here. With me."

He came to stand beside her and a small breath of relief rushed out of her as his arm settled at her waist. This was the man she loved, the man she always wanted at her side. Without him only half of her would exist.

"Honey," Ward began, "you didn't leave any word about where you were going. You wouldn't answer your phone. I thought you were still hiding out somewhere just to spite me. I had no idea that you were lost. That you'd had some sort of accident. If I had, I would have been here immediately."

Lass glanced up at Brady's strong profile. "Maybe it's best you hadn't known where to find me," she said softly.

Ward's narrowed gaze traveled back and forth between his daughter and the deputy who'd rescued her. "How are you feeling now?" he asked Lass. "Ready to make the trip back to Porter Farms?"

"I don't think I want to go to Porter Farms with you," she said flatly.

Brady shot her a stunned look while Ward impatiently shook his head.

"Let's not start this again, Camille."

"I'm not Camille anymore. I prefer the name Lass now," she bluntly pointed out.

Gasping with outrage, the older man looked to Brady. "What have you people done to her? What have *you* done to her? Brainwashed her? Can't you see that she's confused? She's not even sure of her own name!"

Something about the sound of her father's angry voice pierced her and suddenly layers and layers of images were rapidly unfolding in her mind. They were coming at her with such a rush that she was close to being ill, yet at the same time relief was flooding through her, replacing all her doubts and uncertainties with a furious sort of confidence.

"No one has tried to brainwash me, Daddy. Except maybe you. Brainwash me into thinking that your and Jane's trysts were something acceptable, that your long-term affair had nothing to do with Mother's death. Well, you can tell yourself that if it makes you feel better, but you'll never convince me! Mother let herself die because she didn't want to live with a cheating husband. You were her whole life and you betrayed her with an old family friend. You betrayed me."

"Camille! This is not the time or place to be sorting our family laundry! Now get your things. We're leaving. Before we say something that can never be taken back."

Completely ignoring Ward, Lass whipped around to Brady. Excitement, amazement and joy all swept across her face as she gazed up at him. "There's no need for me to go back to Porter Farms now, Brady! I remember everything. And I can tell you now that I'm free. Free to stay here and love you."

A tender light filled his eyes and then before Ward could say anything about the matter, Brady swept her into his arms and kissed her. As the tender touch of his lips lingered on hers, Lass felt contentment so sweet and pure that tears flooded her eyes.

"What is going on here?" Ward demanded.

Just as Brady lifted his head to explain, the doorbell rang. Since Reggie was nowhere to be seen, Brady set Lass aside to go answer it.

"Excuse me," he said as he quickly strode toward the foyer. "I'll be right back."

Once Brady was out of sight, Ward stepped closer to his daughter. "Do you love that young man? Is that why you don't want to come home with me?"

Lass's lips trembled. Her father had hurt her, had managed to destroy her admiration for him, scar all the good years when her family had been happy, when her family's love was whole and strong. And yet, a part of her still loved him, didn't want to lose her only parent.

"I do love him, Daddy. But I—" She swallowed hard, then dismally shook her head. "My life at Porter Farms is over. I think we both realized that once Mother died and I…found out about Jane." A rueful grimace twisted her features. "I'm not saying I want to shut you out of my life completely. I'm trying to tell you that I need time. Time to try to make sense of all that's happened to our family."

He reached out and gingerly touched her cheek. "All I ask is for a chance to make it up to you, honey," he said brokenly. "You and your mother—you've always been my whole life. All I've ever worked for—the farm, the horses—it was for you."

Her throat burning, she turned her face away from him and blinked her eyes. "Yes, I know," she murmured thickly.

The sound of footsteps came from across the room and both Lass and Ward turned to see Brady emerge from the foyer. Another man was following directly behind him, but his head was hidden by Brady's broad shoulder.

Since the Donovans didn't carry out ranching business in the house, Lass wondered if the unannounced guest was Sheriff Hamilton, wanting to question her father. But then Brady suddenly stepped to one side and she could see the visitor was not the rugged sheriff; it was her nightmare come to life.

"David," Ward greeted warmly, "did you have a good look at the Donovans' stables?"

Lass stared numbly at the man, her throat too paralyzed to utter a sound.

He glanced over at Lass, then gave her a sympathetic smile as though she didn't have her full mental faculties and needed to be treated with patience and understanding. Clearly he'd made this trip with Ward confident that Lass still had amnesia and wouldn't be able to recognize him, she thought wildly.

Turning his attention to her father, he answered, "It was great, Ward. You really need to let Mr. Donovan show you around before we leave. They have an aquatic pool for the horses and I want you to see it. I think it's time Porter Farms invested in one. If we plan to compete—"

The muscles in Lass's throat finally released enough to work and she screamed loudly as she stumbled backward, away from David and her father.

Brady leaped forward and caught her by the arm. "Lass! What is it? What's wrong?"

Horrified, she flung a finger toward David, who was already backing cautiously away from them. "David—he's the one who attacked me! At the car—in the mountains!"

Feigning a wounded expression, David stepped forward and held his palms upward in a gesture of innocence. "Camille, I'm so sorry about your—accident. Your father tells me you can't remember anything and I can see for myself how tangled your thinking is right now. But you'll get well and then you'll see how much I care about you."

He reached a hand toward her and Lass shrank back against the comfort of Brady's solid frame.

"Liar!" she flung at him. "You—you're psychotic. Tell my father what you were planning to do to me! To him!"

Totally confused, Ward turned to his daughter and said in a soothing, placating voice. "Honey, you're confused. That's David. Our assistant. Our friend. Remember? He couldn't be the man who tried to harm you."

"He's not a friend, Daddy," she spoke through gritted teeth. "All he wanted was to get your ranch and he planned to do that through me. I tried to tell you about him months ago, but you refused to believe me! Now after all that's happened, you're still taking his side!"

Apparently Ward's spoken defense of him was enough to give David the courage to stop his backward progression out of the room and he stared at Lass as though he couldn't believe she would have the gall or the courage to accuse him of anything.

He said, "Camille, you're still a sick woman. You obviously have me confused with some other man."

Her voice trembling, Lass shouted at him, "I'm sick all right for not screaming to high heaven at the track when you strong-armed me into your car!"

Ward's bewildered expression suddenly turned suspicious as he looked at his assistant. "A few days after Camille left the ranch, you made a trip to Florida to visit your family. Or so you said. Maybe Deputy Donovan should give them a call and straighten out this matter," Ward suggested.

David's gaze was suddenly darting nervously around the room. "This from you, Ward? I'm going outside for some fresh air and while I'm gone maybe you'll come to your senses and realize your daughter is delusional."

"Come here!" The order to David came from Brady, his

voice steely soft and so menacing it could have been a weapon. "You have a few questions to answer."

"Not to you, buddy!"

At that moment David turned and started to run toward the foyer, but Brady instantly leaped into action and halfway across the room, he caught Lass's attacker by the arm and spun him around.

David immediately resisted and attempted to throw a punch at Brady's face, but he quickly dodged the blow. David attempted to swing again, but by then Brady was plowing into him with both fists, until he staggered backward then fell against an antique table. The piece of furniture, along with an ornate lamp, crashed to the floor. David followed close behind and lay sprawled and groaning among the broken pieces.

"My God!" Ward bellowed in stunned disbelief. "What is going on here?"

Heaving from anger and exertion, Brady glanced at him. "You're witnessing an arrest. Lincoln County style."

"Then I'm here at the perfect time," Kate announced as she hurried into the room. She was carrying a large silver tray and there, among the drinks and snacks, lay a pair of handcuffs. With a catlike grin, she shoved the tray toward Brady. "I heard the commotion and thought you might need these."

Wiping his sweaty forehead against the sleeve of his shirt, Brady looked at her and the handcuffs, then started to chuckle. "Grandma, are these the cuffs I gave you as a gag gift?"

Kate chuckled along with her grandson. "I knew someday I'd have good use for them."

Grabbing up the cuffs, he planted a kiss on her cheek. "I can never get ahead of you, can I?"

She tossed him a grin full of love and pride. "Don't even try."

Quickly, Brady plucked the woozy man from the floor and cuffed his hands behind his back. Once he was certain his prisoner was securely shackled, he shoved him down in the nearest chair and turned to search the room for Lass.

She was standing only a few feet away, anxiously waiting and watching for the ordeal to be over. As soon as he held out his arms, she ran to him and buried her face against his chest.

"Oh, Brady," she sobbed with relief. "My nightmare is finally over."

Pressing his cheek to the top of her head, he held her tightly. "And our life together is just beginning, my darling."

Later that night, in the privacy of the foreman's old house, Lass and Brady lay snuggled together on the small double bed. An arm's width away, moonlight slanted through the bare windows and bathed Lass's face in a silver glow that matched the radiant light in her eyes.

Even though she was drowsy from their lovemaking, she couldn't seem to wipe the smile from her face or to let herself actually fall asleep. There was too much to think about, too much to experience to waste it on slumber.

Drawing lazy circles across Brady's chest, she tilted her head back far enough to see his face. His tawny hair lay in rumpled waves over his forehead while his relaxed features were a total contrast to the fierce expression he'd had when he'd lunged for David.

"Are you sorry that Grandma invited Ward to stay on the ranch with us for a few days?" Brady asked in a dozy voice. "She really wasn't trying to butt in, you know. She loves you."

The corners of Lass's lips continued to curve upward. "Yes, I know she loves me. And she wants me and my father to have a chance to talk things over and hopefully make a new start of things. She believes that's important to my happiness."

"So do I." His fingers gently stroked her hair. "Do you think it's possible for the two of you to start over?"

"I didn't before. But I do now. I think…when the awful truth about David finally sunk in, I believe he realized how he'd been looking at things in the wrong way. You see, my father has always been a hard-driving, ambitious man. And David is that same type. I suppose that's why he liked him so much. Why he wouldn't believe me when I told him that he was making overtures that were making me… uncomfortable."

"Had David worked for your family long?"

"Probably three years. And in that time I made the mistake of going out on one date with him. It took me about an hour to realize he wasn't my type at all. But he refused to accept that I had no interest in him." She sighed. "What will happen to him now, Brady?"

Earlier this afternoon, after things had calmed down, Brady had hauled David to the jail in Carrizozo. As of now, the man was still behind bars, waiting for bail to be set.

"That's for a court to decide, Lass. As far as I'm concerned they should lock him away for a long while. But I can't believe that all this while he was checking in to make sure you still had amnesia and couldn't identify him. It took a lot of nerve to come face you again. He sounds like the kind of man who thinks if he wants it hard enough it will come true."

Lass shivered. Now that her memory had returned, the images of what had happened continued to haunt her. Yet a part of her was glad that she could remember the whole incident now. Remember it and hopefully come to terms with it all.

"When he showed up at the track, I was stunned, Brady. I was standing there at the saddling paddock watching the jockeys and the horses and then suddenly David showed up out of nowhere. I had no idea that he knew I'd come here to New Mexico. The only thing I can figure is that he overheard my phone conversation when I was making flight plans."

"What did he tell you? I mean, the reason that he was there?"

"He'd said that my father had taken ill and that he'd come to fetch me home."

"The man hadn't heard of telephoning?" Brady asked.

"Exactly," she answered. "I was immediately suspicious, so I told him I wanted to call my father first. That's when he jerked the cell phone from my hand and forcefully walked me to his car."

Brady made a tsking noise with his tongue. "Bad mistake, Lass. Never get into a car with someone you don't trust."

"I certainly learned that lesson," she said wryly. "I made a huge mistake by not making a scene at the track and alerting someone that I needed help. I should have never allowed him to get me into the car. But I went along. Because deep down, I never suspected he would try to physically harm me. But then as we drove east from the track, he begin to tell me how much he loved me, how once Daddy was dead, the two of us could have Porter Farms for our own. I was terrified. He seemed so calm, so sure that once he'd had me on his own I'd be willing to stay with him and let him have control of me and the ranch. He talked about giving me tranquilizers and telling everyone I'd had a breakdown after my mother died, but he was going to care for me. Or that I'd even have an accident if I ever tried to leave him."

Brady propped himself up on one shoulder to look down

at her. "God, Lass, do you think he meant to murder your father? Or did he only mean when your father grew older and passed away?"

Lass shook her head. "I'm not certain. But when he said those things, there was evilness in his voice that I'd never heard before. After that my mind began to work furiously to find a way to get out of the car and away from him. I knew if I ever had a chance of escape I would have to do it while we were still in the mountains. Once we got out on the flat desert there wouldn't be anywhere to hide. So I feigned nausea and told him to pull the car over before I retched everywhere."

"Yes. Johnny found the spot where the car was parked," Brady said. "He said a scuffle happened there."

Lass closed her eyes against the vivid memories. "David got out of the car, too. I guess by then, he didn't trust me. I walked to the trunk area and began to cough, but it wasn't convincing enough for him. He grabbed me with intentions of putting me back in the car. He told me it was time he had a bit of fun."

"Bastard," Brady cursed. "I should have hit him again, just for good measure."

She slipped a hand down his muscled arm. He was a strong man, this man that she loved and he would always be there to fight for her, protect her in every way. It was a heady thought.

"That's exactly what I did," she told him. "Hard. I guess he wasn't expecting me to fight back. Especially me jabbing my fingers in his eyes. While he was howling, I ran. The sun had gone down, but there was still a bit of light left. He chased after me, but I suppose he couldn't see very well because of what I'd done to his eyes. Once I climbed out of the ravine, I lost him and kept running up the mountain. Until I fell. Then the next thing I remember is waking up to see your face hovering over me."

A tender smile curved his lips. "And now you're here. Still in my arms. I just can't get rid of you, can I?"

"Do you want to?" she asked in a voice that was half-teasing, half-serious.

Brady's eyes twinkled. "I'm not sure. Maybe you'd better let me think about this before I answer."

"I probably should. Since you know very little about my past."

"What's there to know that I need to know?"

"Hmm. Well, let's see, I made straight A's in high school and I took choir all four years."

One of his brows arched upward. "You can sing?"

"Only in the shower."

He grinned. "Good. That means you can serenade me."

She laughed softly. "And I graduated from TU with a degree in business. I used that knowledge to help with the business side of Porter Farms. But horses are my first love. Working with them is what I've always wanted to do the most. Does that bother you?"

"Only if you spend more time with them than me."

She trailed the tip of her index finger across his chin. "I promise to never let that happen."

"Does it bother you that I'm a lawman?"

Suddenly serious, she said, "It worries me that your job sometimes puts you in danger. But I've seen a jockey break his neck. Everything has its dangers. That's why we need to live and love and enjoy each other as much as we can, whenever we can."

"You got that right," he murmured, then tilting his head, he kissed her softly, slowly, as he tried to convey with his lips all the love he was feeling in his heart.

Once he lifted his head, he announced, "We're going to be married. As soon as we can make the arrangements."

Her hands came up to cup gently frame his face. "Are you sure that's what you want, Brady? There's no urgency for us to become man and wife right now. And you've been a bachelor for a long time. Maybe you need to wait and think about this," she suggested.

His brows pulled together. "Lass, I'm asking you to marry me! And here you are trying to talk me out of it?"

"I only want you to be happy. And before I came along you were a free man. You liked to date. Different women."

His frown deepened. "Before you came along, I didn't understand anything about needing, loving. I thought playing the field would be all I'd want for a long, long time. I didn't know what it meant to have someone become a part of me. I didn't know that just the thought of having that part of me torn away would be too much to bear."

"You wanted me to go back to Porter Farms. Apparently you believed you could get along without me."

He groaned. "That's because I wanted you to be happy. And I thought it could never happen until you reacquainted yourself with your old life. I never dreamed that everything was suddenly going to come back to you. But I thank God that it did."

He lowered his head, until his lips were poised over hers. "So what is your answer to my proposal? Am I going to have to beg to get a yes out of you?"

"No," she said with a happy sigh. "All you have to do is love me."

"For the rest of my life, darling."

Epilogue

Three months later, on a cold December morning, Lass and Brady stood in the middle of the ranch yard and waved to Dallas as she pulled away in a truck with a horse van attached to the back.

As Lass watched her sister-in-law's vehicle turn a curve and disappear from sight, she said thoughtfully, "Dallas never quits looking for the perfect horse to use at Angel Wing. When Maura mentioned to her that Jake Rollins had an extremely gentle horse for sale, she couldn't wait to drive over to his place to see it."

Brady's mouth took on a rueful slant. "Well, just between you and me, I'd prefer she not do business with Jake."

Lass looked at him with a bit of surprise. Jake was his sister Maura and brother-in-law Quint's ranch foreman. What could Brady have against the man? she wondered.

"Why? He wouldn't do any underhanded horsetrading with Dallas, would he?" she asked.

Brady shook his head. "Not at all. Jake's an honest man. And he's damned good with horses. But he's hell with the ladies. His motto should be too many women and not enough time."

Lass chuckled knowingly. "Seems like I once knew another man around here that was described as a ladies' man."

Wrapping his arm around the back of her waist, he snuggled her close to his side. "Yeah. But that was before I found the love of my life."

She smiled dreamily up at him. "That's probably all that Jake needs to cure his roaming ways—to find the love of his life."

Bending his head, he pressed a kiss on her forehead. "You could be right. After all, you certainly cured me."

Lass said, "Well, if I'd known you were so concerned about Dallas's virtue, I could have made a trip with her to Jake's place this morning. Just to act as chaperone."

Brady laughed. "Oh, no! I'm not that worried about my big sister." With his arm curved possessively around her shoulders, he urged her in the direction of the house. "We both have the day off today and I'm going to take you shopping."

"Shopping!" She shot him a wry look. "You don't care anything about shopping!"

"I do when I go with a purpose. And Christmas is coming. We have all sorts of gifts to buy."

As they continued on toward the house, a dreamy expression drifted over her face. It would be her first Christmas as Brady's wife and this morning she'd learned she was going to be giving him a special gift. Now she was waiting for the right moment to tell him.

"Oh, well, I'd better get my thinking cap on," she told him. "Because I don't have a clue as what to buy you."

He chuckled. "Forget about getting me a gift. I'm a man who has everything."

Lass only smiled.

At the house, they warmed themselves with short cups of coffee, then climbed the stairs to the bedroom they shared. While Brady showered, Lass changed into a long black peasant skirt and topped it with a bright red sweater.

After she'd brushed her hair loose on her shoulders and attached sparkling earrings to her ears, she walked over to the plate glass door leading out to the balcony. This morning the sky was overcast with high gray clouds. Every now and then tiny bits of snow flew through the air.

Already the mountains surrounding the ranch were capped with white and Ruidoso was full of skiers come to enjoy the fresh powder on Sierra Blanca. For Lass, becoming accustomed to the high mountain climate had taken some getting used to. Already the area had been doused with several inches of snow, but she'd learned to dress for the cold and enjoy the winter season. Just as she was learning to be a Donovan and take pleasure in being part of a big family.

Thankfully, even distant Conall had accepted and welcomed her in his own stern way. She felt truly at home now, yet there were moments like this morning, when she'd used the pregnancy test, that she ached to have her mother back with her. There were so many things she wished she could tell her. Like how happy Brady had made her, how much she loved him and how much he loved her. She longed to tell her about her work at the stables, about all the horses she'd grown so attached to, the lovely children who looked to her for help and guidance. And she also wanted Judith to know that her marriage to Ward had not been a complete failure.

These past few months, Lass had tried to open her heart and her mind to her father. They'd had several lengthy talks over the phone and she was beginning to realize that, in spite of his mistakes, Ward had loved his family. After David had pled guilty to his crimes and was sentenced with jail time, her father had taken a new turn with his life. He'd seemed to suddenly realize that he needed to change, to take time for the things that are most important. He'd completely cut ties with Jane and hired a new assistant to fill David's vacancy. He was even coming out to the Diamond D for a visit during the Christmas holiday and this time Lass was actually looking forward to seeing him.

Forgiveness was not an easy thing, she thought, but it was the right thing. She could see that now. And how could she not forgive, when she'd been blessed with so much happiness?

Behind her, she heard the door to the walk-in closet open, then close. Glancing over her shoulder, she saw Brady shrugging into a dark green shirt that made his tawny hair look even more like a wild lion's mane.

Her eyes full of pleasure, she watched him button the shirt as he walked toward her.

"My, my, you're looking too pretty this morning to be going out with a guy like me. Maybe I'd better go back to the closet and pick out something a little fancier than this ol' shirt."

Turning, she reached to fasten the button in the middle of his chest. "I don't want you to change anything. You happen to look very handsome in this shirt."

Smiling, he bent his head and placed a soft kiss on her lips. "Spoken like a true, loving wife."

"I am a true, loving wife."

"You don't have to convince me of that. But you do need to tell me what you'd like for Christmas. I want to give you something really special. Something you'll love for a long time."

Love swelled in her chest. It didn't matter what sort of gifts Brady gave her. The love he put behind them was the thing that made them precious to her.

"Now what are you planning to give me? You don't have to tell me outright. Give me a little hint and let me guess first."

Dimples carved her cheeks as she gazed up at him. "Well, it's already ordered. But I can't tell you precisely what the gift will be until it gets here."

"Hmm. That sounds intriguing."

"More like shocking," she replied as she struggled to keep an ecstatic smile from breaking across her face.

He arched a skeptical brow at her. "Okay, now you've done it. Why can't you tell me—precisely? Because you want it to be a surprise?"

Chuckles bubbled in her throat. "No. Because I wasn't able to make an exact order. I had to leave it up to God to make the final decision. And that's a fifty-fifty tossup. I can only tell you that it will either be a little deputy or a little cowgirl."

Confusion puckered his features and then suddenly it all fell in place. Stunned elation swept over his face as he grabbed her by the shoulders.

"A baby?" he asked incredulously. "You're telling me that we have a baby coming?"

Once Lass nodded, he threw back his head and howled with glee.

"Oh, darling! You've made me the happiest man alive!" Bending his head, he kissed her, then kissed her again. "How will I ever be able to top this Christmas gift you've given me?"

Her eyes misty, she smiled at him. "Oh, I don't know, try for another one next Christmas, I suppose."

Laughing, he ran out of the room and onto the landing. "Hey everybody, come here and listen to this!" he shouted at the top of his lungs. "We're going to have a baby!"

Her heart overflowing with love, Lass left the room to help her husband spread the news.

* * * * *

First published in Great Britain 2011
by Mills & Boon, an imprint of Harlequin (UK) Limited,
Eton House, 18-24 Paradise Road, Richmond, Surrey TW9 1SR

ISBN: 978 0 263 88904 8

23-0811

Harlequin (UK) policy is to use papers that are natural, renewable and recyclable products and made from wood grown in sustainable forests. The logging and manufacturing processes conform to the legal environmental regulations of the country of origin.

Printed and bound in Spain
by Blackprint CPI, Barcelona

Dear Reader,

Pleasant Valley, New York, is a very real place that's near and dear to my heart. And while this quaint town has grown up in the years since I've spent time there, it's a place filled with warm memories and wonderful people living life to the fullest.

Her Second Chance Cop combines my love of action and suspense with the very thing I love best about Cherish™—falling in love while dealing with the struggles and issues women know intimately. For Riley, returning to Pleasant Valley means facing a devastating loss and finding her footing as a single parent. She accepts those challenges and comes face to face with a few others she hadn't anticipated. That's life. Learning to roll with the punches. Riley does and in the process learns to live, and love, again. Life is too precious to waste a second.

Ordinary women. Extraordinary romance.

I hope you enjoy Riley and Scott's love story. I love hearing from readers so visit me at www.jeanielondon.com.

Peace and blessings,

Jeanie London

To the real Camille and Jake
because I love you both so very much ;-)

Jeanie London writes romance because she believes in happily-ever-afters. Not the "love conquers all" kind, but the "we love each other so we can conquer anything" kind. Which is why she loves Cherish™—stories about real women tackling real life to fall in love. She makes her home in sunny Florida with her romance-hero husband, their two beautiful and talented daughters and a menagerie of strays.

PROLOGUE

SHE KISSED MIKE GOODBYE, arms still immersed to the elbows in soapy dishwater at the kitchen sink. The twins hopped up from the table, eager to make the daily pilgrimage to the porch to see Daddy off to work. Mike, the twins, even the dogs, clustered around her, surrounding her as if she was the sun in their universe. Seraphic chaos, Mike always called it, and she could practically hear those unspoken words when he handed her the dish towel. A perfect moment.

"Got to run," he said.

Without another word, she herded the troops toward the door. He needed to get out early to make court on time, and the traffic getting into downtown Poughkeepsie could be hellish. Judge Callahan ran an orderly courtroom, and Mike didn't want to be late the day he'd be taking the stand. Not when he and Scott had worked for over a year to collar the gang leader on trial.

"Good luck," she said once they made it to the porch, lifting her face for another quick kiss. "You'll be great."

He met her gaze with a deeply amused look as if he'd known she wouldn't say anything else, and that he appreciated how she always thought he was great. No matter what.

Then he scooped up the twins, one in each arm, because at three they were still small enough for him to do that. She wondered what he'd do when they grew too big. Pick up Camille first because she was the princess and the oldest by twenty-two minutes? Or Jake, his little guy? Knowing Mike, he'd take turns and always manage to remember who went first.

Now they'd never know for sure.

Letting her eyes drift shut, Riley blocked out reality for another desperate instant, clinging to the details of that morning, details that had been looping in her head nonstop until she couldn't sleep, eat, *feel*.

Had it only been days since life had been normal?

"Riley," a voice prompted, forcing her back to reality.

Opening her eyes, she found Chief Levering extending a neatly folded American flag. He didn't offer condolences to the widow. He didn't have the words. She knew it, recognized the grief he bore in the worn lines on his face, the heartbreaking weight of a job that cost more than he had to give.

She wanted to thank him for caring, thank the entire force that had loved and respected Mike. She didn't have the words, either. When she accepted the flag, her hands shook.

The chief stood there a moment longer, finally signaling his men to begin the salute to honor their fallen brother.

A gunshot cracked the silence, then another and another, each exploding before the whine of the previous one had faded. The deafening blasts rattled the morning, should have rattled her. But each came as if from a distance, the volume almost too low to make out.

She was disconnected, numb, the only person left alive on the planet though a thousand people surrounded her, fanned out in every direction from the grave site. But they were just background noise, too. Not one of those people could come between her and the reality of that gaping hole in the ground.

Not one could come between her and the extravagant flower sprays with their blossoms so jarringly alive, the bright colors violent against the misty gray morning.

Not one could come between her and her husband's wooden casket, polished to a high gloss that reflected her image, an image as disjointed as she felt.

Had it been only days since Riley Angelica's dream had become a nightmare?

CHAPTER ONE

Two years later

"DADDY'S HERE?" Camille sounded unsure, so Riley glanced in the rearview mirror to find her daughter peering through the minivan window with a disbelieving expression.

Despite grief counseling, Camille's idea of a cemetery clearly wasn't lining up with the sight of lush forest and crowded gravestones whizzing past.

"Daddy's in heaven," Riley prompted. "Remember what we talked about with Ms. Jo-Ellyn? This is his special place on earth so we can visit him whenever we want."

"Like God at church," Jake explained, the caring brother.

"That's exactly right, sweet pea." Riley caught her son's gaze in the mirror and gave him a smile. "We can always talk to God because He's everywhere, but church is His special place."

Jake nodded slowly, looking so serious that Riley knew he wasn't convinced about this cemetery business, either. Tough little guy was just looking after his "girls." She didn't think he could actually remember when his daddy had charged him with that responsibility….

"You're the man around here while I'm gone," Mike had always said. *"Take care of our girls for me."*

Obviously Jake had been affected on some level. One thing Riley had learned during the past two years of grief counseling was that the human mind had an amazing capacity to cling to long-ago details. She also knew caring for "his girls" was a big responsibility for a five-year-old.

She maneuvered the minivan down one of the narrow paths winding through St. Peter's Cemetery. Left. Left. Right. Left. She made each turn as if she'd just visited the grave site yesterday.

Her mind definitely had an amazing capacity for the past.

In some ways Riley felt as if she'd lived a lifetime since that last time she'd been here. Yet she didn't even have to close her eyes to see the place as it had looked then. Stark during that bleak time of year before spring breathed even a hint of promise. Just mere months after Mike's death, when she'd finally accepted she wasn't going to forge through the healing process like the strong widow.

Riley had intended to deal with grief head-on. She knew it would be hard, the hardest thing she'd ever tackled in her life, but she was practical and had every reason in the world to cope with this unexpected turn their lives had taken.

Two very precious reasons—both securely strapped in the back seat of the van.

Much like Jake felt the responsibility of caring for his girls, Riley's responsibility was to care for the family in Mike's absence, to make their dreams happen even though he wouldn't be with them.

It had never even occurred to her that the healing process wouldn't be hers to manage and control, that the process had a mind and a will all its own.

The Law Enforcement Support Network provided a variety of services for family members who'd lost loved ones in the line of duty. She'd read every word of the literature, followed every counselor's suggestion, listened attentively to other grieving folks in the support group. She'd accepted the help of loving family and friends though her inclination was to put on a determined smile and tell everyone, "I'm good. It's all good."

She hadn't been good at all.

It had taken months to accept that fact, months to realize that her decision to grieve in a healthy fashion for herself and her kids didn't matter. Not when everywhere Riley turned she'd been bombarded by memories of Mike, their wonderful life together and all the dreams they'd made for the future.

Riley could barely stand to be inside the house. She couldn't sleep. She couldn't eat. She couldn't concentrate long enough to write a 1200-word article. No matter how hard she tried, she simply couldn't believe that Mike wasn't coming home. Ever.

Part of the problem, she knew, had been the investigation. While Mike had managed to kill his murderer on the courthouse steps, there'd been other gang members who had organized the shooting behind the scenes, a revenge killing against the cop responsible for building the case that would send one of their own to prison. Mike's partner and the entire police department had been determined to bring down each and every one.

Even if she could have avoided the newspaper headlines and television and radio sound bites, she would have had to burn the city to the ground to avoid the reminders of gang graffiti on street signs and bus stops and the sides of buildings.

Every time Riley drove through downtown Poughkeepsie—and her job as a reporter for the *Mid-Hudson Herald* brought her there often—she'd witness the visible displays of anger and violence that had cost Mike his life.

In that fragile emotional state, she hadn't wanted to make decisions about selling their farmhouse in Pleasant Valley, Mike's twenty-five-acre dream home for the horses he loved.

Fortunately she hadn't had to. Their college-age nephew had become caretaker as a way to move out of his family home since he hadn't earned scholarships for dorm housing.

Riley had made arrangements to stay with her mother and stepfather in Florida. On that long-ago day, she'd come to the cemetery on her way out of town to apologize to Mike for abandoning their life until she could figure out some way to heal and go on. But Florida wasn't meant to be forever, and now she and the kids were coming home.

Steering the van off the path, she came to a stop in the grass so a car could squeeze past if one happened along, not that she could see another living soul around. The place was quiet, but with that lively silence of summer. Birds twittered. Insects chirped. Fat squirrels scampered around trees. Though there wasn't much of a breeze, leaves rustled sharply as a squirrel leaped in a daredevil arc from one branch to another.

These antics of nature were familiar reminders of the life they'd left behind in Florida. A life spent largely outdoors with play group visits to parks and the beach. The twins couldn't remember the reality of an upstate New York winter, and Riley hoped the novelty of snow would ease their transition through the upcoming, and unfamiliar, season changes.

"We're here." She forced a brightness into her voice she didn't quite feel and turned the key in the ignition. "Let's grab the things we made for Daddy."

She'd barely gotten the words out of her mouth before seat belts snapped open, the minivan door rattled on its hinges and sneakers hit the ground, ready to run.

She didn't bother repeating her direction, didn't stand a chance against the twins' curiosity and excitement. She just said, "Hang on," while retrieving the backpack from the floor of the van.

"Where is he?" Camille scanned the sea of gravestones impatiently.

Riley handed her daughter a bouquet of bright tissue-paper flowers and her son the Popsicle-stick frame showcasing him displaying the foot-long bass he'd caught on his latest fishing excursion with Grandpa Joel.

"Follow me." She directed them down a winding path, careful not to tread on other folks' resting places. Her two high-energy little kids grew eerily quiet.

"Here we are," she finally said, placing a hand on each small shoulder as they gathered around Mike's grave.

Riley couldn't bring herself to look down, not yet, so she watched her kids instead, the sun glinting off their pale blond heads as she tried to gauge their reactions.

Jake frowned intently, the spattering of freckles across his nose crinkling with the effort. Camille's crystal-blue eyes took in every detail, and she could barely contain her need to move, a need that had her bouncing up on her tiptoes excitedly.

As fraternal twins, Jake and Camille resembled each other as any brother and sister might, but they were entirely their own little people. While both were towheaded with fair skin that held enough of Mike's Italian heritage to let them tan to a deep golden brown, they had distinctly different features. Jake's eyes were a deep, almost sapphire blue while Camille's were startlingly light, the sparkly blue of ice.

The last time Mike had seen them they'd been adorable three-year-olds. Not quite kids, but no longer babies, either.

Now they were all kid, each with his and her own personality and opinions, both raring to get out into the world, which at this age meant kindergarten—the very reason Riley had decided now was the time to come home and get settled.

Unsurprisingly, Camille was the one to make the first move. She launched forward with a hop-skip and sank down in front of the headstone, propping her bright bouquet against it.

"Hi, Daddy," she said in her singsong lilt. "I made this for you at Chiefie school. Jakie made one, too, but Ryan knocked over his juice bag and grape juice squirted all over it. The flowers melted on the table."

"Ms. Kayleigh said it wasn't my fault so it was okay," Jake added in a hasty defense, taking a few tentative steps toward his sister.

Chiefie school had actually been a child-care class in a public high school. The program was designed to give student teachers hands-on experience in child care while gearing up preschoolers for kindergarten. Since Chamberlain High School's mascot was a Native American chief, the preschoolers had been known as chiefies. With four student teachers caring for each little chiefie, the mornings the twins attended the program had been filled with structured fun and a lot of caring attention.

"Here, Jakie. Give Daddy your present." Camille mothered her twin every step of the way, even reaching out to take the frame he held tightly in both hands. Jake pulled away and held it away from her. Camille just shrugged, familiar with her brother's unwillingness to accept help, and told her daddy, "Jakie made you a frame for his fish picture."

"It was a bass, Camille," Jake corrected, still clearly put out that she'd tried to take his gift. Slanting his gaze toward the headstone, he steeled his nerves and said, "Grandpa

Joel said it was the biggest bass in the lake, and he showed me how to bend the hook so his mouth didn't have a big hole when we threw him back in."

The thought of Mike watching this show from heaven helped Riley shift her gaze down to the headstone, too.

Michael Jacob Angelica
Beloved Husband and Father
4/4/1975—2/2/2008
Always in our hearts

She'd chosen that tombstone for the simple design. Two angels poised on top, wings touching to create an arch over the marble memorial. That was the only ornamentation other than the inscription, and somehow seeing those words brought all the expectation she'd tried not to feel, all the anxiety that had been building to fruition. Riley exhaled a deep sigh.

Mike's place was peaceful.

Taking a step forward, she ran her fingers along the smooth arch of an angel's wing, felt the warm marble beneath her touch. A headstone that marked the resting place of the man she'd loved with all her heart. Then she noticed the bottle of Guinness Stout propped against the side of the headstone.

And smiled.

That would be a gift from Scott Emerson, Mike's partner on the vice squad of the Poughkeepsie Police Department, a longtime friend and drinking buddy. Since the label wasn't weathered, Riley guessed this unusual memento must be a recent addition. Leave it to Scott to continue the friendship despite death. That quiet loyalty had always been a part of her husband's partner and friend.

"Mommy, aren't you going to say hi to Daddy?" Camille asked.

"Hi, Daddy," Riley said softly, brushing aside a cluster of tiny leaves from an angel's wing. "We miss you."

"He knows that, silly." Camille rolled her eyes. "We tell him when we say our good-night prayers."

"So, Camille," Jake shot back. "He still likes to hear it."

"Oh, shut up, Jake."

"Camille," Riley cautioned.

"He's grouchy."

No argument there. Riley shifted her gaze to her son, assessing whether or not the emotional letdown was the cause of this mood swing.

Jake shifted from one foot to the other, clutching his picture frame against his tummy. "I'm starving, Mom. We haven't eaten in forever."

Riley bit back a smile at the exaggeration. Apparently now that his apprehension about the situation had been dealt with, Jake's mind was back on the priorities.

Camille pivoted on her sneakers and raced back to the minivan. "I'll get the cooler. We can have a picnic with Daddy."

That wasn't exactly what Riley had had in mind while making peanut butter and jelly sandwiches in their Maryland hotel room this morning, but a picnic with Daddy sounded like just the thing to kick off their return home. And with the canopy of leaves filtering the sunlight overhead, Mike's grave was the perfect place to take a deep breath before gearing up for the next big challenge.

Facing the house and the memories.

Riley took that deep breath, then sidled close to Jake. He'd inherited her hair color but Mike's cowlicks, and his thick blond hair always wanted to stand up like a rooster's whenever it started to grow out from a cut. She ruffled her fingers through it, making it spike even more.

"Mom," he groused, ducking away.

Riley smiled above his head where he couldn't see her. "Are you going to tell Daddy about your bass? Grandpa Joel was really proud of you. He said you reeled in that big boy like a pro."

Jake frowned down at the headstone, at the bright bouquet there. Riley didn't rush him, just slipped an arm around his shoulders when he glanced down at his photo.

"I miss Grandpa Joel," he said.

"I know, sweet pea. Do you want to call him after we get home? He and Granny want to know that we made it safely."

Jake nodded, still clutched his photo.

Riley's father had been a career naval officer, a larger-than-life man as fast to laugh as he'd been to issue orders. He'd died during Riley's sophomore year in high school, and her mom hadn't remarried until Riley's sophomore year at Vassar College, the year she'd met Mike, who'd been playing rent-a-cop at a campus concert.

Riley's stepfather was an Oklahoma farm boy who was as laid-back as Riley's father had been intense. There was no question why Mom had fallen in love with him. Not only was Joel charming, but as senior VP of international relations for a Fortune 500 company, his travel schedule was more active than Riley's dad's had been. Mom got antsy if she stayed in one place too long.

Riley had no doubt that her military upbringing was the very reason she was so set on rearing her kids in one place. In the States. Overseas. You name it, and if Riley hadn't actually lived there, she'd probably visited at some time or another during her early life.

Grandpa Joel had stepped in as the man in Jake's life

whenever he was in town, inviting her son along in the mornings and evenings to help water the yard. He'd taught Jake how to plant and tend tomatoes, how to fish and how to tell the difference between venomous and friendly snakes.

As if any snake could be friendly.

"Is Grandpa Joe as nice as Grandpa Joel?"

Camille reappeared and plunked down the soft-sided cooler. "Grandpa Joe and Grandpa Joel. That sounds funny."

"It does, doesn't it?" Riley laughed, knelt down and unzipped the cooler. "Camille, would you please grab the beach blanket. Then we can sit and have a real picnic."

Her daughter took off again like a bolt, granting Riley a few private moments to deal exclusively with her son—alone time was always a challenge with twins.

"Don't you remember how much fun we had at the Magic Kingdom when Grandpa Joe and Grandma Rosie came to visit? You liked them both then."

Jake nodded.

"Grandpa Joe was a lot of fun. You told me you liked looking for shells on the beach with him. He was the only one who'd climb up those scary nets with you in the tree house at Busch Gardens."

That got a smile.

"His feet kept poking through the holes."

Oh, Riley remembered, all right. She'd been convinced the next ride they were going to take was in an ambulance on the way to the emergency room because her father-in-law had been determined to keep up with his grandkids.

Joe had wanted to make memories, he'd told her, inadvertently driving home the point that by leaving New York Riley had taken away the only remaining connection to his son. Until then, leaving hadn't felt like running away, only an unavoidable necessity. But her father-in-law's comments made her realize the time had come to decide where she wanted to raise the kids, to get them settled before school started.

In her heart she'd known the time had come to go home. And home was the Mid-Hudson Valley, where Mike had lived his entire life, surrounded by his family and friends.

It was all his children would ever have of him.

Slipping an arm around Jake's shoulders, she squeezed. "Sweet pea, Daddy will understand if you've changed your mind about the picture. A reminder of your big bass would be nice, but he doesn't need it. He already knows you caught the biggest fish in the lake because he's keeping his eyes on us from heaven. I know he's really proud of you."

Jake slanted his gaze her way, indecision written all over his face. He glanced down at the photo then at the headstone. She knew the instant he'd made his decision because he squared his shoulders and set his mouth in a firm line.

So like his daddy.

"I want Daddy to have this," Jake said. "Then he won't ever forget how big my bass was."

Riley pressed a kiss to the top of his spiky head and said, "Go ahead, then. Give it to him."

She watched him cover the distance in two determined steps and position the photo frame carefully beside the tissue-flower bouquet. Add the beer bottle and Mike's grave made a festive sight. She'd bring along some mementos of her own next visit.

"I want the cherry juice bag," Camille shouted on her return, the blanket a haphazard tumble in her arms, ends trailing in a threat to those little feet.

Riley launched forward and hauled the blanket from her arms. "Thanks, little helper girl. I'll spread this out while you get those juice bags, okay?"

Camille obliged while Riley settled the blanket, trying to avoid picnicking on top of Mike or his neighbor. She finally managed an acceptable compromise, and as the kids tussled over who got the only cherry yogurt stick, Riley decided that she'd probably be too busy dealing with life as a single working parent to spend too much time obsessing about the past.

She hoped.

CHAPTER TWO

SCOTT EMERSON PUSHED out from under the pickup, the wheels of the floor dolly grinding over the concrete beneath him. Setting aside the wrench, he wiped sweat from his brow and glanced through the open garage doorway where Brian had gone outside to take a phone call on his cell. Scott didn't blame him. It was hotter than hell in this garage, despite the industrial fans whirring overhead.

He sat up to give his back a break from spending too damn long under the antiquated truck used to transport hay for the horses. Why the kid had waited until the last minute to load the hay was beyond understanding. A few days earlier and a broken pickup wouldn't have been a crisis situation.

Scott squelched his annoyance by taking a cooling swig of water. Brian was a twenty-year-old kid who'd been shouldering a lot of responsibility around the farm since his uncle had died. While both Brian's maturity and foresightedness could use some fine-tuning, he'd been remarkably reliable. And that was saying something. Four horses were a lot of work.

After eavesdropping on half the conversation, Scott wasn't surprised when Brian snapped shut the cell and announced, "Aunt Riley just passed Purple Parlor."

"About ten minutes, then."

Brian nodded, uncharacteristically subdued, and Scott couldn't tell if the kid was relieved to be getting some help around here or depressed not to have the house to himself anymore. At Brian's age it was probably a good measure of both.

Scott motioned toward the truck. "Crank her up. Let's see if we got it."

Brian circled the flatbed with a few easy strides and climbed into the cab. He'd been a kid when first offering to help out at the farm after Mike's death. Two years of tending horses and baling hay, and Scott had to wonder if Riley would even recognize her nephew.

The engine roared to life, growling loudly in the lazy afternoon heat.

"All right, Scott." Brian goosed the accelerator for good measure, sending a blast of heated exhaust from the tailpipe.

Tossing the wrench into the toolbox, Scott got to his feet. "Don't wait until the last minute next time." He tapped on the hood with a palm. "Give this old girl a break. Leave yourself some time in case she's having a bad day."

Brian shut off the engine and stepped out, saying, "I know. I couldn't deal with the hay until I finished cramming for a test in Anthropology."

Yeah, right. Always an excuse. Brian was going to do things his own way because he was twenty and he could.

After hanging the keys on a hook above the workbench, Brian cast a forlorn look at the steps leading to the upstairs apartment.

His new home.

"What do you think about moving into the apartment?" Scott asked. "Beats knocking around that big old house by yourself."

Brian scowled, and Scott guessed nothing could be further from the truth.

"It's a bachelor pad with everything a college guy needs," Scott added. "Kitchen. Heat. Private entrance."

"Aunt Riley watching over me."

True. She could glance out any east window to see what her nephew was up to. And knowing Riley, she would. Often.

"I think your aunt will have her hands full enough with the twins to spend too much time worrying about you."

"You think?"

"The twins are starting school so, yeah, I think."

Brian didn't look reassured, and Scott conceded that the garage apartment was a demotion from having a 150-year-old farmhouse to himself, but he couldn't feel too bad. Lots of kids would think Brian had a sweet setup. College. Tending horses in exchange for room and board. Too many kids of Scott's acquaintance would have given their left nut for a shot at college if it meant hauling ripe trash.

Scott dropped the subject. "You going to tell me when you want the posse to work on the yard or should I ask your aunt?"

"I'll tell you," Brian said quickly. "I don't want her thinking she doesn't need me around anymore."

There was the real trouble. Brian was worried about his meal ticket. Good. Worry might motivate him to get organized. Riley didn't need to add another kid to her brood.

"Let me grab my things and I'm out of here," Scott said. "Just call me if the old girl acts up again."

"You should stay. Don't you want to see Aunt Riley?"

"Your grandmother told me she warned everyone not to bombard Riley until she had a chance to get settled."

"There are only two of us, Scott. That's not bombarding."

The kid wanted backup, plain and simple. "I'll stay long enough to say hi."

"Pound it." Brian raised his fist in the air.

Scott pounded Brian's fist in a familiar salutation just as a white minivan slowed on the road before making the turn into the circular drive.

The Angelica family had come home.

Scott reached for the degreaser and a rag to clean his hands as the minivan doors burst open and kids hopped out.

For a moment, he stared, frozen with the rag trapped between his fingers, surprised by the jolt of emotion he felt. These were not the chubby children who used to trail behind Mike while he performed chores in the barn.

These were kids in every sense of the word, from lanky bodies that appeared to be growing with rapid-fire speed to energetic curiosity that had them taking in everything all at once. If not for the blond hair that was bleached almost white against their Florida tans, they'd be unrecognizable from the toddlers Mike had been so crazy about.

Until Scott took a closer look.

Mike was all over these kids. The boy—Jake—came to a screeching stop the instant he saw Brian. Folding his arms over his chest, he gazed out of Mike's eyes with a thin-lipped expression Scott had seen too many times not to recognize. The kid took in the lay of the land with the same deliberation that had made his father such a good cop and trusted partner. Mike had never missed a beat, which was why no one but he and the shooter had died in front of the courthouse that day.

Camille, on the other hand, clearly the more social twin, propelled herself forward on sneakers with wheeled soles, riding to a smooth stop in front of Brian. "Are you my cousin who takes care of Daddy's horses?"

"Yeah," Brian said. "You remember how to ride them?"

Camille might look more like Riley with her delicate features and light eyes, but the look she shot her cousin was pure Mike. "I don't turn six for two months."

She held up two fingers to emphasize her words in case Brian was too thick to understand what she meant. Scott was definitely too thick to understand.

Maybe she was too young to remember living here?

"I'll teach you." Brian seemed to get it. "On Baby. She's the sweetest."

Camille squealed excitedly, while her brother noticed Scott inside the garage. Jake narrowed his gaze and stood his ground, glancing at his sister to make sure she didn't need help.

Scott tossed aside the rag, about to join the party, when the driver door opened and Riley emerged from the van. Mike used to joke that the day he'd met Riley was the day he'd figured out dreams really did come true. It was one of those statements that could have sounded so corny but never did.

Because Mike meant what he'd said.

Scott, and anyone who'd ever been around Mike and Riley together, had understood Riley was the kind of woman to stand beside a man and help him make his dreams come true. And Mike was the kind of guy who appreciated a wife who believed in him.

Sure, it hadn't hurt that she was drop-dead gorgeous, too, long and lean with a head full of wild blond hair.

"You know my wife, Riley," Mike used to say. *"The one with hair bigger than she is."*

Ironically her hair did seem bigger than she did right now. Dressed casually in long shorts and a short-sleeved blouse, she didn't appear to notice any of them while pausing with her hand on the door as if she needed to hang on for support. She stared at the house, looking lost in her memories.

Scott could only stand there, galvanized by the sight of her. The monthly phone conversations they'd had during the past two years hadn't prepared him for seeing her again.

Or for feeling this forgotten but all-too-familiar awareness.

Scott had been telling himself that Mike's death had changed everything, helped him overcome an unwanted desire for a woman he had no business having.

He'd been wrong.

Riley's voice coming at him over a bouncing satellite signal had only placed distance between them, and distance only masked the symptom. The problem was still there. He supposed that shouldn't surprise him, given who he was.

But he was surprised. The moment stretched forever. He practically held his breath, waiting. He had no clue for what, but he did know that the only thing he could control in life was the choices he made. A valuable and hard-won lesson. He'd already made this choice. Long ago.

No man he'd want to know would covet a friend's wife. Period. The words echoed from a barely remembered youth, when he'd had someone who'd cared enough to point out the differences between right and wrong.

A young voice blessedly shattered the stillness. "Mommy, can my cousin teach me to ride Baby?"

Riley turned to her daughter. "We'll see, sweetie." She moved away from the van, all smiles for her nephew. "Brian, ohmigosh, what happened? You're all grown-up."

Before the kid could get away, he was wrapped in his aunt's arms and hugged exuberantly.

Scott found himself breathing a little easier as Brian mumbled some incoherent greeting and started to blush.

Riley and the twins looked as if they'd been on an

extended vacation with their tans and summer clothing, but Scott knew these past two years hadn't been any kind of holiday for Riley. Their phone conversations had revealed how hard she'd been struggling after Mike's death. He could see evidence of that struggle etched behind her smile now. She was thinner. And that tan didn't hide the shadowed circles around her eyes.

Why had she come home to face the past instead of starting fresh somewhere new? And a town where the sun shone most of the year sounded perfect. He knew firsthand time couldn't erase the stink from some places, which was why he'd put New Jersey behind him.

Poughkeepsie had once been his fresh start.

"Come here, Jake." Riley finally let up her death grip on her nephew. "Come meet your cousin Brian."

Jake dutifully stepped forward and extended a gentlemanly hand. "I'm Jake."

Brian shook, looking amused.

"Where are the ducks, Mommy?" Camille wanted to know. "You said there were ducks. Can I go see them?"

"I'll take you down to the pond in a minute." Riley glanced around and spotted him. "Scott."

She hadn't expected to see him, he could tell, but her smile flashed fast and real. He shook off the last thought of anything that was unworthy of a man greeting his friend's long-absent wife and met her halfway.

"Welcome home" was all he had a chance to say before she was taking his hands and leaning up on tiptoes to press a kiss to his cheek.

"What are you doing here?" she asked.

He inclined his head toward the garage. "Pickup decided not to show up for work today. I dropped by to give Brian a hand."

"Come here, kids. Come meet…" She hesitated, shooting him a quirky look, then said, "Uncle Scott."

Scott managed a smile. Uncle worked for him. Gave him a proper place in their lives, a place with clear-cut boundaries. His own upbringing hadn't prepared him for the reality of loving families, so he learned on the fly.

"Hey, you guys have grown up since the last time I saw you. At first I thought you were Brian's friends from college."

That scored him a few points, with Camille, at least. She giggled, gifting him with a beaming smile before bolting away to see what was around the side of the house. Jake hung close to Riley and eyed him warily. Or protectively, Scott decided.

"There's a problem with the truck?" Riley asked.

"Don't worry, Aunt Riley," Brian said quickly. "Scott fixed it, and I was just headed down to load the hay."

Riley didn't blink, but Scott got the impression she caught pretty much everything Brian hadn't said. Giving Scott's hands a squeeze, she released her grip and mouthed the words *Thank you* while turning toward Brian.

"Get going, then," she told her nephew. "Don't let us keep you. We're going to take our time unloading our stuff and getting settled."

Brian looked ready to bolt, but before he could manage a getaway, Riley asked, "Where are you staying?"

"I moved my stuff over the garage."

She nodded thoughtfully, not bothering to hide a wistful smile. "My best arguments didn't change your mind, hmm?"

The kid didn't meet her gaze. "Well, you know… It's your house and all."

Riley chuckled. Stepping forward, she gave him another quick hug. "I do know. You're older now, and you like your independence. Just promise me you'll pop in now and then."

Brian nodded, and Scott guessed the kid would be showing up whenever he got hungry.

"You want some help?" Brian asked.

Riley shook her head. "Thanks, but no thanks. If you've got to get hay, then the horses win. We don't have too much to unload. Just enough to keep us going until the moving company drops off our boxes. There weren't too many of those, either. The Angelica family travels light."

She sounded all breezy, but Scott didn't miss the subtext that seemed to suggest that traveling from her home was a skill she could have lived without.

"Hey, can the kids come?" Brian asked. "We can get some corn to feed the ducks after I'm done with the hay."

"You're just loading?" Riley asked.

"Please, Mommy." Camille circled Riley on those wheeled sneakers before Brian even got a chance to reply. "I want to feed the ducks with my cousin."

"Your cousin's name is Brian."

"I want to go with Brian. Jakie, you want to go, too, don't you?" Camille gave her brother a sly look, trying to implicate him in her efforts.

This twin was a total live wire, Scott decided, and for a moment, he thought her brother might resist on principle. But Jake finally nodded, a willing accomplice.

"I'm just loading," Brian said. "They can help me bale."

"Okay, but you two ride in the cab and share the seat belt. Got that?" Riley knelt down so she was eye level with her twins. "You won't be going out on the road, but it gets bumpy riding down to the barn. It's really important that you listen to what Brian says and don't wander off. Okay?"

Both kids nodded. Riley gave them each a quick kiss, then said to Brian, "They haven't had being-around-horses 101 yet. They can help you bale, but that's it." She patted the cell phone attached to her waist. "Any problems and you call. I'll come down and get them. Got it?"

Brian placed a hand on each twin's shoulder, clearly eager to prove his trustworthiness. "No problem, Aunt Riley."

She said, "Have fun, then, and no fighting," but the words were barely out of her mouth before the twins were chasing Brian to the garage.

Riley watched thoughtfully as they clambered into the cab, and Brian made a dramatic display of strapping in the kids. Then he fired up the engine and drove out of the garage, him and his excited passengers waving as they passed.

Riley chuckled. "That poor kid doesn't have a clue what he's in for. The top of his head's going to blow off. Camille never stops talking."

"They're a handful." That wasn't a question.

She rolled her eyes. "High energy. I don't know who they take after."

She looked serious, and Scott bit back a smile. He knew exactly who those kids took after. He'd never seen Riley do anything at less than sixty miles an hour.

"Brian can handle it," he said. "He's looking for ways to impress you so you'll know how much you still need him."

"Is he, now?"

Scott nodded.

"That's pretty ironic considering I couldn't have done the past two years without him." She stared after the pickup as it made its way down the dirt drive toward the barn. "I'm impressed by how responsible he's been. I'd have had to sell the place or…"

Come home.

She didn't have to finish that thought.

"You're ready to be back now?" The question was out

of his mouth before he had a chance to assess whether or not he was getting too personal. He was. This wasn't his best buddy, Mike, but Mike's wife. And she looked so vulnerable standing there.

He knew the look, just as he knew the struggle to master unwanted feelings and take a step forward. He hadn't missed how she didn't seem too eager to get inside the house.

"You've been helping out Brian a lot?" she asked.

"Here and there. When he comes up against something unexpected."

She didn't believe him. Scott wasn't sure if his training as a vice cop gave him the edge, or if listening to Mike talk about her all these years gave him an advantage, but he didn't have any trouble reading her.

"It's mutual," he reassured her. "Brian always helps me out when I need him at Renaissance. He gets the volunteer hours for school, so it's win-win. I mentioned that I've had a crew of the Renaissance kids dealing with the yard. They appreciate a steady landscaping gig."

She nodded, sending glossy blond curls tumbling over her shoulders. "The place looks great."

Scott glanced around the yard of the farmhouse, which was situated at the very front end of twenty-five acres, close to the road. Riley was right. The hedges around the house and two-story garage were neatly trimmed, and bright annuals lined the circular drive. The place could have been professionally landscaped, and Scott felt pride. Not of himself but of the street kids who'd earned a place on the landscaping crew.

"Yeah, it does, doesn't it?"

Riley nodded. "I know Brian appreciates the help, too. Dealing with the yard during the summer is a lot to ask on top of the horses."

Scott didn't contradict her, although he knew Brian hadn't ever taken summer classes so the additional workload wouldn't have killed him and would have saved Riley some money. But Scott had been happy to put together a crew that had earned the trust and privilege of being employed for fair wages.

Those opportunities didn't come along easily for former gang members.

Renaissance was a fresh-start program designed to keep inner-city teens off the streets. It began as a Poughkeepsie Police Department program over ten years ago, and Scott had been on board ever since, helping at-risk kids break away from gangs or avoid them altogether. The programs offered kids more productive things to do like getting through school and earning wages for hard work. Things that helped kids build self-esteem and earn the respect of the community.

The program volunteers provided encouraging role models and helped these kids realize they could live the kind of lives that didn't involve gangs, drugs and prison.

Scott thought Riley had been particularly decent to allow the Renaissance kids to come and work on the farm, considering Mike had been killed for his work against a local gang….

"So tell me what's new with you?" she asked.

"Nothing much since we talked, but thanks for asking."

"Nothing at all?"

Scott knew exactly what Riley was avoiding so he obliged. "Chief Levering got another civic award. They had a luncheon to roast him."

"Oh, how nice."

The chief hadn't thought so, but Scott kept that to himself. "And we got a local cosmetic surgeon to sit on the

Renaissance board of trustees. He's been offering free tattoo removal services to the kids."

"Wow. Good for you. That's quite a coup."

Scott nodded. "Rosie warned everyone not to bombard you until you got settled in."

"Did she? Probably afraid they'll scare us off."

"Probably. She and Joe have missed you."

"I know," Riley said softly.

"And the pickup broke down, but we got it running."

She finally met his gaze, laughter sparkling in her eyes. "That's it?"

"That's it."

"I hoped to keep you talking so I could avoid unpacking."

"Figured that part out."

She gave an exaggerated sigh. "It was worth a shot."

Scott gave an equally exaggerated sigh, and she laughed, a sound that rippled through the sunny quiet like bells in the wind. Riley was easy to be around. He'd always loved—*no,* liked that about her.

"Want some help unloading your things?" he asked.

"Only if it's no trouble. There's not really that much."

Scott stared down at her, recognized the strong woman who'd picked up the pieces and returned home to get on with life. But he also glimpsed so much vulnerability in the shadows beneath her eyes, the unaccustomed fragility. He had the wild urge to be the guy to step in and take away her burden, let her rest her head on his shoulder. So not appropriate.

Long before Mike's death, Scott had made a promise to watch over Mike's family if anything ever went south on the streets.

It had been the promise of one partner to another.

It had been the promise of a friend.

Helping Riley and the kids had been easy when they were in Florida. Keeping an eye on the farm. Giving Brian a hand. But now they were home. Scott would have to figure out how best to keep his promise without losing his head. He wouldn't do that to Mike.

With a newfound resolve, Scott anchored himself to his purpose. This was a job he was trained for, and he kept that thought in mind as he held her sparkling gaze.

"No," he said, and he meant it. "It's no trouble at all."

CHAPTER THREE

RILEY CRADLED THE PHONE against her shoulder and cast a panicked glance at the kitchen table, where bread crusts, half-eaten carrots and browning apple slices still graced the kids' lunch plates. The past weeks since arriving back in Pleasant Valley had been hectic to say the least. "I can be there in forty minutes, Max. Will that work?"

"If that's the best you got, darling," Max shot back. "This is about to go down, so get moving or you'll miss the action."

"On my way." Riley disconnected and waited impatiently for a dial tone. Then she called her mother-in-law, hoping—no, praying—Rosie would be available to watch the kids.

"Of course, dear. No problem," Rosie said.

"You're a lifesaver." Riley hung up, taking her first real breath.

She still cradled the receiver against her shoulder while snatching plates from the table. Tipping the remains into the trash, she put the plates in the dishwasher and called, "Code Tasmanian Devil. Use the bathroom and grab your things. Pronto."

Code Tasmanian Devil relayed that Mommy had been called into work, and they all needed to be out the door with fire-drill speed.

Excited shouts echoed from the farthest reaches of the

house, and Riley plunked down the telephone receiver in its base, grateful the kids were still young enough to view rushing out the door as an adventure.

She wanted to brush her teeth, but decided not to take the time; gum would have to suffice. Sailing into the foyer, she snatched up the briefcase she kept beneath the antique bench for such speedy exits.

Recorder?

Check.

Camera?

Check.

Laptop?

Check.

Everything a reporter needed to get the scoop on breaking news. If she got out the door and to Hazard Creek in time.

"How are you guys coming?" she asked as Camille wheeled around the corner, backpack hanging from one shoulder.

Riley pressed a quick kiss to the top of her silky head, smiling at the haphazard ponytail.

"Good girl. Your hair looks lovely. Is that what you were doing in your room?"

Camille nodded, clearly pleased by the praise. "I'm going to do my nails at Grandma and Grandpa's."

"Oh, a manicure. Can't wait to see. Jake, where are you?"

"Coming." He appeared in the hallway in front of his room, hanging on to a CD and looking surly.

This one obviously missed the memo about the adventure and had decided he didn't want to be rushed today. Or maybe he just wasn't in the mood to cooperate. Riley didn't know yet.

"Where's your backpack?"

"In my room."

"Go get it, Jake. Camille's already in the car."

Their lives had degenerated into bags packed and ready for action. Hers with everything she needed to cover a story, the kids' with activities for Grandma's house, along with spare clothes, CDs and DVDs. Fishing bag and tackle box. Dance bag with ballet slippers, acro shoes and leotard. T-ball bag with Jake's uniform, helmet and glove. And she hadn't even packed the schoolbags yet.

That would be next week's project.

Time. There simply wasn't enough of it nowadays.

If Riley could have turned back the clock, she'd have had Mike beside her, running through the checklists. There'd have been no need to rush the kids out the door. She'd always tried to work her schedule around Mike's shifts.

For one striking instant an intense physical feeling of longing swept through her. She missed him so much. She always would. That was the reality. She'd expected to feel this way again, being back home, but to Riley's credit and surprise, she hadn't felt it all that often in the weeks since they'd been home. She was living in the present. She'd come a long way in the two years since his death. Further than she'd thought.

Jake reappeared, and Riley herded him out the door onto the front porch to the tune of: "Go, go, go."

After activating the security system, she made her way to the minivan, where she found her daughter already buckled in and her son hard at work with the CD player.

"Jake." She exhaled his name on one long, exasperated breath. "I'll put in your CD after we get going. Get your seat belt on."

He finally got settled, and Riley glanced at the digital display while cranking up the van.

"Great job, guys. We were out the door in less than five minutes. That's a record."

"Will you buy us Popsicles for our reward?" Jake asked.

Riley slipped on sunglasses and glanced over her shoulder, considering. "If you have any room left in your tummy after Grandma Rosie gets hold of you. If not, we can buy snow cones at the summer festival this weekend."

"Yay." Camille clapped.

That seemed to content her son, too, who quickly moved on to the next order of business. "Turn on the music."

"Please," Riley prompted, looking both ways down Traver Road before pulling out of their driveway.

"Please," he said.

She depressed the power button. The noise that blared from the speakers at an insane volume shot her blood pressure—which was already pretty up there—skyrocketing.

In the time it took to turn down the volume, Riley's head pounded with gravelly rap vocals so hard and raw she hadn't been able to make out a word, just the pulse-pounding beat that threatened to blow off the top of her head.

"What on earth is this?" she asked.

"It's Daddy's."

Riley frowned. "Where did you get it?"

"Daddy's office."

"Not in the case where the others CDs are?" She caught Jake's gaze in the rearview mirror.

He shook his head, and Riley didn't see anything about his freckled face that made her think he wasn't telling the truth.

She cranked up the volume again, enough to make out the words. She'd heard rap music before, but never like this. Crude. Vulgar. Unpolished. As if someone had recorded it in a basement rather than a studio. Definitely not the sort of music appropriate for her almost six-year-old.

In a few measures she heard lyrics she could barely understand. But she got the gist. Criminal activities made to sound cool.

Was it Mike's? More likely Brian's. And hopefully not from anyone he was hanging out with. She couldn't even imagine what her sister-in-law would say. Or worse yet, her brother-in-law, a strict Italian dad in every way. Riley made a mental note to ask Brian about it.

"Why don't we listen to Radio Disney?"

Camille's approval drowned out Jake's complaints, and Riley flipped over to the AM radio station.

"Thanks for compromising, Jake." Grudging though that compliance was. "Mommy's got to work, and I need to collect my thoughts before I get there."

Only her second week back and already she was scrambling to keep up. Thank God they'd come home before school started to settle in. Not that she felt settled yet. Not even close.

She glanced in the rearview mirror again at those sweet faces that meant more to her than anything in the world. They were all rolling with the punches. Trying to, anyway. She needed to take her own advice and work on her spirit of adventure.

Mike's folks didn't live far away, and their house happened to be located in the very direction she needed to go today—the Taconic Parkway. She caught the light at the end of her road and made it to her in-laws' place in less than five minutes. Now if she could just get in and out quickly, she might actually get to Hazard Creek in time to get the story.

"We're here, guys." Riley brought the van to a stop but left the engine idling, hoping to save time. "I know you'll both be good for Grandma and Grandpa."

"Can we call you?" Jake popped open the seat belt and leaned into the front seat to retrieve his CD. He made a last-ditch grab, but Riley stopped him.

"Play your other CDs for Grandma Rosie." Grandma Rosie couldn't watch the kids again if she died of a heart attack from listening to *someone's* idea of music. "You can call me if you need me, sweet pea, but I won't be long. We'll be home in time for dinner."

"Pizza?" Camille asked hopefully.

"Tacos." Healthy ones with beans and lettuce. Riley kept that part to herself.

Camille gave a good-natured shrug and hopped out of the minivan. Riley followed with Jake in her wake just as the front door opened and Rosie appeared.

"Hugs, please. I want hugs from my beautiful family." She extended her arms and wouldn't let the kids pass until they'd been greeted in proper Rosie fashion.

Riley's mother-in-law was a woman who knew what it was to love and to lose what she loved. That experience was etched in the lines on her face, in her warm hugs and in the hope that seemed to glow from the inside out. She was determined to wring every moment of joy from every day, to savor every second as if it was a gift. She'd been that way ever since Riley had met her. She was still that way today. It was a quality Riley had always liked, but one she'd grown truly to admire since Mike's death.

"Give me kisses before you go, guys. I'm not coming in." Riley knelt and gave each kid a big squeezy hug. "Love you bunches. Give Grandpa Joe a kiss for me."

"Grandpa Joe is in the kitchen." Rosie stepped out onto the portico to let the kids pass into the house. "Why don't you go find him then we'll decide what we want to do for fun."

The kids didn't need to be asked twice and disappeared without a backward glance.

"Big assignment?" Rosie asked.

"A scoop that the DEA and HCPD are going in on a crack cookhouse."

Rosie scowled. "I thought you weren't covering this sort of stuff anymore."

"Max's making a spot for me on staff, Rosie. I can't turn down hard news."

"I can't believe he wants you covering that sort of stuff."

Max Downey was an Angelica family friend whose family owned the *Mid-Hudson Herald*.

"I appreciate your concern, Rosie, but I need this job."

Rosie narrowed her gaze but didn't say another word. They both knew jobs weren't so easy to come by in this economy. And as both Rosie and Joe had helped Riley manage Mike's death benefits, they knew better than anyone that Riley's days as a stay-at-home mom in Florida had been numbered.

She gave Rosie a hug. "I can't tell you how much I appreciate your help. Please thank Joe for me."

"I will. But it's our pleasure. You know that."

Riley gave her another squeeze. "Oh, and before I forget, Camille has nail polish in her bag. She's planning a manicure."

Rosie nodded knowingly. "Thank you, dear. I'm on it."

Riley checked off that worry from her mental list. Rosie wouldn't want Kiss Me Pink all over her tile or, heaven forbid, the furniture.

Then Riley took off, grateful she didn't have to angst about the kids being in good hands. Driving toward the Taconic Parkway, she tried not to speed, though her impulse was to put the pedal to the metal. She did not want to explain to her boss, family friend or not, that she'd arrived on the tail end of the action because she'd been pulled over by a state trooper, leaving the *Mid-Hudson Herald* to parrot the reports of the other local news services.

No, Max had gotten the scoop about the bust, which meant if Riley did her job—and he was counting on her to do that—they'd break the news online first. One part of her was pleased he had so much faith in her work. The other part had to question whether his faith was well-placed. Once, she'd been on top of her game, but she'd been off her beat for a while now. No one knew that better than Max Downey, managing editor of the paper.

She'd interned under Max during the summer between her junior and senior years at Vassar. That internship had been the opportunity of a lifetime, and she'd jumped all over it. He'd hired her straight out of college, and she'd worked her way up the rungs at the paper, establishing her reputation and finding an unexpected and very dear friend in Max.

That was why he'd rolled with her during pregnancy and motherhood, allowing her to scale back her assignments to accommodate her family. That was why he was taking her back after a two-year leave in a down economy when the Internet was making print media scramble to stay relevant.

Riley had to earn her place on the paper again, and that meant getting to Hazard Creek and covering this breaking news. Fortunately luck was with her, and in less than twenty minutes from the time she'd taken Max's call, she was following GPS directions through the streets of an older residential community on the outskirts of the township.

Max's source had come through big because Riley spotted several cruisers from Hazard Creek's PD and a truck that must belong to the DEA. She was surprised the sheriff's department wasn't here, too. A cluster of spectators—most likely folks evacuated from the surrounding homes—stood beyond the perimeter beneath the watchful gaze of the HCPD that had parked a cruiser to block access to the neighborhood.

Riley circled the minivan around before getting caught up in the roadblock. After glancing at the GPS, she cut down a side street that brought her around to the other end of Alban Lane, where she hoped to get a better view of the house.

She'd no sooner brought the minivan to a stop against the curb when she heard shouts. Crackling radios. The screech of tires over the road. Grabbing her gear, she slid from the minivan and cut across someone's front yard to get close to the officer manning this side of the street.

To get closer to the action.

After flashing her press pass, she nodded when the officer told her to keep behind the caution tape. She slid down to the very end where the tape hung from a wooden blockade that had been set up to cut off access to the sidewalk. Aiming the digital camcorder at the house where DEA agents and police officers garbed in Kevlar swarmed the yard, she started to record, already deciding to pull stills from the footage for her story.

If she could catch anything on video, *Herald Online* would run it. That would make Max happy. Especially since she saw no other media personnel. Heck, she'd barely made it.

But as she watched the agents swarm the house, Riley knew something was wrong. Those in the doorway disappeared inside, but those on the lawn seemed to freeze, as if someone had pressed the pause button on a video.

Anxiety crawled uncomfortably at the base of her neck, but she had no time to question the sense of premonition, no time to make sense of what she was seeing in the view screen of the camcorder before the sound of locked brakes shrieked, and the grind of tires screamed over the street, way too close.

Snapping her gaze to the direction of the sound, she froze, unable to register the sight before her. All she could see was the face of a teen, a boy who could be no older than Brian, his expression pure determination as he clung to the steering wheel of a car…

And headed toward her.

Riley could only react, twisting around to get out of the way, lurching into motion so fast that her knees almost buckled beneath her. She staggered for an instant but managed to make it onto the curb just as she heard the wooden barricade shatter behind her. She heard shouting, too, but couldn't make out who or what. All she heard was the solid thunk of a groaning axle as the car jumped the curb.

Run, run, run.

The random thought that she should have worn sneakers popped into her head, followed by the sounds of Camille and Jake's sweet voices crying out in time with the pulsing throb of her heartbeat.

"Mommy died. Mommy died like Daddy."

CHAPTER FOUR

"THE CHIEF WANTS TO SEE YOU," the desk sergeant said, and Scott only nodded as he and Kevin Rush exchanged an uncomfortable glance.

His partner was a decent enough guy, a good cop with a feel for vice that not all cops had. It wasn't entirely Kevin's fault they'd spent the morning chasing their tails, but a more seasoned cop would have recognized that the prostitute they interviewed had been lying through her teeth. She'd claimed to have witnessed a direct purchase between a known street peddler and a suspected head of a drug supply ring.

Her story had been fiction. She was a hooker with a vendetta, Scott had quickly decided, but Kevin believed there was something in her story, something worth their morning. It had taken him hours to admit he'd been duped. Literally. A more experienced cop would have known that shooting in the dark was all part of the game. Sometimes it made more sense to back up and admit a wrong turn rather than barrel ahead.

Scott needed to rein in his irritation because the chief was guaranteed to notice. Then he'd start up with the twenty questions about how Scott was adjusting to his new partner.

There was no way in hell he was going there again. Not when the past two years had been an exercise in humility, starting with the day the chief had paired Scott with an older vice cop who'd known what it was like to lose a partner.

When that match had proven *not* to be made in heaven, the chief had tossed another partner Scott's way. Kevin was a few years younger and had just earned his promotion to detective.

The chief had been giving Scott a vote of confidence by assigning him someone fresh, someone to train into the kind of partner Scott wanted to work with. Turned out he wasn't really in the mood to train. Just as he hadn't been in the mood to change the way he did things to fit in with a hardheaded cop with an eye on retirement.

Scott wanted to work, to immerse himself in his cases and do his bit to clean up the streets. That was what he did, what gave him a sense of purpose.

Kevin had potential, no question, but he got distracted too easily by nonsense—tripping over his own ego for one. The wasted morning wasn't such a big deal. Scott had spent his fair share of mornings going around in circles. Still, he hadn't exactly come away empty-handed today. No, he had an attitude he couldn't shake and a truth he didn't want to admit.

Kevin's biggest offense was that he wasn't Mike.

But that was an old problem that would have to wait for another day. They arrived at the chief's office, and right now Scott had to contend with the expectations of a boss who wanted him to accomplish the sort of miracles that he and Mike had in their heyday. Figuring out why he couldn't settle in with a new partner when even Riley was managing to get on with life would require more time and energy than Scott had right now.

Kevin didn't say a word as he knocked and pushed open the door. In all fairness to the guy, he wasn't the only one feeling the weight of the chief's expectations.

"What did you come up with?" Chief Levering glanced up expectantly from the report he held.

Scott stood there silent, keeping his face carefully blank. He'd give Kevin the chance to spin this however he thought best.

"Nothing," Kevin said. "Dead end. She didn't have anything except a grudge against our guy."

The chief glanced at the clock. "You went in at nine?"

"Yes, sir."

To Scott's surprise the chief just nodded. "Kev, you can go. I need to talk with Scott."

Kevin narrowed his gaze, clearly concerned whether this dismissal boded ill for him, then headed out the door. Scott knew better than to ask the chief what was up. He waited.

Chief Levering was generational law enforcement. He'd worked his way up the ranks from homicide, the son of a son of a son, and someone with a foot still on the streets while hanging on to the oh-shit handle with city bureaucrats.

The chief inspired an insane amount of loyalty from his men, probably because he was insanely loyal himself. He was the kind of cop to take a bullet as quickly as chew out a cop for doing the same. The chief wasn't afraid to get his hands dirty. His men respected that.

He also didn't miss a trick. "Kevin thought something was there and you didn't."

Scott shook his head.

"You tell him?"

"Yes."

The chief eyed him appraisingly with a look Scott knew all too well, and he expected the chief's next words to start up an interrogation about how the two were gelling as partners.

Interestingly the chief only nodded and said, "DEA went in on a crack operation in Hazard Creek."

Since Hazard Creek was a township southeast of Poughkeepsie and out of their jurisdiction, Scott knew there must be a point to this news. "Hadn't heard anything over the radio."

"They just went in."

"How'd it go down?"

The chief scowled. "Not like they hoped, I'm sure. Place was completely cleaned out. Neighbors said the renters scattered like roaches not an hour before the cops showed up."

"Who tipped them off?"

"No clue, but the Narcotics Commission has had a team working on this bust for months."

The Narcotics Commission was big news in the Mid-Hudson Valley. The task force had been instituted by the governor a handful of years ago, a coalition of police agencies charged to stop drug trafficking into Dutchess County. The governor had appointed Jason Kenney, police chief of Hazard Creek, as the most recent commanding officer.

It was a nice nod, no question, even though it was a lot more work on top of an already demanding job. But Jason Kenney thrived under a spotlight, so Scott was sure he'd grabbed the reins of the Narcotics Commission with both hands.

Jason had once been on the force with Scott. He'd been a good cop, instrumental in cracking a few highly visible cases, which had shot him to the forefront of the local media. Jason liked seeing his face on the front pages of the *Mid-Hudson Herald* and *Poughkeepsie Journal,* so he'd accepted the position of police chief with the village of Hazard Creek.

The department might have been smaller than the

Poughkeepsie PD, but Jason also liked being a big fish in a little pond. Scott considered him somewhat of a fame whore, but Mike, who'd known the guy for years, had always taken a lighter view. Every time Jason opened his mouth in front of television cameras, Mike would just roll his eyes and say, "You know Jason."

Scott hadn't known Jason, but knew enough to guess that their limited past history didn't explain why he should care about a bust going south in Hazard Creek.

"Why are you telling me this, Chief?"

Beneath a heavy brow, the chief leveled a stoic gaze, and Scott braced himself. "Whatever went down didn't filter through the drug operation. Some mules arrived for a pickup and found the place shut down by the law. They tried to run for it, and Riley got in their way."

Scott just stared. "She okay?"

"From what I hear. DEA's still got the scene locked down."

Scott was already to the door before the chief said, "Don't kill yourself getting there."

Scott didn't have to. He shoved the light on the dash of his unmarked cruiser, turned on the siren and made Hazard Creek before the HCPD had finished taking witness statements.

He didn't understand why Riley had been at the scene. He was going to kill Max, who should be assigning her city council stories or entertainment reviews. Not drug busts, which around here had everything to do with gangs.

But there she was, sitting in the open doorway of the emergency vehicle, talking to Jason and another man, some fed wearing Kevlar and a vest with the stenciled bold letters: *DEA*.

Scott shut off the siren, swerved the cruiser against a curb and jumped out, taking in the scene as he made his way to the emergency vehicle. Skid marks had left rubber on the asphalt. Deep tire gouges on a lawn where the runaway car had jumped the curb. Not one but two wooden barriers splintered over the street. Scott flashed his badge at the uniform who made a move in his direction.

"Jason," Scott said as he approached, eyeing the DEA agent.

Jason performed the introductions, and Scott gave a barely civil nod to Agent Barry Mannis before kneeling in front of Riley. He took her hands and asked, "How are you?"

She shook her head. "Okay. All good."

She didn't look okay. *Not okay* was all over her face, from the tight set of her mouth to the way she avoided directly meeting his gaze. There were grass stains on her khaki slacks and a tear that revealed white bandages below. Bandages that matched the ones on her arm. Likely where she'd fallen.

Her hands were cold, delicate, fitting in his so neatly, silky skin against skin. He squeezed slightly to reassure her.

"Riley," he said, a whisper between them.

She finally met his gaze, and Scott saw so much in her eyes, in her expression. She was rattled. And relieved to see him. *That* got a reaction deep in his gut, and he tried not to notice how smooth her skin was against his, telling himself she'd have been glad to see any familiar face right now.

But it was *his* face she stared into, *his* hands she clung to, and rationalizing her response didn't stop his pulse from lurching expectantly, didn't stop him from hanging on to her as if magnetized.

And for a stunning few heartbeats the world seemed to disappear, just completely vanish, leaving nothing but him and Riley connected by a touch and a glance.

"Damned hoods freaked when they saw the roadblock." Jason's voice shattered the moment like a gunshot. "Riley had to make a quick exit."

Their gazes broke away to find Jason staring uncomfortably at the remains of the wooden blockade that littered the street.

Riley slid her hands from his as a paramedic reappeared from inside the vehicle.

"Ma'am, I need to—"

"We're done," she said, clearly bristling. "I'm good."

Jason cast an annoyed look at Scott that translated into *Will you deal with her? I've got my hands full.*

Scott glanced between the expectant paramedic and Agent Mannis, and managed to squelch his own annoyance at Jason's lack of concern. This was *Riley,* not some random pain-in-the-ass reporter. Then again, Scott wouldn't want to be in Jason's shoes right now. Bust going balls-up on the DEA's time. No wonder Hazard Creek's normally imperturbable police chief looked perturbed.

Deciding to cut the guy some slack, Scott inclined his head in another silent communication. *Got her.*

Jason nodded, looking relieved as he escorted the DEA agent away from the ambulance to where the HCPD was mirandizing a group of kids handcuffed against two cruisers.

Scott shifted back, and Riley popped to her feet as if detonated. "I need to go home."

She still didn't sound like herself, and Scott raked another gaze over her tight expression. He couldn't miss her agitation or pallor.

"No problem, Riley. Let me wrap things up with these guys." He turned to the paramedic. "Where are we? Did you get everything you need from her?"

The guy seemed to understand that Scott was asking whether or not his resistant patient was in shock. "Vitals are good. Cleaned up the surface scratches. She has some bruising."

Not so bad considering she'd outrun a car full of panicked drug dealers. Scott glanced back to where the HCPD were loading the last of the young hoods into separate cruisers. Scott didn't recognize any of them. That at least was good.

He spotted a brightly colored tote bag sitting inside the ambulance. "This yours?"

She nodded.

Grabbing the bag, he placed a hand on her uninjured elbow, steering her away from the ambulance and toward their cars.

"Did you get your story?" He needed to get her talking.

"The little there was."

"I'll bet this wasn't the outcome Jason was looking for."

She nodded, then reached for her bag. He handed it over, frowning as she plunged a hand inside and fumbled around. He heard the rattle of keys.

If Riley thought she'd be driving herself home, she'd need to rethink her plan. He didn't care what the paramedic said.

"Come on, ride back to town with me," he said.

She stopped short and glanced up at him with a frown. "I have to pick up the kids at Rosie and Joe's."

"No problem. I'll take you."

"My van."

"I'll make the trip back to pick it up with Kevin."

She shook her head and inhaled deeply, visibly steeling herself. "Thank you, Scott, but no. I'm fine."

He didn't believe her. She knew he didn't but wasn't backing down. Had she always been so stubborn? He looked into her clear blue eyes, sparkly eyes that couldn't hide how rattled she was no matter what she said. How would Mike have handled his willful wife?

"How about if I follow you back?" Scott suggested a compromise. "Just to make sure you get there okay. My day will be shot if I'm worried about you making it home in one piece."

She held his gaze for another moment, and her expression eased up. "Fine. I promised the kids I'd get them before dinner. We're having tacos."

He wasn't sure why she was sharing the menu and considered this another good reason why she shouldn't get behind the wheel. He was about to have another go at persuading her to let him play chauffeur when Jason showed up.

"You okay?" he asked Riley, earning back a few points in Scott's book. The guy wasn't always a jerk. Nice to know.

"Yes." She lifted up on tiptoe and pressed a kiss to Jason's cheek. "Sorry things didn't work out as you'd hoped."

Jason flashed the smile that folks on both sides of the Hudson River were familiar with, a smile as fake as if it had been carved on a Halloween pumpkin. "Just remember we go way back when you write your article. I really don't want to see my face all over the front page associated with this mess."

Riley gave a weak smile while depressing her key fob. She reached for the handle as the lock on the van door clicked, but Jason got it first, making her wait.

"How'd you hear about the bust, anyway?" he asked.

"Max. He didn't share his source."

Jason frowned, but Scott was frowning even harder by now. He'd thought the guy would be too busy with the feds, who were swarming the HCPD cruisers almost ready to leave the scene, to be playing twenty questions with Riley.

Jason glanced Scott's way, then pulled open the door. Riley slipped inside.

"Sorry we had to meet up again like this, Riley," Jason said, leaning on the open door. "Welcome back."

"Thanks," she said.

Jason blinked hard, then he eased shut the door before asking through the open window, "Are you all right to drive back?"

"I'm following her," Scott said. "Pull over if you need to stop, Riley. And don't lose me in that hot rod, okay?"

She rolled her eyes. Scott headed toward his car, not really good with letting her drive but unsure what the hell else he could do. Short of handcuffing her, anyway.

CHAPTER FIVE

JASON KENNEY BACKED AWAY from the van while Riley cranked the engine. He came to a dead stop as a roar of sound blasted from the stereo. Riley jerked back in her seat, and for a stunned instant Jason froze as raw rap music rocked the suburban quiet.

A string of words that had no business pouring from any young mother's minivan.

Words from the streets.

Riley slammed her palm against the steering wheel to shut down the noise.

"Too much convenience isn't always a good thing," she said wearily while popping out a CD from the stereo. She tossed it onto the passenger seat with a muttered, "That kid."

Jason didn't ask what she was talking about. He didn't need to know. He only needed to know why she had that CD.

And did Scott know?

Casting a quick glance at the unmarked cruiser, Jason found Scott inside the car with the door shut.

Was this some sort of setup? What else could it be?

"Take care, Jason," Riley said, and he stepped away from the door automatically to allow her to pull out.

The gleam of red taillights flashed as Scott followed her, and Jason remained immobilized by indecision. About the only thing he knew right now was that he had no time to figure out what to do and how it would to come back to bite him in the ass. And it would. That much he knew. Lately everything he did circled around like a damned concrete boomerang ready to smash him in the face.

He could feel Barry's gaze burning a hole through him from across the street. The DEA agent from hell wanted answers. Jason stubbornly decided to let him wait and buy himself a few extra seconds to think.

He couldn't be mistaken. No. He hadn't heard much of the poison blasting from Riley's van before she'd stopped the show, but he'd recognized what he'd heard.

Veteranos got it down. Ace cool in the game. The Busters hooked up. For a piece of curb service.

The lyrics of that pounding rap beat were a language all their own. The language of the streets. And Jason was well versed in what those lyrics meant.

Cops had backed up veteran gang members during a drug delivery, protecting the criminals and their cut of the action from drugs that would be sold on the streets.

Jason couldn't be sure without listening to the complete track but guessed the lyrics would provide details about the specific crime. And specific cops.

HCPD.

In a perfect world, the idea of any law-enforcement officer getting into bed with the hoods would have made him see red.

But this wasn't a perfect world, and the cops perpetrating illegal acts weren't always corrupt. Sometimes they were simply following orders. Bad orders, maybe, but orders nevertheless.

Homemade CDs like the one Riley had came from gangs who circulated them on the streets to boast of their exploits. A gang friendly with local law had a built-in safeguard against other gangs that might want to intrude on their operations.

Those CDs were also insurance policies. Bad cops might be in on the street action, but when push came to shove, they also had the power. Gang members didn't trust cops—particularly ones who betrayed the law they'd sworn to uphold—when those same cops could send them before a judge. Gangs understood loyalty. Sometimes Jason thought that was all they understood.

So what was Riley doing with that CD on the day she'd turned up at a bogus bust?

Jason was sure Scott hadn't heard, and that might be Jason's only decent luck lately. Scott would have known what was on that CD. He worked knee-deep in gangs. Hell, he even dealt with them for fun with that volunteer group Chief Levering had started when Jason had been with the PPD.

Or was this whole thing a setup? Had Scott given the CD to Riley? Had she played it to get a reaction from Jason? Did they suspect what was going down in Hazard Creek?

No, Jason decided. That was paranoia, plain and simple. How could they have possibly known he'd show up at Riley's van?

Then again, they shouldn't have known about this bust. But Scott had only arrived after Riley had gotten hurt, and Jason seriously doubted Riley would have put herself in harm's way for any reason. Not after what had happened to Mike.

But someone had spilled something to the *Mid-Hudson Herald* and Riley had that CD…

Damn it. This situation was a mess.

"How did they know about this hit?" Barry Mannis aka Agent Asshole asked from a distance, barreling across the street like an out-of-control semi, which was what the

DEA agent looked like. Short. Thick. Muscular build making up for what he lacked in height. Fast, though, as if he rolled along on eighteen wheels.

Agent Asshole couldn't wait for answers, so Jason was out of time. He shrugged. "Editor at the paper got an anonymous tip and sent a reporter."

"You know her." It wasn't a question.

"Not really. I worked with her husband back in my PPD days. Haven't seen her in years."

"What about the cop with her? He PPD, too?"

Jason nodded.

"Let me get this straight. Not only do we have the media showing up at what was supposed to be a surprise hit, but now we've got Poughkeepsie's department involved, too."

What was Jason supposed to say? He'd cast his vote that this was a stupid move. Insane. Agent Asshole hadn't wanted to hear it. Not when he was getting pushed around by DEA brass and needed to look as if he was doing some honest work around here.

Pumping drugs into the area wasn't honest work.

But Agent Asshole didn't care who he risked. Why should he? It wasn't his team that would look stupid when they came up empty.

Jason took a step forward, forcing the DEA agent to sink back on his heels to maintain eye contact. And though he couldn't see the man's eyes through the polarized aviator shades, the reminder of how short he was would irritate the hell out of him. Jason knew Agent Asshole always stood at a distance because he didn't like looking up to anyone.

Petty, maybe, but it was all Jason had right now.

So he stared down at the thickset man, absolute loathing burning through him like battery acid. How had he ever thought this man might be a useful contact? How had he missed that nothing in life, especially appointments to high-profile commissions, would ever come free?

"So who tipped off the media? One of yours?" Mannis held his ground and looked pissed about it.

"Not one of mine," Jason retorted. "You're the one who set up the bust, then tipped off the hoods. My men aren't in the loop. I told you that. Not one of them."

That was the only thing that let Jason look in the mirror at night. He might have gotten sucked in with the wrong bunch of high-powered pricks, but he wouldn't implicate his men. If anything went wrong—and with his luck it was only a matter of time—then his men could honestly stand before Internal Affairs and say they weren't involved.

Jason had a responsibility to the good, loyal men serving Hazard Creek. He wasn't going to drag them down until he could figure out some way to make this nightmare go away.

Until then he had no choice but to play the game.

"You better hope like hell you're right, Kenney," Mannis finally said, and Jason could almost see the agent's eyes narrowing behind the dark lenses. "I don't want to call in an anonymous tip of my own. Got some shots from Atlantic City that would make a much better story than what happened here today. That streaming video of you with those pretty *cholas* would make you really popular on YouTube. You'd be a cyber-celebrity."

The blood drained from Jason's head and, for one blind instant, all he could see was himself surrounded by a bunch of naked young women. Prostitutes, most likely. Jason couldn't be sure. He'd been so stoned on ecstasy at the time he'd thought he'd stepped into a friggin' wet dream.

He shut his eyes against the sight, against the vision of what *that* night would look like immortalized on video and playing in a courtroom, and in that moment, he would have given his reputation, his job and every man on his squad to unload his service weapon in Agent Asshole's face.

But until Mannis wound up the victim of a public service murder—and he most definitely would if there was a God—Jason had to deal with damage control. At least until he could figure out how to safeguard the incriminating evidence he'd unwittingly given this man to use against him.

"I'll find what went down," he said flatly.

"Get on it," Mannis said. "I don't want trouble right now."

No damn doubt. Jason hadn't been trusted with all the details of the seven-hundred-and-fifty-thousand-dollar shipment coming into their area, but he knew the operation had been in the works too long to screw up at the finish line.

"Keep me informed," Mannis repeated when some of his agents emerged from the abandoned cookhouse.

Jason collected himself as he headed back to the crime scene, snapping at Hank Llewellyn as he passed. "Get those blockades out of the street."

His department would look stupid enough without his office being flooded with complaints about trashing the neighborhood.

The HCPD would certainly get real estate in the news. Some talking head would tell the world about how the Narcotics Commission had let a drug manufacturing ring slip through its fingers. Then the governor would be calling for an explanation.

Jason didn't know how this day could have turned into any more of a nightmare than it already had. But he had figured out one thing—he wasn't sharing the bit about the CD. Nothing else was getting out of his control if he could help it.

He didn't know what the hell was going on with Riley and Scott, but he was going to find out. Riley had gotten that CD somewhere. Its contents would tell him exactly what he was up against. If Scott and the PPD were involved…

CHAPTER SIX

ABOUT THE SAME TIME Riley had taken the phone call from Max, drug dealers had been clearing out their operation in an older residential neighborhood and driving away. She might have even passed them on the Taconic Parkway in her rush to Hazard Creek.

All that scrambling around to catch the action, stressing the kids out as she hurried them out the door… For what?

Mommy died. Mommy died like Daddy.

Her eyes fluttered shut as she endured yet another blast of anxiety so physical it rushed through her like a cold wave.

Maybe she needed a new career. She'd come home to start a new life. *Her* life. She could be a teacher. Journalism or maybe English. Better yet, she could work in an elementary school. Then she and the kids could be together in the same place all day, have the same schedules. A career where she wouldn't get in the way of law-enforcement officers doing their jobs and drug dealers doing theirs…

Riley couldn't shake the memory of scrambling to get away from that out-of-control car. The details had etched themselves in her head. Always too many details.

The scooter carelessly discarded on the front porch as if a child had dropped it without a thought.

The baskets hanging from the gables, filled to overflowing with cheery summer blooms.

The violent ruts in the carefully tended grass where car tires had dredged deep into the dirt.

That drug operation had been hidden in a neighborhood where folks reared families and moms walked the streets with strollers and kids riding scooters.

How did such a dichotomy exist in one place? Families living alongside drug dealers? Such a wholesome environment coexisting with a destructive one?

Riley felt the same incomprehension she'd faced with the reality that her husband, such a vital and loving man, could be there one day and be gone forever the next.

Merging with traffic on the Taconic, she glanced in her rearview mirror to see Scott's unmarked car stuck like glue to her bumper. She couldn't see him, of course, with all the tinted glass, but felt such a profound wave of relief that the feeling came as another shock, so wildly out of proportion to what she should have felt.

Scott had been Mike's partner and friend, but in this moment, when she felt so off center and anxious and unsure, she knew he was more.

Riley glanced again in the rearview mirror, the relief still so completely there red flags were flying. When had Scott become *her* friend, a part of her life? When he'd made it clear he'd intended to keep his eyes on his best friend's family? By regularly calling her in Florida? By listening to her unload about the details—big and small—of her days? By helping Brian around the farm?

Or maybe this relief was simply a side effect of the anxiety she felt right now. Though she'd covered her fair share of drug busts, even had a few run-ins where she'd been in the way, she'd never been this rattled. She couldn't cover breaking news without getting into the thick of things, and breaking news had been all she covered in her prekid life. But now…

Mommy died. Mommy died like Daddy.

Sometimes the voice was Camille's, sometimes Jake's. And the only thing that helped Riley get a grip on her emotions was knowing that the man in the vehicle behind her had cared enough to drive to Hazard Creek to make sure she was okay. Him, and deciding to spend the night researching the requirements to become a teacher in Dutchess County. She had a master's degree, after all. Shouldn't it be a matter of getting some sort of teaching certificate?

But her anxiety melted away the instant she pulled into her in-laws' driveway. The front door swung wide and her kids burst out at a run.

"Mommy, Mommy! Are you all right?" Camille called out, ponytail bouncing as she clomped down the porch steps in sandals not meant for breakneck speed.

Jake, in sneakers, raced ahead, eyeing Riley with such a look of worry that her heart ached. He made it to the driveway so fast Riley had to shoo him back to get her door open.

"I'm good, guys. How was your afternoon?"

"Grandma said you got boo-boos. Where?" Camille caught up and gazed at Riley, who tugged her ponytail in greeting.

Hiding what had happened hadn't been an option. Not while adorned with gauze and grass stains. Still, she didn't want to make a big deal and worry the kids.

Reaching for Riley's hand, Camille urged her to her knees. The adhesive pulled painfully against her skin, tugging the raw flesh along her thigh, but Riley schooled her expression to meet two worried gazes.

"Not big boo-boos." She lifted her elbow to reveal the gauze bandage. "Just some scratches."

Camille pressed a careful kiss to the wound. "There, all better."

Jake didn't say a word, just rubbed her shoulders, comforting her in a way that would have comforted him.

"Were you worried?" she asked him.

He gave a stoic nod.

"Mommy's fine." She gave him a smile then pressed a kiss to Camille's hand where the tiny nails had been polished a blinding shade of pink. "Your nails look lovely."

Camille lifted a sandaled foot and wiggled her toes. "Look, my toes match."

"Beautiful." She glanced up as Rosie appeared in the doorway with Joe behind her.

Riley waved and gave them a reassuring smile just as Scott joined her.

"Are you okay?" Joe huffed to a stop as he joined the small party congregating beside the minivan.

Mike's dad looked a lot like Riley imagined Mike would have looked at the same age. Tall and fit even well into his sixties. His northern Italian heritage was all over the gray hair that had once been a tawny blond, the warm eyes and sturdy olive skin that did a lot to conceal his true age.

"I'm fine," she said. "But how did you know?"

"Scott called." Joe nodded toward the man in question.

Again, that feeling of relief. Riley kept the smile on her face. She guessed Scott had wanted to reassure everyone. Of course, no one would have known what had happened had he not given them a heads-up. But knowing Scott had her back, that he'd stepped in to calm the people she loved…

"Appreciated you getting over there." Joe clasped his hand and thanked him for the call.

Scott waved off the gratitude with a grimace.

Riley seized the chance to distract her father-in-law from the discussion she sensed forthcoming. A conversation that made Scott seem uncomfortable.

"Come on, kiddos," she said. "Collect your things so Grandma and Grandpa can have their day back. What's left of it."

"Oh, no, dear." Rosie looked aghast from her perch on the front steps. "You're staying for dinner. Ground beef's all thawed and Camille's been helping me cut up the veggies. The kids told me we're having tacos."

Okay. Riley was not up for a party at the moment. All she really wanted to do was get home and surround herself with normalcy. But what could she say? Everyone wanted to help, so she kept her mouth shut and followed the group as they headed toward the front steps.

"Scott, you'll stay, too," Rosie said then frowned. "Unless you have to get back to the station. Got twenty minutes or so? That should be enough to get things together."

"You know I'd never turn down food in your house, Rosie," he delighted her by saying. "I don't think the chief will mind me taking a break."

Rosie laughed, giving Scott a hug when he reached the top step. "Not unless he wants to answer to me."

As it was just past four in the afternoon, this break qualified as less a late lunch than an early dinner. But Riley took each of the kids' hands and led them inside, unable to help noticing the way Scott preceded Rosie into the heart of the Angelica home well familiar with the way.

Rosie immediately began issuing orders.

"Camille, you help Grandma Rosie get everything on platters. Jake and Grandpa, you get the table set. Oh, and make sure you put out extra napkins. Riley and Scott, you two wash up for dinner."

"Yes, ma'am." Scott spun on his heels and disappeared down the hallway where the guest bathroom was.

Riley stood for a moment, watching all the activity,

feeling disconnected, as if she was an outsider looking in on this warm family scene.

While Rosie and Joe had always had an open-door policy, Riley had never known Scott to be one who readily accepted social invites or dropped in anywhere for casual visits. But he seemed more at home than she could ever recall seeing him.

When Mike had been alive he'd regularly had his buddies over for barbecues, dinners and whatever game was on TV. Their house had often been pleasantly full with friends and family. Scott certainly had been a guest, but now that she thought about it, she realized he'd rarely been there on his own—instead being one of many visitors. And until she'd moved to Florida, she could easily count on one hand the number of times she'd had a private conversation with him.

So why this connection now? Why was he the one to help her get her equilibrium? And why did she *want* him to be the one she could turn to? Why did it seem so natural for him to be here, at the Angelicas', with her?

No, wait. He wasn't *with* her. No. He was simply looking out for her and the kids. Fulfilling some promise made between friends and partners. That's all this was.

Still, when he brushed past her to enter the kitchen, the brief physical connection felt intense and far from casual. It felt strong, intimate…a man-woman touch rather than a friend's touch. That surprised her.

Because she wasn't sure when she started noticing Scott as anything more than Mike's partner.

CHAPTER SEVEN

"YO, BIG HOME," General E. called to Scott while launching himself into the air to sink an easy basket.

Groans erupted from the nearly half-dozen teens with chests bared beneath the blistering afternoon sun swarming the court. General E.'s team wore T-shirts. A few players cheered.

It didn't take long for Scott to decide where he was needed. Yanking off his T-shirt, he tossed it onto a bench.

"Hey, homie. Hey, homie." The acknowledgment went up among the "skins," and Scott laughed, pounding a few fists before Mateo passed him the ball.

Throwing himself into the game, Scott was grateful for the activity and some downtime for a brain that had been steeping in frustration from one too many stalled cases.

And too many thoughts of the woman he shouldn't be thinking about.

A hard-nosed game of basketball would be just the ticket, and these guys were hard-nosed about everything. Everyone always wanted to come out on top. But all things considered, this was a good group of kids, which was a break for Renaissance. All too often the tough job of turning around inner-city kids was made even tougher by past history on the streets.

Scott and the other volunteers who kept the program

going tried to create an environment that didn't invite gang rivalries inside the walls of the leased warehouse that housed the program. The Center, as it was known, was a place filled with counseling rooms for support groups and classrooms for tutoring programs that helped kids get through school or earn their general education diplomas.

The Center had even carved out a few niches for specialty interests. A local artist volunteered time to teaching younger kids how to paint. A martial artist taught tae kwon do. A nurse-practitioner not only performed triage on kids without access to reliable health care but taught parenting classes to kids who had kids themselves.

Renaissance was a safe haven for anyone who didn't want to die behind bars or from drugs or in a gang war. In a perfect world, it would be Poughkeepsie's equivalent of Manchester Bidwell, a social program that had originated in Pittsburgh decades ago and still boasted a mind-blowing success rate.

Funding didn't allow Renaissance to compete on the same scale as Manchester Bidwell, but Scott and the other volunteers didn't need money to adopt the concept. So they raised their expectations for the kids who found themselves here, sometimes without being able to explain why they'd come. Those expectations were high, because the simple fact was, when the volunteers believed in these kids, the kids learned to believe in themselves.

The results got better and better each year.

Of course, Scott got older and older each year, too, which meant he was sweating a lot more than these kids by the time General E. sank the basket that irrevocably widened the point gap. But age and experience wasn't always a negative. It helped him recognize the instant the tenor of the cheering changed. He was already wiping the sweat from his eyes with his T-shirt by the time the snarling started.

Sure enough, General E. was in Cakes's face. Instinct took over, and in the blink of an eye, team members were taking sides.

"Don't make me start breaking heads." Scott grabbed a fistful of General E.'s collar and hauled the big teen backward.

"What you gonna do, Big Home?" General E. tried to pull away, hostility a few steps ahead of rational thought. "Kick me to the pavement?"

"Hell to the no." Twisting the kid's collar tighter, Scott forced him around until they could make eye contact. "I'm going to pull my service piece and shoot off your ear. The one with the gauge."

It stung Scott's pride to acknowledge that might have been the easiest way for him to take down this kid, who had a good four inches and fifteen pounds on him. General E., whose real name was Eric, stood six foot four with a build that had made him a natural in command, hence the nickname. He'd been on his way to senior status in 16 Squared, the gang that owned 16th Street around town square, before a judge had sent him to Renaissance for his one and only chance to straighten up.

"Get a grip, Eric." Scott held his gaze.

With any luck, General E. would funnel all this natural talent for leadership in a productive direction. If these kids could get a break, a decent job or enroll in community college, they usually created new identities for themselves and fit back into their real names again. Not all kids did, but General E. looked as though he might make it as he sucked in a deep breath.

"You breaking your own rules, Big Home?" General E. sounded genuinely shocked. "You brought a piece into the Center?"

"Not hardly." Scott twisted his collar harder for good measure. "I wouldn't bring a gun around you thugs. Wouldn't trust you not to steal it and blow off your damn feet."

That got a round of laughter and made General E. growl out, "What? You going to take me down with your busted self, old man? Like your boys shut down that cookhouse in H Creek."

Cakes threw down his arms and backed off, shaking his head. "Hell with you, chump."

So word had gotten around the streets about Jason Kenney's nightmare bust. That got Scott's attention.

"You go, Cakes." He released his grip on General E.'s collar, and backed up enough for the kid to straighten up.

Cakes raised a fist and said, "Pound it."

Scott connected fists and didn't have to say another word. Renaissance was all about teaching these kids to expect more from themselves than society did. Cakes had every right to feel good right now. It was too easy for them to get sucked into not-so-old habits.

General E. was still visibly wrestling with his pride, but Scott let him be, content when the other kids started breaking away, grabbing shirts that littered the perimeter of the court. The pack mentality evaporated as fast as it started. Good. Scott wasn't in the mood today to deal with this crew out of control.

Pulling his shirt over his head, he turned toward the sound of wolf whistles and found a group clustering around the fence as two girls walked by. "Dudes, you really need to act like gentlemen in front of the ladies."

"Man, who are you calling ladies?" Mateo yelled out, loud enough for the girls to hear.

One of the girls flicked him off, and a bunch of the guys hooted with laughter.

"I think you're pretty, ladies," Do-Wap said. "So does Big Home here. Forget those losers."

"You need a life, Do," Cakes called out.

Cakes's real name was William Brown, and Scott had never understood the nickname. Some handles made sense. Devonte "Do-Wap" Smith was from Wappinger Falls. Easy for his "busted old self" to figure out. But all Scott had heard about Cakes was that he was a world-class liar who could cover up anything. Like icing covered a cake?

Scott had no clue.

"You need a life, too, Big Home." Cakes fell into step beside him as the guys started filing inside the Center.

Scott, of course, was Big Home. He couldn't remember who'd started calling him that because it had been so long ago, but he answered to Big Home. Kept him one of the crowd.

"What, you're tired of seeing my smiling face around here?" he asked. "I'm hurt."

"Dude, you called Shae Cherry a *lady*."

"Do-Wap seems to think she—"

"Do-Wap's the only one in town who hasn't tapped it." Cakes shook his braided black head sadly. "Do-Wap and you, looks like. He's angling, but you need to hook up with someone who can show you the difference between a lady and a ho."

"That's harsh." Scott motioned to the hallway filled with teens coming in from the court and emerging from a tutoring session. "Exactly when do I have time to *hook up?* If you hoodlums aren't keeping me busy running the streets, you're wearing me out on the basketball court."

"You need to chill with your lady, dude." Cakes's eyes widened in horror. "You do have a lady? You know what I mean…*tending the farm*."

"Don't you worry about *the farm*." Scott wasn't having any part of this conversation.

The only woman in his life right now was the one he couldn't think about. Big difference between feeling and *acting on* a feeling, exactly what he preached to these kids. He knew firsthand because he hadn't been any different than they were before learning that he had control of his life, that he could turn things around with the choices he made.

He'd chosen not to think about Riley. He valued looking himself in the mirror more than letting his feelings get control of him.

"The cows are mooing, man, so let it rest." A lie. "General E. mentioned H Creek. Lot of talk?"

Cakes eyed him narrowly as if he suspected the motive behind Scott's change of subject. "Word's out the busters screwed up."

"Suppose that's one way to call it."

"Sheeeet. What else do you call Drano in your cop shop?"

"It's not *my* cop shop," Scott clarified. "And that's what you're hearing—a leak?"

"H Creek ain't Mexico," Mateo added, obviously keeping up with the conversation. "You all brothaz in blue."

Scott had no problem discussing gang-related activities if these kids needed to talk. Not only was a leak in the Hazard Creek bust news to Scott, but his senses were tingling.

Mateo was right about one thing—law around here was tight. No surprise when Hazard Creek, Hyde Park and Pleasant Valley orbited like satellites around Poughkeepsie.

Then there was Riley. She might only have been in the wrong place at the wrong time, but in his mind she was now involved. Any word on the streets that might impact her was his business.

"Who's talking leak?" Scott asked.

Cakes gave him a sidelong glance.

"Why you scared, Angel Food?" Mateo demanded with a laugh then turned to Scott. "Everything is everything. You know talk's out about how the chefs in that cookhouse did a ghost."

"Who heard they were tipped off?" Scott asked.

"Some peripheral was running her mouth about how she'd hooked up with a prince from Big House. She was way fine, too."

Do-Wap gave a low whistle, another eavesdropper to the conversation. "I'd buy anything that sweet piece was selling."

Cakes snorted. "You'd sell your mama for a piece o' anything."

Do-Wap elbowed him, and Cakes sidestepped the blow, nearly taking Scott down in the process.

He scowled. A girl who hung in the periphery of any gang wasn't likely to have a bead on the inner workings, even if she was sleeping with a senior member. "A peripheral? You think there's something to that?"

Mateo shrugged. "The Big House brothaz all up in H Creek's grill, Big Home. Everyone knows that."

Not everyone. Big House operated on Scott's beat, and this was the first he'd heard about any connection to Hazard Creek. If the gang was operating out of Poughkeepsie proper, there had to be some solid link to the area.

The link wasn't likely to be a bunch of similar-minded drug dealers, otherwise Scott would have heard. Any connection between Poughkeepsie inner city and H Creek had to be one that could enable these thugs to branch out operations into new turf without a lot of press. That meant only the most senior gang members were in on the operation.

Had these kids heard right? Could there be a leak in one of the departments?

CHAPTER EIGHT

THROUGH TEARY EYES, Riley stared in the rearview mirror, her stomach sick.

Just four days ago, Mrs. House, with her kind smiles and soft voice, had seemed to be the most perfect kindergarten teacher in the world. Today, she seemed more prison warden while leading Jake through the car-rider line execution style.

"Mrs. Angelica," she'd said oh-so diplomatically on the telephone last night. "I think it might be better if you drop Jake off at school. Camille and I will get him to class, and he'll have a little time to adjust before we get inside."

All the excitement of kindergarten had disintegrated into a raging case of separation anxiety for her son. Riley assumed he'd feel better when he had a clearer idea of what to expect. But the situation wasn't working out that way, despite Riley's best efforts at reassurance. She'd given Jake checkpoints to look forward to during the long day.

Smiley-face notes in his lunch box.

One of Daddy's handkerchiefs in his pocket.

Unfortunately, after three days of panicked tears at the door, the teacher had decided to assume control.

In her heart, Riley knew Mrs. House was right. Camille, who was genuinely excited about school, became worried and sad whenever Jake melted down. Then there were the other twenty-five little kids in class to consider. This wasn't the best start to anyone's day, nor did Riley want Jake labeled a problem this early in his school career.

So last night she'd spent the night prepping him for today's change of routine. She'd placed her picture in his pocket so he could pull it out whenever he missed Mommy. Then she'd bypassed the parking lot and headed for the car-riders' line, where Mrs. House stood waiting as promised. Riley had given each kid a kiss and hug. Camille had jumped out of the minivan eagerly. Riley had nearly had to throw Jake out.

This was not how life was supposed to be. Riley should be walking her kids to class, then hanging around to help out as homeroom mom whenever she didn't have an early assignment. *She* should be comforting her son, not relying on a kindhearted but all-too-busy teacher to do the job.

An impatient horn sounded behind her, and she dragged her gaze away from the kids and quickly glanced at her blind spot before pulling away from the curb.

That sick feeling in her stomach intensified at the stop sign. Her own separation anxiety spiked as she faced the decision to drive home or wait at the nearby coffee shop until she knew for certain Jake had calmed down. Did she want to be too far away if she had to pick him up?

Uncertainty echoed in her head, and the horn beeped again, impatient, forcing her to make a choice she didn't want to make.

Riley wheeled the minivan into the flow of traffic.

Of course Jake would calm down, she told herself, physically willing herself to drive past the coffee shop. He had to make peace with school, and Mrs. House was trained to help him. She also understood the unique aspects of the situation, and the factors that made leaving mommy difficult. And Jake wasn't alone; Camille was in the same class. Thank goodness Riley had kept them together instead of separating them as so many parenting guides suggested.

No. She'd go home. She'd hope for the best, and if she was needed, she'd only be fifteen minutes away.

The best obviously wasn't on the schedule today, though, because as she rounded the last bend before her house, she was greeted by the police.

Cruisers parked haphazardly in her driveway, on the street, on the lawn between, as if the entire police force had been dispatched to her place. For one breathless instant, her memory flashed back to the day Chief Levering had shown up to tell her about Mike....

Had something happened to Brian?

Her heart pounded out an uncomfortable rhythm. She couldn't remember if she'd seen her nephew's car in the driveway this morning.

One of the uniformed officers recognized her and flagged her to a place on that semicircle of grass between the driveway and street. He was at her door by the time she'd set the emergency brake.

"Riley, it's good to see you again." He was smiling. That took her by surprise.

"Charlie, what happened—"

"Everything's okay," he reassured her. "459a came through dispatch." He glanced around and gave a sheepish shrug. "Everyone recognized your address."

"My alarm went off? Why didn't the security company call?" She slid a hand automatically to her waist to check her cell phone, then realized it wasn't there. In the turmoil of the morning's anxiety, she must have forgotten it.

Charlie frowned. "Intruder attempted to gain entry

through a bathroom window—the one over the basement door. Looks like the alarm scared him off."

"A burglary?"

Charlie nodded. "Got through the window on that overhang. Don't worry. We don't think he got into the house."

Don't worry? That was the twins' bathroom.

She had to stop her imagination from leaping straight to the worst possible scenario, to an image of Camille or Jake walking in on an intruder.

But they were safe at school, settling in for the day, or trying to in Jake's case. No worries.

"Riley?" Charlie asked. "You okay?"

She forced herself to move past the fear, forced herself to reply, "The point of entry makes sense."

Charlie nodded. "No question. No one's getting in around back without a ladder."

The house was situated on a descending slope that left the front porch ground level and the back of the house a full story higher with a magnificent view of the duck pond and the surrounding acreage. Since the front of the house was visible from the street, the bathroom window provided some cover.

"Have there been burglaries in the neighborhood, Charlie?" She didn't want to overreact, but the idea of someone inside the house… "I need to call Brian and make sure he's okay. May I go inside and get my phone?"

Charlie didn't get a chance to reply because just then another uniformed officer—Janet DiBenedetto—noticed Riley and called out, "She's here, guys. Riley's here."

That began an avalanche of greetings. Riley had never seen so many of Mike's former coworkers together at one time except at police functions. And his funeral.

They welcomed her home and sought to reassure her

they'd be working double-time, no *triple*-time, to keep watch on her place after this break-in so often that she couldn't help but be overwhelmed.

She felt as if she was repeating the same words over and over. But "thank you" wasn't nearly good enough in the face of so much support, and just as the lump in her throat grew almost impossible to talk around, she spotted Scott circling the side of the house.

He came to an abrupt stop when he saw her, and their gazes met across the distance. One brief instant and the crowd seemed to vanish. All the greetings and laughter faded to white noise. From where Riley stood his eyes seemed almost black, but she knew they were really deep, deep brown. He searched her face, assessing, and he was relieved by what he saw, the look in his espresso-colored eyes somehow liquid.

She knew how relieved he was. Though his expression never changed. Though the sharp lines of his face might have been chiseled from stone.

As though held by some bodily connection, she just stood there, trapped by his gaze, feeling so aware of him, so glad he was here.

She could barely acknowledge that this wasn't the first time she'd felt so *relieved* to see him. So grateful he kept showing up exactly when she needed him. How, Riley couldn't say, but he seemed to know with an uncanny knack because he headed straight toward her. Suddenly he was at her side, assuming a quiet control over the well-meaning chaos simply by inserting himself into the conversation.

He complimented Janet on her suggestion to notify the neighborhood crime watch for some extra eyes. He thanked Roger, who offered to have his son, a friend of Brian's, spend a few nights. He ragged on Charlie for offering to drive by Riley's place at three in the morning when he was coming off duty. And his good-natured presence gave Riley time to catch her breath before she had to deal with the matter at hand.

The *matters* at hand.

Someone had broken into her home.

And she was far too grateful to have Scott beside her.

Charlie's waist crackled a static interruption, and he withdrew from the group, taking the transmission where he was out of earshot.

Scott glanced down, his dark eyes looking over her, not assessing but gently, as if they stood alone. "You okay?"

Two simple words, but somehow they were a caress, no different than his gaze. She found her voice. "I need to call Brian, but my cell phone is in the house. May I use yours?"

Scott nodded, adding, "I spoke to him already. He's been on campus since the crack of dawn. Doesn't have a clue what went down. He tried calling you. He was worried."

Again she felt that sense of appreciation. For Scott. For his becoming a part of her life. "Oh, thank goodness he's okay. And thank you for checking on him."

"Called you first. When I couldn't get you, *I* got worried."

Riley didn't get a chance to reply, didn't get to dwell on the fact that Scott so obviously cared, when Charlie circled the cruiser again. "Neighbor reported seeing a motorcycle tear-assing toward Route 55 not long after dispatch got the alarm."

"Motorcycle?" Janet narrowed her gaze. "What makes you think it's our perp and not some kid out for a joyride?"

"The neighbor said she didn't hear the bike coming

down the road. It sounded as if it pulled out from somewhere right before the bend. That would be Riley's place."

Riley guessed the neighbor must be Peg Haslam, the widow who'd parceled off some of her own land after her husband's death to add to Mike's acreage.

"Sal." Charlie radioed the officer investigating the shoulder of the road leading away from the house. "That fresh rubber look like a motorcycle to you?"

"You betcha," the voice transmitted. "Our intruder must not have been looking to score stuff he could hock."

"Money or jewelry, then," Charlie said. "That would be easy to carry."

Janet nodded. "Jewelry's an easy enough pawn."

Scott frowned. "He obviously didn't know the security system routes a silent alarm to the precinct. A normal system would have given a burglar a good five or six minutes before the security company dispatched the police. Time enough for Riley to get a call and confirm whether or not this was a false alarm."

"I didn't get that call, either," she admitted, frustrated by her own absentmindedness. Leave it to her to forget her phone the day she actually needed it. She had so much on her mind that things were slipping through the cracks. "But I don't know anything about a silent alarm. What are you talking about?"

Scott met her gaze. "The chief authorized it as a precaution after Mike. Until we figured out exactly what went down and who was involved, we didn't want to take chances."

"It's active?" She wasn't the only one looking at Scott.

"We talked about disconnecting after we closed the investigation, but you were gone, and Brian was alone in the house." He shrugged. "Seemed a good idea to leave it.

"Which raises a question." Scott leaned against the

cruiser and folded his arms across his chest, looking strong and capable, a man in control. "So as far as the perp knew, he should have had time to get in and out. But if that was the case, we'd have caught him. So why'd this guy run?"

"Petty hood got spooked?" Sal offered as he joined them.

"By what?" Janet asked.

"Or he knew the cops were on the way," Scott said.

Sal frowned. "You thinking he had a radio?"

Scott nodded.

"He must have been looking to make a fast getaway," Charlie said. "Why else the bike?"

Scott usually wore a poker face, but right now Riley could see through his intensity. She wasn't sure why. Perhaps only because she was getting to know the nuances of this man who was becoming her friend, establishing his own place in her life. He wasn't going to let this go until he had answers.

And knowing that reassured her. So much.

"It's not possible to predict your work schedule, Riley," he said, his gaze holding hers. "You don't always know when you're heading out on assignment. So how long have the kids been in school—a couple of days now?"

"Since Monday." Four days that had passed in a blur.

"So whoever tried to break in didn't know about the silent alarm, but he knew the exact time you'd be gone. How long does it take you to drop the kids off and get back?"

"Thirty minutes round-trip give or take."

That got everyone's attention. Riley could see it in the way everyone focused on her. Even the latest arrival, a man appearing from around the garage, wore a frown. A detective, judging by his casual dress.

"That's not a very large window," Scott said. "And not a very established routine."

Riley thought she understood what was troubling him. “Brian only takes early classes on Tuesday and Thursday mornings.”

“And the semester started last week.”

She nodded, feeling her heart rate speeding up again.

The new guy extended his hand to Riley. “Kevin Rush,” he said. “Scott’s partner. Pleased to meet you.”

Riley introduced herself. Mike had been Scott’s partner for as long as she’d known them. She’d never thought to ask how his new partner was working out, hadn’t thought of Scott in any role other than the one he’d always played—as Mike’s friend.

But now she wondered how this man compared. How did their work measure up? How did Scott pass his days now—with camaraderie or stoic professionalism?

Then Kevin said, “Whoever this guy was, he had a pretty tight bead on your schedule.”

“That’s what I’m thinking.” Scott reached for Riley’s elbow as if he knew she was putting two and two together and didn’t want her to worry. “Come on, Riley. Let’s unlock the house. We need to do a walk-through.”

“You said he didn’t get past the bathroom.”

He squeezed her elbow, a gentle touch. “He didn’t. Barely had time to break the window let alone get inside. It’s a precaution.”

“We’re the best. You know that.” Janet laughed. “We want to be thorough.”

“The chief’ll fry our asses if we’re not,” Sal added. “You don’t want to make us deal with him, do you? We’ll wind up in front of the review board.”

“Or suspended without pay,” Charlie added. “Can you imagine what Sarah-Lynn would have to say about that?”

Riley smiled, knowing the performances were for her

benefit. Charlie's wife would be as bad as the chief, she knew. Maybe even worse since Charlie actually lived with her.

"Come on." Scott guided her to the front porch door. "I want you to check your messages."

That snapped Riley back to her right mind. "Ohmigosh. My phone. What if Mrs. House tried to call me? Who has the time?"

"Eight twenty-four," Janet offered, clearly puzzled.

But Riley didn't bother to explain, just grabbed her keys off her belt and headed toward the front porch. She'd left school nearly thirty minutes ago. What if Jake hadn't settled down? What if Mrs. House had been trying to reach her?

She was yanked from her thoughts when Scott plucked the keys from her hand.

"If you don't mind." He didn't give her a choice as he unlocked the door.

Suddenly she found herself flanked by a personal security force made up of Poughkeepsie's finest. They kept her from entering until assured the coast was clear.

Riley finally entered and beelined straight for her cell phone charger, which she kept on her bedside table. The phone read Charge Complete on the display. She cleared the screen and, sure enough, found her missed calls.

Home security.

Scott.

Brian.

No calls from the school. She exhaled a pent-up breath.

"Everything okay?" Scott asked, startling her.

She hadn't heard him approach and turned to find him framed in the doorway, his broad shoulders filling the opening, that serious expression hinting at how much he cared.

"Jake had a rough morning. I was afraid the teacher might have called."

"She didn't?"

Riley shook her head, appreciating his concern.

Scott didn't move. He didn't quite meet her eyes, either, as if there was some invisible line that kept him from even glancing inside the private domain of her bedroom. He shifted from foot to foot, looking so uncomfortable that Riley keenly felt the distance between them, the way he no longer seemed like Scott, who'd been around forever. Her husband's partner. His friend. Scott had been many things through the years. A handsome, sometimes somber man, who wore his loyalty to those he loved on his sleeve. But he'd never been *her* friend.

He'd always kept his distance. She didn't know why. Yet now, as Riley watched him, she knew things were changing between them. And she was very, very aware of those changes.

CHAPTER NINE

WHAT IN HELL was wrong with him?

Scott didn't have a ready answer, but he stood at the threshold of Riley's bedroom, more physically affected by the sight of her than he should have been. Way more.

She glanced down at the display again, scrolling through her telephone messages. Her wildly curly hair fell forward, covering much of her face. Still, he could see the tight set of her jaw, the delicate profile set in anxious lines.

In that moment there should have been only the two of them. There should have been only relief that the perp hadn't broken into the house, hadn't harmed her or given her anything else to worry about. She was already struggling to settle in.

She hadn't said anything, not to him or Rosie or Joe as far as Scott knew, but tension was all over her. In the way she had to work for smiles that used to come so fast and easy. In the way so much attention from overzealous and well-meaning cops seemed to swallow her up. In the way she looked fragile right now, as if she stood there holding her breath just waiting for something else horrible to come at her.

So what was wrong with him that he was standing here, almost painfully aware of the neatly made bed, the silky blouse hanging from a bedpost, the toiletries scattered over the dresser that seemed so much more personal than if they'd been on a grocer's shelf?

And why in holy hell was he suddenly hearing the words *tending the farm?*

Damned kids.

Scott shook his head to clear it. But he didn't move from that doorway as he swallowed past the lump in his throat and tried to ignore those words.

What was wrong with him? He needed to back up and get out of this room. But he was still standing there when Riley glanced up again, curls tumbling over her shoulders, the tight lines of her face relaxing as sunlight spilled through the window, bathing her in a glow that made her tanned skin seemed cast in gold.

Their gazes met, and a frown tugged at the corners of her mouth. His gut gave a hard twist.

"Scott?"

"Yeah," he forced out.

"Is anything wrong?"

"No. Just need you for the walk-through." Stupid ass he was. Doing exactly what he didn't want to do—worry her.

"Of course. I'm sorry."

He was pushing too hard. "No hurry. No one's going anywhere."

A small smile. "No real crime to fight out there, hmm?"

He could only snort.

Her smile widened. "I appreciate everyone responding the way they did. Please tell the chief. I can't tell you how much better I feel knowing everyone's got their eyes on us. I mean really, Scott."

"Everyone's glad you're back." He responded on autopilot. "But seriously, you should take a few extra precautions. Let Roger's son stay with Brian a few nights. Brian will go along. Do whatever you can to shake up your routine."

The smile vanished as fast as it had appeared. She sank down onto the side of the bed, a boneless motion that made her look tired. "You're worried."

"I'm always worried."

She lifted her gaze, and those crystal-blue eyes weren't sparkling. "I mean more than your normal worrying. Things aren't adding up. I know the look."

No doubt. "We should pay attention."

"What else can I do?"

"You know the drill. I'll have a unit assigned to patrol your place. No problems there. Vary your routine and keep the security system armed even when you're at home. Any chance of getting your dogs back?"

She gave a wry chuckle that didn't reach her expression. "Not hardly. Caroline thrives on playing big sister. Her 'babysitting' turned into a little more than I expected. Hershel and Oodles Marie are hers now. I wanted to bring them down to Florida once I knew we'd be staying, but she insisted they wouldn't like the heat." Riley shrugged. "They're her only connection left to Mike. I'm trying to be gracious. So, no watchdogs. I can't handle puppies."

"Can't blame you there. I don't want you to worry, though." He'd be worrying enough for them both. "PPD's got your back."

He sounded a lot more assured than he felt, but his words had the desired effect. Riley visibly relaxed. With a graceful motion, she straightened and stood.

"Thank you," she said earnestly, an appreciation he didn't deserve. "I feel a lot better. And that's saying something. It's been a rough week."

"Jake going to be okay?"

She cocked a hip against her dresser and clipped the cell phone to her jeans. "Yeah. He just takes a little more time to settle in than Camille. And I'm never sure if I'm doing everything I should be to help him along."

Scott wasn't sure how to respond to that. He had about zero experience with little kids, although he was pretty savvy about the older ones. But when she folded her arms across her chest and took a deep breath, Riley gave the impression she just needed to talk. Sure enough…

"Camille's really excited, you know. She loves school. But when Jake gets upset, she feels bad, like she shouldn't be so happy about something that bothers him. She doesn't understand the problem even though I talk with her about it. They're so different that a lot of the time what works with one doesn't work with the other, and it's hard to get any alone time with either of them." She lifted a hand and rubbed her temples. "My impulse is to fix things, but I can't always do that. I have to help them learn to cope. But it breaks my heart watching Jake struggle so much."

Scott nodded. He thought he understood. She was a good mom. She even shoved aside her own feelings to teach her kids. Sure, it might be easier for her if she fixed the situation, but in the long run, Jake wouldn't have the skills necessary to handle the things that came up in life.

That was exactly what Scott dealt with at Renaissance. Kids whose parents hadn't prepared them to deal successfully with the world. Sometimes parents died or took off, or their own addictions got in the way of their responsibilities. Sometimes they were still around, but didn't know any better. Whatever the reason, the result was the same—kids fighting to cope with life and making a lot of wrong choices along the way.

He'd been a kid like that himself once.

Life had taken away all the people who mattered and left him with a family that had been the antithesis of Mike and Riley's. Scott might have lost a parent—a mother in his case—but the father who'd been left behind hadn't been the least interested in parenting.

But Scott had been one of the lucky ones—he'd had a decent enough start to realize that he wanted more for himself. He'd been smart enough to figure out how to get it. That hadn't happened without a fair amount of good people to help him along the way. People like the chief, Mike and, in her way, Riley. He'd been Mike's friend, never hers. How could he when he'd always been so aware of her, and so ashamed of feeling that way? But he'd made the choice to keep his distance from her long ago, and while Riley might not have known how he felt, she'd always welcomed him unconditionally, always respected the distance he'd kept between them, accepted what he'd had to offer.

"You're doing your best, Riley." That much he did know. "What more can you do?"

She shrugged. "It always feels like I could be doing more, like I'm missing something."

"Trust me on this," he said softly, denying the urge to share details about his own upbringing to convince her. "Jake and Camille are two cool little people. That speaks for itself. You're raising good kids."

She gave a rather lopsided smile, looking sheepish. He wasn't sure why. Maybe because she'd needed reassurance. Or maybe because they were talking about personal things in a way they never had before.

Either way, Scott knew she'd not only lost her husband when Mike had died, but her best friend. Sure, she had other friends, but most had taken off after college, heading back home or launching careers elsewhere. Pleasant Valley had been Mike's town, not Riley's.

She eyed him thoughtfully. "You know, maybe I should ask Rosie to help me arrange some alone time to spend with each of them. I'm sure she'll help out."

"No question there. She'd probably jump at the chance." As Riley had said, the Angelica family didn't have many connections left to Mike.

"Hey, man," Kevin called from down the hallway. "We ready to get this show on the road?"

The moment was over. Pushing away from the dresser, Riley gave a light laugh. "You're so sweet. Thanks for listening."

"I'm here, Riley." It was all he could think to say.

But Scott wasn't thinking, that much was obvious when he stepped forward and reached for her hand, gave it a reassuring squeeze. Her fingers felt lightweight and warm against his, so alive. So Riley. Had Scott been thinking, he'd have remembered he had no business touching her, not even casually.

He couldn't be casual with Riley.

"You ready yet?" Kevin asked when he appeared in the doorway.

Scott slipped his hand from Riley's and turned. "Yeah. Let's do it."

"What do I need to do?" Riley asked.

"Give us the ten-dollar tour." Kevin seized the chance to take control, even going so far as to loop his arm through Riley's. "You can double-check that nothing looks disturbed while I get to know you better. It's a pleasure to finally meet you. I've heard a lot about your family."

"Good, I hope," she said.

"Naturally." Kevin flashed a blinding smile that gave

Scott the sudden, and unexpected, impulse to plant a fist in his cosmetically perfect teeth.

Kevin led Riley through the door, forcing Scott to fall in step behind them. This wasn't going to work.

"Riley, want me to get a jump on the broken glass?" He reached for his cell phone. "I'll give Tony at Father and Son Glass a call. He'll send someone out. I don't want you home alone with that window out."

She glanced over her shoulder, a smile plastered on her face. A forced one, Scott was pleased to note. She wasn't stupid enough to fall for Kevin. "I'd appreciate it very much."

"Done." He made his way to the foyer to place the call.

By the time he reconvened with Riley and Kevin, he had a glass guy on the way.

"They didn't make it inside," Kevin informed him.

"No surprises there." Scott met Riley's gaze, found her looking drained. "Not the best way to start the day."

She only gave a wan smile before accompanying them onto the front porch. She thanked everyone who hadn't taken off yet and waited inside the open doorway as her driveway cleared. Scott wished she would go inside and lock up, so he would at least know she was safe. But he couldn't think of any way to tell her to get inside without looking like an overprotective jerk. An overly possessive one, anyway.

So he slipped into his car, barely giving Kevin a chance to get in before he gunned the engine and took off, watching Riley recede in his rearview mirror.

Kevin sank back in the seat and gave a low whistle. "Wow. The widow is everything I heard and a bag of chips."

Scott shot Kevin a look, not a little surprised he was heading down this road. "You're an idiot."

Kevin's turn to look surprised.

Scott relented. "What'd you hear?"

"That Mike was a seriously lucky man. I didn't know the dude. Not really. Seen him around the station, but I was new with the department. You two were legendary."

Scott snorted.

"No, really, man. You two came and went as you pleased, and always had the chief on your side. Looked pretty good from where I was standing."

What did he even say to that? "Yeah, well, what it looked like and what it was were two different things."

"Maybe, but not with the widow." Kevin closed his eyes. "Heard she was a stunner. I'd say so."

This wasn't news. Not to anyone who knew Riley. Everyone in the PPD had known Mike was a lucky bastard. They'd ragged him about it endlessly. Mike had always told everyone to take a damn hike. He knew they were jealous.

But not Scott.

He might have had unwanted feelings for Riley, but what kind of person would be jealous of a friend? Especially a friend like Mike.

"So you've been keeping your eyes on her," Kevin said. Not a question. "That's decent. Not like you'll go blind, though."

Another image flashed of what Kevin would look like with a few broken teeth. Scott blinked a few times to erase the vision. The rational part of his brain knew Kevin meant nothing more than to pay Riley a compliment. But that rational part got its ass stomped by the irrational part, which didn't want to face the fact that Kevin was all too right.

Watching over Riley wasn't hard. It was easy. Too damned easy.

"WHAT DO YOU THINK, Chief?" Hank Llewellyn emerged from the questioning room wearing a scowl.

"I think you're up against a player," Jason said. "The guy told us he didn't know a thing about guns the first time we questioned him, and he not only hunts but has an NRA membership. Give me a break."

Hank nodded. "I'm booking him."

Jason was about to reply when message traffic over the police radio caught his attention.

10-17.

29 Traver Road, Pleasant Valley.

Attempted burglary. Suspect fled the scene.

Jason's heartbeat upped a notch, though if Hank noticed the frequency for Pleasant Valley's patrol zone, he gave no clue.

Jason might be looking at Hank, but didn't hear a word his officer was saying as the radio relayed details of the call.

10-17. PPD had responded to a suspected prowler.

Jason had been monitoring the sheriff's band, but supposed he shouldn't be surprised the PPD had taken the call. All it would take was one cop to recognize Mike Angelica's address. Half the force had probably shown up before the sheriff had gotten there.

Not all towns in the Mid-Hudson Valley had their own police forces. Smaller townships, such as Pleasant Valley and LaGrange, relied upon the County Sheriff's Department, the state troopers and neighboring departments to serve them.

Jason had been hoping for a little luck today. He'd hoped that when the security company called Riley, she'd assume a false alarm and give her code word. Still, there should be time for Tyrese to find what he was looking for inside the house. *"Attempted burglary. Suspect fled the scene."*

"Damn it," he ground out.

"Chief?" Hank frowned. "You're not okay with that?"

Jason stared, so wrapped up in his own thoughts that he had to shake his head before seeing Hank again, who was looking at him from not two feet away. He shook off his distraction. "No. It's all good. You got it, Hank. Good work."

Jason had no clue what he'd just signed on for, but had to trust Hank's discretion. The fact that Hank looked pleased by the praise only served to ramp up Jason's anxiety. Friggin' domino effect. This grief was taking over his whole life.

He issued a few more statements to get Hank out of his face. Sure enough, no sooner had the door to the questioning room closed when the disposable cell phone in Jason's pocket rang.

Retrieving the phone, he headed into his office and shut the door. "Give me good news, man."

"You want good news?" the voice said, gruff and annoyed. "Then you came to the wrong place."

Tyrese Griffey had been one of the few surprises in Jason's law-enforcement career. He was old-time 16 Squared—a peewee since long before his voice had changed. Few gang members ever lived to see the opposite side of twenty, especially one like Tyrese with a rap sheet as long as his arm before he'd been old enough to get a driving permit.

The various law agencies around the area had collared him so many times he practically had his own police ten-code. His young age would put him right back on the streets again.

Then, during one night in the Hazard Creek lockup, not long after Jason had become chief, Tyrese claimed to have had a divine visitation. He began to witness salvation on street corners, declaring the love of Christ Jesus for all mankind, and becoming another sort of nuisance entirely.

So when he showed up for his day in court, Jason convinced the judge to give him a shot at redemption with the Renaissance program. Chief Levering knew Tyrese personally and didn't want any part of this serial offender, but Jason had managed to convince him to take a chance.

Tyrese had surprised them all. He hooked up with a church that seemed to appreciate his enthusiasm and abilities. They put him to work as groundskeeper and handyman, a sort of living testimonial to the love of Christ. Tyrese had been doing what he could to improve the world ever since.

Until the night some neighborhood thug had raped his baby sister and beat her within an inch of her life. He'd gone to preach mercy and forgiveness and wound up killing the guy.

Tyrese had freaked and called Jason. And when Jason had weighed all the good Tyrese had been doing against this thug from Big House…well, Jason wasn't God or anything, but he thought Tyrese had done the world a public service by taking out one of the bad guys. So he'd given the kid a second chance and helped him make the whole situation vanish.

It had never occurred to Jason that he'd call in the favor.

But now he half sat on the edge of his desk, feeling sick. "What happened?"

"Wasn't any problem getting the place empty," Tyrese said. "Broke a window and had cops breathing down my neck before I'd gotten inside. Good thing I had the radio."

Under any other circumstances, Jason might have complimented the foresight, but not now. Not when he was in way over his head. He needed to know what was on that

CD and if it implicated him. He needed to know if Riley knew what was on it.

"Must have had a silent alarm wired straight to PPD dispatch," Jason said. "It would explain why the cops responded as fast as they did."

But it didn't explain why the house was wired. Jason could understand the PPD adding the precaution while investigating Mike's death, but that had been over two years ago. Why now?

Maybe he was just being paranoid or maybe someone was worried about Riley's safety because she was investigating stories that put her at risk.

"Yeah, I figured that part out for myself." Tyrese sucked in a deep breath. "Listen, Chief. I've got a shot at a life here, a real one. I'm not going down for you."

"You got a shot because I gave it to you."

There was silence on the other end. Jason could practically hear Tyrese's divinity warring with his worldly self. But Tyrese couldn't hang up. Jason needed him. Tyrese was *his*. Not someone Agent Asshole could blackmail or buy off. It didn't matter that he was one more on the growing list of people whose lives Jason was screwing up because *he'd* screwed up.

Callie. The kids. His parents.

So he said the only thing he could think of that might convince Tyrese not to hang up the phone.

"I'm in trouble, Tyrese."

CHAPTER TEN

RILEY HAD ALWAYS LOVED the chaos of Angelica family get-togethers. This Labor Day celebration was no different, if for an unexpected reason. Once upon a time, she'd enjoyed being with immediate and extended family because she'd loved the camaraderie, a welcome change from her solitary and mobile upbringing as an only child in a military family.

And while she still enjoyed that camaraderie with people she'd come to love dearly, today she also appreciated how the chaos distracted her from thinking—about Jake's difficult first week of kindergarten, about available career choices, about how different this gathering felt without Mike.

Different yet somehow the same. As if she still belonged here. That was a good feeling, a hopeful feeling, as if the future would sort itself out as long as she kept putting one foot in front of the other.

"Aunt Riley, I thought you said these kids went to school in Florida," Brian called out from the pool.

"They did." She smiled as Brian hefted Jake into the air and flipped him head over heels into the water.

Her son's laughter rang out, ending as quickly as it began when he landed with a splash. Water exploded onto the deck. Groans and growls erupted from the group playing pinochle not far from the splash zone.

Brian propped himself up on the side of the pool. "I don't think these kids did anything but swim. They're kicking our butts at water tag."

Riley laughed. "It's summer all the time down there, Brian. They went to school and swam pretty much every day."

"Oh, man. That's just wrong."

"My turn." Camille launched herself onto her cousin's back and tried to drag him underwater. "Throw me."

Brian good-naturedly went under, coming up with dramatic sputters that made Camille squeal.

Riley covered her ears. "Dunk her, Brian. Before she does permanent damage."

Brian obliged, and they got a split second of blessed silence before one of the cousins, who'd been congregating at the opposite end of the pool, declared the break over.

"Jake and Camille are it." The cry rang out as energetic swimmers propelled themselves into the water, starting the mayhem again.

Riley plunked down into an Adirondack chair to watch the carnage, hanging on to a glass of water she wasn't drinking.

Camille and Jake had the obvious advantage. They dove in and around their older cousins like little piranhas, delighting everyone—particularly themselves—with their speed and prowess.

"You can't catch me," Camille shrieked when her head broke the surface, clearly wanting her big cousins to do exactly that.

Jake was so much more subtle. He was on the warpath and out for blood.

"Don't you know how to swim, dude?" he taunted Brian, then dove underwater, only coming up for air when he was clear on the opposite end of the pool.

Her kids got their time to shine, their time to connect

with cousins they couldn't remember and, in the process, earn a place for themselves. They had a big Italian family to love them. And Joe and Rosie's family was definitely big. They'd had five kids total. Mike and his twin, Lily Susan, had been surprise blessings, as Rosie always referred to them, twins who were eight years behind the pack. Everyone lived close by with the exception of Lily Susan, whose destination-wedding business was based out of Manhattan.

"Mind if I join you?" Caroline appeared at her side, collapsed into a nearby chair.

"Game over?"

Caroline scowled. "So it would seem."

Riley glanced up in time to see Caroline's husband, Alex, storming into the house, leaving behind a picnic table with various in-laws staring after him, still holding cards.

"Everything okay?"

"Fine, thanks. But I would caution your kids about choosing their life mates at the tender young age of sixteen."

Riley only gave a slow nod, knowing better than to comment. Caroline had met Alex Bosse during her sophomore year in high school. Alex had been a junior at the time, and they'd gotten married not long after Caroline's graduation, so she could go off to college to live with him.

"Then may I say thanks again for lending me Brian?" Riley said to break the silence and distract her sister-in-law from what appeared to have been an unpleasant scene. "He's been a treasure. I couldn't have done the past two years without him."

"He feels the same about you, Riley. Taking care of the horses is a small price to pay for his independence, don't kid yourself. He has a sweet deal and he knows it."

Riley smiled. “A mutually beneficial arrangement. Can’t ask for more than that.”

“No, I suppose not.”

“Do you see him much?”

Caroline scowled harder. “Sunday dinners here unless he needs something. I should be grateful. I’d barely see him at all if he’d have gone away to college.”

Which Riley could see invited mixed emotions, and she could certainly understand. Her kids weren’t close to college yet, but she filed the information away and hoped to remember a few years from now. Enjoy the moment. It would all too soon be over.

Or all too unexpectedly.

That was a lesson she’d learned well.

“It’s good that he’s keeping close with Rosie and Joe.”

“Yeah. But I wish he would spend more time with us.” Caroline shifted her gaze to the patio doors where her husband had disappeared. “Then again, I guess I can’t really blame him. No one wants to be home much anymore.”

There was so much in that statement. Riley eyed her sister-in-law closely, wishing she could read her mind. “Want to talk?”

“Thanks, but no thanks.” Caroline’s golden-brown eyes narrowed. “Same shit, different day.”

She reached out and grabbed Caroline’s well-manicured hand and gave a squeeze. “Well, I’m around if you change your mind.”

But Riley knew Caroline wouldn’t call. They were fond of each other and had been close before Mike’s death. Maybe the years of distance had taken their toll. Maybe Caroline thought Riley had her hands too full to add anything else to the mix. She was thoughtful that way. Or maybe Caroline simply didn’t want to talk. Whatever the reason, it served as another reminder of how quickly life marched on. The twins weren't the only ones who needed to reestablish places within the family.

"I'll sit in with pinochle," Riley said lightly. "If you'll teach me how to play."

That got a better response. Caroline's warm eyes crinkled around the edges in real amusement. "I can't teach you during a game. We'll be too busy playing."

An old problem. "What about Max or Rosie?"

"Max isn't coming because Madeleine has a tummy bug," she replied, referring to Max's young daughter. "And forget about Mom. She won't leave the kitchen until dinner is on the table. Speaking of..." Caroline glanced at her watch. "She's running late. She's probably stalling because of Scott. He's late."

"Scott's coming for dinner?"

"Yeah. He usually calls if he's not going to make it, but I don't think he called."

"How'd you all manage to get him here?"

"Dad caught him helping Brian out at your place one Sunday. You know Dad." She rolled her eyes. "He made Scott come with Brian under threat of death. Scott humored him, but he's been coming around more and more. Dad's pretty pleased with himself."

No doubt. Riley had tried for years to get Scott to feel as welcome in her home was Mike's other friends. But Scott had never dropped by without a formal invitation. He'd been prone to waiting in the cruiser outside rather than coming in to pick up Mike before a shift no matter how often Riley invited him in for coffee.

Water sluiced over the side of the pool followed by gales of laughter, and both Riley and Caroline lifted their feet to avoid the flood streaming beneath their chairs.

"Leave some water in the pool, guys," Caroline told them.

Riley only smiled, mulling what her sister-in-law had said about Scott. Was that what she'd noticed the night they'd eaten tacos after the Hazard Creek debacle? That sense of Scott being comfortable in the house, familiar with the dinner routine. She'd been right.

"Exactly how much has he been helping Brian out around the farm?" Riley asked. "I'm getting the sense it's a lot more than I realized."

Caroline met her gaze with that honest stare that reminded Riley so much of Mike. Like her brother, Caroline didn't pull any punches. "Nothing ridiculous or I'd have stepped in. Trust me. But the bottom line…well, Brian's a kid. There's a lot of stuff he doesn't know even though he'd never admit that."

"Oh, Caroline, I knew he was taking on a lot. If it was too much I'd have made other arrangements. You've been telling me everything is fine."

"I've been telling you everything's been fine because everything has been fine." Caroline leaned forward with a conspiratorial glance at the pool. "My son wants to be independent. He was leaving the day he turned eighteen no matter what. That left him with taking care of the farm or moving out with one of his buddies and killing himself to pay rent."

She shrugged. "At least when he's working for you, he's got boundaries. You flat-out told him he has to stay in school or the deal was off. Every last person in this family will narc on him if he screws up, and he won't get any mercy if he kills one of Uncle Mike's horses because he's lazy."

"That's awfully heavy for a kid…." Riley let her words trail off when Caroline shook her head.

"He's learning responsibility. That's a good thing. One of his parents spoiled him." She had the grace to look abashed but quickly added. "Cut me a break. He was my first. Besides, when he gets stuck, he calls Scott. At least he's calling someone to help and not toughing it out on his own. We really would end up with dead horses then."

"Remind me when my time comes, okay?"

"I will. Though I might not get the chance to boss you around." Caroline smiled. "Well, to be honest, I hoped you'd never come back so I wouldn't have to tell you that Hershel and Oodles Marie are mine now. We've bonded. You'll scar them for life if you take them away."

Riley sighed. "I made peace with your betrayal a while ago. But for the record you were only supposed to be babysitting while I got settled at my mother's. It was only a few weeks."

"What can I say? I'm hard to resist."

"You are that, which must be why I'm here now. I do appreciate everything you and your son have done for us. And Scott's really good with young people, so I'm not surprised Brian likes him so much. The feeling seemed mutual."

Caroline sank back in the chair and tipped her face toward the sun. "No question. That's all he has—work and those kids."

Riley shouldn't ask. From the depths of her soul, she knew she shouldn't ask. But she couldn't resist. She wanted to know, plain and simple. "Not involved with anyone at the moment?"

Caroline waved an impatient hand. "Not that I've heard, and I'd have heard."

"Can't say I'm surprised. He was always a dating junkie. Never knew who he'd bring to police events. Hard to keep up."

"I have no clue what his deal is," Caroline admitted. "He's dated some nice women, but I don't think he's been doing much lately. Not since Mike…"

"It's been rough on him?"

"He's on his second partner."

"Oh" was all Riley could think to say. She'd asked Scott how he was doing, of course. Every time they'd spoken on the telephone for the past two years, but he always said he was okay, never went into any specifics. She'd let it go at that. It just wasn't that way between them. He'd been Mike's friend.

Now she wanted to know why he dated but never seemed to have relationships.

"I really wish he'd get more balance in his life," Caroline said thoughtfully. "And that's not gossip, by the way. I've said as much to him."

"Really?"

"Really. Come on, Riley. He's a good-looking guy. Hardworking. He's a volunteer, for God's sake. A guy with a social conscience. But he's never been married. Doesn't have kids. We're the only family he has, and we only see him on Sundays. Doesn't that make you wonder?"

"When you put it like that."

"Commitment issues, do you think?"

"I don't see it. He's committed to so many things—the department, Renaissance, his friendships. Doesn't seem to have trouble to me." So what, then? Riley was surprised by how much she wanted to know. "But what do you mean he doesn't have any family? I knew he didn't have anyone around here. Mike said as much, but he doesn't have any family anywhere?"

"That's what he said. His mom died when he was five, and he lived with his grandmother until she passed away.

Then he came to Poughkeepsie. Been with the department ever since."

Wow. "I've known Scott since I met Mike, and I've never heard one word of that. He told you?"

"Heck no. But you know Mom. When she wants to know how smother someone, she's relentless."

"You mean *mother* someone, don't you?"

"Oh, yeah, right." Caroline cracked a grin, and Riley was about to ask for more details, unable to resist the temptation of getting to know more about this man she was befriending, but the patio door slid open and the man himself came through as if on cue, wielding a bouquet of summer flowers.

"Hey, everyone. Sorry I'm late."

"Should have brought flowers for us, detective," Joey, Rosie and Joe's eldest son, said. "Mama's starving us so we can wait on you."

"That's why she's waiting on him." Caroline smirked. "*Because* he brings her flowers. You're an ungrateful mooch. You should at least bring a bottle of wine or something."

"What in hell are you talking about?" Joey scowled. "I brought the sausage. Freaking *ten pounds* of it. From Bastian's Road House no less."

"Be patient, Joey," Rosie told her son. "You won't starve."

Joey's wife made a show of patting his stomach, which was hanging somewhat over his belt. "No, he won't starve."

Laughter tittered around the table, and Joey scowled. Scott, Riley noticed, had the good sense to keep his mouth shut. Instead, he gave Rosie a hug and presented her the flowers.

"Sorry I'm late. You should eat and not worry about me."

Rosie accepted the bouquet and gazed up at him fondly. "But I do worry. Everything all right?"

"One of the kids let his pride get in the way of his good sense. Now he's in trouble with the law." Scott shook his head. "Needed a character reference."

Rosie reached up and patted his cheek. "You're a good boy."

"And you're turning my stomach here, Ma," Joey complained.

More laughter. Then Rosie asked, "Any hope for this one?"

Scott shrugged. "Maybe. He's got a shot, but you know how it goes. You can lead a horse to water…"

"Good luck with that," Joey said.

Rosie nodded. "I'll hold a good thought."

"Thanks."

"Well, come on, then." Cradling the bouquet in her arms, Rosie headed back toward the patio doors. "Get the kids out of the pool and washed up. Everything's ready, but I could use some help getting it out on the table. We're going buffet today."

"I'll help, Mom." Caroline pushed herself up out of the chair with effort.

"Want some—"

"Don't worry about it, Riley. You take care of the twins."

Caroline sidestepped the patio, reaching up on tiptoe to kiss Scott's cheek. "Glad you made it. You'll sit in for pinochle after dinner?"

"Didn't see Alex inside. He being…difficult?"

"Got your gun?"

Scott laughed. "Locked in the car. And, no, you can't have my keys."

"Not helpful, Scott. *Not* helpful." Caroline gave a laugh and headed inside.

Riley got to her feet, dragging the beach towels from the back of the chair so she could corral her kids.

Catching Scott's gaze as she turned, she smiled a greeting. "Nice to see you."

"You, too," he said.

Then silence engulfed them, the rowdy laughter from the pool fading from her awareness. It was a striking moment, a weird moment, filled with the past and the present. Scott must have been as struck by the weirdness as she was because they just stood there staring at each other. He seemed equally at a loss for words.

Riley wasn't sure why, but all the easy chitchat that had carried them through the years didn't seem to be working now. Not with a man who knew more about what was happening in Caroline and Alex's marriage than Riley did. Not with a man who'd stood in her bedroom and let her share her worries.

Not with this man who stared down at her with eyes so dark and serious that she barely recognized him. Definitely didn't recognize how he'd opened up to the family in the years she'd been away. He seemed comfortable around everyone, well liked and respected.

That part at least shouldn't come as a surprise. Scott was good people. She's always known that. No, the surprise was the way he was inserting himself into her life, becoming more than Mike's friend. She liked the man she was getting to know and couldn't help but wonder what he'd think if he could read her thoughts right now.

CHAPTER ELEVEN

SCOTT HATED STAKEOUTS for a variety of reasons. Topping the list was the fact that he didn't like to sit still for extended periods of time, so cramped in the front seat of his cruiser translated into the worst form of physical torture. Added to the physical torture was a mental one—stakeouts meant maintaining an alertness that was impossible to achieve without moving around to keep the blood flowing.

As such, he was forced to drink copious amounts of coffee to avoid slipping into a coma, but then he wanted to relieve himself way more than was convenient for sitting on a side street trying to look inconspicuous.

Then there was his partner.

Mike had understood the finer points of a stakeout. Even Roger, with his barely-two-years-until-retirement mentality, had understood that spending the night jammed in the front seat of a cruiser waiting for something to happen was a delicate balance of tolerance, patience and not doing anything to make an already bad situation worse.

Kevin hadn't figured that out yet. Scott wasn't sure he ever would. Kevin viewed the stakeout as the land of opportunity. Time to talk shop. Time to brainstorm stalled cases. Time to "bond"—whatever the hell that meant. They hadn't been sitting in front of the hardware store they suspected of being used as a drug drop for an hour before Scott was itching to point his service weapon at his new partner with the directive to shut up or be shut up.

Scott had tried to be reasonable. He understood Kevin was young and didn't seem to sit still any better than Scott did. Then there was the fact that Kevin was new to vice and wanted to impress the chief. One way to do that was to fit in, which Scott guessed had led to the whole "bonding" thing.

He tried to make a game out of it: *How many ways could he convey to Kevin that he didn't want to talk without actually saying the words?*

He'd lost count somewhere around midnight. Kevin refused to get the message. By 3:00 a.m., Scott had dispensed with the subtleties and flat-out said, "Will you shut up, man? You're too busy talking and not busy enough doing the surveillance. A damn cow could stroll by ringing a bell and you wouldn't hear it."

Kevin had just laughed and shut up for a grand total of ten minutes. And Scott knew that Mike was up *there* somewhere, laughing his fool head off.

Maybe that was why Scott had Riley and the kids on his mind after finally dropping Kevin off at the precinct a few hours later. Scott decided to cruise by Riley's place to reassure himself all was well at the farm, even though Pleasant Valley wasn't remotely close to his place out on Salt Point. But he had gallons of Starbucks Sumatra blend pumping through him, so he wouldn't be sleeping anytime soon, especially now that the sun was up and most of the world was starting the new day.

Scott wasn't sure what he'd expected to be going on at the crack of dawn, but it definitely wasn't finding the minivan doors flung wide and Jake loading up the back seat with pillows, blankets and a bucket. Brian's car was nowhere to be seen.

Scott had planned to drive by, but a little kid with pillows and a bucket invited a visit.

Slowing as he cruised into the driveway, Scott lowered the tinted window so Jake could see him.

"Hey, kiddo," he said. "What are you up to?"

Jake hopped out of the minivan, surprise melting into recognition on his face. "Oh, hi, Uncle Scott. I'm making a nest for Camille. She's sick."

"That doesn't sound good."

Jake shook his head solemnly, expression set in a grimace. "She has a headache. They make her puke."

That explained the bucket. "Brian's not around?"

"Mommy said he had a cook-off at college. He's gonna bring us leftovers."

Scott nodded. "Where's your mom—"

"Jake, where are you?" Riley's voice interrupted him from inside the house.

There was no missing the frantic edge to her voice. Jake didn't miss it, either, because he didn't say another word, just dumped the things he held inside the van and spun on his heels.

Scott slipped the car into Park and got out. He heard Jake announcing him when he got to the door and held the porch door wide, "Hey, Riley. I know it's a bad time—"

"No. No, it's not. Come on in."

He found her in the living room, with the shutters closed and the lights off. She knelt beside Camille, who was curled up in a tiny ball on the couch, a pitiful bundle of bright pajamas, colorful quilts and seemingly well-loved stuffed animals. She had a wet washcloth over her eyes and a bucket within easy reach. Her little mouth was drawn and pale even in the darkness.

Riley was smoothing hair away from her daughter's

forehead, and though she was playing the part of "mom" with her gentle touch and frazzled expression, she certainly wasn't dressed the part. The business suit she wore neatly hugged her curves and left the long expanse of her legs bare. She'd pulled her hair back, exposing her features in a way that normally got lost beneath all the hair. High cheekbones. Graceful curve of her jaw. Slender lines of her throat. Lots of smooth skin.

"She okay?" he asked, a distraction.

Riley glanced up. "Migraine."

"Isn't she a little young?"

"Don't I wish." Riley rearranged the stuffed animals on her daughter's pillow. "Try to sleep, sweetie. The medicine will start to work soon, I promise."

Camille barely managed a weak groan, and Scott just stood there, surveying the scene, not a part of it, but from the outside. He watched Riley rearrange the stuffed animals again, recognized the action as busywork for hands that wanted to be doing more.

"Mom, I'm gonna be late." Jake's urgency seemed to be apace of Riley's, and Scott remembered Riley's words about Jake's tough week at school. Walking in at this hour probably wouldn't do much for morale at this stage of the game. Moving Camille didn't look like such a hot idea, either.

"I'll take Jake to school," Scott offered. "If it'll help."

She glanced up at him, and there was so much in her expression, too much to make out. But Scott made his career out of reading people. She was overwhelmed.

And in that moment she was no longer the Riley he'd always known—laughing, genuine, competent, crazy in love with her husband. Right now she was a woman with responsibilities and a lot of people depending on her.

She was a woman he wanted to help.

"Sweet pea, we'll leave in a minute," she told Jake, standing with an agitated burst of energy. "No worries. Will you sit with Camille for a second while I talk with Uncle Scott?"

Jake plopped down beside the sofa with a huff.

Riley led Scott to her bedroom and motioned him inside. He stood on the brink of a room he didn't want to enter, a room that encouraged thoughts of Riley that he couldn't allow himself to think. But Scott's best interests weren't the priority right now, so he braced himself and stepped inside. The door had barely closed behind him before she erupted.

"Oh, Scott, thank you so much. I'd love to take you up on your offer, but I'm not sure it'll help," she said on one pent-up breath. "Jake gets so worked up. Maybe being with you will distract him. But getting him to school isn't the problem. The county head of criminal justice is giving a press conference in an hour. He's addressing the charges of accepting a bribe to push that food contract through his department. Have you heard about it?"

Scott barely nodded before she forged ahead.

"I've got to get into town before eight, and I was already pushing it with a side trip to school. Then Camille woke up with a migraine. She's so sick, and I've called everyone I can think of to watch her. Rosie and Joe are in Atlantic City. Caroline's hosting a pharmaceutical company brunch at the hospital for Alex. The aunties are at work and the kids are in school. Brian's not even around. I don't want to take Camille to work with me, but what else can I do? I can't leave her."

She exhaled an exasperated groan. "I hate this! What kind of mother leaves her little sickie? But I can't leave Max hanging. He won't be able to get anyone to cover the press conference with this short of notice, and I can't be in three places at one time—"

"Riley." Scott stepped forward and clamped both hands over her shoulders to brace her.

His touch seemed to startle her. It startled him. The feel of her beneath his hands, solid, warm and so completely real.

"Riley," he repeated, trying to block out the way his hands molded easily over her shoulders. A perfect fit. "Take a deep breath."

She lifted her gaze to his.

He met the worry in her expression and found his own breath coming with effort. "Let me help. Does Camille need to go to the doctor?"

She shook her head, finally coming around. He forced himself to let her go, to let his hands slip away.

"No. She needs to sleep. She's had migraines before. I'm pretty sure she's through the worst of it."

"Would you like me to stay with her?"

She narrowed her gaze, a look that, at the same time, was hopeful and suspicious. "Don't you have to work?"

"All-night stakeout" was all he said. "I'm too wired to even think about sleep, so I decided to play patrol and make sure all my favorite people were okay."

Her eyes closed, black lashes shuttering those sparkling eyes for the briefest of instants. A look of such relief crossed her face, as if his action was so much more than a simple offer to help out, as if *he* was so much more than he was.

"Would you, Scott? I can't leave her with just anyone, but she trusts you. *I* trust you. And I won't be long. I swear. Just a few questions after the press conference, and I'll come straight home."

But he wasn't anything more than a friend who'd driven by at the right time. "No problem. Do what you need to do. If the little sickie just needs some sleep, that's easy."

"I have my cell. Call me if—"

"We'll be okay. What's the worst-case scenario?" he asked. "I call 9-1-1. I might not know much about little kids, but I do know everyone at emergency dispatch. They'll fix me up."

That had the desired effect. Riley visibly relaxed and gave a smile, a blinding one that made her seem to glow from the inside out. "You're an answer to a prayer."

Scott didn't know what to say to that, so he pulled open the door and stepped aside. He wanted out of this bedroom. He wanted away from any reminder of Riley as a woman, and that big bed only made his thoughts travel in places they had no business traveling. She was a worried mom, and only a depraved jerk would be pumping his ego up at her expense right now.

Thoughts about riding in to save the day were the stuff of eight-year-old fantasies. He was an adult who'd made a promise to a friend. One he intended to keep. Period.

But Scott couldn't deny the wave of pleasure he felt when she hurried past, the smile still on her face and relief fueling her with purpose as her heels tapped sharply over the wood-beamed floors.

"Okay, kiddos." She reentered the living room with a take-charge stride, her control no longer just a facade for her kids' benefits. "We're back in action."

One fluid motion and she was on her knees beside Camille again, peering cautiously under the washcloth. "Sweetie, how's your head? Any better at all?"

Scott couldn't be sure, but he thought he saw Camille's eyes squeeze tighter against the light.

He resisted the urge to do the same, to block out the sight of Riley, all lean curves and bare legs.

"Uncle Scott is going to stay with you for a little while. Just till Mommy gets back, okay?"

Camille managed a weak nod.

"I have my cell, so you call me if you need me, okay? Uncle Scott will get you whatever you need, but your medicine should kick in soon, so you'll probably sleep." Riley pressed her lips to Camille's hand. "I love you. I'll be back as fast as I can." She kissed that pale little hand again, then tucked it beneath the quilt.

"C'mon, Jake. If we hurry, we'll make it." She rose to her feet, glancing around at Scott. "Please, make yourself at home. There's plenty of food if you're hungry. If she wants something to drink there's Gatorade in the pantry. Not cold. She likes the berry kind. The red stuff."

He nodded. "Got it. I'll call if I have any questions."

She gave him another one of *those* smiles.

"You really are a godsend, Scott. Thank you." She disappeared out the door, leaving Scott standing in the foyer, fighting so hard not to be impressed with himself for making her smile that way.

He was still staring at the door when the minivan ground out of the driveway and took off down the road.

And a huge part of him felt relieved that she was gone, relieved for the chance to get a lid on reactions that were so unworthy of Riley and himself. Of the man he'd chosen to be.

Pulling the door shut, Scott sucked in a deep breath to regain his focus, to release the conflict and send unwanted thoughts on their way.

Okay, so here he was…*babysitting*.

He could handle this. Riley would never have left Camille with him if she hadn't been sure he could handle the job.

Of course, Riley had been desperate.

An answer to a prayer.

Mike—wherever he might be—would be getting a lot

of laughs at Scott's expense today. No question. As long as he couldn't read minds.

Scott definitely needed to get a grip. So he locked the front door, armed the security system with the motion detectors disabled and went to check on his patient.

The little sickie was exactly where her mommy had left her, and he sank to his knees, made sure she was still comfortable. Hard to tell. She was so tiny in that massive bundle of quilts and stuffed animals....

"Uncle Scott?" Her voice was as tiny as she was, a throaty croak in the early-morning stillness.

"Hey, kiddo. How're you feeling?"

She pulled a face, barely discernible except for the effort it took.

"Can I get you something? How about some red Gatorade?"

A few pale blond hairs moved over the pillow as she shifted her head. "Lie down."

"You want me to lie down?"

The living room had been arranged with comfort in mind, and two plush couches created an L-shaped grouping against one wall. Camille lay on the couch facing the fireplace. Scott decided he could stretch out on the other couch and still face her.

"How about over there?" He pointed to the other couch.

"In a nest."

Scott frowned. "A nest?"

With a weak hand, she pushed aside the washcloth and tried to open her eyes. "Mommy has blankets in the closet."

Her voice was a throaty croak, and he knew he was making her work too hard to explain what she wanted. What in hell was a nest? Should he call Riley? Blankets in the closet… Then it clicked. Jake had been making a nest in the van. Little kid wrapped like a mummy in blankets.

A nest.

"I'll be back."

It took three tries to find the right closet, but he soon returned with an armful of blankets. Camille had turned her head to the side to watch him, so pitifully still, as if just the effort of observing sapped her strength.

He spread out the largest blanket, tossed a few throw pillows on one side, kicked off his shoes and lay down. Then he pulled the other blankets over him. "How's this?"

She gave a wan smile. Then she let her eyes close again.

Scott lay there and watched her as the light beyond the shutters brightened the room in slow degrees. But Camille seemed to be resting comfortably. Surprisingly, lying down in the warm comfort of his "nest" was also having an effect on him. He didn't think it was a good idea to sleep, in case the patient needed him. He could last a few more hours. But only if he got up and moved around.

He would. In a minute. Right now, he was struck by the silent familiarity of the dim room. It seemed like a lifetime ago that he and Mike had sat in here with the chief, watching the NFL draft or the play-offs while anyone who wasn't on duty dropped by to catch updates on the game.

Riley would keep the kids occupied or be in the kitchen cooking or brewing coffee, always in the background during those visits, always there making sure Mike's guests had what they needed for a good time.

He watched Camille sleep, knew she had no clue about how lucky she was to have a mom who loved her. But Scott knew. He knew from dealing with the kids at Renaissance. He knew firsthand from his own upbringing. And along the way he'd formulated his own ideas about families, about the way they should be. Mike and Riley had created the sort of family he admired. They'd wanted their kids to grow up in the comfort and security of a home that offered unconditional love and support.

Riley was carrying the torch now.

Scott hated seeing her so upset this morning, guilt tugging at her from all directions. She was an amazing mom, the best, but she hadn't felt that way. He was so damned glad he'd dropped by. But he wasn't Riley's answer to a prayer.

He was someone who had no business being here.

This was Mike's life, and Mike should be living it. Then Riley wouldn't be torn between a job she needed and her sick kid. She wouldn't always have that haunted look behind her expression, as if she hadn't figured out how to be happy again.

Scott didn't have a death wish by any stretch, but he'd worked on that case with Mike…and he hadn't had anything more to lose than his life. Literally. He didn't have a wife and kids who were crazy about him, who waited for him to come home after a shift, who depended on him.

And that had never felt as empty as it did right now.

Because he wanted someone to care about him?

Throwing his arm over his face, Scott tried to block out his thoughts. But the trouble wasn't something he could shut out by closing his eyes.

Had he envied Mike? The loving wife. The cute kids. The whole crazy package including extended Italian family. Or was it that seeing Mike's life up close and personal had been working him over subconsciously, making him rethink choices he'd made long ago? He dated his fair share of women, but always kept it simple. He didn't get involved. Scott had reasons for handling life the way he did.

He came from bad blood. While he'd grown far from his roots, he didn't trust himself. Couldn't. Any man who could covet a friend's wife… While Scott would never act on his feelings, the fact that he felt the way he did proved him untrustworthy.

And maybe that was the real trouble. Riley wasn't married anymore. She was just a woman. And one he cared about.

So much more than he should.

CHAPTER TWELVE

RILEY FINALLY GOT Jake to school, and he'd pulled through when she'd needed him to tough out the situation. Not only had he been worried about Camille, but he'd known Riley was upset. She hadn't said a word, but he'd known.

So, her tough little guy had given her an extra big squeezy hug before getting out of the minivan. He hadn't uttered one word of complaint. It was as if the separation anxiety he'd felt last week had never been.

Riley never failed to be amazed by how many emotions she could feel at once. Pride that her son had found his courage. Gut-wrenching worry about her darling girl at home. Appreciation that Scott had blown in to save the day.

And guilt, guilt, *guilt* for leaving.

She had no clue whether or not Camille was finally asleep or if her head was still throbbing hard enough to make her tummy sick. Riley hadn't hung around long enough to know whether her daughter had managed to keep the medicine down. If not, Scott was likely now holding the bucket, treated to a gritty reality of parenthood no serial single man should have to face.

Serial single.

The phrase popped into her head from nowhere, maybe some unmemorable article or bit of research. But it described Scott. She recalled her conversation with Caroline, but couldn't reconcile the Scott she knew with a man who had trouble committing—not given the relationships he had in his life. He was a solid, loyal man who was in for the long haul. That much he'd proven over and over again. His dedication to the PPD. To the kids at Renaissance. In his friendship with Mike and his continuing and evolving friendship with her.

Then again, Riley reminded herself, Scott had always been a closed book. She couldn't assume anything about him or about life. She'd learned that firsthand. She'd never imagined choosing a press conference over her sick child, yet here she was. The past two years had been nothing if not an exercise in recognizing that life wasn't obliged to follow her plans.

But despite the unexpected start to the morning, she managed to make the press conference. Of course, she had to bypass municipal parking for a place on a side street, but she scooted through the door seconds before the executive director took his place in front of the podium.

Then she put everything from her head and worked.

The executive director—former director, now that the man had surprised everyone by resigning his appointment—fielded too many questions about the charges of contractual corruption. But Riley lucked out and was called upon several times. And she got answers that would enable her to pull together an article that should make Max happy.

She slipped out a side door as the press conference wound down, hoping to avoid both the departing rush and a parking ticket on her windshield. What she found was a puddle of glass on the ground behind her minivan.

For an instant she stood there, unable to do anything but stare at the wreckage of her back window in disbelief. Who would break into a white minivan that looked like a giant refrigerator on wheels?

There was nothing of any value inside that would attract a thief.... Except her work bag, which contained everything she hadn't taken inside the conference center. And since all she'd needed was her handheld recorder that left her laptop and camera. If the alarm had sounded, it had long since stopped. Obviously no one had bothered to call the police.

She stared at the broken back window, wondering if she should scream now or save the meltdown until later.

Every shred of her wanted to hop inside the van and head home, but after checking inside to find—no surprise here—her work bag missing, she had to call the police and report the incident. Not that she thought they stood any hope of retrieving her equipment, but she would need the incident report for the insurance company.

Reaching for her cell, she snapped it open and scrolled through her contacts.

"Poughkeepsie Police Department nonemergency line," the perfunctory voice answered on the first ring.

Riley explained the situation, still trying to understand this turn of events. All her work...research for the articles she was working on. Had she backed up everything to her briefcase on the *Herald*'s server last night? She couldn't remember. If not, how much would she lose? And what about the photos she'd taken of the kids' first day at school? Were they still on the memory stick?

How could she have been so careless?

The answer to that question wasn't hard to figure—she was doing too much and not giving her best to anything. Riley was trying to decide how best to fix that problem when a unit arrived to take her report. Janet DiBenedetto.

"I couldn't believe it when I heard your name." Janet gave Riley a quick hug. "You okay?"

"Fine. Just not my week, I guess." Not her two years by the looks of it. "I left my daughter at home sick."

Janet smiled, a mom herself. "Don't worry. We'll make this quick."

And she did. Riley was on the road within ten minutes, a copy of the report on the passenger seat beside her and Janet's promise to question some people in the area to see if anyone had seen anything.

Riley didn't have much hope, and as the sounds of traffic echoed with the rush of wind through the smashed back window, she reminded herself that the situation could have been a lot worse. She and the kids could have been in the car. She had everything in the world to be thankful for.

Two beautiful, healthy kids. A home. A job. A wonderful family. Scott, who hadn't jumped ship but had been making an effort to segue into her life as a single parent. A caring person like Janet, who went out of her way to help out.

Riley had no business feeling as if the whole world was against her because of a broken window and stolen electronic equipment. If she hadn't taken the time to back up her work, she had nobody to blame but herself. She knew better. And she still had her handheld recorder. She could write today's article if she pulled research from other news services.

She'd managed to talk herself into a better frame of mind by the time she pulled into the driveway to find Scott waiting for her, the cell phone cradled against his shoulder, looking sleep ruffled with his dark hair listing to one side.

He snapped the phone shut as she parked the van. Then he was there, opening the door. "You okay?"

"Janet called."

He only nodded, glancing at the broken window, the worry in his gaze at odds with the pillow creases on his cheek.

"You got some sleep," she said softly.

Running long fingers through his hair, he made the whole glossy mess stand up even more. "Camille had me make a nest. Mistake. The minute I sat, I was down for the count. But she's okay. Still sleeping."

Riley could see her sweet little girl, even in the throes of a debilitating headache, turning the moment into a game.

A nest.

Riley wasn't sure what it was about Camille wanting Scott to have a nest that unglued her, but suddenly, tears prickled at her lids. The distress she'd been staving off in degrees all day formed like a wave from so deep inside. But she wasn't going to cry, refused to give in to the urge. She might be overwhelmed and having the run of luck from hell, but she was blessed. *Blessed.*

She inhaled raggedly, waved her hands as if she could physically fight off the tears.

Who cared about a stupid back window, anyway?

But her struggle must have been evident because for one stricken instant, Scott, a man with no clue what to do for a woman on the verge of melting down, stared at her. A small part of her mind, a rational part that managed to stand back from the encroaching tidal wave, chided her for being so weak. She had no right to burden him with her weakness.

But as quickly as Riley recognized that, as fast as she decided she would absolutely not burden this poor man any more today, he had her wrapped in his arms, cradling her against his warm, hard chest.

"It's okay, Riley," he crooned in a low voice.

He stroked her hair, and she felt the uncertainty of his touch. A friend. He wanted to comfort her, and the feel of his strong embrace was exactly what she needed to fight back. She melted against him, powerless to resist his solid strength, though she had no right to depend on him.

But in his arms, Riley wasn't thinking about right and wrong. She was thinking about him.

Slowly the emotion subsided, the anxiety quieted, smothered by her conflict over burdening Scott. But if he felt burdened, he certainly didn't show it. He held her close, creating a warm shelter with his embrace as one hand lightly stroked her back, as if he wasn't entirely convinced that touching her was the right thing to do.

But standing in his arms felt right. More right than she could have imagined. She was so aware of the unfamiliar feel of his hard body against hers. And she was so aware. Of how tall he was, taller than even Mike had been. Her heels brought her just high enough for him to rest his cheek easily on the top of her head. Her face rested on his shoulder, and she could feel the warmth of him radiating against her skin, feel the steady rise and fall of his chest.

Riley should step out of his arms, offer him a smiling thanks to transition through this intimate moment. She should cut the guy some slack so they could segue back to normal again.

But she didn't move, didn't speak, didn't want to do anything to ruin this moment, a moment where she felt as if she wasn't all alone for the first time in such a long time.

Reality finally intruded. The sound of a passing car. A horse neighing in the distance. Worry about Camille. And Jake. How was he surviving the day? Guilt because she was being so weak and selfish, because Scott had been working all night, and she'd sucked him into her chaos. The guy had only meant to cruise past the house to check on them.

"Thank you," she finally said. "You've been really sweet."

He chuckled, a throaty sound that rumbled deep in his chest. "I'm not so sweet. Nests are...comfortable."

That was even sweeter. "I'm beginning to think I should never have come back."

She tried to smile, but he must have known it was an act. Hooking a finger beneath her chin, he tipped her face up until she met his gaze. Those dark eyes were so still, so serious, a caress. "No," he crooned, still comforting her. "Everything will be all right. Trust me."

She did trust him. Too much. He'd been Mike's friend. While he was bridging the distance he'd always kept between them, he was still just a friend. She needed to keep that straight in her head.

She managed a small smile this time, one she hoped would reassure him. But Riley didn't trust herself to reply. Not when she wanted to tell him how much she appreciated his friendship, how much she liked the caring and strong man she was getting to know. Not when one simple admission would cross the boundaries of friendship and change things between them.

CHAPTER THIRTEEN

"DIDN'T YOU BLOW OUT of here about seven this morning?" Chief Levering asked. "What are you doing back?"

Scott lifted his head from the files scattered over the desk in front of him. Sleep hadn't been possible after leaving Riley's, so he'd headed to the precinct to burn off his surplus energy. "Looking over some recent B and E's and auto thefts."

The chief's eyebrows rose halfway up his forehead. "You don't have enough on your desk keeping you busy already?"

"You're kidding, right? That's why I'm here on my day off."

Scott braced himself for the reprimand he knew would come. An ongoing argument about too much time at the station and not enough living a life outside of work. An ongoing, *old* argument.

The chief surprised him. Glancing down at the files, he frowned and said, "You're worried about Riley?"

"Something's not right."

"Any ideas?"

Scott shoved the files away from him, disgusted. "Nothing but this knot in my gut."

Pulling the door to Scott's office shut, the chief dragged a chair around the side of the desk, then lowered himself so slowly Scott expected to hear creaking joints.

"You need something?" Scott asked.

"I'm a longtime fan of your gut, so why don't you pass a few of those folders this way?"

The chief was full of surprises today. "Don't you have somewhere to be? Busy police chief and all that."

"Got all kinds of time to burn today. Go figure. Now pass me some of those reports."

Scott shoved over a stack with the warning: "I have no clue what I'm looking for."

"Me, either. I'll fit right in."

Scott opened the next folder and scanned the details of the report. The chief did the same. They worked in silence for about five minutes.

"I wasn't okay with the break-in," Scott said suddenly, interrupting the quiet.

"No?" The chief didn't bother looking up. He didn't sound surprised, either.

"The window of opportunity was too narrow. It's not like Riley's routine is written in stone. The kids haven't settled into school yet. Brian, either. That means the perp had to be watching her closely."

"Not if he saw school-aged kids at the house. Doesn't take much of a leap since district elementary schools all start at the same time."

"He would have had to know they didn't take a bus."

"True." The chief inserted a report back in its sleeve, then reached for another. "Did you consider that it might have been random? The perp lucked out and came across the house when it was empty, took a chance, then got spooked. It's a nice place. It would be attractive to someone looking for fast cash."

"No way," Scott scoffed. "The perp went through all that trouble to break a window where he wouldn't be easily seen. He could have gotten in but took off before we got there." Scott shook his head decidedly. "He knew we were on the way."

"Okay. I buy that. Most kids looking for drug cash aren't so prepared."

Scott snorted. He didn't have to point out that most kids looking for drug cash usually kicked in the front door and stuffed whatever they got their hands on in grocery bags.

"Okay, so you got a perp who avoided our silent alarm," the chief said. "Did I mention I'm glad you talked me into keeping the place hardwired to the precinct?"

"You're welcome." Scott skimmed through another report, looking for any similarity to the attempted break-in at Riley's. "So, the question is—what was the perp looking for?"

"What'd he get from the car again?"

"Laptop and camera."

"Purse?"

Scott shook his head.

"He didn't need her identification, so he obviously knew who he was going after. Didn't take any money or credit cards?"

"No. Janet said it looked like he went in the back and didn't bother with anything else. Probably was long gone before her car alarm stopped blaring." Scott leaned back in the chair and met the chief's gaze. "That's what's bugging me. Riley said she normally keeps her laptop bag up front with her. She pushes it under the passenger seat, and there's usually so much of the kids' stuff around that she hides whatever's left sticking out. But she parked on the street this morning because she was running late. That's the only reason she moved her equipment into the back. It's the only place in the van where it's really hidden."

"And the only way the perp would have known that is if he watched her put it there."

"You got it." That knot in Scott's stomach clenched like a fist.

The chief frowned. "You don't expect to find anything in these reports."

"No. But I didn't want to overlook anything before I start interrogating Riley. She's pretty shaken up already."

"The break-ins?"

He shrugged, feigning a casualness he didn't feel, but he wasn't going into details with the chief. Not when they would force him to think about this morning, when he'd been trying all day to stop thinking about it. What had gotten into him? He'd crossed all the lines by touching her. She might think he wanted to console her, but he was a selfish bastard who'd wanted to touch her and hadn't been able to resist. Now that Mike wasn't around, Scott was chafing at the boundaries he'd set.

"Not entirely," he admitted. "But you know Riley. Truth is she's got her hands full with the kids and work. It was tough enough coming back to town without all this added aggravation."

The chief let the folder he held fall to the desk and sank back in the chair. It was one of those moments where he looked the part of aging police chief who'd been worn down by his years on the force and the constant demands.

"Let's come up with something." He massaged his temples. "Unless you've got some ideas you haven't shared with me yet."

Suddenly Scott knew exactly why the chief had sat down in the first place. He knew better than anyone how Scott worked and had wanted to give him someone he felt comfortable to bounce ideas with. So much for thinking he'd been keeping anything from the chief about his work with Kevin.

"You weren't just burning time." Not a question.

"Blew off the mayor for you." The chief glanced at his watch. "Figure he gave up on me about five minutes ago."

"I didn't need any help."

"Didn't say you did." The chief cracked a smile. "That's the best part of working with you. I never actually have to do any work."

"I have a partner. If I wanted him here, I'd have called him."

"I don't think so. Not when it has to do with Riley."

The hairs on the back of Scott's neck stood on end. "What in hell does that mean?"

The chief shrugged, making light of an assessment that felt too much like an accusation. "It means I've noticed how you've made it your new quest in life to watch over her and the kids."

"How is that any different from what the rest of us are doing? Half the department showed up on her doorstep when that alarm went off."

The chief chuckled. "Heard all about it."

"Then what's your point? I promised Mike if anything ever went south, I'd look after his family. And if things had gone the other way two years ago, he'd be your second-in-command at Renaissance right now."

Again, Scott couldn't help but be struck by how empty that sounded. The only people who would shed a tear if he suddenly wound up under a headstone were his coworkers in the department and the volunteers with Renaissance. Maybe the kids there, too. The members of Poughkeepsie's gangs would probably throw a block party. It was something, he guessed, but nothing like what he'd watched the Angelica family go through.

Or Riley.

The memory of the way she felt in his arms tore through him. And the chief just sat there, fingers steepled in front of him, gaze never wavering as if he was seeing so much more than he'd been meant to see.

"You done yet?" he asked casually.

Scott scowled.

"I understand, Scott. Believe me. I like to think that if I go down, you all will keep your eyes on Deb. But I also know how tough this is on you. Unlike your new partner, though, I also know you're a one-man circus. You're not alone with this. I'd have thought you'd gotten that with the party on Riley's front lawn the other day."

"A one-man circus?" God, could this get any worse? Not only did he have to deal with the fallout from his stupidity with Riley earlier, but now the chief was starting up this crap again.

"Liked that, did you?" A smile played on the chief's mouth. He was impressed with himself, no question.

Scott wasn't going to contradict a man who'd just blown off the mayor. "Okay, I'm not alone. Appreciate that. So, got any thoughts about who—"

"No, no thoughts. Told you, that's why I like working with you. The mayor would have had me jumping through hoops right now. You…" He shoved the chair back and stretched his legs out before him. "Well, it's damn peaceful in here."

"Thanks…I think."

"You're welcome. So what do you have in mind?"

"Work. What else is there?"

The chief frowned. "She's only been back, what…three weeks at best?"

Scott nodded.

"Hardly seems like enough time to start pissing people off with her articles."

"I agree. But after what happened last week in Hazard Creek…" Scott let his words trail off. The memory of her sitting in that ambulance made his stomach clench with almost brutal force. "She jumped right back in the thick of it. She covered Lundquist's press conference."

"I thought you said you hadn't interrogated her yet?"

"I haven't. I was at the house when she left this morning."

"Really?"

"Babysitting."

That got a reaction. "You *babysit?* What was she thinking?"

"She wasn't," Scott admitted, not in the least offended. "Camille got sick. I happened by at the right time."

An answer to a prayer.

"Kid still alive?"

"One-man circus yourself."

The chief chuckled wryly. Then they fell silent again, scanning through the rest of the reports, looking for something that wasn't there.

"I'll have to talk with her," Scott finally said.

"Yup." The chief agreed. "Keep me in the loop. That's an order. I don't want you alone on this, and I know what a pain in the ass you can be."

"You're hurting my feelings."

"If I thought you had any feelings, I'd apologize."

"Damned barrel of laughs."

The chief got to his feet. He gazed down and asked, "Do you know why I made you Mike's partner?"

"You always said it was because we were the same shade of green."

"Yeah, well, you both were that." He gave a gruff laugh.

"I put you two together because I knew you'd be good detectives. Damned good. There was only one difference between you."

"What was that?"

"Mike believed it. You didn't. You're never convinced you're doing enough."

There was so much truth in that statement Scott didn't know what to say. "And the reason for this trip down memory lane?"

The chief nodded. "Mike considered you a damned good friend. I know because he told me. And you've always done right by him. When he was alive. While you were investigating his death. You're still being a good friend."

"Yeah, and…"

"I thought you needed a reminder."

"I have no idea what you're talking about." But he did. A weight was settling on his chest, making it hard to breathe, almost impossible.

"Then you need to make some time to think about it." The chief gave a huff as if he didn't think Scott capable. "Mike made you a part of the family the minute he decided you were good people, Scott, someone he wanted around. You're the one who doesn't play well with others. I understand why, but it's time to learn. Stop tearing yourself up. You care about Riley and the kids, and that's okay." He pulled open the door, but paused, glancing over his shoulder with a narrowed gaze. "Remember what I said. And good luck."

The closing door echoed with a finality that jarred Scott's already fried nerves. His few hours' sleep after the night from hell was wearing off in a big way, evidenced by his inability to accept what the chief had said.

"You care about Riley and the kids, and that's okay."

Scott stared at the stacks of folders on his desk. He'd

known he wouldn't find anything about who might be stalking Riley. But he'd spent the afternoon going through them anyway, to be thorough, to investigate all the possibilities because he wouldn't take chances with Riley's or the kids' safety.

"You care about Riley and the kids, and that's okay."

He did care. He didn't want to dump this on her when she was so clearly struggling to get back on her feet. But he couldn't figure out what she might have stepped into without her help.

So why was he still sitting here? Why was there a vise crushing his chest, cutting off his air until he could barely think? Why did he hesitate to pick up the phone and call her when he knew the next step was to delve into her work, into what had been on her stolen equipment?

Then Scott knew. With a sickening certainty, he knew.

And there was no more running from the truth. No more hiding. So he sat there, hands stretched before him on the desk, lifeless, as if they belonged to someone else. Someone who hadn't been so disconnected from his feelings that he'd managed to deny the obvious. He'd been telling himself he had his feelings under control. He'd made the choice to act honorably, the only choice he could make and still look in the mirror.

The very silence in the office mocked him. How long? A day? Three weeks? Or had he been denying the truth even longer, burying feelings he didn't know what to do with for *years?*

How long had he been in love with Riley?

The truth. Undeniable. He'd have known by the sheer absence of anything like this in his life before. He'd simply never felt this way.

But it was there, had always been there. He'd noticed

her from the day Mike had introduced them. He'd lived with that truth, dodged it at every turn. Only a scumbag would have feelings for his friend's wife, and Scott had chosen not to live life as a scumbag. Simple. So he'd never allowed himself to get too close, had sidestepped her invitations time and time again. But he couldn't let go even after she went to Florida. He'd stayed connected through phone calls, had let himself get sucked into Sundays at Joe and Rosie's.

Helping Brian with the horses. Bringing a crew to maintain the lawn. Fixing the truck. All stupid little things that had meant so much to him. He told himself he was being a good friend to Mike, watching over his family, but he was a liar.

That didn't surprise him.

What kind of friend fell in love with another man's wife? The mother of his partner's kids?

Scott knew that answer, too—the diseased kind, the kind who'd inherited poison instead of blood running through his veins. The kind of man *he* was, the reason he hadn't allowed himself to get in deep with anyone, not once in all these years.

"You care about Riley and the kids, and that's okay."

No, it wasn't.

CHAPTER FOURTEEN

JASON STEPPED OUT OF his unmarked cruiser when the familiar motorcycle roared into view, pulling into the parking lot. Jason had chosen this long-abandoned tire plant as the meet point for a reason. The place was so remote this meeting with Tyrese should go unnoticed, and there were several access roads. They could go their separate ways, eliminating any connection between them should anyone take notice. Not that there was anyone around. This parcel of industrial acreage tucked away on the outskirts of town had been on the market so long, Jason wasn't even sure the owner—or the Realtor for that matter—was still alive.

Tyrese maneuvered the bike up close to the cruiser, cut the engine and removed his helmet. His expression was solemn. "You just used up your Get out of Jail Free card, Jason."

Through all the years of their acquaintance, Tyrese had called Jason a lot of things, starting with Buster and winding up with Brother in Christ. But Jason could never remember Tyrese ever using his first name. Not once.

"I don't know what kind of trouble you're in." Tyrese began unraveling the bungee cords that held a bulging laptop bag to the back rail of his bike. "But I'm praying for you, and I'm going to keep praying. I want you to know that."

Jason inclined his head but didn't say anything. He honestly didn't know what to say.

"I want to help you." Tyrese set the laptop bag at Jason's feet. "But I'm not doing any more of your dirty work. My account is closed. Paid in full." He fixed his dark eyes on Jason, eyes so dark they seemed almost black, eyes that suddenly saw through him to the quick. "You know what was with all that stuff you had me steal?" Emphasis on the *steal*. "Kids' stuff. Fishing poles. Roller-blades. And dolls, man. Little girl dolls. I had to dig through it all to get to that bag because your mark hid it under that stuff to protect it from thieves."

Thieves.

There was irony here. A mouthy hood with a rap sheet as long as his arm lecturing a police chief on ethics. There was definitely irony here. The kind that made him itch to defend himself, to explain to Tyrese exactly what was going down, so he'd understand why Jason had become a thief, had turned Tyrese into one again.

But there wasn't any defense. How could he defend turning Riley Angelica into a *mark?*

So Jason stood there in his neatly pressed suit that Callie had picked up from the cleaners just last night, a suit that had probably cost more than Tyrese grossed for six months of work at the church.

Tyrese, on the other hand, wore one of those casual shirts old men liked to wear. Neat-looking and light-weight, comfortable in the summer heat. The short sleeves didn't cover the elaborate tattoo adorning his left arm to the wrist, a jumble of thick black mathematical symbols that was a souvenir of his days as a member of 16 Squared. He'd have had to wear gloves to cover the prime numbers etched on the backs of his fingers in black ink, more souvenirs that marked him for exactly what he'd once been.

If Riley Angelica or any other soccer mom had spotted Tyrese in a grocery store parking lot, she'd have steered her cart in the opposite direction.

Jason knew better than anyone there was a lot more to Tyrese nowadays. He was getting through community college one class at a time. Yet, he'd used Tyrese's past against him because he had specialized skills. Skills that Jason needed because now he was the thief.

"We're square, Tyrese. You have my word." As if that counted for much anymore. "You head back to your life and forget that any of this ever happened."

Tyrese inclined his head. "I hope what you need is in that bag because I'm for real. I found the CD under a seat. It's in the bag, too."

"Thank you. Ditch the phone. We're square." On a debt that hadn't needed to be repaid. Jason had never once in all these years thought of what he'd done for Tyrese as a debt. Until now.

"Listen, brother. I'm going to tell you something some-one told me back when I needed to hear it." Leveling that inky black gaze at Jason, he said simply, "'Own up, take the heat, then get on with your life.'"

At first Jason could see nothing but images of what he'd look like on the news when production ran clips of *that* video, of him having the time of his life with four hookers.

"Today, the Hazard Creek police chief was indicted on charges of criminal obstruction...."

Jason just stood there until Tyrese's voice broke in, all too real and surprisingly self-assured, a man with a message.

"It was good advice when you gave it to me all those years ago," he was saying. "It's still good advice."

Shoving the helmet onto his head, he kick-started the bike. "Good luck, man. I'll be praying for you."

Then he wheeled around and drove off, leaving Jason staring at his receding figure, the dust kicking up in his wake as the powerful engine growled through the buzzing, late-afternoon quiet. Jason stood there in his crisp suit, wondering what had happened to the man who'd cared enough about a mouthy street punk to give him a chance when no one else would.

RILEY KNEW SOMETHING WAS WRONG the instant she opened the door to find Scott on her doorstep, looking much the same as he had when he'd left earlier. Same rumpled shirt. Same faded jeans. Same hiking boots. His hair looked as if he'd shoved his fingers through it a few dozen more times.

"What's wrong?" she asked without preamble.

"Nothing. I need to talk with you about today."

Their gazes met.

Today?

Did he mean her stolen equipment and the time she'd spent in his arms?

"Come on in." She stepped aside and held the door wide.

He passed with a long-legged stride, gaze averted, tension all over him. While she might not know what part of today he wanted to discuss, their earlier exchange was between them in a big way. She was aware of him in every cell, the feel of his arms around her so much more than a memory.

"Any luck with getting the glass replaced?" he asked. "Your van isn't out front."

"I parked it in the garage. Gene from Abb's Auto Glass came this afternoon to install it. Popped it right in. Took a grand total of ten minutes."

"I'm glad it wasn't a hassle."

She forced herself to stand her ground, to meet his eyes, to get a grip, willing a sense of normalcy she didn't feel. "Not at all. But at this rate, I'm going to be on a first-name basis with every glass guy in town."

"I hope not."

"You're not the only one."

"How's Camille feeling?"

Scott moved through the front porch, and Riley pulled the door shut and locked it. "Much better, thanks. After a good night's sleep, she'll be good to go."

"I had no idea kids even got migraines."

She exhaled hard, trying to get hold of her breathing. Honestly. "Me, either. Not until she started getting them, anyway. It's a family thing from Joe's side. He got them when he was a kid. Caroline still gets them."

Scott stepped aside to allow her to enter the house before him. "Nothing they can do?"

"Medication once one starts. That's about it unless I'm willing to keep her medicated. I'm not. She doesn't get them all that often. And there are triggers—whenever she gets overexcited or eats too much sugar. Or spends too much time in the pool. The chlorine, I think. We can usually control that."

Scott didn't get a chance to reply before Camille's shriek echoed across the living room. "Mo-om. Jakie won't give me the dental rinse."

Riley seized the moment to catch her breath and regain her composure. "Everyone's ready for bed around here. Beyond ready. If you have a few minutes—"

"Go do what you need to do. No rush."

She motioned him toward the kitchen. "I won't be long. Brian's here. Why don't you—"

"Yo, man," Brian said around a mouthful of pizza when he appeared in the hall holding a massive slice. "Aunt Riley cooked. It's awesome."

"Scott, if you're hungry, help yourself. There's plenty." She did a double take at the pizza stone, where her ravenous young nephew had been eating his fill. "Brian, grab a plate for him, please."

Then she beat a hasty retreat, allowing the routine of tucking in the kids to calm her runaway nerves. Camille was down for the count the minute her head hit the pillow. Jake, on the other hand, was still wound tight from his first day of school without his sister. He got chatty, and Riley didn't have the heart to rush him, so she let him talk himself out while she talked herself down from her own racing thoughts about Scott.

Friends supported each other. Scott was a friend, and she'd needed support this morning. No reason to obsess over the exchange or read more into one hug than was there.

Except that she'd been aware of him as more than a friend. She'd been aware of him as a man.

Enough!

She finally kissed Jake and arrived back in the kitchen to find Scott washing the dinner dishes and Brian drying.

"Thank you so much," she forced herself to say lightly. "But you could have put them in the dishwasher."

"I told Scott." Brian scowled. "He wouldn't listen."

Scott didn't say a word, but Riley didn't miss the smile playing around his mouth. She knew exactly what he was doing and liked the influence he had on Brian. He knew teenagers, which shouldn't be a surprise with all his work at Renaissance.

"Well, less work for me, and I appreciate the help. I haven't gotten the kids trained to load the dishwasher yet.

Well, they're trained," she corrected. "Let's just say I don't trust them completely. Anyone want coffee?"

Another diversionary tactic.

Brian tossed the dish towel onto the counter. "No thanks. I'm out of here. Got an assignment due in the morning."

"Get going then, sweetheart," she said. "Jake already put in his request for French toast in the morning if you find yourself hungry again before class."

Brian bent down and kissed the top of Riley's head as he passed. "Glad you're home, Aunt Riley. Take it easy, dude."

Then he disappeared down the hallway.

Leaving Riley and Scott alone.

She wasn't sure why the sound of the front door seemed to echo as if in a cavern or why her insanely large kitchen suddenly seemed to be shrinking, but that's exactly how it felt.

Maybe the dark night from beyond all the windows was closing in. The kitchen had actually sold her on the house when Mike had brought her to see the place. It was the hub, wide open to a dining room that had a dozen windows looking out over the duck pond and the stables. A gorgeous view no matter what the time of day or the season.

Except on moonless nights. Like right now when the darkness pressed in until the big room felt like a closet with Scott only mere feet away.

"Scott, would you like coffee?"

"Only if you were going to make some for yourself. Otherwise, I'm good."

Very diplomatic, but not a no. "Let me ask you a question. Am I going to need coffee for whatever you want to discuss? I have to admit that it's been a pretty long day."

"Make the coffee."

She nodded and headed toward the pot. He went to stand in front of the windows, restless for a man who hadn't slept in a while. She could feel every inch of the silence stretch between them, not sure why. But, coward that she was, she was in no hurry to end it. Scott appeared to be so deeply in thought, his back to her as he stared out into the night. Things were changing between them, and she wasn't sure how she felt about that. Let alone what *he* might think.

His shoulders were so broad he appeared showcased by the window frame. His glossy black hair, longer than she was used to seeing it, curled around his neck. His hair was really wavy, and she wondered why she'd never noticed before.

"Did you get your article written?" he asked without turning around.

"Yes, believe it or not. E-mailed it off not long after I picked up Jake from school."

"How'd that go? Did you take Camille with you?"

She was surprised he'd thought of that. Then again, the man was a detective. Details were his business. "Thankfully Brian came home. He kept an eye on her. Don't know what I'd have done without all the men in my life today." She gave a light laugh. "Even Jake was a trouper this morning. He headed off to class without a peep. I was so proud of him."

"So he's settling in?"

Scott was making conversation, and she sensed that he was as unnerved by the quiet as she was.

"I think that will take some time for all of us. We'll be okay."

Scott inclined his head but didn't reply. He looked thoughtful standing there.

She brought two mugs to the table and sat down. He finally turned to face her, glanced absently at the table before pulling out a chair and sitting across from her.

"Thanks," he said.

"So, are you going to keep me in suspense any longer?"

"I need to know what was on your laptop and your camera."

An interrogation. Okay, she could handle this. "I use my laptop mainly for work because the kids play games on the desktop. The camera had both personal and work-related photos."

"By any chance did you have backups? I need to know as much as I can about the events you're covering."

"You don't think today was a random theft, do you?"

He leveled his gaze at her, and there was so much in his expression, so much she'd never noticed before. She just had to look past the vice cop persona, past the familiar seriousness, to see a man who was paying attention to the details, to her details. She saw a man who cared.

"I'm sorry, Riley," he said quietly. "The last thing I want to do is alarm you, but things aren't adding up. You wound up being treated by paramedics in Hazard Creek. Then you had a break-in. Now a car theft. We need to pinpoint what's going on."

She sank back in the chair. She'd nearly melted down over a migraine this morning. Where was she going to find the energy to deal with the frightening reality that someone wanted something from her, enough to break into the house and the car?

"Mommy died. Mommy died like Daddy..."

Riley inhaled deeply to dispel the voices in her head. She wasn't alone. The entire Poughkeepsie Police Department had her back, as Mike used to say.

But knowing that didn't feel so important right now. It was the man sitting across from her. The man who'd cared enough to drive by the house to make sure she and the twins were okay. The man who'd easily stepped in to babysit her sick daughter. The man who'd wrapped her in his strong embrace to make her feel better.

"Okay." She pushed away from the table and stood. "Come into the office so we can figure this out."

CHAPTER FIFTEEN

SCOTT WATCHED AS Riley sat on a blue exercise ball in front of her office computer.

"Why don't you take the chair," he suggested. "I'll grab one from the kitchen."

"I'm good, thanks. Strengthens the core muscles." She sat even straighter, sucking in her stomach a little for effect.

He shook his head. "And limits the amount of time you spend in front of the computer, I'll bet."

That got a small smile. "Saves me from dragging my children away from their games. They usually get up on their own after a reasonable amount of time."

"Smart."

"Desperate." She rocked forward on the ball and gave a little sigh. "I'm outnumbered around here."

If Scott hadn't appreciated what that meant, he'd seen the results firsthand earlier. "You've got it under control."

She shot him a surprised look. "Yeah, when tired vice cops ride in to save the day."

He hadn't thought of what he'd done in that way, but suddenly the morning was square between them. He braced his hands on the back of the chair while the computer blipped and beeped through the start-up menu.

He couldn't miss the flush of pink suddenly staining her

cheeks beneath the fading tan. "There's nothing easy about this situation."

For her or for him. But at least her situation wasn't self-inflicted torture.

Mike would never have asked Scott to watch over his family if he'd known how his best friend had felt about his wife. But he hadn't known. Scott thought he'd had a grip on his emotions, but he hadn't.

He'd been lying to himself all these years about how much he cared. And that said a lot about his capacity for self-denial. An ability he wasn't going to complain about. Not when he'd go right back to ignoring the way he felt about her. His feelings didn't matter. What mattered was Riley's safety. And the kids'.

Even if he couldn't get back to the blissful ignorance he'd been living in for all these years, he still had the single most important tool in his arsenal.

Free will.

The ability to make the right choice was his and his alone. No one could take that away. No person. No life circumstance. He'd learned that lesson the hard way. That's why he worked so hard to convince the kids at Renaissance that they had everything they needed to break away from the lives they'd been living. Free will might not seem like much, but it was everything. And for the kids he worked with, it was a start down the path to a new life.

Just as it had once been for him.

That's why he was here with Riley tonight, making the right choice and doing right by his friend. He was going to scan her backup files and assess what story had made her a target.

Scott sat down.

He wasn't going to notice how close they were, so close

his knee almost brushed hers. He wasn't going to remember the way she'd felt in his arms or the way her slender body had lined up against his in all the right places. Instead, he fixed his gaze on the monitor and watched windows flash open as Riley maneuvered the system.

"So, what have you got?" he asked, sounding impressively controlled.

"I've got so much stuff here," she said. "I really need to sort through my files instead of uploading everything and forgetting about it."

Scott scanned the thumbnails. "This is all stuff you've been working on since you got back?"

She nodded. "It's a mess, I know, but that's only because I don't work on the server. I have to attach everything to e-mail and send it to the paper, so things aren't organized the way they are on my hard drive."

He snorted. "I meant because there's so much. You've barely been home a month."

"Oh. Well, yeah. Every article requires a fair amount of research and fact-checking. It's time-consuming." She waved a hand at the monitor. "That's what most of this is. I open files and dump research inside from the various wire services. Then I use it to pull an article together when I sit down to write."

He'd read her articles before, knew she was good. "I understand. Do you have any completed articles here?"

She nodded.

"That's what I want to see first."

"You got it." She moved a few thumbnails around then brought up the word processing program and tilted the monitor his way. "How's that?"

"Perfect." He scanned the story about a prominent money laundering case where two local businessmen had been using offshore trusts to launder millions of dollars for U.S. citizens to help them avoid paying taxes.

Scott nodded, and Riley moved him on to another story. He found himself skimming the leads on stories he'd either read about or heard on the news. He forced his attention to the display, refused to notice the cool scent of Riley's hair or the way the lamplight played over the curls, making them look as if they'd be soft to the touch.

There were only two stories she considered hard news. The resignation of the chief executive that she'd started covering today, and what she called a "takeout" on a pharmaceutical company that had been offering free training and some other over-the-top benefits to doctors who prescribed its drug.

"What's a takeout?" he asked.

"Basically it's a running story. I write about the developments as they come up and put the news into context."

"Got it. That seems the more likely of the two. What are the chances you've inadvertently uncovered something that might implicate someone who doesn't want to be implicated?"

She leaned forward on the ball, and he refused to react when their fingers brushed as they both reached for the mouse at the same time. He would simply ignore the warmth radiating through his fingertips, ignore the blush of color in her cheeks, which suggested she'd noticed their touch, too.

He waited while she opened file after file and skimmed through the text with a frown. "If I'd uncovered anything that was news, I'd be writing about it, trust me. I'm trying to earn my keep at the paper. But I don't see anything here."

"I need to review those files and do some digging of my own."

"There's a lot of information here, Scott. Can I organize it for you? I'm serious. I cut and paste. I don't even reformat. Takes too much time for something I typically use only once."

Scott took the opportunity to take a breather. Shoving the chair back, he stood. "I've got a flash drive in my jacket. You can copy those files onto it. Want more coffee while I'm up?"

She nodded absently, attention still on the information she'd culled for that article. Scott took both their cups and headed out of the office, appreciating the quiet stillness of the house, the way the temperature had dropped enough so the cool air cleansed Riley's delicate scent that still lingered in his senses.

Grabbing his jacket from the coat rack in the foyer, he threw it over an arm before heading into the kitchen to refill the coffee mugs. He glanced at the refrigerator, where a magnetized frame that read World's Greatest Dad hung.

Glancing at the photo of Mike, a photo from way back, probably not long after the twins had been born, Scott anchored himself to his purpose.

Keeping Riley and the kids safe.

This was a job he was trained for. He needed to remember that. He needed to put his imagination on lockdown. He needed to shut away any and all unworthy thoughts and be the friend that he'd always claimed to be.

With that renewed resolve, he followed the warm glow of the light spilling from the office into the hallway.

"Here you go." He placed the cup in front of her. Then he produced the flash drive. "Will you copy those files onto this? I know it's late. Not too much longer, I promise."

"No worries, Scott. I'm much better off busy. Nothing worse than lying in bed having an anxiety attack."

She tossed that out so casually he knew she must be intimately acquainted with late-night anxiety. And that was exactly why he was here. To figure out what was going on so she could get back to her life.

And he could get back to being a sometimes visitor. He couldn't seem to handle any more than that.

"Take a look at these, will you?" Displaying two stories at once, she plugged the flash drive into a USB port.

He recognized the first. The failed DEA bust had turned into a news bit hardly worth the gas it had taken for her to drive to Hazard Creek. Or the risk to her safety.

The second was a longer piece on the painful unraveling of a criminal identity theft case, where a gang thug was arrested for a break-in and gave the victim's information to the police instead of his own. The criminal record and an outstanding warrant was attached to the innocent victim and not discovered until months later, long after the thug had done a ghost.

"What's Max doing assigning you all these gang-related stories?" Scott hadn't meant to sound annoyed. It really wasn't his business what Riley covered, but gangs…

"It's not Max's fault." She stared at the display, giving him a view of her delicate profile backlit in the golden glow of the lamp. She looked tired, worried, and the need to reassure her hit him again. Unbidden. Hard.

"The schedule's flexible," she explained. "Which is really helpful while I get the kids settled at school. After that, well, I've been giving that some thought. Maybe it's time for a career change."

"You're considering leaving the *Herald?*"

She turned to face him, met his gaze above the rim of the mug. "Let's just say I've been researching options. Between you and me, Scott, ever since that day in Hazard Creek, I'm not entirely sure this job is in all our best interests."

She cocked her head to the side and tried to look casual, a gesture he saw right through. She'd been as spooked as he'd known she'd been that day. As spooked as he'd been.

"I'm thinking life is dangerous enough without me placing myself in situations where I have to outrun drug dealers on foot. I don't want my kids to be orphans if I can help it." She didn't give him a chance to react, just forged on. "I'm looking into what it will take to get a teaching certificate. I've got my master's. So far it seems to be a realistic option."

"You want to work with kids?"

"I like them, and I could take mine to school with me. We'd have the same schedule and summers off together. Solves a lot of problems." She gave a smile that seemed a little strained. "Then if one gets sick, I can call a sub instead of recruiting the first nice guy who happens along."

He hated that she felt pressured to make these kinds of choices because she was scared for her safety. "Listen, Riley. The chief and I talked today. We'd feel better if you had protection until we figure out what's going on." He hadn't intended to put the chief's name in there, but he wanted her to know he hadn't been the one to come up with the idea.

She inhaled deeply, the sound of inevitability. "What do you have in mind?"

"Nothing crazy." But it was crazy. More crazy than she would ever know. "Just me. You can stand a few days of seeing my face, can't you?"

"You don't mind, Scott? It seems like an awful lot to ask."

That wasn't the argument he'd expected, which told him she was a lot more worried than she was letting on.

"No. I don't mind. Just like I didn't mind being recruited today. I'm not going to get any sleep anyway until we figure out what's going on. You don't want me lying in bed awake having anxiety attacks."

She only nodded. "Camille's got a trundle bed, I can put Jake in with her—"

"If you don't mind, I'll bunk on the couch."

She searched his face as if trying to determine how worried she should be. "I'll make you a nest, then."

A nest. A loving gesture that epitomized the sort of care and concern he'd always associated with this family, a family that was stretching its arms to include him with no clue how much he wanted to be included.

VETERANOS GOT IT DOWN. Ace cool in the game. The Busters hooked up. For a piece of curb service.

Jason finally clicked off the CD player after realizing he'd looped around to this same track for the third time. Or was it the fourth? He didn't know. He only knew he felt incredible relief.

He couldn't think, didn't want to move, didn't want to do anything to disrupt this stunned sense of hope. He just needed to catch a break. One break to help him crawl out from under the mess he'd made of everything.

Had he finally gotten it?

Pulling off the earphones, Jason let them fall to the desk. He could only stare at the portable CD player until his brain started working enough to process more stimuli. The desk where he'd been poring over his appointment book, figuring out how to schedule necessary meetings when his life had been taken entirely out of his control.

The moonless night, inky beyond the open plantation shutters that Callie had had installed last spring. A jaw-dropping expense, but a deal she simply couldn't pass on with the window treatment place going out of business. She'd wanted to upgrade from the stock blinds for so long.

The quiet that had settled over the house meant the kids were asleep. Callie would be puttering around, working on some project or another. She'd mentioned something at dinner, but he couldn't remember what she'd said.

Jason couldn't focus on anything but that CD.

He'd been expecting to hear a detailed and documented account of the "services" he'd been forced to provide Barry Mannis and his team. He'd expected to learn that the drug dealers who'd been picking up and delivering their poison at prearranged drops had known exactly who'd been providing the protection. He'd been expecting to learn that his unmarked cruiser hadn't fooled anyone.

Drug dealers were supposed to be afraid of the police—not looking to them for help. But that's exactly what had been happening since Agent Asshole had sunk his claws into Jason.

He'd been turning a blind eye to the local residences and businesses where powder cocaine was being transformed into the crack that went into the streets. He knew where the vessels and chemicals that were used to prepare the crack were being stored.

He knew where the new cookhouse had sprung up to replace the one cleared out for a fake bust. He'd even helped equip the place with a sophisticated surveillance system so the drug dealers wouldn't be surprised by the law. The "real" law. Not the bought-and-paid for kind he'd been providing.

He knew Agent Asshole and his team had been abusing federal resources to run drugs and get rich, but he had no way of knowing how deep their operation went or how long they'd been operating in the area.

But now, compliments of Riley's CD, Jason had a better picture of what was going on.

And it had never once occurred to him that he wasn't the only poor Joe on Agent Asshole's hook. The power-hungry bastard had been running his scam, getting bolder and greedier and including more people than was smart. It was only a matter of time until Mannis screwed up.

Jason knew that from personal experience.

CHAPTER SIXTEEN

RILEY DUG THROUGH the drawers of Jake's dresser, through the stacks of neatly folded clothes. Should she pack him an extra pair of jeans? It was September, and the temperature dropped at night. Would he be inside most of the weekend or outside? She couldn't be sure, so she grabbed a pair.

"Are you sure you want Camille and Jake to go with Rosie and Joe this weekend?" Scott appeared in the bedroom doorway.

"It's probably not necessary." She kept her voice light, didn't want Scott to know the idea of sending the kids away was rattling her in places she hadn't realized could still be rattled. They'd never been apart. Not since before Mike…

"I'm a big believer in going with the flow. Rosie and Joe have an unexpected chance to see Lily Susan, and the kids haven't seen her since we've come home. They'll only be two and a half hours away at Lily Susan's place in the city, and until we figure out what's going on…" She shrugged, another gesture to make her appear casual. Or maybe she hoped by acting that way, she might begin to feel that way, too. "The kids don't remember Lily Susan except from photos. And some time with Rosie and Joe will be a good thing, too. Everyone will have a chance to bond."

Scott eyed her with that dark gaze as if he didn't quite

believe her. Detectives. She inwardly sighed. Always looking for what was below the surface, regardless of whether or not she wanted to share. And she didn't. She needed to figure out how she felt about the way things were changing between her and Scott. She'd never expected this. Not once.

"Just so you understand we don't have much to go on here," he said. "Both attempts seemed directed at theft. Whoever wanted your equipment has it now. I don't want you to feel pressured or scared."

She felt both but wouldn't admit it. Not when Scott was being so sweet by addressing the issue, and by dropping everything to play her bodyguard. Again. She layered the new additions neatly into the duffel bag. "What time do you expect the lawn crew to be here?"

"Soon. They'll stay outside though. You won't have to see them."

"I should thank them for all their hard work, don't you think?"

He looked surprised. "I don't want you uncomfortable."

"Uncomfortable?" Her turn to be surprised. "Is there something about these kids you haven't told me?"

He frowned. "They're from Renaissance."

"I know that."

He frowned. "Gang kids. Well, *former* gang kids. I hope."

"I know that, too." She was surprised by Scott's perception and his thoughtfulness.

How had she missed so much about this man?

He stood inside the doorway, arms folded across his chest, radiating a quiet strength that made her smile.

"I'm okay with former gang kids, Scott. I appreciate the work they've been doing and would like to tell them that."

His eyes traveled over her, and she knew that slow,

searching gaze took stock of what she wasn't saying. "They'll appreciate the chance to thank you, too. It's tough for these kids to get honest work. You're a steady gig that pays well."

She knew it must be hard to get a chance to make different choices with their lives. "It all worked out, then. I really hated to put any more on Brian's shoulders."

Scott scoffed. "I haven't seen him straining himself."

"Is that Scott the Renaissance coordinator talking or Scott the cop?"

He gave a short laugh. "Both, I guess. He's a good kid, don't get me wrong, but he's got such a sweet deal here. I don't think he appreciates it as much as he should."

"Fair enough. He's barely twenty."

"I'll keep that in mind."

Whether or not he agreed, and she suspected he didn't, which said something about Scott the man she didn't know. Had he been the kind of kid who'd had to grow up fast? One with a lot of responsibility thrust upon him at an early age? As a parent she knew there was such a fine line to walk, balancing enough with too much. Had someone loved him enough to find that balance?

Riley knew nothing about his family. Mike had always said Scott didn't have any, but he must have some. Rosie had managed to drum up more about him than anyone, and Riley was surprised by how much she wanted to know about the events that had shaped this man before her, an honorable, dependable man, who bore the weight of her family's trouble with such ease and concern. Adding pajamas into the duffel bag, she zipped it shut. "I'm glad you suggested the Renaissance kids."

"That's generous."

"Not really. I have more understanding than most about

why kids wind up in gangs. Because of my work and yours. I don't blame them for their life circumstances. And I certainly don't blame all gang kids for what happened to Mike."

His expression softened. He didn't say anything, just kept watching her thoughtfully.

"Don't look at me like that. It's not anything special," she said. "Just healthy. I do try, and in some ways I'm actually surprising myself."

"Really? How's that?" He sounded amused.

"The grief counselors and the other folks in the support groups all said time would make the difference. I don't think I ever actually believed them. Now sometimes I surprise myself by how healed I am. I don't miss Mike any less, but I don't hurt so much. Instead of always seeing how he's not here, I remember when he was here. I feel…well, grateful. We had so much to be thankful for. I can't help thinking that time was so perfect because we weren't going to get a lot of it."

He was silent so long that Riley wondered if she'd made him uncomfortable, and felt uncertain by this intimacy of their changing relationship. In some ways she felt so at ease around him. But in other ways…

"May I ask you a question?"

She was grateful for the distraction, didn't want to overthink how much things had changed between them. "Of course."

"Are you glad you came home?"

She considered that for a moment, considered him, knew she would be honest. "In some ways. I liked our life in Florida. It was all shiny and fresh. We were making new memories, and trust me when I say you can't beat year-round sunshine and the beach. But I don't think I would have known how much I'd healed if we'd stayed. I needed to test myself. I needed to be healthy about the situation because the kids are taking their cues from me."

"You're doing a good job, Riley."

His comment seemed so random she could only glance up at him, found him watching her with an expression of quiet appreciation, one she found surprisingly intimate.

One that made her notice his dark, dark hair. And how he might be almost too thin if not for those broad shoulders, those long, strong legs that left no doubt that he was an active man. Even if she hadn't known how many team sports he was involved in through the department and Renaissance, she knew he was physical by the way he'd always helped out Mike, then Brian, with cars, tractors, trucks and the four thousand other things that could go wrong around here.

She wasn't sure what surprised her most—that he was even thinking about her parenting skills or that he thought she'd needed to hear that she was doing a good job. It occurred to her that it might have nothing at all to do with her and everything to do with his appreciation of family. He seemed to have fullness and balance in all the other areas of his life. Strong relationships with people he respected at the department. Through his volunteer work. On all the team sports he participated in. He was a good man. And if she hadn't fully appreciated how good before, she'd been getting an education the past two years.

It was such a surprising moment, one where Riley seemed to see him as she never had before, a stranger, not someone who'd been a part of her life for so long.

Perhaps because *this* Scott was different.

This Scott was a man, who'd been carving a place for

himself in her life. A man, she was coming to realize, she wanted in her life.

"May I ask you a question?" she said.

He didn't hesitate. "Sure, shoot."

"You and Mike discussed the possibility of him being hurt at work, didn't you?" *Hurt.* Not dying. She couldn't get that word out of her mouth.

He held her gaze steadily. "Yes."

That one word righted their equilibrium and put Mike between them where he'd always been. And it felt so comfortable to have him there.

But there was a part of Riley, a part that she wasn't sure how she felt about yet, that liked this new direction her relationship with Scott was taking, that liked the man she was getting to know.

ON A NORMAL FRIDAY, Jason would have been long gone by the time his son was heading to school, but he'd spent the night going through every file on Riley's notebook computer. File after file after file until his eyes had crossed.

But he hadn't found anything to make him suspect she had a clue he'd been working with the DEA on that bogus bust, nothing to hint she had any idea what was on that CD. He'd read her every article, every shred of research, which all seemed neatly tied to her articles.

He'd scanned photos of her kids, who were just a year younger than Kyle. Cute kids who looked more like Riley than Mike with that blond hair. They'd been pictures of the first day at school. Jason knew because he'd lived through the whole scene just a year ago himself.

Photos and video files that Riley must have uploaded from her camcorder. He wondered if she'd deleted them from her hard drive yet. If she had then she'd lost everything because he had her camera, too. He'd stolen more than equipment; he'd stolen memories. She wouldn't be able to replace those.

He'd finally passed out while sitting upright at his desk, his eyes scratchy and unfocused, his thoughts tortured with questions of how he could get this equipment back to Riley without leaving a trail of breadcrumbs back to himself or Tyrese.

Callie had found him like that, slumped, still dressed, in his office chair.

He'd lied, of course. Told her he was bypassing the office this morning to head straight to a meeting. She'd seized the opportunity to let Jessica sleep in, taking Kyle to school while Jason was in the shower.

That was the only reason why he was still home when the doorbell rang. He opened the door to find the FedEx guy with a package addressed to Callie.

Jason glanced at the sender's name then did a double take, his blood running icy through his veins.

Chola Party Babes
Maharaja Hotel
Atlantic City, NJ

Signing for the package with trembling fingers, Jason stared blankly at the courier before slamming the door in his face. Maharaja Hotel in Atlantic City was the name of the place where he'd screwed up his whole life. He didn't need to ask who the Chola Party Babes were. Just like he didn't need to ask who'd sent this package.

The man who'd set him up.

He had the envelope opened by the time he got to his office and, sure enough, there was a DVD inside a jewel case. He wondered what Callie would have thought had she opened the package. There was no accompanying documentation, nothing to give a hint what the DVD contained. Would she have popped it into the television or the computer, curious?

Jason had the overwhelming urge to check it out for himself to see if Agent Asshole was bluffing. He didn't. He scooped the cell phone off his desk and dialed.

Agent Asshole answered on the second ring.

"What in hell are you doing sending that…that *garbage* to my wife?"

"I told you to keep me informed," he replied in a cool voice.

"And I told you I would," Jason exploded into the phone. "I've been taking care of it. I haven't informed you of anything because there's nothing to tell you."

His words echoed sharply off the walls. He took a deep breath, tried to control the rush of blood behind his ears.

"Y'know, you're really a dumb-ass, Kenney. What part have you been taking care of? I must have missed it. Your busted attempt to get into that reporter's house ended up with the PPD on her doorstep. Now that cop's guarding her around the clock."

Jason froze where he stood, the anger draining away as fast as it had come. "You're tailing her?"

"I told you I didn't want any mistakes. You're a mistake. I'm just cleaning up your mess."

"Jesus, Mannis. What did you do?"

That cool chuckle bounced over the satellite signals with the force of a comet. "That problem isn't yours to worry about anymore, so put it out of your head. You just worry about doing what I ask you to do because the next time you might not be so lucky. Your wife might get the mail."

It took Jason a minute to realize the line had gone dead.

"Daddy," Jessica screeched so loudly that Jason jumped. He dropped the cell phone and it skittered loudly across the wood floor just as his daughter tore into the office on bare feet, her Dora the Explorer nightgown tangling around her knees.

"Daddy." She launched herself at him with complete abandon, arms outstretched, silky dark hair flying behind her.

She never once questioned whether or not he'd catch her. Jason hoisted her barely forty-pound body into the air, her giggles piercing his shame, anchoring him in the present.

When she finally stopped squirming, she threw her arms around his neck and hugged him tightly. For one heart-stopping moment, he felt like a man worthy of so much love.

"Good morning, my Jessie," he whispered into her hair.

"Morning, Daddy." She leaned back in his arms, would have landed on her pretty head had he not held her securely. Then she planted a big kiss on his cheek.

But Jason wasn't worthy.

In that instant, all the running, all the lying, all the hiding from the ugly reality of this situation reached a zenith. He'd betrayed his beautiful daughter's trust. He'd betrayed his wife. And the men in his department. And Tyrese, who'd proven himself to be a much better man. And Riley, who wasn't guilty of anything except running into him.

He was toxic, poison to everyone he came in contact with, people who should have never been dragged along for this ride.

All for a weekend of high-stakes poker and sex. No. Even worse. The gambling and the sex had merely been side effects of his ego. His greed. He'd wanted to be one of the guys with high-powered connections. He'd wanted more of that power for himself.

How had he gotten so far away from what was impor-

CHAPTER SEVENTEEN

SCOTT COULD HANDLE THIS. All he needed to focus on was keeping Riley safe. Doing a job. Honoring a promise. *How* he felt didn't matter. He didn't always feel like getting out of bed to go to work. Or leaving a good basketball game at the Center to take some phone call that would send him to a crime scene where a drug deal had gone balls-up and left body parts everywhere.

Then again, Scott hadn't actually bargained on spending so much time with Riley. He didn't blame her. The situation had just been throwing them together. And one thing was for sure—talking to her from up the Eastern seaboard hadn't exactly tested him the way watching her walk down to the barn, carrying a pitcher of iced tea for the crew, the sun glinting off her hair did.

He'd never actually had to stand around and see a half-dozen kids vie for her attention. They'd been charmed by Riley, by her goodness—who wasn't? And these kids were nothing if not savvy about spotting the sun through cracks under the doors.

How had Mike handled it?

That didn't take too much thought. Mike had been secure in Riley's love. He'd never minded men ogling his wife, in fact, he'd been amused by it. Proud, too, Scott thought. He would have been if he'd been a family kind of man.

That reminder helped steel his resolve, helped keep him focused on the job at hand. Leaving the cool recesses of the barn, where he'd been returning some tools, he took stock of where each member of the crew was with the work.

Cakes was almost done bundling the shrub and tree limbs to stack beside the road for the trash pickup.

Mateo and Do-Wap were still on their knees weeding in the back bed. Wouldn't be much longer and all this work wouldn't make a difference. The weeds would soon be dead, along with the flowers they'd planted at the start of summer.

General E. was driving the lawn mower. Week after week his age and experience gave him his pick of jobs. The one he chose usually involved being in the driver's seat of the riding mower.

"Hey, Scott," Joe's familiar voice called out.

Scott shielded his gaze and turned into the sun. Joe was coming down the slope from the house.

"How are you holding up?" Joe asked. "Tired of farm life yet?"

"What's to get tired of when all the kids do the work?"

Joe laughed, his gaze darting around to see the kids attending to their various tasks, taking casual notice of this newcomer. "Sounds like a plan. Maybe I should get them over to my place."

Scott nodded. "You bring the kids from school?"

"Yeah. Figured it would be easier than making you pack things up here. Riley didn't think you'd want her to go alone."

Scott didn't reply, although Riley had been right. He would have left the kids here alone before allowing her to go off anywhere without him.

"Listen, Scott. I really appreciate all you're doing. Rosie and I both do. But talk to me. How worried should we be?"

"Don't worry—"

"Cut me a break." He frowned. "When Riley agreed to let us take the kids, we knew there was trouble. How much?"

In Scott's opinion, there were only two kinds of fathers—the ones who cared about their kids and the ones who kids were better off without. Joe was one of the good ones.

"I'm trying to figure out why someone would want her equipment," Scott said. "Some story she's covered. Some evidence she's come across. I haven't found anything solid to point me in a specific direction. Kevin's running a few leads. Hopefully something will turn up."

"What about what happened in Hazard Creek?"

"Looks random as far as I can tell. Like she was just in the wrong place at the wrong time."

"She was the only press there. You don't think that's suspicious?"

Joe was just trying to help. He'd already lost his son. He didn't want to lose a daughter-in-law he loved, too.

"It's suspicious, no question," Scott admitted. "But I don't have anything to tie it to the other incidents. If someone wanted to hurt her, they wouldn't go from trying to run her down to breaking into her house and car. And I could think of much better places to go after her than in front of the DEA and the whole Hazard Creek PD."

Joe snorted. "Got a point there."

"We'll figure it out. Most likely she came across something while researching one of her stories that someone doesn't want to get out. If that's the case, it'll just take time to make the connections." He tried to look reassuring. "You know the PPD. We'll be on red alert until we get this sorted out."

"I know you will. My son was fortunate in his friends."

"Your son was a good friend."

Joe just inclined his head, letting the words linger.

"Taking the kids away this weekend is a big help," Scott

said. "Riley's really worried about them, even though she's not saying as much. I wish she'd go with you. A break would probably do her good, but she's determined to be here while I go through her work files until I find something solid."

"And you will." Joe rocked back on his heels to meet Scott's gaze. "She couldn't be in better hands. Both Rosie and I feel that way. We appreciate everything you've done since Mike passed. Don't you forget that."

Scott felt uncomfortable with such a blatant vote of confidence. Joe was a good one definitely.

"You got my cell number. Call if you need anything. I mean it, Scott, anything at all."

"I will, but don't worry. And don't let Rosie worry, either. Have a good weekend."

"We will. Lily Susan's excited about seeing the kids. She's been making plans all day. Lots to do in the city for young people."

Didn't take much to envision visits to parks and toy stores and Broadway shows. A real family that enjoyed being together. Scott knew what a family should be like, even if he hadn't lived the reality himself; he'd seen it up close with the Angelicas.

Joe clamped a hand on Scott's back. "I'm out of here, then. Good luck."

"I'll come say goodbye to Rosie." Scott walked with him back to the house, found everyone all packed with the bags waiting on the front porch.

"Didn't want to put the kids' stuff in the car until you got here," Rosie said with a twinkle in her eyes. "Figured you'd want everything in a special way."

"Of course." Joe glanced at the two duffel bags sitting side by side, identical except for the colors—one blue, the other pink. "Jeez, Riley. Look at the size of these. They're only going away for two nights. What do you have in here?"

Riley seemed ready. "Only the essentials. I promise."

"Grandpa, we have to take Franny," Camille explained.

"And Gentle Ben," Jake added. "And my special pillow."

"Important stuff, Joe." Scott reached for the duffel bags and hoisted them over his shoulder. "And not nearly as heavy as they look. The kids could even carry them."

Riley cast him a grateful glance before she said, "They *should* be carrying their bags."

Both kids only laughed and cut off Scott as they ran out the door. Scott followed, not minding his turn as pack mule for the few short steps to Joe's Cadillac. As Rosie predicted, he made a production of stowing everything in the trunk.

But Scott was more interested in watching Riley in his periphery, the way she'd knelt down in front of the kids and talked to each of them in hushed tones.

He strained to hear and, with effort, could make out her whispering voice. Telling them what to do if they wanted to talk to her, reminding them how they should behave, promising that she wasn't so far away if they needed her.

She couldn't seem to keep her hands off them. Adjusting Jake's belt. Brushing strands of hair from Camille's neck. Finally taking their hands in hers, a routine they'd all obviously played time and time again.

Then she was kissing and hugging them and telling them how much she loved them before letting them loose. They raced to the car as if they'd been fired from a gun.

"Have fun, you guys," she said while Joe held the door for Rosie. "Stay in touch and kiss Aunt Lily Susan for me."

Joe rolled the windows down and reached for Riley's hand. "Don't you worry. We'll take good care of them."

"I know." Riley squeezed his hand. "Have a great time."

Then she let go and stepped back from the car, blowing kisses to the kids, both of whom had stuck their arms out the windows on either side as if trying to make the car fly.

"Bye, Mommy. Love you, Mom," came the excited voices as the car pulled out of the driveway.

Even Scott gave a wave, smiling as the Cadillac took off with a gleam of red taillights. That was until he heard a strange gulp of breath and glanced at Riley. She stood beside him, still waving, her smile collapsing.

"Riley?"

She wouldn't look at him, just waved him off.

"Riley, they'll be fine."

She nodded, but didn't say a word as she visibly fought to control her expression.

Scott knew she trusted Rosie and Joe to care for the kids. Was this some sort of mom thing? Could she miss them already? Or was this about all the pressure that had been on her lately, all the responsibilities of parenting alone and going back to work and facing the past and outrunning drug dealers on foot and break-ins at the house and in the car and her equipment stolen…

"Riley." He reached for her like he had only days before, without thought, just wanting to take away her pain.

The instant she was in his arms, Scott knew that touching Riley was playing with fire. She melted against him with a breathy sigh and pressed her cheek to his chest. He could feel her shudder, feel every curve of her slim body as if she was some missing piece of him.

He had no business feeling this way, imagined Mike up *there* somewhere, that place his grandmother claimed existed when he'd been a kid, the place where his mother watched over him, always loving him, no matter how shitty life got. And it had gotten really shitty after his grandmother had died and he'd gone to live with the old man. Scott had always kept that thought close. But in this moment, with Riley in his arms, he hoped his grandmother had been wrong. He didn't want Mike to look down and see his friend taking advantage of his wife's need.

Because that's what he was doing.

He didn't let her go. He only held her close, a man without the will to resist temptation, a man who savored this time, knowing he'd never get another chance.

He couldn't stop from running his hands over her hair, down her back—simple, forbidden touches. He'd never felt this way, wouldn't have allowed himself to feel this way if he could help it. But he couldn't. Need left him helpless. He just wanted to hold her close. To soothe away her pain. Riley didn't stop him, though he wished with every shred of reason he had left that she would.

And still he couldn't let her go.

He stood with his cheek pressed to the top of her head, the breath trapped in his chest as he fought his desire to keep touching her.

RILEY STOOD IN THE DRIVEWAY long after the kids, Rosie and Joe had driven away, surrounded by Scott's strong arms. His hard body blocked the fall breeze as the sun began its late-afternoon descent.

She should move. She should say something, do something, *anything* to end a silence filled with a desire that she could no longer deny.

She could hear his steady heartbeat throbbing beneath her cheek, feel the softness of his T-shirt and the warm strength of the man beneath it. With every breath, she inhaled the smell of him, musky and almost overpowering, the smell of a man who'd been doing yard work all afternoon. It was a new smell, Scott's smell, not unpleasant.

His body was hard with the muscular strength of an active man, a man whose arms held her so close her breasts pressed against him, her stomach lightly grazed his, their thighs brushed together. She could feel everywhere they touched as if a current ran between them.

What was this? She only knew what *this* wasn't—the grateful reaction to the comfort of a friend. *This* was something so completely different, something so unexpected that she simply stood there unmoving. Something so much more.

This was a feeling she hadn't felt in so long…a feeling she'd never expected to feel again. Not since Mike, the man she'd loved with her heart and soul.

Arousal.

For Scott.

Every nerve ending in her body tingled, and she could only tighten her grip around his waist, an instinctive move to feed the pleasure. He shuddered, a full-bodied motion as he anchored her even closer, one big hand trapped in her hair, the other securing her around the shoulders, molding their bodies together intimately.

Bringing their bodies to life in an unexpected way.

His breath came in a ragged burst. Riley's caught in her throat, a sigh of surprised pleasure, an exhalation of profound relief to rediscover such a forgotten part of her.

A sound that echoed between them.

And jolted Scott from the moment. His entire body went rigid, and he sprang away as if he'd been detonated, leaving her staring up at him in surprise.

She felt trapped beneath his dark gaze, every tingle that shouldn't be happening, every raw breath that lifted her chest and drew attention to breasts that felt full, showcased beneath eyes that saw everything.

"Riley—" The voice broke from his lips, a plea.

Still, she could only stare, overcome by the need pouring through her. She tried to make sense of what was happening, of what she felt…of Scott's broken expression. Then, in the wake of the need, came panic.

She hadn't misread his reaction to her, but what if he hadn't wanted to react? What if he'd only wanted to comfort her?

"I'm not normally such a wimp." The words erupted from her, a desperate bid to fill the silence to distract them from what had just happened.

"I don't think you're a wimp." His reply sounded just as raw, just as grateful.

"I can't imagine why. I've been totally acting like one."

"We could argue that I smell like a goat. I've been outside all day working on the yard."

She laughed stupidly. "I honestly didn't notice. Shows you how far gone I was."

It was the most stupid exchange ever between a man and a woman in the history of mankind. There was no question at all about whether he was as sideswiped as she. Not when they kept staring at each other like deer caught in headlights, nonsense pouring from their mouths.

Scott came to his senses first. "I need to check on the crew."

"I've got to start dinner. The least I can do is feed you." But she was staring at his broad back before the words were all out of her mouth because he took off so fast, long strides chewing up the ground and putting distance between them.

The instant she could no longer see him around the side of the house, Riley waved her hands in front of her as if she might shake off the crushing wave of embarrassment. She headed straight for the house to get as far away from the scene of her humiliation as possible.

CHAPTER EIGHTEEN

THE PHONE IN JASON'S POCKET vibrated. Not his personal cell phone, but the untraceable one that Agent Asshole had provided to tell Jason when to jump. He flipped it open by the fourth ring to find out how high.

"Yeah."

"Got details for you." The harsh voice shot over the line. "Going to need a few more men for protective detail. You can handle that."

Jason stared at the highway unwinding in front of him, faded yellow lines anchoring him to the reality of his world. He willed himself to reply normally, when he felt anything but normal. "When?"

"Tomorrow night. Late."

"No problem."

Agent Asshole didn't reply. He didn't have to. Jason knew he'd expected no other answer, not when Mannis had already bought and paid for services rendered.

"Where?" Jason asked, impressed by how businesslike he sounded when his stomach roiled violently. His pulse pounded so hard behind his ears he had to strain to hear the details of this all-important drop.

Agent Asshole relayed the coordinates of a private airfield in the northern part of Jason's jurisdiction, an airfield where the high profiles who did business and vacationed in the area were afforded the sort of privacy they needed to come and go without fanfare. They paid for that privilege.

The fact that this DEA team gone bad was shelling out the price for this added protection confirmed what Jason had suspected all along.

This drug shipment wasn't coming through the same channels as the others. This must be coming straight out of Mexico from one of the more well-known cartels. This posh private airstrip would be the perfect place to enter the area unobtrusively, a place where they'd be able to unload the drugs then disperse them in every direction—upstate, into the city, local stash houses and into the prison system if the information on that CD was correct. If Jason had had any doubt before, he didn't now. Agent Asshole was uptight. That's why he sent the DVD to Jason's house and stepped in to deal with Riley. He'd known he needed extra protection, and wanted to make sure he'd taken care of any wild cards and had Jason well under his thumb.

Jason hadn't thought Barry Mannis possessed any conscience and found it somewhat reassuring to know the man did care about something—if only his three-quarters of a million-dollar shipment and his reputation with the bad guys.

"You got that?" Agent Asshole asked.

"No problem."

"Keep me informed. This needs to go off nice and neat. Trust me, you won't be sorry."

But he was. About this whole mess. "Got it."

The line disconnected.

Jason flipped the phone shut and tossed it onto the passenger seat as he passed a sign marking an approaching Poughkeepsie exit.

He wanted to know what Agent Asshole planned to do

about Riley, but he hadn't asked, hadn't wanted to give the guy one whiff of suspicion that would cause him to question Jason's loyalty when he probably wouldn't get a straight answer anyway. But Jason knew that with the drop scheduled to go down tomorrow night, Agent Asshole wouldn't leave any loose ends. Riley was exactly that.

Funny that his moment of truth had come while sitting behind the wheel of his cruiser, heading south on a highway that could take him away from this nightmare.

The only sane thing to do was arrange for the extra security and show up for tomorrow night's drop. Agent Asshole would expect him to bring his men. He could simply tell them they were assisting the DEA like they had in that bogus sting. No one would question that. Jason would safeguard himself from another copy of the DVD showing up at his house. Worse yet, Agent Asshole might send the DVD to the media, where everyone in the world would be treated to his downfall. If he stuck with the program, he might even get tossed a bone for good behavior. Agent Asshole had said as much.

The trouble with this was two-fold. Compliance left an innocent woman at risk and gave Agent Asshole license to continue the blackmail. Jason would like to think eventually this DEA unit from hell would leave the area, but this could go on forever. Or until something went wrong and the situation blew up in his face. Jason wasn't stupid. Blackmailers would keep blackmailing as long as their victims let them.

That left him only two choices. He could keep driving and forget this nightmare had ever happened. He could lose himself and start up someplace new, where no one knew him, or what he'd done. Canada, maybe. Or South America. He could give up his life. Callie. His kids. His parents.

The very thought should have killed him. Giving up all the people he loved, who loved him…he was numb. He'd unloaded all over his confused wife this morning, leaving her worried and scared and without answers. Such a selfish bastard.

"Own up, take the heat then get on with your life."

Tyrese's words had been replaying in his head. *His* words. From back when he'd known there was more to life than believing his own press. Honor. Something he'd forgotten along the way.

Jason could come clean, but he wouldn't have a life to get on with. His career would be over—even if he managed to avoid jail time. His marriage, too, most likely. How could Callie ever forgive him? How could he forgive himself?

"Own up, take the heat then get on with your life."

Jason hadn't had any clue the kind of courage it would take to follow that advice when he'd given it to Tyrese. But could he live with himself if something happened to an innocent woman? Could he look himself in the mirror every day, knowing he'd been too much of a coward to do the right thing?

He saw the exit sign ahead, wondered if he'd take the turnoff ramp toward Poughkeepsie or hit the gas and keep driving.

RILEY PROWLED THE ROOMS of the house, thoughts racing. She washed her hands and brushed her teeth. She arranged the kids' stuffed animals on their pillows, marking the spot where those sweet little heads would lay once they returned home from their trip. She emptied the dryer of a load of whites, folded and put them away before finally remembering she really did need to start dinner.

With a goal to ground her, Riley headed into the kitchen and willed herself to focus. She opened the fridge and took stock of what she had available. Sauce, mozzarella and a chunk of parmesan left over from the pizza. Several pounds of frozen chicken breasts that wouldn't take long to defrost. Without a great deal of work, she could put together chicken parmesan that should satisfy a hungry man.

Satisfy a hungry man.

Those few innocent words conjured up memories that sent another wave of heat flooding through her and started the whole sorry process of obsessing all over again.

She tossed the chicken onto the counter, where it landed with a solid thunk, and headed toward the coffeepot. No, she didn't need any caffeine when adrenaline was spiking her anxiety quite nicely, thank you very much, but coffee always made everything better. And with any luck the caffeine would constrict her blood vessels so she could focus for two minutes to make sense of…*that.*

She got the coffee brewing then arranged the chicken in the microwave to defrost, willing herself to calm down, to think clearly. She was an adult with some problems that needed resolutions. She couldn't afford the luxury of freaking out because she'd responded in Scott's arms, had been taken by surprise by her reaction to him.

And Scott's reaction to her. A shiver coursed through her as she remembered the expression on his face. Shocked. Stricken. And as embarrassed as she'd been. That much she hadn't imagined.

And aroused?

Yes. She hadn't imagined that, either.

Definitely aroused whether or not he'd wanted to be.

Pulling a skillet from the cabinet, Riley assembled everything she needed to bread the cutlets. Spear a cutlet.

Roll it in flour. Submerge it in egg. Coat it with seasoned bread crumbs. Then place it in the skillet.

She caught sight of a glossy black head in her periphery and glanced up from her task to see him crossing the yard toward the barn with a boy who was even taller than he was.

Flour. Egg. Bread crumbs. Skillet.

She willed the repetitive action to keep her attention and calm her jangled nerves. Once she got a few swigs of coffee in her, she'd be able to think more clearly.

Scott was an attractive man, a gorgeous man. Riley had always known that. Anyone with eyes would know that. Admittedly, she had to wonder why someone hadn't scarfed him up long ago. He'd dated some really nice women. Most hadn't been around long, but there'd been a few who'd hung around so she'd remembered their names from one police function to the next. Jennifer. Stephanie. Who was the one with the exquisite taste in shoes? *Dana*.

Mike had always told her not to worry about Scott. He'd said that Scott had some issues to sort through before he could commit to a woman. And then finding one might be a problem because he'd set his sights extraordinarily high.

That instantly recognizable black head caught her attention again. This time, Scott left the barn with two young men, probably Brian's age or close to it, in tow. The one who was taller than Scott—what was his name again? Eric. And the Hispanic boy, Mateo. She speared a cutlet from the skillet, accidentally spattering oil when she didn't drain it long enough.

What idiot had thought shutters would only detract from the view of the farm through all these windows? The idiot standing here with a fork in her hand, catching glimpses of a man she didn't want to see. Every single time she caught sight of him, those broad, broad shoulders, Riley found her thoughts circling right back around to *that*.

True, their relationship had been changing lately, but she'd gone from zero to sixty in his arms. There was no other way to describe it.

Riley had to get a grip. She wasn't a sixteen-year-old with moody hormones, and Scott wasn't someone with whom she had the luxury of losing control. He was involved with her family. He was a friend. She couldn't damage their relationship over some…she still didn't have a clue what *that* had been.

Flour. Egg. Bread crumbs. Skillet.

Darn it. What was wrong with her? Was she so emotionally vulnerable that she physically reacted to the first attractive man she felt comfortable with? And here she'd been telling Scott how healthy she was.

But that didn't ring true. Not really. No question they'd been growing closer. No question that she liked the man she was getting to know. But she was honestly surprised *that* part of her hadn't died along with Mike. Of course the grief counselors and people at the support groups had all said time would eventually help her get back to living. She was young. Her kids were young. They had a future meant to be lived. Riley hadn't believed them.

"Riley?"

She spun around, almost upending the bowl of flour. Scott stood in the doorway of the kitchen, and she'd been so preoccupied with her thoughts she hadn't heard him come in.

"Crew took off and I have good news." He sounded normal.

"I'm all ears." She sounded normal, too.

He leaned against the doorjamb, still not meeting her gaze. "Kevin found a possible answer—he just called to tell me. A local drug rep from one of the companies under investigation has a connection to someone we've gotten to know pretty well down at the department the past few years. Someone who'd know to bring along a radio to a cop's house."

"The pharmaceutical case?"

Scott nodded. "It's weak at best, so don't get your hopes up. But it's something. Kevin's on it."

"Thanks, I—"

"Listen, Riley," Scott cut her off. "I'm sorry about today. I was totally out of line."

"Scott, I—"

"I don't know what happened." He shoved his hand through his hair, upending the thick waves almost comically. "I shouldn't have invaded your personal space. I...well, I wanted to make you feel better."

He was taking the responsibility for what had happened? "But, Scott, you weren't—"

"I'm going to put the security on." He was already turning, ready to bolt. "I really need to shower. Do you mind?"

Whether she minded or not didn't seem to be at issue because he was gone before she could reply. Again she stood there staring after him as she heard the rapid beeping of the security panel as he set it, then the door to the kids' bathroom slamming firmly shut across the house. And some rapid-fire sputtering it took a moment to identify.

"Oh, no." She spun toward the skillet to find two cutlets burning.

She rescued them with a fork, shaking her head. What kind of conversation had that been? Why was Scott assuming the blame? She'd been the one to ignite like a spark to kindling in his arms. Could he have possibly misinterpreted her reaction?

Replaying the exchange over and over in her head, she finished assembling the meal and put it in the oven to bake. Then she washed the dishes. All she knew was that had been the second stupidest exchange between a man and woman in the history of mankind. Only this time she hadn't been the one with the stupidity pouring out of her mouth. She hadn't been able to get a complete sentence out thanks to Mr. Noble Gentleman.

So what was she supposed to do now? Just accept his apology and pretend nothing had happened? That didn't even make sense. Normal people discussed situations that needed discussion. But if he wasn't willing, then maybe she should figure out what was going on with her before addressing the issue with him or trying to.

He didn't seem to mind having conversations all by himself. Or assuming all the responsibility for something that had clearly happened between the two of them.

It was nearly five o'clock when Scott resurfaced. She intended to sit him down at the dinner table and try to revisit the subject, but the sight of him looking so freshly scrubbed from the shower derailed her.

There it was again. That *awareness*. Of how shiny and black his hair was with the waves still damp from the shower. How pink his cheeks were where he'd shaved. His jeans were clean. His shirt was fresh and neatly pressed. She could remember exactly how his hard chest would feel beneath that crisp white shirt.

"Smells good in here." He met her gaze this time, seemed to have collected himself. Apparently he intended to follow through with his pretend-nothing-ever-happened strategy.

"Hungry?" she asked. "Or is it too early for you? I'm on kid time myself."

"I'm starving, but don't go to any trouble for me."

Hadn't she said she would cook for him? Hadn't he even noticed that she'd been cooking for the past hour and a half since the kids had left? "No trouble. The least I can do is feed you—"

His phone rang. He reached for it with an apologetic expression, and she decided she wasn't going to catch a break right now. Not to talk with him.

Scott was frowning, so she asked, "Kevin again?"

He shook his head, sending a damp wave curling over his forehead. "I don't recognize the number." Flipping open the phone, he said, "Emerson."

He went utterly still while listening to his end of the conversation, and Riley, too, went on red alert. She knew the look, knew this call involved something he was invested in. His mouth compressed into a tight line, his jaw clenched as he responded in monosyllables. She noticed his knuckles grow steadily whiter as his grip tightened on the phone.

"I'll get him there," Scott said. "Chick's. Forty minutes?"

Chick's in the Valley was a tavern that had been around a lot longer than Riley had, a total hole in the wall that had become a Pleasant Valley institution.

Scott ended the call and for a moment was silent, as if he still hadn't transitioned from the call back to reality. He finally met her gaze. "I've got to leave for a little while. There will be a unit parked outside until I get back. Just a precaution. I won't be long."

"Is everything all right? I assume that call didn't have anything to do with me or you wouldn't be leaving."

His dark gaze bored into her with such intensity that Riley's pulse kicked up a notch. "I'll know more soon, but I've got to make some calls myself."

Then he left the room, leaving her staring after him again. What was this man's problem?

CHAPTER NINETEEN

JASON FOUND A PARKING SPOT beside the back door that led upstairs to the apartments above the tavern. He still wasn't sure if he'd made a mistake by agreeing to this meet at the height of Friday-night rush-hour traffic. He'd thought about waiting until after dark, but decided it would be easier to hide his movements in the traffic rather than try to slip away from home at night.

He wasn't worried about Callie. She was used to the demands of his job and wouldn't think anything strange, but he didn't trust Agent Asshole not to have put a tail on him. For precisely that reason, he'd asked Tyrese for another favor—borrowing the man's motorcycle, a favor much more to Tyrese's liking. That's why he'd jumped on board the "reform Jason" train with more than prayers. But Jason appreciated the prayers. He needed a miracle.

Once inside the back entrance, he pulled off the helmet.

Jason made his way down the narrow hall, finally pushing through swinging doors to the bar. Chick was behind it, where he'd been for the past forty years, maybe longer.

"Bud." He slapped down a ten, waited until he had the icy longneck in his hand before saying, "I'm meeting—"

"Private room." Chick cocked his balding head toward the swinging doors. "They're waiting for you."

Jason tipped his bottle in salute, then took a deep drink as he went to meet his fate.

Scott and Chief Levering were both inside the small dining room. The chief was sitting, nursing his own beer, while Scott prowled the perimeter. Jason closed the door.

"Chief." Chief Levering saluted Jason in a greeting that was a joke between them ever since Jason had left the PPD to lead Hazard Creek's department.

"Chief." Jason made his way to the table and extended his hand. "Thanks for coming on such short notice."

"What do you have?" Scott asked.

The moment of truth.

Jason set down the beer. He cocked his hip against the table and folded his arms across his chest. Taking a deep, fortifying breath, he felt the silence stretch, knowing the time had come to commit to the decision he'd made.

To do the right thing.

"I stepped in a pile of shit and need your help getting out."

To Jason's surprise that admission didn't get as tangled up with his pride as he'd expected. His voice sounded almost normal as he detailed the situation from the setup in Atlantic City to his appointment on the Narcotics Commission to Agent Asshole blackmailing him to provide law enforcement protection at various drug drops into the area.

When he finished, there was more of that silence.

"Shit, Jason?" Chief Levering shook his head, looking disgusted. "You're not kidding. What the hell do you think we can do for you?"

"Help me bring this asshole down," Jason said simply, all the humiliation, all the tension, all the goddamn months of sick pressure lessening with every word. "I'll give you everything you need and then some to set this guy up. I've got details on three-quarters of a million in drugs coming in. I want to go in with your best men undercover and bring every one of these hoods down."

"You'll be going down with them," Scott said, scowling.

It took effort to get the words out. "I know, man. I screwed up. But I don't want the media wiping the floors with my family. If you help me bring these assholes down, I'll have something to offer the D.A. We can keep this reasonably quiet."

Chief Levering's gaze narrowed. "You know the way this works, Jason. You're well-known around here. Do you think swinging a deal is even possible? What else do you have?"

Jason wasn't going to dwell on where basking in the local limelight had gotten him or the irony that all he wanted now was to disappear into a hole. "Enough to blow open something that's going to solve problems you didn't even know you had."

"You mentioned Riley on the phone," Scott said.

Jason nodded. He took a step away from the table, that feeling of relief getting lost somewhere beneath the sober admission he needed to make.

"I'm responsible." He met Chief Levering's gaze. "I sent someone to break into her house and car. I needed to find—"

He'd been too busy battling down guilt and pride as he faced his old boss to notice the powerful right hook coming at him. Then the side of his head exploded and he was tripping backward over a chair. He crash-landed against the wall with a thud that rocked the door in its frame. He had time to register Scott bearing down on him when Chief Levering's command rang out, "Knock it off."

Scott stopped short when Chief Levering caught a hand in his collar. "Don't make me say it again."

"Son of a bitch," Scott growled, visibly shaking.

Jason rubbed his jaw. He couldn't meet either man's gaze. Not when he hadn't even gotten to the good parts yet.

"Get up," Chief Levering said to Jason just as the door opened and Chick stuck his bald head into the room.

"You want me to call the cops?" He gave a short laugh.

"Aren't you a comedian." Chief Levering scowled. "Bring us another round, would you?"

Chick disappeared again, and Chief Levering pointed to the table. "Both of you sit and get a grip. Now."

Chick returned a few minutes later with three beers on a tray and left with a muttered, "Do not tear up my place or I'll kick all your asses, cops or not."

"You got it, buddy. No problem." Chief Levering glared down at the table as the door slammed shut. "You finish talking," he charged Jason. Then he directed Scott, "And you don't open your mouth again until he does."

Jason gulped down half a beer before explaining how the CD in Riley's van had begun a chain reaction.

"Damn it." Scott swore, clearly forgetting the part where he was supposed to keep his mouth shut. "I heard something when she cranked up the radio in the car that day, but I never gave it another thought. Just figured one of the kids had been pushing buttons."

"I didn't think you'd heard, but with everything going on I couldn't be sure if you were setting me up or not. I needed to get hold of that CD to find out exactly what was on it."

Scott sank back in the chair, glaring. "That was what you were after."

Jason nodded.

"Well, you got it," Chief Levering said dryly. "Don't keep us in suspense."

"The CD wasn't what I expected." Coming across that CD and learning what it contained were the luckiest breaks he'd had lately. Jason reached inside the inner pocket of his jacket and pulled out an envelope. "Turns out it had nothing to do with me and everything to do with the assholes blackmailing me. Details about operations that went down when they first got into this area nearly three years ago."

That got a reaction. Both Chief Levering and Scott stared at him as he withdrew two burned copies of the CD and slid them across the table. "Here you go."

Scott took it. "Riley had this?"

Jason nodded. "When you hear what's on it, you'll draw the same conclusions I did."

"Cut to the chase," Chief Levering ground out harshly, and Jason didn't miss the way his face had drained of all color, making him look old and tired.

"It had to be Mike's. That's the only way to explain why it surfaced now. Riley must have come across it after she got home. I'm willing to bet money she doesn't have a clue what it is because she'd have never left this sort of incriminating evidence lying around under the car seat. She's a reporter. She's not stupid."

"Incriminating evidence about this DEA agent," Chief Levering repeated.

"And about the people responsible for gunning down Mike."

The sudden silence seemed alive. Then Scott was shaking his head. "No way, man. We brought down everyone. Every damn one."

"That you knew about. Because if you'd have known about the DEA, you'd have fried them like you fried everyone else involved in Mike's murder, and saved me a boatload of trouble."

Jason snorted. "My guess is you didn't know Agent

Asshole was blackmailing a parole officer. But those hoods who recorded this CD did. They detailed everything they might need to make sure they weren't nailed if any shit went down. If you'd known about that parole officer, you'd have blown open this whole thing. I'm thinking Mike must have come across this CD. I'm thinking that's what got him killed."

That silence again. Jason wanted to tell Chief Levering to sit down before he fell down, just as the older man dropped heavily into a chair.

Scott slammed a hand down on the table. "The CD that went missing from the evidence room."

"You knew about it?" Now it was Jason's turn to be surprised.

Scott nodded. "It was the only loose end we had after the investigation. A CD that was picked up in a bust and logged in as evidence. We never could find it."

"What happened?" Jason asked.

"I'm thinking Mike must have taken it home," Chief Levering said.

"Mike would never have taken anything from the property room without signing. He was by the book." Scott scowled. "That CD was never checked out. I know because I went through every damn entry myself."

"It wouldn't have been Mike's job to log it out, but the officer on duty in the property room," Chief Levering pointed out. "We questioned everyone about that CD. Maybe no one could remember anything because someone screwed up. We don't have any clue when Mike might have taken it. And we've got a couple of cops who aren't even with the department anymore. Maybe someone was covering his ass because he screwed up and forgot to log that entry and was afraid to say something."

It happened, Jason knew. Just like he knew if that CD

had been logged out of the property room the way it should have been, Mike Angelica might still be alive and Jason himself wouldn't be staring at the end of his own life as he'd known it.

"And you're willing to testify about all this if I help you set up the DEA?" Chief Levering eyed him levelly.

"I want to cut a deal." There was only one way he stood a chance with Callie. That was by owning up and taking the heat. "I'm not one of these assholes, no matter what you think. I have to try to salvage something from the wreckage. I've got details about the biggest shipment he's brought into the area that I know of. A well-known drug distribution ring operating out of Mexico. Your department will be shining stars."

"Why?" Scott said.

"Why what?"

"Why are you coming to us now? You've known this DEA agent and his team went bad ever since they set you up. Why the change of heart now? Why not *before* you involved Riley—" Scott turned to stare at Jason, understanding all over his face.

Jason didn't have to say a word. He half expected Scott to come after him again, but Scott was already on his feet, cell phone at his ear, voice raw as he barked into the receiver, "Charlie, talk to me. Everything okay there?"

Jason just sat there, feeling sick all over again when Chief Levering's gaze swiveled to him. "Tell me that agent didn't make you target Riley."

He was saved from replying when Scott demanded, "What delivery? Did you check out the driver? What about the flowers?"

Scott shot Jason a gaze that made him marvel at the man's self-control.

"Are you inside yet?" Scott hissed into the receiver. "Is she okay?"

As Scott waited, he covered the receiver and told Chief Levering, "I got a bad feeling. I'm heading back. We can brief for the operation—"

A shock of sound emitted from the phone so loud that even Jason could hear. The phone flew from Scott's hand as he instinctively jerked it from his ear. It hit the table and skittered hard, but Scott caught it in a fast lunge.

"Charlie?" He yelled into the receiver. "Charlie, are you there?" Scott snapped the phone shut, cursing, then jammed a few buttons. He dragged the phone back to his ear. "Come on, Sal."

Chief Levering was already on his feet when Scott announced, "He's not answering, either."

CHAPTER TWENTY

RILEY SET the extravagant basket of flowers on the kitchen table, then stepped back to view the result. She wasn't sure why the *Herald* had sent them. Max had been pleased she'd made her deadline despite stolen equipment, but she didn't think he'd been responsible. It was more likely Shirley Henderson, his assistant.

The card read, *So you know the Herald cares.*

This sweet show of support only added to her conflict about the job. She liked the familiarity and flexibility but didn't want to cover the action anymore. It just wasn't safe. Maybe, like so many areas of her life, the time had come for a new challenge.

She stared outside at her freshly mowed yard shadowed in oncoming dusk and remembered the kids from Renaissance she'd met earlier. They'd worked so hard, had spent hours and hours hacking away brush and weeding beds. They might have looked like hoods that she would have avoided on the street, but they'd been very polite when Scott had introduced them, so appreciative of her efforts when she'd brought them iced tea. Just kids.

They hadn't had the breaks her own kids were getting. Even though losing Mike had unexpectedly and irrevocably altered their family, her kids still had a parent to help them make sense of the tragedy of losing their dad. They had extended family who loved them. They had stability.

Not the kids Riley had met today. She didn't know their individual circumstances the way Scott did, but she knew those kids had been forced to face the hard side of life at too young an age, might not have had parents who loved them or who could take the time to teach them how to live purposeful lives.

That didn't make them bad people. Scott knew that. She liked that about him. And he was right about something else, too. Whatever she decided about her job ultimately, she shouldn't decide because she was scared.

Setting a good example for her kids was the most important thing. She didn't want to teach them to run away from life's difficulties. Move on, yes—sometimes they wouldn't get a choice—but never run because they were scared.

"Riley?" A sharp knock echoed down the hallway. "Open up."

She recognized Charlie's voice. Smiling at that bright floral arrangement, she spun on her heel and headed out of the kitchen. She'd give the circulation desk a call while she was folding the laundry. Shirley would already be gone for the weekend, but Riley would leave a message.

Then the house literally shook beneath her feet. The walls vibrated around her, and a rush of heat filled the hallway as the security alarm, wired to sense fire, shrieked a warning. But Riley didn't need the alarm to know what was happening. She could hear the roar of flames, and froze for an instant, her muscles utterly rigid as panic and reason collided.

Get out. Call 9-1-1.

Her cell phone was in the bedroom. She didn't need it. Charlie or Sal would radio emergency if they hadn't already.

Launching herself into motion again, she covered the distance to the front door in a few bounding steps. She flipped the dead bolt and yanked the door wide.

She expected to find Charlie, but not lying in a heap on the floor. For another stunned instant she stared down at the collapsed officer on her front porch. How had the explosion harmed him here when she hadn't been hurt inside the house?

She noticed the cell phone discarded beside him, and the ajar porch door just as it swung wide, slamming into her with such force that she rocked backward. Staggering to catch her balance, her feet tangled in Charlie's inert form, and she yelped, bracing herself as she fell.

"Sorry, ma'am." Strong hands grabbed her arm, dragged her upright with enough force to nearly yank her shoulder from its socket. Riley cried out again, glancing up to find a muscular man in a paramedic uniform hanging on to her.

He pulled her through the open doorway, then let the door swing shut again. Charlie disappeared from sight.

"I'm okay," she insisted over the steady shriek of the security alarm. "But Charlie—"

"Don't worry, ma'am. He'll be taken care of," the paramedic said coolly. "Right now we need to assess your condition."

Don't worry? Her house was burning down and there was a family friend lying unconscious on her porch floor. *Don't worry?*

Riley glanced around, the panic tightening like a vise around her chest. She struggled to draw in a good breath, to make sense of the sight before her.

An ambulance idled beside the police cruiser in the driveway, but she didn't see any sign of Sal, who'd ridden with Charlie. Had he radioed in the explosion? Was that how the ambulance had gotten here so quickly?

"The fire department—?"

"Already on its way," the paramedic said, steering her around the cruiser and toward the ambulance.

She noticed another man behind the wheel of the emergency vehicle, but something wasn't right. Riley didn't know what it was, only that panic was well and truly taking hold of her.

Something wasn't right.

That thought lodged in her brain as she stumbled along on clumsy feet as the paramedic rushed her toward the ambulance, keeping up a steady stream of chatter. How had it gotten here so quickly? Even if Charlie had radioed the instant he'd heard the explosion…

Charlie was unconscious. Unconscious? Or dead?

The thought finally pierced Riley's confusion, and she pulled away. The man's grip was a vise around her upper arm. When she resisted, he simply tightened his grip and lent his considerable bulk to the cause, shoving her toward the waiting ambulance.

"Come on, ma'am. We need to check you out."

"Let me go." She fought with every ounce of her strength, kicking out as the certainty that something was terribly wrong drove away all thoughts of the man on her porch and the fire raging in her kitchen.

"Sal," she screamed, relieved by the power of her voice. If he didn't hear her, someone else might. "Sal. Help me."

As quickly as she started fighting, Riley stopped, becoming a dead weight against the man's grip, drawing on every ounce of defense training Mike had ever taught her. The paramedic staggered, caught by surprise, his balance uncertain. Riley slammed the heel of her hand into his face while pulling away. She heard a sickening crunch, and the man grunted loudly. This time she broke free.

Lunging into motion, she managed to get almost to the cruiser when the sound of a blaring horn startled her. But she didn't even flinch, just kept running.

Until the paramedic tackled her.

The breath fled her lungs with a whoosh as his muscular frame slammed into her, knocked her to the ground. She hit the concrete hard enough to make her see stars, and for a stunned instant she didn't move, didn't fight back.

That was all he needed to drag her upright by the hair. In one skilled move, he locked his arm around her throat and half dragged, half carried her to the ambulance.

He hefted her up and tossed her inside without a word. She landed in a heap, her chest still seized around a breath. She couldn't expel any air, couldn't drag any in.

He slammed the doors shut, sealing her in darkness. Then the vehicle accelerated with the screech of tires, and Riley was slammed backward, hitting something—a gurney, she thought. With her feet, she anchored herself upright, fighting unconsciousness, refusing to leave herself so vulnerable. She needed to remain alert, to look for the opportunity to escape, or at the very least signal help.

Scott.

Just the thought of him helped focus her, and she fought for that breath, to control her panic and fear, to relax her chest enough to breathe, breathe, *breathe*.

In slow degrees, the vise eased. Oxygen flooded back into her lungs, sharpened her vision, or maybe she was just growing accustomed to the darkness. She willed herself to think, though her brain didn't seem to be working yet. The lack of oxygen or the fear, she didn't know.

She just knew she couldn't panic. Who had her and why? The medical scam she'd been investigating? The ambulance. Made sense. Her abductors were professional.

That much she knew. This was no random abduction but a well-planned attack.

The ambulance skidded around a curve so hard Riley flung an arm out to brace herself. The gurney rattled noisily. Equipment, wires and hoses and belts, swung wildly until the ambulance righted itself. They were probably taking the curve near Mrs. Haslam's place.

She tried to focus, but disjointed thoughts kept racing through her head. Thank God the kids were away. If they had been inside the house, that explosion… She hadn't been able to protect herself. Thank God the kids were with Rosie and Joe. They were the only things that mattered. She could live without the house, without her mementoes of life with Mike. As long as she had her kids and her memories.

An emergency siren screeched, and for a heart-stopping second, Riley felt a wave of hope so strong, she gasped aloud. Help had arrived. Scott had come.

She knew he would find her.

Then she realized the sound was coming from *this* ambulance, a diversion that would give her abductors the advantage.

With a cry, she flung herself at the doors, hoping to unlock them. It didn't matter how fast they drove. She'd throw herself into the path of oncoming traffic if it would get her out of this ambulance before they merged onto Mountain Road, which would lead them to the Taconic Parkway where her abductors could drive eighty miles an hour to anywhere they wanted.

She pulled on the door latches, tears springing to her eyes when they levered ineffectually against her grip.

Locked.

She pounded her fists against the door, drawing a laugh

from one of the men in the cab, a laugh she could hear over the blaring siren and the sounds of two sweet little voices.

"Mommy died. Mommy died like Daddy."

CHAPTER TWENTY-ONE

"CAN'T YOU GET THEM on the radio yet?" Scott demanded.

"Damn it." The chief braced himself against the dashboard as the cruiser's wheels lifted off the ground, then landed again with a jarring thump. "No wonder you can't keep a partner when you drive like this."

Scott didn't comment. He was too focused on keeping the car on the road after his left wheel caught the shoulder, kicking up gravel and dirt and practically ripping the steering wheel from his grasp. From Chick's in the Valley to Riley's house was barely a five-minute drive, but all of Traver Road wound through a mixture of hilly woods and farmland. Not an easy road to travel at high speed, especially when it was getting dark.

The chief's answer was to radio through to dispatch again.

"Still no contact with Charlie's unit, but we've got our first report of a fire at Riley's address," the chief said grimly. "A neighbor. She wanted to know why the ambulance took off before the fire truck got there."

"How the hell did the paramedics get there when they're still two minutes behind us?" Scott glanced away from the road and found the chief staring back, gaze narrowing.

Strangely, Scott had Jason to thank for being with the chief right now. And he couldn't think of anyone he'd rather have sitting beside him. Except for Mike. Not when his heart was pounding the rapid-fire rhythm of an automatic weapon. Not when only long years of training kept him focused with the roar of that explosion looping in his memory. The sound of Charlie cursing. Then the awful silence.

Having the chief beside him took some of the pressure off. Scott didn't have to think of everything. He didn't have to explain himself. He didn't have to battle through this unfamiliar panic. Together he and the chief wouldn't miss any detail with Riley at risk.

"Sheriff's got units on the way," the chief said.

Scott nodded and slowed enough to take the switchback turn, the last turn before the farm.

He spotted the smoke coiling from the back of the house before turning into the driveway. He hissed in relief that the entire house wasn't up in flames. Charlie's cruiser sat unmanned. Beside it was a dark stain he couldn't quite make out in the fading light. Blood?

His heart thudded a single hard beat, but he didn't get a chance to put his gearshift into Park before the porch door burst wide and Sal appeared, one side of his face angry and swollen.

But no blood.

"We were sandbagged," he called out. "Two men disguised as paramedics. Armed and dangerous. Professional. She's gone. They took her in an ambulance. Toward Freedom Road."

"Was she hurt in the explosion?" Scott asked.

"I'm sorry. I didn't see her. I came around when the ambulance was pulling out."

"Charlie?" the chief called through the open window.

"Unconscious. Got a pulse. I'll get him out." Sal waved them toward the road. "They're not two, maybe three minutes ahead of you. Go, go, go."

"Fire department is right behind us. Sheriff, too."

With a scowl Sal waved them off again, and Scott shoved the gearshift into Reverse and gunned the engine. He corrected the wheel and spun back onto Traver Road. He could hear the wail of sirens in the distance.

The fire department, most likely.

He didn't think, just drove while the chief put an APB out on the ambulance. Three minutes could mean the difference between Riley's life and death.

Scott gained time on the open stretch that ran alongside a dairy farm on approach to the turn at Freedom Road. No sight of the ambulance, but a choice of three different roads.

"Taconic?" the chief asked.

"They're not going far in an ambulance," Scott said. "They'll have to make a switch somewhere. The nearest medical facility is an urgent care on Route 55."

The chief placed the emergency light on the dash as Scott slowed to maneuver the intersection. He was about to gun the engine and speed toward LaGrange when he caught sight of fresh tire tracks in the field off the shoulder, as if someone had pulled off the road in a hurry.

"Get an ID on that ambulance," he ground between clenched teeth. He didn't want to be responsible for running down a legitimate emergency vehicle and possibly killing someone.

Instinct had him making a wide turn down Mountain Road, which led straight toward the Taconic Parkway. The back of his neck prickled as he scanned the area, taking in the rising and rolling hills that blocked the distance from view. The sprawling barns that dotted those slopes.

Kondas Brothers' Dairy Farm.

The perfect place to make a switch?

"Vassar Hospital is missing an emergency unit." The

chief grabbed the overhead handle when Scott turned off the road into the field. The car's suspension bucked wildly as he descended the first slope, but while the ruts faded, he could easily follow the indentations in the grass.

There were houses in the distance, likely the folks who owned the farm. But an ambulance could have easily hidden behind either, especially the ranch-style house on the highest rise before the forested slope of the mountain began.

Scott circled the first of the two barns and just as he made the curve, a vehicle cut him off.

"Shit." He jammed his foot on the brake as a pricey four-wheel-drive with tinted windows narrowly missed his quarter panel.

It must have been lying in wait, watching their approach, and now it circled around and bore down on them, keeping them occupied as an ambulance started bouncing wildly down the hill to get away.

"There she is," the chief said, on the radio again, this time calling for backup.

Scott's pulse slammed against his inner ears, the rush of blood throbbing so loud he could barely hear the roar of the engine as he spun the wheel again, tires grinding through dirt and grass as the car spun in a three-sixty. He managed to avoid taking a hit by the taller vehicle.

But as he jammed his foot on the gas, intent upon shooting out of the 4X4's way, he heard the chief issue a stream of curses. Scott glanced out of the corner of his eye…just as the ambulance sent dirt spewing upward as tires skidded along the ground, vainly spinning for purchase.

His heart stopped beating as the back of the ambulance pitched over the lip of a small gulley and went straight down.

"Shit," the chief ground out as the crash resounded through the field, and all they could see of the ambulance was the underbelly of the cab pointing straight toward the sky and the tires spinning in the air.

Riley.

Scott was so focused on the ambulance that he didn't see the 4X4 spin out in reverse. He gunned the engine to get out of the way, but several gunshots rang out, distracting him. The steering wheel bucked in his hands, and he fought to stop the car as the 4X4 rear-ended him hard. Once. Twice. Each crash resounding louder than the last as it finally pushed his front end through the fence and into the side of the barn.

Wood splintered around them. Glass shattered when some sort of shelving collapsed, spewing glass all over the hood of the cruiser. Scott slammed the car into Reverse and glanced in his rearview mirror simultaneously.

Sure enough, the 4X4 had bought enough time to speed to the ambulance. It stopped in front of the wreck, blocking it from view.

"Go, go, go," the chief yelled as Scott gunned the engine. More wood splintered. Something was trapping the front bumper, and Scott had to rock the car to break free.

He cleared the fence, but not before the 4X4 circled the gulley, its back door slamming shut as it took off with a shuddering jolt and began a speeding ascent toward the houses.

"Riley?" Scott followed the 4X4 automatically, but had no way of knowing if they'd taken her or left her in the ambulance.

"I don't know," the chief said. "Give me the wheel."

Scott pulled the cruiser in front of the crash site and ground to a halt. He jumped out, and the chief took his place in the driver's seat. The entire exchange had taken only seconds, but already the 4X4 was disappearing up the slope. If it headed into the woods, the chief might lose them completely.

"Riley," he yelled. His entire body started to shake when he glanced down to see how tightly the ambulance was wedged in the gulley, the clearance so compressed it would take heavy machinery to remove it.

The only luck had been the backward descent. Had it gone in cab first, the ambulance would have likely exploded on impact.

"Riley?" Scott called again as he yanked back the door of the cab. "Riley, are you here?"

Silence.

"Riley." He tried to gauge the stability of the vehicle, but with the darkness descending, he could only see shadows. He scrambled gingerly into the cab, relieved when the vehicle seemed solid, shoving aside radio equipment that hung from the instrument panel. He sprawled across the front seat and peered down into the darkness.

"Riley."

No reply. Then, after a breathless instant, Scott heard movement. A metallic clatter. The thud of some smaller items hitting the back door. Then a moan.

"Riley." No longer a question, but a sigh. "Riley, are you injured? We have to get you out of here. Can you move?"

"Scott?" She sounded a little dazed but alive.

Alive.

"Yeah, it's me," he choked out, the words lodging in his throat. "Are you hurt? Talk to me."

"No, no. I'm okay."

His eyes shuttered instinctively, a prayer of thanksgiving.

"You're here."

"I'm here." Those words tangled with a breath in his

throat, threatened to choke him. Or was that relief because she was alive? "I'm here. I'll help you climb out. Or do you need me to come down to you?"

"No. No. I'm okay."

"Is there anything on top of you? Anything I need to move?"

He heard her grunt of effort then the sound of something heavy being shoved aside. "If I can swing my legs around..." Her words trailed off.

"Just go slowly. Make sure you're okay."

The shuffling sounds of her maneuvering. He prayed the doors underneath her were solidly locked or crushed shut against the gulley bottom. There was no way to know.

"Got it. I'm okay. Just a little banged up."

Thank God. "Okay, good. Can you see my hands?"

He forced himself to remain calm, to keep his voice steady when his heart was pounding too hard and his throat was tight. Anchoring his thighs against the backrest of the seat, he leaned down into the darkness, stretching his arms out before him.

Her hair was a pale blur in the shadows, a beacon that drew him toward her. "I want you to grab on to me. I'll pull you out."

His lungs compressed against another crushing wave of emotion, making it so hard to breathe as he waited.

Then her fingers were brushing his, soft, warm, and he was threading his hands firmly around her wrists as if his life depended on it.

"Riley." His voice was a whisper in the darkness as he pulled her up inch by inch. She used her feet to find footholds, to steady herself against the equipment that shifted with their movements, impeded the speed of their progress.

But she came to him. Slowly, ever so slowly she

emerged until he was forced to slide out of the cab to bring her the rest of the way.

"You got her, Scott?" The chief's voice called out and a flashlight beam slashed through the darkness.

"Yeah, I got her. I guess that means you didn't find them."

The chief gave a grunt and didn't bother replying. He just shone the flashlight into the cab. "Need a hand?"

"Yeah. If you could hang on to me while I pull her out."

A few solid moves and they had Riley seated in the grass, looking unsteady but alive.

"You need medical attention." The chief sliced his light across her.

"No, no. I'm okay. I'm okay. The house. And Charlie."

She could barely get the words out. She was going into shock if she wasn't there already. Scott knelt beside her and shoved hair from her face, running his fingers along her temples, her cheeks, down her neck, over her shoulders. He could feel nothing but the smooth curves of this beautiful woman, this beautiful, breathing woman.

"Anything hurt?"

"No. Really, I'm okay."

"What about the explosion at the house?"

She shook her head. "Charlie called me. I was out of the kitchen when the fire started. He was…hurt."

"He's fine," the chief reassured her. "In a real ambulance on the way to a real hospital, but he'll be okay. His head's as hard as a rock. Trust me. And your house…well, from what I hear, the only damage is in the kitchen. And the smoke. Don't worry. We'll lock it up tight."

"Lock it up," she repeated. "No. I need to go home. Brian will be coming home to deal with the horses."

"You need to be checked out, Riley," the chief said sternly, glancing at the ambulance. "You may be concussed—"

"Chief, I didn't hit my head. Honestly, you two, I'm okay. Just banged up a bit. I'll go see my doctor tomorrow."

"Tomorrow's Saturday."

"Then I'll have my brother-in-law check me out if something doesn't feel right. All I want to do is go home."

The chief cut a meaningful glance at Scott, who said, "Listen, Riley. You and I are going to take a ride. I'll give Brian a call on the way. Sound good?"

She turned those sparkling eyes to his, and even in the darkness he could see the shock taking hold. She was running on adrenaline at the moment, but he needed to get her someplace safe, where he could assess her before she crashed.

"Backup on the way?" he asked the chief, who nodded.

"Go. Trooper's pulling off the Taconic. Two minutes max."

Scott slipped an arm beneath Riley's and helped her stand. The chief came at her from the other side and they guided her back to his cruiser. She quickly strapped herself into the passenger seat.

The chief shut the door on her and met Scott's gaze. "This cruiser took a beating tonight. Is it still going to get you where you need to go, or do I need to call in—"

"It'll be fine. I don't want to wait."

"Then let me know where you wind up."

Scott circled the car. He slipped behind the wheel, then headed out of the dark field and back onto the road. He saw the trooper's visibar flashing in his rearview mirror as he sped toward Overlook Road, wanting to avoid Riley's place, which would still be surrounded with emergency vehicles.

She didn't need any more surprises tonight.

He gave Brian a synopsis of the situation and worked out an arrangement for the kid to deal with the horses and pick up some things while a patrol unit stayed tonight. He told Brian to go to his parents' or a friend's to sleep, then meet up with another patrol in the morning. Just until they had a lock on the men who'd abducted Riley.

That wouldn't happen until they rounded up everyone at Jason's bust.

"Okay, Brian's all set," he told her.

"The kids, Scott," she said, voice shaky. "They're going to call so I can tell them good-night."

He held up his phone. "Want me to call Joe?"

She shook her head. "I need to talk to them."

He handed her the phone, frowning when her hand shook. "You're still feeling okay? Not dizzy or anything, are you?"

"No. I'm okay. Really."

But she struggled to dial. He knew what was happening—the adrenaline was wearing off. He knew because his was on the way out, too.

Yet she was so determined. Cradling the phone against her ear, she rested her head against the window and closed her eyes. "Hi, sweet pea. It's Mommy," she spoke softly, looking so relieved. "You and Camille okay?"

Scott drove through the city, listening to her as she mothered her kids long distance, talking to them in turns, getting excited as they related their stories of the day, loving them, all while her hands trembled and her breath came in ragged bursts. They had no clue about what had happened tonight. How close they came to losing their only remaining parent. She bore that burden right now. Alone.

"I love you so much," she finally said. "Call me if you need me. But call me at Uncle Scott's number, okay? I misplaced my phone. I know, silly Mommy. I love you. Tell Jake I love him, too. Sweet dreams, pretty. I'll talk with you in the morning."

Then she flipped the phone shut. She just held it in her

lap as if it were a solid connection to her kids. She never opened her eyes.

"Joe and Rosie?" he asked.

"I'll tell them when I talk with them next. No need to stress them out just yet."

Scott wasn't surprised she was thinking about others, even when she was coming apart herself. But she was so still as he drove through the city to the outskirts of town.

The silence was complete, as if someone had pressed a mute function. The blue and red blasts of the emergency light sliced through the darkness at rhythmic intervals, the only sign of life except for the sound of Riley's shallow breathing.

He wanted her safe. He thought about taking her straight to a hospital, but didn't want her exposed until the chief had a lock on the situation. He compromised. Putting a call in to Brian's father, Scott made arrangements for Alex to check Riley out in his office at the hospital. She argued, but Scott didn't want to find out that she was more banged up than he could handle without assistance.

After a perfunctory examination, Alex declared Riley in the clear of any major trauma and let Scott take her. Then he drove to the only safe place he could think of. Wheeling off Salt Point Turnpike, he headed down a dirt road. The path followed a creek that wound through the parcel of wooded acreage, not too far from the Clinton townline.

He pulled up in front of the stone bungalow that overlooked the creek, a place that had once been a guesthouse for the larger residence on these acres.

Riley never asked where they were, and he understood why the minute he opened her door.

She was shaking, a lot.

"Come on. It's just mild shock. Alex said to expect that, so don't worry." He hoped. "We'll get you feeling better."

With his arm tightly around her, he helped her climb the front steps. He unlocked the door, flipped on a light then led her straight into the living room.

"Sit. I'll be right back." Scott headed into the kitchen, turned on the stove light and pulled open the refrigerator. Where was it… There. He withdrew a cardboard container, remnants of takeout dinner from the Canton, his favorite Chinese place in downtown Poughkeepsie.

Pouring the broth into a mug, he withheld the wontons then shoved the mug in the microwave to nuke for a few minutes.

He went to the bedroom and yanked the comforter off the bed, then brought it to Riley, who gazed up at him, plaintive eyes gleaming in the darkness.

"I c-can't s-stop shaking."

"You need a nest." With a hand on her shoulder, he helped her lean forward so he could wrap the comforter around her. Then he slipped off her shoes. "Pull up your legs."

He tucked her feet beneath the heavy comforter, too, then went to retrieve the broth when the microwave beeped.

"Drink some of this."

She shook her head, tangled blond hair coiling around her neck. "N-not h-hungry."

"I know. Trust me. It'll help."

She couldn't hold the mug, so Scott sank down beside her and pulled her onto his lap. Slipping his hands over hers, he helped her steady the mug as she brought it to her lips.

"Just take small sips."

The glow from the kitchen barely penetrated the living room, and he willed the dark quiet to calm her, calm *him*. The adrenaline was wearing off too fast, leaving him wired and overwhelmed by how close he'd come to losing her.

The memory of that ambulance… It was a miracle she was alive, unharmed.

"It's okay," he crooned in a whisper against her hair, as much to himself as to her. "Everything is okay now."

He tried to block out the memory of staring down into the darkness of the ambulance, not knowing if he would find her, and if he did whether she'd be alive or dead. He just focused on the way she folded into the curve of his body, fitting neatly against him as if she belonged there.

"N-no m-more," she said weakly, pushing the mug away after only a few sips.

He didn't try to convince her otherwise, even though her tremors were growing more violent rather than less. He set the broth down on the coffee table and ran his hands over her shoulders, down her arms. He tried to warm her, wanted to soothe her fears away.

"Shh. Everything is okay now," he whispered over and over.

But it wasn't. Tremors became spasms. Her teeth chattered.

"F-freezing."

Had he made the wrong choice by bringing her here? For an instant of blinding uncertainty, Scott froze with his arms around her. Should he call 9-1-1 or take her to the emergency room?

No. Alex would never have let Riley leave the hospital if she wasn't okay. Until the chief called, she was safest here. If the DEA was responsible for her abduction—and who else would be so skilled as to make use of emergency equipment for a kidnapping?—Scott had no way of knowing how ambitious they would be. If that CD was the reason Mike had been killed, then Scott couldn't take any chances with Riley's safety.

But once this was done, he would kill Jason Kenney himself.

Riley's spasms and chattering teeth gave way to dry, heaving breaths, and Scott shifted out from under her, reached down and lifted her into his arms.

"It's okay," he crooned, over and over, willing her to believe him, willing her to calm in his arms.

The need to do something finally spurred him to his feet and he carried her into the bathroom, cradled her against him as he shoved open the shower door so hard the glass rattled in its frame, and turned on the water one-handed. Soon clouds of steam billowed from the stall, and he shoved the comforter off her, kicked it away, along with his shoes.

"Close your eyes." He stepped under the spray, and she buried her face against his chest.

Hot water pounded, quickly soaking their clothes, the fluid heat blasting through fabric and skin, a heat to sink bone deep.

Riley's hair plastered against her head, the water turning natural curls into dark, unfamiliar waves that twined around her cheeks and neck and made her skin seem unnaturally pale. Her thick lashes formed dark crescents beneath her eyes, and she nestled closer against him as though they might actually fuse into one so she could share his warmth.

And she trembled.

Scott had no clue how long they stood there, him crooning nonsense, his hands never ceasing their travels over the smooth curves of her back, her arms, anywhere he could reach while still holding her tight. He couldn't stop touching her.

He'd never known such powerful relief, a sensation that robbed him of reason, of speech, of everything but the knowledge that she was *alive,* here in his arms, and for this moment, this forbidden moment, he could touch her. He could inhale the scent of her hair, caress the slick wetness of her neck. Pretend that he had every right to feel the way he did.

Scott was so caught up in his own thoughts he didn't notice her trembling had eased until it stopped completely. He was so caught up in the feel of her body that he didn't notice when her hands had joined his, traveling over his wet clothes, trailing along his shoulders and down his back, mirroring his strokes.

He only came fully to his senses when she started to move, pushing out of his arms and stretching her legs underneath her. She slid down the length of his body, ready to stand on her own. And he steadied her during the descent when their sodden clothes dragged together, her shirt pulling up to reveal flashes of her smooth stomach, the strap of her bra. He stood transfixed by the long, sensuous unfolding of sleek curves and firm muscles. But Scott knew exactly when Riley came back to herself.

She tilted her face up and kissed him.

CHAPTER TWENTY-TWO

THE EVENTS OF THE NIGHT FADED. Her racing thoughts. The anxiety. The fear. All gone beneath the steady pounding of the hot water.

Riley was tired, so tired, but the heat and the feel of Scott's strong arms around her anchored her to the moment. A moment where she was safe and standing in the only place in the world she wanted to be.

The feeling didn't make sense. Not if she started picking it apart with her head, but Riley knew her body. And just as she'd been certain she hadn't sustained any hidden injuries from the night's events, she knew that being in Scott's arms was exactly where she should be.

She couldn't think beyond that. Wouldn't. She had only this second. Didn't want reason. Didn't want any more fear or worry. She wanted to feel the way she felt right now.

Good.

She never dreamed her body would ever awaken, would ever feel alive this way again. But the water warmed her until the heat became so much more, a fire that pulsed thickly through her veins, until all she was aware of was the strength of Scott's arms around her, the way he held her close.

She might come up with a thousand reasons why she shouldn't feel this way. Scott might refuse to discuss the awareness that had flared between them so unexpectedly. But she recognized this feeling on a purely instinctive level.

This wasn't fear. This wasn't weakness. This wasn't grief.

This was *want*.

She wouldn't resist. Not now. Not after tonight. Not after the twists and turns her life had taken the past few years. She'd learned one valuable lesson at least, and she wouldn't waste a second because she might not get another.

So she stretched languidly against him, forced him to let her down, greedy to feel him against her, to discover the hard contours of his body, to test this awareness and learn if he was as aware of her as she of him.

She hoped. The intensity surprised her.

Her feet touched the floor of the shower stall, but his arms still held her steady, so she rose up on her tiptoes and pressed her mouth to his.

He tasted wet with the water that sluiced over them, so unfamiliar yet so male. And for a stunning instant, Riley simply stood there, waiting for him to react. Her breath trapped in her lungs. Her heartbeats throbbed hard between them.

Then he sucked in a sharp breath that stole hers. And his mouth came against hers with such unmistakable need that a memory of the hurricane chamber at the Florida science museum flashed in her head, of hundred-mile-an-hour winds whipping around with fierce intensity. The way Scott seemed to explode around her as if his need had been so tightly contained one touch was all it took to shatter his control.

Suddenly his hands were everywhere, one banding around her waist, the other spearing into her wet hair, and he brought her up against him with a force that dragged another gasp from her, a crazy exhalation that burst against his lips. His body was a solid wall of muscle, wholly unfamiliar with its long contours. Tall, lean strength. So much contained power.

He kissed her with a possession that surprised her. Their tongues tangled as their lips glided silkily beneath the steady stream of water. Until Riley could taste this kiss in the pit of her stomach, in the wild heat pooling even lower, in the way her legs grew molten and heavy beneath her.

She could only sink against him for support, suddenly unsteady, but she found no respite because he leaned back to brace himself against the wall, an action that crushed her breasts to his chest. Her stomach cradled the hardness of his growing desire. Her thighs stretched out against him with an intimacy that was intensely physical.

Riley couldn't think, only feel, knew a need to touch him that drowned out everything else. Her breath fluttered in her throat, and with a forbidden thrill as she slid her hands between them, coaxed her fingers beneath the dripping hem of his shirt and brought her hands in contact with his bare skin.

His stomach contracted at her touch, a hard expanse of muscle that invited exploration. She skimmed her hands upward, felt the crisp ruffling of hair beneath her palms, the hollows of definition, the supple skin that barely masked the throbbing heartbeat and told Riley he felt her touch the way she felt his. She dragged her palms slowly over his nipples, shivered when his low moan burst against her lips.

Suddenly his hands were on her face, dragging her mouth more deeply into their kiss, and the force of his need sparked her own until she gasped, the ache inside suddenly overwhelming.

Slipping her arms around his waist, she let her hands glide over his butt, tightly encased in wet jeans. She pressed him close, rocking her hips to ease the need within.

Scott followed her lead because his hands began a traveling descent, raking down her throat with firm strokes, over her shoulders and down her back. They mirrored each other stroke for stroke, drank in the long-forgotten feel of arousal.

Scott sighed against her lips, and then his hands were everywhere. Reaching for the hem of her shirt and tugging it upward. She raised her arms into the air to assist, and he broke their kiss to drag her sodden shirt over her head. It hit the floor with a wet thud. Her bra followed. She worked the buttons on his shirt until she could shove the whole wet mess over his shoulders and down his arms, baring the expanse of his chest.

Then, as if they'd been magnetized, they came together, their bodies drawing close, the tips of her breasts pressed against his warm, wet skin.

Now it was her turn to gasp. His hands contained such unleashed strength as he caressed her back, her waist, her ribs. He stroked the undersides of her breasts and she trembled, such a blatant admission of her desire.

She wanted him. He wanted her. That much she knew.

There were no questions, no indecision.

Only too many clothes.

Popping the button at her waist, she worked her dress slacks over her hips. They were so weighted with water they slipped down her legs with little effort. Scott's jeans proved much more of a challenge, and Riley sank to her knees to peel away the stubborn fabric, freeing his maleness with an intimate touch that made her heart beat so hard it actually hurt.

His groan carried over the sound of the pulsing water, and she glanced up, startled, aware of this desire. She wasn't the only one. His eyes fluttered shut, as if he was too overwhelmed, too caught up to resist.

She didn't want him to. She wanted him to give way to

this pleasure. Didn't want to think, didn't want to be reminded that anything but the two of them existed right now, and the unexpected surprise of what burned between them.

She couldn't resist trailing her mouth down the length of his thigh, entertaining herself with this slow task, smiling when a shiver rocked his entire body.

Impatiently, he kicked away the jeans, then dragged her up against him. His breathing grew ragged, his chest heaving as their slick skin came together in a fluid glide. Riley could feel him everywhere, feel his whipcord arms bracing her closer, ever closer. His eager hands exploring her with greedy abandon. The heavy length of his need branding her with its heat.

She just melted against him, so caught up in the moment, in the feel of him. What else could she do in the face of such unexpected, powerful need? Only give in. She had no fight left. Not tonight.

Pressing kisses along his shoulder, she tasted the pulse at the hollow of this throat. Her body was alive with desire, awakened to a need she hadn't known existed. She'd forgotten that she was a living, breathing woman.

A woman who wanted this man.

Riley wasn't the only one who wanted. With an abruptness that startled her, Scott broke away. She heard the faucet snap shut. The water stopped its flow and the shower door shot open. He stepped through, dripping everywhere and not seeming to care. He didn't grab towels. He didn't say a word. He simply reached for her hand to lead her from the stall, then lifted her into his arms.

The cool air assaulted her. Burying her face against his neck, Riley tried to contain the trembling that had begun again, a trembling so different from the physical reaction that had rocked her earlier.

This time she felt only eager.

There was no question. No need for discussion. There was no past between them. No worries about the future. There was only right here and right now. The soft bed beneath her. And then Scott's warm, wet body surrounding her, so hard and heavy in all the right places.

SCOTT STARED INTO his dark bedroom. Not morning yet, which bought him a little more time. Stolen time. Time to imprint in his memory the way Riley felt in his arms. Her sleek curves pressed against him. Her thigh casually tossed over his. Her cheek pressed to his shoulder. Her arm draped across his waist. The shiny hair that had dried into wild disarray.

He smiled into the darkness. Her hair was everywhere. Draped over the pillow. Trapped behind her shoulder. Tucked around his neck. Even in his face. Whenever she moved those spun silk curls would go into his mouth and up his nose. He kept trying to blow them away so he wouldn't sneeze and wake her.

He didn't want to do anything to bring an end to this night any faster than it was already coming.

He had no justification for his actions. No excuse that would wash. He'd been so affected by his fear for her that when she'd kissed him, he'd flat-out lost it.

How could he resist Riley?

He couldn't. He'd lost control, plain and simple.

Scott's eyes squeezed shut against the emotion, a brutal combination of relief and awe and gratitude and an unavoidable truth. A truth he wanted to block out for a little longer.

The night would only complicate things between them. Try though he might, he'd been projecting his feelings for

Riley ever since he'd realized how he felt about her. It was only natural she'd react. His need for her was so powerful.

And that's where the guilt was coming from. It wasn't about Mike, which surprised Scott. It was all about Riley. She deserved someone so much better. A man from a normal family, not someone who would only open the door to a world she'd been lucky enough to avoid.

She shifted again, this time nestling her face into the crook of his shoulder. After she was comfortable again, she exhaled a sigh that warmed his skin. Scott held her. Just held her. Tried to burn the feel of her silky curves into his brain. The way she stretched out against him, all sleek, toned skin. The arm that draped across his stomach, hand outstretched, fingers curled ever so slightly. The slim foot she rested on his ankle. The annoying little curls that kept tickling his nose.

The darkness began to fade beyond the blinds. Morning had finally come. Scott pressed his lips to her head, smiled when she sighed. Then he untangled himself from her and slid from the bed. He had a job to do.

To protect the woman he loved.

Scott made coffee and started with the phone calls. He needed to get a grip on himself, to get his head back in the real world before tackling the shower with its memories of Riley. Trembling from shock. Trembling from desire.

She was still sleeping when he finally emerged and dressed quietly, hoping not to disturb her, and he'd have left her that way, except this time when his cell rang the call was for her.

"Riley." He knelt beside the bed, not trusting himself near her, not when he still ached to touch her. "Kids on the phone."

Though she'd been dead asleep, she instantly blinked to awareness. Scott placed the phone in her hand, unable to take his eyes off her.

She was gorgeous with a drowsy-soft expression, mouth still full and pink from his kisses, bare shoulders peeping through the wild mass of her hair, which had dried into a shape not unlike that of the pillow.

He put some distance between them, half sitting against the dresser while she talked with each kid in turn, gave reminders about their plans for the day.

And loved them so completely.

It was in everything she said, the look on her face, the tone of her voice. Such a loving woman, so willing and passionate in his arms.

And she finally sat up, looking like a fantasy that had parked square in the middle of his bed. She wrapped the comforter around her, and it drooped in places that gave him choice views of bare curves and tan skin.

He left the room and poured coffee, which he brought to her. Lifting her gaze to his, eyes sparkling, she smiled a smile of such welcome that his heart gave a single hard beat.

She took a sip, then another, looking grateful. Then she was kissing the kids goodbye and flipping the phone shut.

"Good morning," she said huskily.

"Good morning." He folded his arms over his chest and filled her in on the news. He didn't give her a chance to address the night, interjected reality between them as a distraction—for her and for him. "Charlie's home. Concussed but completely fine. So no worries there."

"You've been working this morning?"

He nodded.

"Do you have any idea who those men were last night?"

Given his way, Scott would have let Riley believe the pharmaceutical story she'd been working on had invited the trouble. He didn't want to reopen old wounds about Mike based on Jason Kenney's word. At least until after the bust when Scott and the chief could break open Mike's case again and go through everything until they figured out exactly what had gone on.

But Riley was a reporter. And a good one at that. She wanted answers. As much as he wanted to spare her the uncertainties, he wouldn't outright lie to her.

"It's a long story, Riley. The chief and I don't have all the pieces in place, and a lot of what we do have I can't tell you yet. Not until after tonight."

"What happens tonight?"

"Undercover bust with Hazard Creek PD."

"You're going?"

He nodded. "The chief needs a strong team. We'll be dealing with some skilled criminals. We don't want any gunplay."

She sank back against the pillows and took a swig of coffee. "Hazard Creek, hmm. Did I step into something the day I showed up to cover that DEA bust?"

"Yes and no. I'm sorry to be cryptic, but I don't have all the answers. Let's just say it wasn't all about the bust."

"So it wasn't the pharmaceutical story I was working on?"

"No. Doesn't look like a story you were working on at all."

She was silent for a moment, staring down into her coffee mug, looking thoughtful. Then she said, "What about me? If you're working tonight, does that mean no one's after me?"

He forced himself to meet her gaze, felt her hope deep down in his gut. He wanted to sit next to her, take her in his arms and reassure her. He gripped the edge of the dresser to keep himself from going to her. "I've made arrangements for you to catch up with Joe and Rosie in the city."

"You told them what's going on?"

He shook his head. "They already knew. Alex told Caroline after we left last night—"

"Got it." She held up a hand to stop his explanation.

"I gave Joe a call this morning to fill him in. Sal and Janet are going to pick you up at noon and drive you into the city. You'll catch up with everyone and stay there until we get the situation under control. How does that sound?"

"Sal and Janet are staying, too?"

He nodded, watching the understanding dawn on her beautiful face. "The chief sent a disaster recovery company to your house this morning to assess the damage. They met up with Brian when he came over to feed the horses. Your insurance will handle it. You'll get a new kitchen and a clean house out of the deal. The bomb was meant more as a diversion than anything else."

"Good to know that no one wanted me dead."

Scott didn't point out that if they had, they'd have had ample opportunity to kill her yesterday. Not when the thought made him grip the dresser even harder.

"Please tell him thanks for me when you next talk to him."

"I will."

"And Janet and Sal are coming for me at noon?"

He nodded. "Are you hungry? I can fix you something to eat while you get ready."

"No thanks." She set the mug aside and glanced around. "Is this your place?"

He nodded again.

"Mike told me about it. It's beautiful." She gave a shrug. "What I saw of it in the dark, anyway."

"Not big. Grand tour will take all of five minutes. Feel free to look around." He glanced at her mug. "Want more coffee?"

A tiny frown creased her brow. "Scott, we made love last night. We slept together in this bed. Are you really going to stand there and act like it never happened?"

He met her gaze then, surprised by both her candor and

his own stupidity. His head flooded with a thousand things he wanted to say, but not one he could actually admit aloud.

"Why won't you talk with me about this?" she said. "Please tell me. I want to understand. You shut me down yesterday, too."

"Riley, I—" He what? He loved her, but couldn't bring himself to tell her when it meant revealing that he wasn't the man she thought she knew, but a man who'd come from a dark past.

She swung her legs around and stood up, dragging the comforter with her. It revealed more than it concealed, but she didn't seem to notice. He did. A gut-deep ache started inside, and he had to fight the urge to cover the distance between them, to admit he'd loved her forever, that he wanted nothing more than to continue loving her forever.

"Are you intentionally trying to make this weird?" she asked in a clipped tone he'd never heard before. "You care about me. You wanted me last night as much as I wanted you. I'm not imagining any of that."

"No," he admitted, forcing the words out. "You're not."

"Then what's the problem, Scott? Just talk to me."

He stared at her. At the confusion and anger on her beautiful face. What could he say? She was a strong woman. A woman who believed in people. She wanted to believe the best in him, too. And knowing that made him feel more powerless, more toxic than he'd ever felt before.

"Riley, I'm not who you think I am."

She shook her head, trying to shake off her confusion, as if she wasn't sure she'd heard him right. "I don't understand."

"No. You don't," he agreed. "You've been through so much. There's no happy ending with me. I'm no good for you."

Scott didn't give her a chance to reply. He left the room.

CHAPTER TWENTY-THREE

JASON STOOD UNNOTICED in a side room, peering through the ajar door, for once out of the glare of the spotlight of news crews that had been assembled for this press conference.

"Last night's operation dismantled an organization that has abused its power and connections for the past several years by importing powder cocaine from Mexico, converting this material into street drugs and distributing it throughout our city and surrounding communities," Chief Levering told the reporters. "The D.A. will bring charges against the individuals involved. The success of tonight's operation is thanks to the cooperation of the FBI, Poughkeepsie and Hazard Creek Police Departments. Federal and state authorities will continue working together to attack public corruption and the sale of illegal drugs."

Jason waited through the ensuing question-and-answer period, didn't come out until the room had cleared of the media and Chief Levering was gathering items into his briefcase, looking as if he was about to head out himself.

"Chief," Jason said. "You treated me better than I deserved tonight. I wanted to say thanks."

The bust had gone down with the help of the FBI, and they'd rounded up a total of thirty-two drug dealers and six DEA agents under the command of Barry Mannis. The drug dealers were with a well-known cartel out of Juarez,

Mexico, and Chief Levering had directed Scott to book Jason privately. The chief had already worked out an arrangement with the D.A. and a judge to release Jason on his own recognizance until Internal Affairs began their investigation and decided whether or not to bring charges against him.

It had been much, much better than Jason deserved.

Chief Levering leveled a no-nonsense stare from beneath grizzled brows. "I know you're facing a tough road ahead, but I also know you did the right thing tonight. We shut down an operation that has been pumping drugs into our neighborhoods and the prisons for too long. And you've helped us to get the person responsible for Mike's murder. I appreciate that personally. I know you made some poor choices recently, but it looks like you've got company."

"Are you talking about the parole officer?"

"And a prosecutor with the D.A.'s office and correctional officers at Downstate and Green Haven. That's so far."

"Jesus," he blurted. "That many?"

Chief Levering nodded. "Seems Agent Mannis has been running quite the tight operation, which might explain why he tried to eat his gun when his drug deal went south."

"I missed that."

"Thought you might have. You and your men looked pretty busy with the feds on that plane."

No argument there.

"You came clean. That wasn't easy. It was right. Remember that when you're looking in the mirror." Chief Levering extended his hand. "Good luck, Chief."

Jason shook his hand, surprised that he didn't feel like a hypocrite for the first time in a long, long time.

The sun was coming up by the time he left the police

station by the back exit. He walked out the door into a day that looked like it might turn out to be one of those rare Indian summer days. He wasn't exactly a free man, but he was outside and not locked in a cell.

It was a start.

"Damn it," he swore as he reached into his pocket. The booking sergeant had returned his keys, but his cruiser was still at the airfield. Scott had driven him into Poughkeepsie to be booked.

Jason could have gone back inside to ask someone for a ride, but he pulled out his cell instead. He'd used up a lot more than his fair share of luck with the PPD and didn't want to push it any further.

He was about to call directory assistance for the number to a cab company, but to his surprise, he caught sight of a familiar figure at the edge of the fenced parking lot. A casually dressed black man who leaned against a motorcycle with his tattooed arms folded across his chest. Jason was surprised by the strength of the emotion he felt and headed straight toward this unexpected visitor.

"It's Sunday morning, Tyrese. Shouldn't you be at church or something?"

"Services don't start until ten. But I heard how things went down last night and thought you might need a ride."

Jason didn't ask how Tyrese had heard. The media had only just gotten hold of the story, and they wouldn't be implicating the Hazard Creek police chief, anyway. He could only assume Tyrese still had street connections. "You have a divine vision or something?"

Tyrese flashed a toothy grin and his grill gleamed. "I know how it works around here. Just glad you're walking out the door without cuffs."

"Me, too, man. Me, too."

"Then hop on, boss." Tyrese motioned to the helmet on the bike's back rail. "You're in for the ride of your life."

That was the damned truth. Jason wished he had one-tenth of Tyrese's faith that everything would turn out okay. But the sick feeling he had in the pit in his stomach promised that facing Internal Affairs and the FBI wasn't going to be pretty. And even worse would be facing his family, especially Callie. He was going to break her heart. He might find himself alone for the first time since he'd met his oh-so-competent wife.

Well, not entirely alone thanks to Chief Levering and Tyrese, he reminded himself while climbing onto the bike. And Callie did love him. He didn't doubt that. If his luck held a little while longer, he might convince her to give him a chance to earn her forgiveness, too.

"I DON'T UNDERSTAND," Riley told Chief Levering when he called to tell her and her entourage, which included her kids, in-laws and two police escorts, that the coast was clear and they could come home. "I haven't been able to reach Scott by phone ever since I left his house Saturday."

"I told you, Riley," the chief said. "He's fine. There's nothing to worry about. The sting went down better than we had a right to hope. I didn't want you coming back to town until the FBI rounded up everyone. Just a precaution."

"You're not answering my question."

"You haven't answered mine, either. Did Jake tell you where he found that CD?"

"Yes," she said, chagrined. "Behind the desk in Mike's office."

"Behind the desk?"

"Mike kept his laptop bag on the floor beside the desk.

If he put the CD in an outer pocket, it could have fallen out. Unless he had it on the desk and accidentally knocked it off himself. I don't know. Except that my inquisitive son found it."

"Which turned out to be a good thing."

"Yes, mostly," she admitted. Finding out that a corrupt DEA agent had been responsible for taking her husband's life still didn't bring him back. And considering the break-ins and the abduction and the explosion in the middle of her kitchen… "Now back to Scott. If he wasn't hurt in the sting, then why aren't you telling me where he is?"

"He got a phone call about some personal business he had to deal with out of town."

She glared at the phone, plastered a smile on her face while crossing the living room, where Rosie, Lily Susan and the kids sat poring over old photo albums. She pulled open the door and slipped onto the patio.

"Out of town is a big place, Chief. Anywhere in particular?"

"I understand you're annoyed, but I can't tell you what you want to know."

To say she was annoyed was a dramatic understatement. She simply didn't believe the man had made love to her then disappeared off the planet without a word.

"Chief, my house and minivan were broken into. My equipment was stolen. I'm so scared for my children's safety that I have to send them away and get around-the-clock police protection, which didn't do the trick, I might add. My kitchen blew up. I'm abducted in an ambulance that winds up in a ditch. You find the people responsible for my husband's murder and bring down a drug organization that involves public corruption on local, state and federal levels." Her voice rose in a crescendo despite her best efforts at remaining rational. "After all I've been through, you won't tell me where Scott is?"

"Riley, please, I can't tell you." The chief sounded as helpless as she felt, and guilt pricked her conscience.

It passed quickly. She wasn't going to accept this. She wanted answers. Scott wasn't giving them to her, so the chief was her next best option.

Before he got a chance to make another excuse or hang up, Riley launched into her plea. Not the gory intimate details, of course, but the broad strokes.

"I know Scott cares about me," she told him. "but he has totally shut down. He refuses to discuss what's going on between us, and I don't know if he's flipping out because of Mike. I didn't expect this any more than he did, but we can't pretend it isn't happening. He said he wasn't good for me, and now he's AWOL. Do you understand why I'm worried? You know him better than anyone. Can't you give me something to work with here?"

To her surprise Chief Levering chuckled. "Having cops is more trouble than having kids."

"What does that mean?"

"It means you've convinced me to betray his confidence."

"I did?" She frowned, afraid to believe winning him over had been that easy.

"You did. How much do you know about Scott's upbringing?"

Sinking onto the edge of a planter, Riley stared out at the street with its traffic rushing in all directions. "I know he comes from New Jersey. Caroline told me his mother died when he was young and his grandmother raised him for a while. Mike only said his past had been somehow…difficult."

"*Difficult* doesn't describe it, Riley, but that's Scott's story. Right now all you need to know is where he is."

"Why are you telling me now?"

"Because I know Scott. I don't want him to let a good thing pass by because he's a stubborn pain in the ass."

"And…" She couldn't get out another word around the lump in her throat.

"*And* I hate that he's alone right now. His father died, Riley. He got the call a few hours after the sting."

"Oh, no."

The chief snorted. "Don't get me wrong. He hated the son of a bitch. If he'd had any choice, he wouldn't be dealing with this at all. But he's next of kin. And given the circumstances, there wasn't anyone else."

"What circumstances?"

The chief's sigh made Riley brace herself. "His father was a lifer. Tri-State Correctional Facility in Jersey. Murder one. That's all I'm going to say. You want to know more, then talk to Scott. He went to sign papers and make arrangements. I offered to go with him, but he wouldn't let me. He knows this place is a zoo with the Feds here."

Still clutching the phone, Riley stared into the street, consumed by the idea of Scott alone. Thoughtful, kind Scott, the man who made nests and babysat sick little girls, who helped teens fix cars and get their lives on track. The man who'd always been there for her, who'd held her, who'd listened to her rant, who'd rescued her from an ambulance in a ditch. The man who'd reawakened her ability to feel and brought her back to life with his kindness and kisses.

Had Mike been alive, he'd have been with Scott right now. There wasn't a doubt in Riley's mind.

"I'm on my way, Chief."

"Good girl." He gave a laugh. "Just give me a call when you get close. I'll find out exactly where he is. If he's still at the correctional facility, I'll make some calls to get you in."

"Got it."

"Good luck, Riley."

She laughed. "Sounds like I'm going to need it."

After disconnecting the call, she remained outside, taking time to collect her thoughts and whisper a silent plea to Mike for some idea of how best to be there for Scott.

And Riley knew as surely as if he'd spoken to her directly from heaven what Mike would have done—he would have offered unconditional support and love just as he always had.

That was one of the things she'd always loved and admired about her husband.

But Riley wasn't the only one who loved Scott, and as far as she was concerned things always worked out for a reason. At the moment, she had a whole living room filled with people who considered Scott one of the family.

With an utter certainty she hadn't enjoyed in a long time, Riley headed back inside the apartment and called her kids. "Hey, guys, want to help me make somebody feel better?"

"Who?" Camille asked.

"Uncle Scott. His dad died, so I'm thinking we should try to make him feel better. What do you think?"

Those two sweet little faces reflected so much concern that Riley could only marvel at how mature they were becoming. They understood what it meant to lose a dad.

"I still feel sad," Jake admitted. "Hugs make me feel better."

"And pizza," Camille suggested. "We can bring Uncle Scott pizza. That will make him feel better."

Riley could not have possibly been more proud. Laughing, she met Joe's gaze above the kids' heads. "Those are great ideas. Now go make sure you've got everything in your duffel bags, okay? We don't want to leave Aunt Lily Susan's house trashed or she won't invite us back."

The kids took off for the guest bedroom, leaving Riley to relay the adult version of the situation to Rosie and Joe.

Then she was sitting between her kids in the back seat of Joe's Cadillac heading south on the Jersey turnpike.

The correctional facility turned out to be barely more than an hour outside of the city. She called the chief when they arrived in town to find that Scott had already gone to the funeral home to finalize burial arrangements. When Joe wheeled into the parking lot, Riley spotted his car immediately.

"Why don't you all wait here for a few minutes," she suggested. "Give me a chance to find him."

"You got it," Joe said. "Wouldn't mind getting out and stretching a bit."

Riley kissed his cheek. "Just a few minutes."

"Take your time."

Steeling herself with a few deep breaths, Riley hurried inside. The foyer had been decorated in standard upscale funeral home style, and she couldn't help but remember the last time she'd been inside one—when life as she'd known it had ended. Ironic she'd be back inside one today, hoping that her life as she'd come to know it would change again.

Fortunately she didn't walk in on any services, but a gentleman in a suit emerged from an office to greet her.

"Good afternoon," he said. "May I help you?"

"I'm looking for Scott Emerson. I was told he's here."

"Right this way." The man extended an arm toward a long hallway, and Riley followed him. She found Scott seated at a conference table with paperwork spread out in front of him.

Riley drank in the sight of him, glossy dark hair, broad shoulders, cheeks drawn and tight in a carefully blank expression that revealed nothing and everything all at once.

She knew that look, could visibly see what it cost him to keep detached from the task at hand.

"Mr. Emerson," the funeral director said. "Someone here to see you."

Scott glanced up absently, then did a double take. "Riley?"

"Will you give us a few moments?" she asked the funeral director, who was already retreating from the room. He closed the door behind him.

"What are you doing here?" Scott rose slowly to his feet, clearly rattled.

"I came so you wouldn't be alone."

He stood there, hands hanging helplessly before him, the pain in his expression practically breaking her heart. "Riley, you don't understand."

"No," she admitted. "But I want to."

"You shouldn't have come."

"Can't it be enough that I didn't want you to be alone right now? That I wanted you to know how much you mean to me? Not only to me but to all the people who love you."

He scowled, and she came face-to-face with that stubborn pain in the ass the chief had mentioned.

"I appreciate what you're trying to do," he said. "But you shouldn't be here."

"Tell me why not? You're burying your father, Scott. That's difficult under the best of circumstances. From what I understand, these don't even come close."

He looked stricken, and Riley ached for his pain, pain she was causing him. Stepping forward, she took his hands in hers, felt the warm strength she'd only just gotten to know.

"I want to be here for you," she said. "The way you're always there for me." She meant it. She wasn't sure how it had happened, but she'd come to care so deeply about this man.

He pulled his hands away. "You shouldn't—"

"Yes, I should. You care about me, too. Don't bother denying it. I'm not stupid. I can't explain why this is happening between us. And I don't have any answers about where it might lead. But I do know how I feel."

"Not here. Not for *this*." There was a broken boy inside that gruff plea, and Riley recognized him, couldn't resist the need to comfort and love him.

Slipping her arms around his waist, she pressed close, rested her cheek against his chest. Then she held him. He didn't move, stood so still he might have been carved from stone.

She held her breath, refusing to let him frighten her off, only wanting to help, only wanting him to accept her help.

"When I was in that ambulance," she whispered, "the only thing that kept me from going to pieces was knowing you wouldn't stop looking until you found me. Don't ask me to stop looking for you."

He responded then, arms anchoring her tight, his whole body contouring to hers, such a perfect fit. They stood there, holding each other in the silence, proving without words how much they cared.

And when Scott pressed soft kisses into her hair, down her cheek and finally caught her mouth with his, Riley knew they'd weathered this storm, knew they'd be okay.

"Thank you," he whispered against her mouth.

She had no words, only had emotion to guide her. Rising up on tiptoes, she kissed him until there could be no doubt she meant everything she'd said. Then she stood behind him, with her hand on his shoulder as he finished signing the papers. He set the pen on top of the stack and pushed away from the table.

"Done?" she asked.

He met her gaze and didn't try to shield the emotion there. "No viewing. No service. There's no one to come."

She placed her hand in his and held on while the funeral director reviewed the formalities.

Then they left hand in hand, Riley smiling at Scott's surprise when he recognized who awaited him in the parking lot.

Two generations of Angelicas descended on him. Joe shook his hand and said all the right words, and Rosie hugged him fiercely. Jake must have thought Scott didn't need another hug because he mimicked his grandpa, shaking Scott's hand so stoically that Scott's expression twitched with suppressed laughter.

But Camille sealed the deal when she circled Scott on her wheeled sneakers and asked, "Pizza will make you feel better, won't it, Uncle Scott?"

Scott's smile broke free then, and he ruffled her blond head fondly. "You know. I think pizza's just the thing."

Camille wheeled around her brother with her hands outstretched in an I-told-you-so-gesture. And as they walked to the cars, working out seating arrangements for the ride to the nearest pizza place, Riley found herself beside Joe.

He took her hand and whispered, "Mike would be very proud of his family today."

Riley felt that familiar emotion well in her throat, but today it was a full, good feeling. She knew Joe was right. Mike had always understood what she was now just accepting.

Life was meant to be lived.

And her beloved husband would have wanted nothing less than that for the people he loved.

She kissed Joe's cheek. "I think you're right. He would be very proud of his family. All of them."

EPILOGUE

Two years later

SCOTT SWUNG DOWN from the tree, where he'd been stringing streamers in the branches the way kids toilet-papered houses at Halloween. He stepped back to survey his handiwork. "What do you think, guys? This what you had in mind?"

"It's perfect, Uncle Scott." Camille breathed an excited sigh, eyes sparkling like her mother's when she gazed around the scene at the fishing hole with undisguised delight. "Mommy's going to love it."

"Too much pink, Camille." Her brother screwed up his face in distaste. "It looks like someone puked strawberry Kool-Aid. I told you to get blue balloons."

"Mommy doesn't like blue, Jakie."

Camille was the only one nowadays who could get away with calling her brother by that name. To the rest of the world, this eight-almost-nine-year-old man wanted to be known as Jacob.

"We're never going to catch any fish," Jacob lamented.

Scott wasn't sure the decorations would scare off any fish, but he did have a point. "We need to tie the horses farther downstream just in case the balloons pop. They'll spook."

Two impish faces spun around to stare, clearly curious

about what spooked horses involved, and Scott realized he might have made a mistake giving them any ideas. "Come on, guys. Give me a hand. Jacob, you lead Shadow. Camille, take Baby."

He led Charger downstream himself, until they found a place where the horses could graze and drink while the rest of them got about this day. They'd been planning this for weeks now, and Scott didn't want the kids to forget anything important to them.

Riley knew something was going on—how could she not when they'd abandoned her with the picnic basket at the house? She didn't know what and played along anyway, telling them she would check the picnic basket again to make sure they had everything for their afternoon of fishing.

That had been an hour ago.

"Are we ready to call your mom?" Scott asked. "Can you think of anything we missed?"

"Call Mom, Uncle Scott," Jacob said. "I'm starving."

No news there. "You ready, too, Camille?"

"Ready."

Scott flipped open the cell phone and hit speed dial.

Riley picked up on the first ring. "Hey, you. I was getting worried."

"Just a few logistical things to work out."

"I can't imagine what you're doing. I'm excited."

"Me, too," he admitted.

"Not one hint?" she coaxed in a voice that made him smile.

"Not even one. We want you to be surprised."

"Okay then." She strung the words out, but he could hear the amusement in her voice. "Ready for me?"

"Always ready for you, gorgeous."

She laughed, and the sound spiked his growing anticipation, a feeling of contentment he'd never known before and welcomed fiercely. Life had been so good, in fact, that he was determined never to take one second for granted. "See you in a few, then. And don't go straight to the fishing hole—meet us downstream. We'll be waiting."

"Will do." She blew him a kiss over the line, and Scott disconnected, turning to the kids. "She's on her way."

"Got the blindfold, Jakie?" Camille asked.

"Check." Jacob produced the bandanna he'd rolled up for just this occasion.

"Got the ring, Uncle Scott?"

"Check." Scott patted the pocket of his cargo pants, where not one but three jewelers' boxes were concealed.

"Decorations?"

"Check."

"Flowers."

"Check."

"Mom has the food, right?" Jacob asked uncertainly.

Scott inclined his head. "Check."

It wasn't long until Jacob cocked his head to the side, and his eyes widened. "I hear her. She's coming."

Sure enough, Riley rode into the clearing on Sugar, her eyes sparkling as she glanced around curiously. "Is this where we're picnicking today?"

Scott reached up to take the basket. "No, ma'am. This is the parking lot. Here you go, Jacob. One full picnic basket."

Jacob didn't have to be asked twice. He took the basket so Scott could help Riley dismount.

"Where is it?" Camille hissed to her brother. "The blindfold?"

Jacob wasn't relinquishing his hold on the picnic basket, not even to perform his prescribed part in this drama.

Camille snapped the bandanna out of his back pocket and told Riley, "Kneel down, Mommy."

"You're blindfolding me?" Riley gasped, but she did as asked and submitted to her daughter's ministrations, which turned out to be a fairly haphazard job at best.

"No peeking," Camille instructed. "Ready, Uncle Scott?"

"Ready. I'll grab one side and you grab the other."

With them acting as honor guard, they carefully escorted Riley back to the fishing hole and led her into the center of the clearing where she couldn't possibly miss the full effect of all their hard work.

"Ready?" Scott asked Camille, taking a step back and folding his arms over his chest so he could enjoy the scene.

She exchanged a glance with Jacob, then shook her head. "Okay, Mommy, you can look now."

Riley peeled away the blindfold then opened her eyes. She brought her hands to her mouth and twirled, taking in their carefully executed decorations.

"Ohmigosh," she exclaimed with exactly the perfect amount of surprise for the occasion. "This is amazing. Did it rain pink fairies today?"

Camille giggled.

"But it's not my birthday. It's not even any of your birthdays." She glanced suspiciously at them. "So what are we celebrating?"

Jacob, still hanging on to the picnic basket, glanced Scott's way. "Go on, Uncle Scott. Do it."

Scott made a great show of unfolding his arms and pushing away from the tree. He gave an exaggerated cough to clear his throat, ready to play his part. But he obviously wasn't moving quickly enough because Camille took his hand and led him to Riley.

"Go on," she said. "Do it right. Like we practiced."

Riley met his gaze above the kids' heads. He winked, knowing that in that instant, her surprise wasn't feigned.

Slipping his hand inside his pocket, he felt around for the appropriate box. Then he knelt in front of Riley. Her eyes grew wide and her mouth formed a delightful O at the exact time he flipped open the jeweler's box and held it out to her.

"Riley Angelica, I love you, and I love your kids. I want us to be a family."

"A *real* family," Camille said.

"A real family," he repeated. Then he removed the ring from the box and slipped it onto her finger.

The ring fit perfectly, as he'd known it would, and he pressed a kiss to her fingers and smiled up at her. Those gorgeous blue eyes were glinting suspiciously, and he knew she was too overcome to reply.

He bought her some time by motioning for the kids. "Come here, you two."

He pulled the remaining boxes from his pocket, and when they saw there were more gifts, they were flanking Riley before Scott could take his next breath.

"For us?" Camille gasped, a mini-version of Riley as she brought her hands to her mouth in surprise.

Scott nodded and knelt before them. "Camille, Jacob, I love you both, and I love your mom. I want us to be a real family."

He opened the other jeweler's box to reveal a little-girl-size ring with a pink pearl and two tiny diamonds. He slipped it onto Camille's finger.

"Oh, I do," she squealed, throwing her arms around his neck. He caught her delicate body in a big hug, laughing.

"You didn't get me a ring, did you, Uncle Scott?" Jacob slowly set down the picnic basket, clearly worried.

"Will you turn me down if I did?" Scott laughed.

"Uh, yeah." He sounded as if that should have been obvious.

"No ring. I didn't want to risk it." He handed Jacob the remaining box, waited while he opened it to find one top-of-the-line Swiss Army knife.

"Too cool." The box hit the ground at his feet and he started prying out the equipment for inspection. "Screw-driver. File. Whoa. Look at this knife."

Riley found her voice. "No missing fingers today, please."

"Mom, I have an axe, remember?" This blade was small by comparison.

Camille shifted around to sit on Scott's knee, and he looped his arm around her waist to hold her steady and asked, "So, what'll it be, Jacob?"

"Oh, yeah." He held up the knife with a gleam in his eye that would have made most folks nervous.

Scott wasn't entirely sure that yes had been for him, but he'd take it.

"Oh, no." Camille brought her hands to her mouth in horror. "You're the only one who didn't get a present, Uncle Scott."

"That's not true. I'm getting the best present of all. You guys as my family." He glanced up at Riley, whose eyes were sparkling. "That is if your mom accepts."

Camille hopped off his lap and went straight to Riley. "Mo-om, you're supposed to say yes."

Scott got to his feet, suddenly breathless. His future hung in the balance as he awaited an answer from this woman he loved more than life itself. The woman who loved him unconditionally in return and had helped him recognize that, though he'd loved her forever, he'd never betrayed Mike's trust with those feelings. An honorable choice worthy of the people he loved. He had nothing to be ashamed of and a life filled with love to look forward to.

"Yes," Riley said simply.

One word and his whole life changed, was suddenly complete. Then she was in his arms, her laughter breaking against his mouth as they kissed.

"Yes." She breathed the word again. "Yes."

"What are we going to call you, Uncle Scott?" Jacob asked. "You won't be our uncle anymore after you marry Mom."

"That's true." Scott abandoned his attempts to kiss his new fiancée—he should have known better by now—and twisted Riley in his arms so they could both face the kids. "I'll be your stepfather."

Jacob screwed up his face in that look that said more than words ever could. "That's not working for me."

"He's Lieutenant Emerson at the station," Camille said.

"That's stupid, Camille." Jacob earned a look from Riley that should have made his ears dry up and fall off. "We can't call him Lieutenant Emerson."

"How about we refrain from the name-calling and brainstorm," Scott suggested. "I could use some help here."

And he got his help from the beautiful young girl who looked so like her mother that he melted inside when she turned sparkly eyes up to his and said, "Daddy's Daddy, so you can be…" Her words trailed off as she cocked her head to the side, considering. "Pop. You'll be Pop, Uncle Scott. It's just right."

And it was.

* * * * *